Class 1902

———◆——

"All that is needed to understand World War I in its philosophical and historical meaning is to examine barbed wire—a single strand will do—and to meditate on who made it, what it is for, why it is like it is." —JAMES DICKEY

Class 1902

Ernst Glaeser

NEW INTRODUCTION BY HORST KRUSE

THE UNIVERSITY OF SOUTH CAROLINA PRESS

New material © 2008 University of South Carolina

German edition published as *Jahrgang 1902* by Gustav Kiepenheuer
Verlag A.G., 1928
English cloth edition published by Martin Secker Ltd., 1929
English paperback edition published by the University of South
Carolina Press, Columbia, South Carolina 29208

www.sc.edu/uscpress

Manufactured in the United States of America

17 16 15 14 13 12 11 10 09 08   10 9 8 7 6 5 4 3 2 1

Library of Congress Cataloging-in-Publication Data

Glaeser, Ernst, 1902–963.
 [Jahrgang 1902. English]
 Class 1902 / Ernst Glaeser ; new introduction by Horst Kruse.
   p. cm. — (Joseph M. Bruccoli Great War series)
 Originally published: London : M. Secker, 1929.
 ISBN-13: 978-1-57003-712-2 (pbk : alk. paper)
 ISBN-10: 1-57003-712-4 (pbk : alk. paper)
  1. World War, 1914–1918—Fiction. I. Kruse, Horst. II. Title.
 PT2613.L3J32 2007
 833'.912—dc22

                                                        2007022653

This book was printed on Glatfelter Natures, a recycled paper with
50 percent postconsumer waste content.

Contents

Series Editor's Preface

The Joseph M. Bruccoli Great War Series republishes fiction and personal narratives—the demarcation is not always clear—from the belligerent nations of World War I. Formal military history is excluded.

"The war to end all wars" generated a vast literature—much of it antiheroic and antiwar. The best books of the war convey a sense of betrayal, loss, and disillusionment. Many of them now qualify as forgotten books, although they were admired in their time. The intention of this series is to rescue once-influential books that have been long out of print.

The volumes are drawn from the Joseph M. Bruccoli Great War Collection in the Thomas Cooper Library, University of South Carolina.* This collection is named for a private in the AEF who was severely wounded on the Western Front. Joseph M. Bruccoli's medal has seven battle bars and he claimed two more battles. He was not embittered by his war.

M.J.B.

---

* *The Joseph M. Bruccoli Great War Collection at the University of South Carolina: An Illustrated Catalogue*, compiled by Elizabeth Sudduth (Columbia: University of South Carolina Press, 2005). See also *The Joseph M. Bruccoli Great War Collection in the University of Virginia Library*, compiled by Edmund Berkeley Jr. (Columbia: MJB, 1999).

Introduction

HORST KRUSE

Ernst Glaeser's novel *Jahrgang 1902* was published in 1928. In terms of the development of the antiwar novel as a genre, it is important to note that its publication preceded that of Erich Maria Remarque's *Im Westen nichts Neues (All Quiet on the Western Front)*, which appeared in 1929. Ernest Hemingway, in discussing the prospective publication of his own war novel, *A Farewell to Arms*, later that same year, indicated his awareness of these German predecessors. Arguing with Maxwell Perkins, his editor at Scribner, about retaining certain words that "have not been in print before," Hemingway pointed to both Remarque's novel and the possible publication of a second volume of Arnold Zweig's *The Case of Sergeant Grischa* and then concluded, "I hate to kill the value of mine by emasculating it."[1] Hemingway's argument that "you should not go backwards" suggests that in the ongoing process of writing novels about the Great War there is a progression from "genteel writing" to what he calls "first rate writing." In a September 1929 letter to F. Scott Fitzgerald, he once more refers to Remarque's novel and other "Great German War Books" and then continues with reference to *A Farewell to Arms:* "It's bad luck maybe that mine comes out now and after all these that [I] have not had opportunity to profit by them in writing it."[2]

The title of *Jahrgang 1902* provides a key to both the achievement and the meaning of the novel. Consideration of what the title connotes in German—as well as a brief reflection on its English translation—is essential. A literal translation, "Class 1902," is not

1. Hemingway to Maxwell Perkins, June 7, 1929, in *Ernest Hemingway: Selected Letters, 1917–1961,* ed. Carlos Baker (New York: Scribner, 1981), 297.
2. Hemingway to F. Scott Fitzgerald, September 1929, in ibid., 307.

readily intelligible to English speakers; therefore an American edition was published as *Class of 1902* (New York: Viking Press, 1929). This merely added to the confusion, since in the United States "class of" traditionally refers to students who graduate in the same year from the same institution. A contemporary reviewer of the first British edition (London: Martin Secker, 1929) felt the need to offer the following explanation: "'Class 1902' for Germans means the boys born in that year, whereas for the French it would mean the boys becoming liable for service in that year."[3] The German word "Jahrgang" is also of special importance with regard to military service. "Jahrgang" means the boys to be drafted or called to arms when they have reached a designated age, an age that may well vary according to military needs. It is used and understood as a collective noun, and in combination with a given year it frequently points to a particular experience—such as a war or a time of political upheaval—that is liable to befall all its members and to foster solidarity. Thus, while "Jahrgang" is an important term in view of an impending and an imposed experience (such as the draft), it is equally important in evoking or explaining such an experience in retrospect. In this regard, it is not unlike the term "generation," but it serves as a far more specific marker. The translators of Glaeser's novel, Willa and Edwin Muir, must have seen that "Born in 1902" was inadequate to capture the complexity of the term's military as well as collective connotations. They must also have felt that *Class 1902* was less ambiguous a title in its reference to collective rather than individual experience. Although the novel centers on the experiences of the narrator-protagonist E. and although the exact ages of his friends and companions are rarely given, the story that emerges is the story of the boys (and girls) who were born in 1902 and lived through the war years of 1914 to 1918 but were not in combat—for 1902 was the first "Jahrgang" to escape being drafted into the Great War. This is equally part of their collective experience and part of what *Jahrgang 1902* connotes. The title thus announces that the

3. "A Symposium on the War," *Times Literary Supplement,* November 21, 1929. The French publisher V. Attinger, understanding the differences in usage, translated Glaeser's title as *Classe 22.*

novel hopes to transcend individual experience and to provide a panoramic view of the times. E.'s very personal quest for sexual enlightenment is made to carry the burden of disenchantment with the world of grown-ups and with what E. and his friends come to see as the war of their elders.

Biographical information about Ernst Glaeser is helpful in assessing the author's achievement in *Class 1902* because in his writing he stuck closely to what he himself had experienced and observed, while at the same time he used narrative strategies that allowed him to present a variety of views and to broaden the scope of his novel. Glaeser was born on July 29, 1902. In 1912 his father was appointed district judge in Gross-Gerau, a small town near Darmstadt in Hesse, which became the setting of *Class 1902*. Many actual events and persons from the town figure in the novel. In the fall of 1917, Glaeser transferred from a local school to the gymnasium, the classical academy, in Darmstadt, commuting by train. Darmstadt also figures in the novel, abbreviated as D., and this abbreviation, along with that of E. for the autobiographical protagonist, is one strategy by which the author claims authenticity for his account. After the war Glaeser attended the universities of Freiburg and Munich to study philosophy, German philology, and literature. These studies contributed in a significant way to the writing of *Class 1902*. While working for a newspaper and for a theater in Frankfurt, Glaeser was able to complete the novel, which became an immediate international success.

Much of the national and most of the international response to *Class 1902* was due to its value as a reliable document of life on the German home front, about which very little had been known. The *Manchester Guardian,* in a review excerpted on the dust jacket of the "Cheaper Edition" published by Martin Secker in 1930, noted that the book is "an almost indispensable piece of raw material for the history of the time." But it is as a novel that *Class 1902* was conceived and written, and it is as a novel that it asks to be read and evaluated. An essential part of its achievement in this respect lies in Glaeser's strategy of combining and describing two parallel quests of his narrator-protagonist. E.'s basic pursuit is to uncover the mystery of sex, a preoccupation that persists throughout the text as it describes his development from age twelve to age sixteen. During these years his parents' generation fails him, through lack of interest, irresponsibility, or sheer absence due to the war. Unable to comprehend the aspects of sexual desire or activity he witnesses, he perceives sex, in a fashion typical of so many novels of adolescence, as ugly and evil. What he sees at first is violence and suffering; what he then pays for with stolen money is to witness a scene whose silent fury he fully misinterprets. In his confusion he concludes that the mystery whose revelation he seeks is actual murder. And so with silent ardor he takes an oath never to grow up. In the end he meets Anna, a guard on the commuter train that takes him to his school in D., and slowly they come to love each other.

This development parallels the development of the protagonist's perception of war, another matter that pertains to the adult world and is beyond his immediate comprehension. E. is slow to share in the general enthusiasm that springs up as the prospect of war increases, and over the course of the novel, he is brought ever closer to the reality of warfare as he observes life in his hometown: the departure of combat troops, the return of the wounded, the deaths of two soldiers and a horse, the hunger, and finally the air raids that bring the horror of war to the home front. It is at this point that the two lines of development converge in a dramatic conclusion: Anna is killed in a raid on the city of D. just when she and the narrator had agreed to become lovers and the mystery of sex was to be revealed.

The advancement, the interplay, and the convergence of the two strands as narrative strategy and structural device are not small achievements in themselves, but in the end they are all but subservient to Glaeser's purpose of presenting a portrait of German society and public opinion prior to and during the years of the Great War. Having been set free from strict supervision and guidance, the narrator is also free to move (almost in the fashion of a juvenile picaro) among various groups and individuals and so to observe people in different walks of life. "Through my curiosity," E. remarks, "I was getting hopelessly entangled in the web of society" (100). In his own words, he is both a "seeker" and a "spectator," and these two roles sustain the plot as well as structure the novel. His observations

are presented in a series of episodes (again, much as in the pica-
resque novel) that make up the chapters of *Class 1902*. The title of
part 1, "Marching Away" (and even more so the original German
title, "Der Aufmarsch"), connotes a military buildup, but this section
of the novel is wholly concerned with events in civilian life; only in
the final scene are these events made to culminate in the news of
German mobilization. By using this title and by giving ten chapters
to part 1 as opposed to five chapters to part 2, "The War," Glaeser's
emphasis is made to fall on the various factors and attitudes that
brought about the war rather than on wartime behavior itself. At the
same time it is clear that the author is making an important point:
war begins as an attitude. The military buildup is first of all a matter of mustering and preparing the minds of the people; only second-
arily is it one of the mustering of troops. This observation is brought
out in the opening scene of the novel, the first of a long series of
episodes filled with cleverly selected details and ironic statements.
The count-off drill suggests a military context in keeping with the
title of part 1, but the actual scene turns out to be set among twelve-
year-old boys in a school yard.

The episodes presented dramatize, separately and in their inter-
action, different stances in relation to the impending war and its
meaning: the pacifist attitude of a cosmopolitan Anglophile noble-
man and the antagonism he encounters; the naive belief of a Social
Democrat that the international solidarity of the proletariat will
obviate any war; the outright anti-Semitism of the community and
the hypocritical behavior of people in seeking their own advantage;
the revolutionary views of the labor unionist with his reading of Marx,
Engels, and Bebel and his belief in the power of plain numbers to
tell the truth; the self-righteousness of the autocratic yet deferential
civil servant, who fails as a father; the escape from reality of E.'s
mother in her aesthetic devotion to sublime literature, which makes
her easy prey for chauvinistic rhetoric; the promulgation of fantasies
of German racial and intellectual superiority and the corruption of
the populace by the repulsive professor who exploits both his social
standing and his elocutionary ability—all these and many more
appear in a novel that shows them in their interplay and describes

how the profuse voices nonetheless come together to welcome war
or to suffer it to happen, before the realities of war proceed to dis-
solve the chorus.

What keeps these voices from being one dimensional is Glaeser's
art as a novelist. *Class 1902* is a political novel, and it is a pacifist
document; but it is not a novel whose purpose reduces its characters
to caricatures. Many sections stand out as well written—even brilliantly written—and many sections have kept their relevance to this
day. One of them is the slightly ironic chapter about the Silberstein
family, the Jewish owners of a draper shop. E.—who has been chosen to inform his ailing classmate Leo that he will henceforth be
protected against Brosius, their powerful and sadistic form master
and gymnastic instructor—is eager to demonstrate that he does not
share the covert anti-Semitism of the townspeople; yet the weak but
intelligent Leo succeeds in proving just the opposite. Leo undercuts
E.'s protestations of sincere friendship by leading him to admit that
he would not concede to being protected by Leo. At the same time
Glaeser fashions what amounts to an arresting emblem of Jewish
suffering that in its significance transcends both scene and chapter:
"They all fell silent, as if they had no more breath left, standing rigid
like a group of statuary . . . ; they made a group which was by no
means ugly. All that was ridiculous in Herr Silberstein's appearance
had vanished; I saw no longer his funny little legs, and I forgot the
unmanly crook of his shoulders; even the mother, whose blurred
face always offended me, had a fine air, and Leo, standing pale, thin
and weary between his anxious parents, looked as if he were gazing
into a tomb" (62).

Similarly emblematic is the opening scene of chapter 6, which
describes the Sunday afternoon walks through the cornfields along
narrow, winding paths that E.'s father would take in the company of
his wife and son. Swinging his stick to cut off the golden heads of
dandelions—possibly a reference to Alfred Döblin's disturbing ex-
pressionistic story "Die Ermordung einer Butterblume" ("The Murder of a Buttercup") of 1910—he would then pluck a small cornflower
to fasten to his right lapel. This act is an expression of his love for
the principles of the old kaiser, whose favorite the simple flower
had been. At the same time he shepherds his family through the

fields in ritualistic fashion and in strict observance of all rules and regulations, curbing E.'s desire to run ahead and refusing to discuss "the beast in man" that his wife invokes. What is called "disciplined Nature-worship" is made to epitomize the role of the father in German society in the years before the Great War.

In chapter 8, titled "Gaston," Glaeser apparently responds to Thomas Mann's *The Magic Mountain*. Published in 1924, this novel of ideas was much discussed at the time, and Glaeser would certainly have encountered it. Writing in an often symbolic mode, Mann had brought together an international set of characters in a mountain sanatorium in Switzerland. He had taken the story up to the outbreak of the Great War, describing the impact of the event on the configuration of individuals, and in the final chapter, "Thunderbolt," had ended the story by sending his protagonist, Hans Castorp, into battle, the "universal feast of death," with the slimmest chance of survival. Glaeser, likewise, has E. and his mother stay in a sanatorium in the Swiss mountains in the period between when the shots were fired at Sarajevo and the actual outbreak of the war. While the grown-ups have difficulties overcoming language barriers, E. and a French boy named Gaston easily become close friends and spend carefree days away from their elders without ever having to resort to language: "There was no need of speech, with its malice and ambiguity which so often put human beings at variance; there was none of the vanity of disputation nor any disruptive struggle to 'be in the right' with words. We did not need to translate our desires; we understood each other through our eyes, through our senses, and all that we did was honest" (162). As the war draws closer, there is a sorting out of people according to their nationalities, and when the guests begin to depart, the two boys have to be torn away from each other. At their last meeting Gaston speaks what the narrator in retrospect calls "those unforgettable words of my boyhood: 'La guerre, ce sont nos parents—mon ami. . . .'" (168; "The war is the concern of our parents, my friend. . . .")—words that serve as the epigraph for part 1 of *Jahrgang 1902* and, in some later editions, even as the epigraph for the whole book. Glaeser's novel does not achieve the symbolic density of *The Magic Mountain,* but the implicit references to the earlier work as well as the obvious symbols that do occur, along with the fact that even in its totality (setting, characters, all events) the text may be read symbolically, elevate the "Gaston" section above all others.

Two of Glaeser's techniques—inserting ironic innuendo and subtle symbolism into what appears to be straightforward reportorial narration as well as debunking through anticlimax—are especially apparent in chapter 9, "Das Schützenfest." The title refers to a time-honored German tradition, that of an annual shooting competition staged by the members of rifle associations in their traditional paramilitary uniforms. The several days of general festivities include marching and brass bands, as well as much beer drinking and dancing. All of this is well captured in the translation of the chapter's title as "The Rifle Carnival." But the chapter shows how what is expected to be harmless amusement celebrated in traditional fashion is slowly transformed into frenzied and boundless enthusiasm for war. Flags in great numbers fly in expectation of the conflict rather than for the carnival itself: "We're counting on the French declaring war every hour. Everybody is waiting for that as for a deliverance" (179), as the father puts it. A little later a trumpeter from one of the carnival bands blows the German army charge, and the Social Democrat gets up on the platform to make an announcement: "'Silence!' he cried—then after a calculated pause he said in a devout voice, as if he were intoning a prayer: 'France has just declared war on us. . . .' —'Hurrah!' roared the marquee. The people flung their arms above their heads and leapt up on their stools, as if from there it was easier to see a better future" (182–83). Glaeser develops the scene to undercut further what is considered a great historical moment: the first band plays a hymn of thanksgiving; the second band plays the German national anthem; a toast is proposed to the kaiser; people empty their glasses of beer at one draught; but E.'s beer goes down the wrong way and soaks his sailor suit. In the end he is intoxicated. National history and individual history are shown in incongruous coalescence: "It was the second of August. It was my first experience of being drunk" (186). In the emerging ambiguity of its double reference—to small-scale civilian social event and to large-scale military conflict simultaneously—the term "Das Schützenfest" anticipates, in the cluster of its sardonic implications, the title of Isabel

Colegate's novel *The Shooting Party* (1980), which similarly takes place shortly before the Great War.

In the complexity of its achievement, as literature, as historical document, as a study of mass psychology, and most of all as a plea for pacifism, Glaeser's *Class 1902* has not been adequately understood and appreciated by critics or readers. In his 1929 article "Absage an den Jahrgang 1902," the journalist Hans Zehrer, who was slightly older than Glaeser and a veteran of the war, denounced all those born in 1902 for adapting themselves so easily to the standards of the Weimar Republic and for availing themselves so readily of its economic opportunities; those born earlier, who had seen combat, preferred to stay aloof. Glaeser's *Jahrgang 1902* had given these younger people a certain importance and relevance, but the novel was, according to Zehrer, just "ein kindlich geschriebenes Buch," an infantile work. It appears that prejudice against Glaeser's success—his book was selling extremely well, and it was eventually available in more than twenty languages—stood in the way of a more balanced response. So too did Glaeser's politics. In 1930 Glaeser attended the Second International Congress for Revolutionary Literature in Kharkov in the Soviet Union, and the following year he coauthored a study of the progress of the Five Year Plan. His leanings towards communism as well as the pacifism of *Class 1902* caused the book (along with others that he had written) to be among those consigned to the flames in the book burnings by the National Socialists in Berlin on May 10, 1933. Glaeser left Germany the same year, first for Czechoslovakia, then for Switzerland. He returned in 1939, was drafted into the German Wehrmacht in 1940, and did editorial work on newspapers for the services, later maintaining that he had never identified with Nazi ideology. He lived to 1963 and continued to write, but none of his later books (political and regional novels and stories, as well as historical and political studies) achieved the success of *Class 1902*.

Among the critics who took exception to certain aspects of *Class 1902* was the reviewer of the *Times Literary Supplement* of November 21, 1929. He wrote that "the unpleasantness of the characters, their sexual precocity, and the twist of perversion so common in German books on the War will probably limit the sympathy of the average

British reader." From the vantage point of today, there seems to be very little in the book that justifies this evaluation. What unpleasantness there is, is called for in the interest of truthfulness and serves its purpose in the denunciation of war and all behavior that leads to war. The unpleasantness was one of the aspects that caused Remarque to conclude about *Class 1902:* "The value of Gläser's book is not merely literary, but much more than that: it is an important document of the history of the time."[4] And Hemingway would have felt that the *TLS* reviewer had listed the aspects that brought the novel closer to doing justice to its subject. This is probably why he said of *Class 1902:* "A damned good book!"

---

4. "Jahrgang 1902: Ernst Gläsers Roman," undated review [1928], R-C 2.14/010, Erich Maria Remarque-Archiv, University of Osnabrück, Germany.

Class 1902

PART ONE

MARCHING AWAY

La guerre—ce sont nos parents . . .

GASTON P.

CHAPTER I

THE RED MAJOR

" ATTENTION ! Eyes right ! Number off ! "

" One—Two—Three—Four—Five—Six—Seven
—Eight—Nine——"

" Ten ! "—that was Ferd.

" Eleven ! "—that was me.

" Thirteen ! . . ."

" Halt ! "

Dr. Brosius, form master and gymnastic instructor to the Quarta, runs his eye along our line. He thrusts his head forward, shooting out his neck, which is always somewhat inflamed by his stiff collar—like a parrot craning for a lump of sugar ; and then stamps his foot in the bluish-grey gravel of the school-yard till it flies up. His finely polished glasses tremble precariously ; nothing but the silver chain over his ear keeps them from falling off. The scars on his cheek stand out. In the row of heads rigidly turned towards him one face becomes red as fire.

" Silberstein ! Of course, Herr Silberstein of David Silberstein and Company, Wholesale Drapers, can't count up to twelve ! Forward ! "

And Leo Silberstein, the only Jew in the class, steps forward.

" Back again ! " roars Dr. Brosius. " Which foot do you start with ? "

" The left. . . ."

" Answer me properly ! " yells Dr. Brosius, giving

A *   9

Silberstein a push which sends him flying back into the ranks.

" Please sir, with the left foot, sir," sobs the small Leo, who, as usually in such scenes, is struggling with tears.

" Forward ! "

This time he does it correctly.

" Now what about your number ? "

Leo stands to attention with a face like a turkey-cock and salutes. " Please sir, I made a mistake."

" A mistake ? " Dr. Brosius is seized by one of his fits of horse-laughter.

" A mistake ? In counting ! Doesn't know his own number ! You were asleep, that's all, dreaming in the sun ! "

" I've such a bad memory for numbers," says Leo, in a low voice, dropping his head and out of em-barrassment scratching in the gravel with his left foot.

" Stand at attention while I am speaking to you ! " Leo winces and immediately stiffens his head, feet, arms and back into the required position. A few tears run down his cheeks. He cannot wipe them away because he has to stand at attention.

Brosius grins, and rocks himself twice from the hips. He walks round the wretched boy, screwing up his nose. " Oh, it isn't the Guards you'll get into," he sneers, in the Berlin accent he always assumes when he wants to ridicule anybody. " Oh no, but you've still a chance of the Army Service Corps . . ." he adds, with ironic encouragement to Leo, whose military posture is continuously shaken by suppressed sobs. (For a German youth in 1914 the Army Service Corps was nothing less than a disgrace.) Three times Brosius circles round Silberstein, jeering at his miserable figure, while the line of boys grins

Indeed, Leo was a pitiable spectacle. In his thread-
bare suit the vest always sat awry ; his lean shanks
ended in feet that turned out and were too big ; his
shoulders were nervously drawn up and uneven, and
round his neck ran a dusky ring, for he was averse
to washing anything but his face. Only his eyes and
his hair were beautiful, especially his hair, which
was black and gleamed like jet.

Suddenly Brosius shakes his head. He plants
himself before the line of boys, and says in a nasal
drawl : " Oh, the little Silberstein, what's to become
of him if he can't count ? What will his Papa say,
who does nothing the whole blessed day but count
money. . . . Eh ? "

And Herr Brosius screws up his face, crooks up his
left leg, rounds his back as if he had a hump, pushes
his glasses down on his nose, and rubs his first finger
and thumb together as if he were counting shining
ducats into the hollow palm of his other hand.

Some of the boys emit a duly appreciative snigger.

The whole town knew Herr Brosius for a wag.
As President of the Navy League he made speeches
at its public dinners which coruscated with wit,
throwing the ladies out of one fit of laughter into
another. He could also give excellent imitations of
animal noises, and at the Casino when amateur
productions were staged, mostly consisting of rustic
Tyrolean scenes, his co-operation from behind the
wings was indispensable. But it was at country
picnics that he shone most. On these occasions his
realistic renderings, for the ladies' entertainment, of
the bellowings of many oxen struck his hearers dumb
with admiration. Brosius was in high favour with
Fraülein Hainstadt, the richest heiress in our town.
He was an officer in the reserve, and had lost both

his innocence and the callow smoothness of his
cheeks in an intrigue at Heidelberg. His first name
was Heini. The only boy in our class who dared to
refrain from laughing at his witticisms was Ferd von
K. In return Brosius had a dig at him whenever he could.

So little Leo Silberstein stands like a soldier
at attention in front of the line and sobs. Only his
hands flutter like frightened birds which are unable
to fly. Brosius regards him with mocking concern.
He relishes the boy's abashed distress. Suddenly he
resumes his official attitude, replaces his glasses in
their normal position, and announces : " Twenty-
five knee-bends for Silberstein, because this is the
third time he has fallen asleep at numbering off."

" Stand at ease ! " he shouts to us, and then
draws himself up severely in front of Silberstein and
begins to count : " One, two, three. . . . One, two,
three. . . ." The first five times Leo manages to
bend his knees correctly. After that I notice him
trembling. His knees are shaking. His neck wobbles.
His toes, when he gets right down to squatting
position, shift feebly and bore holes in the ground.

Dr. Brosius laughs. " Keep it up," he cries, " my
little Silberstein ; show that you're a real German boy! "

Leo struggles on desperately. It is pathetic to
watch him trying to do what is beyond his strength.

His outstretched fingers grope in the gravel. His
body hunches up. But Brosius thumps him in the
small of the back and cries : " Straighten up ! "

" Brute ! " murmurs Ferd von K. beside me.

Brosius has now planted himself beside the tottering
Leo and accompanies his own counting with a series
of exact knee-bends. Unquestionably that appeals
to him as the crown of the jest. But not one of us
laughs. The Quarta stands motionless and silent.

Suddenly I am aware that Ferd von K. is grinning all over his face. His small mouth stretches nearly from ear to ear. He snorts through his nose ; his eyelashes are wet and shining as he suppresses his mirth. He punches me in the side, and nods towards Leo. Leo is suddenly doing knee-bends as if he were an india-rubber Jack-in-the-box. Beside him Brosius is counting for the twenty-first time, " One, two, three. . . ." But Leo springs up again undismayed.

A wide grin rippled down the whole line of the Quarta. It cost me an effort to keep from doubling up with laughter. For no sooner had Leo remarked that Brosius was no longer standing in front of him to keep an eye on his exercises than he made shift to help himself by simply sitting down on his heels at the word " Three," and thus securing a steady pose in squatting which overcame the difficulty of balance and gave him a good send-off for the upward movement. Anyone could do fifty knee-bends in that fashion, even a Leo Silberstein.

Brosius observes nothing ; he is much too enamoured of his own performance. At the twenty-fifth repetition he springs exactly to attention, claps his hands, and stares in dismay at Leo, who, abandoning his trick, continues to bob up and down with the help of his unexpended strength. Brosius takes a step backwards and covers his eyes with one hand.

" Twenty-eight . . ." gasps Leo, " twenty-nine . . . thirty ! . . ." then collapses, in exhausted triumph, and shuts his eyes.

Brosius stands as if paralysed. He clears his throat three times, and says, " What ? " He takes a half-turn round the helpless boy, and again says, " What ? "

Then he says, " Sapperlott ! " and stands still, staring at Leo, who lies on the ground in the exhaus-

tion of his triumph, his eyes closed, and beads of
sweat on his forehead. Herr Brosius feels uneasy.
Perhaps the boy has over-strained himself, and has a
heart-attack. That might have awkward consequences, thinks Dr. Brosius, a little alarmed for his
career. For undoubtedly a harmless joke of that
kind with a Jewish pupil would be eagerly snapped
up and exploited by a certain section of the Press.
Only keep it out of the papers, thinks Herr Brosius,
only keep it from coming to a scandal. For like all
the men of his class, he has a boundless fear of
publicity.

He stands there and clears his throat. " Hm ! "
he says. Three times he says " Hm ! " and with a
nervous gesture shoots back his starched cuffs which
have slipped forward.

" Silberstein ! " he cries. " What's wrong with
you ? Get up ! " Leo does not move. Brosius'
voice becomes almost wheedling. " Silberstein, you
did that very well. Bravo, my dear Leo ! But get
up now. . . . You might catch cold. . . ."

Leo's face is as grey as the ground where he is
lying.

" But, good God, I didn't mean it like that ! . . .
It was only a joke. . . . Can't you stand a joke ?
Come on, get up, Silberstein . . . ! "

And he catches the wretched Leo, the little Jew
and the future member of the Army Service Corps,
under the shoulders, and tries to lift him up. The
boy is as rigid as a poker.

" Water ! Get some water ! " I run to the
fountain. The others put on grave faces.

" Such a thing to happen to me ! " murmurs
Brosius, shaking his head.

" He has strained himself," said Ferd von K.

suddenly. " He's always had a weak heart, and often has attacks."

" Then he ought to be excused from gymnastics ! " cries Brosius, springing up in relief. " How should I be expected to know that ? It's not my fault ! I can't understand what his parents are thinking of. The devil take it ! "

" They're afraid the boy will be laughed at if he asks to be excused," says Ferd.

But he gets no answer, for every eye is fixed on Leo.

At Brosius' last words he starts, his eyes fly open, with tottering limbs he gets up—and his body continuously shaken as if beaten by an invisible fist, he forces his legs to remain rigid, salutes, and says in a trembling voice : " Here, Dr. Brosius, sir."

Ferd von K. springs to his side and supports him.

Brosius looks at the boy. His face clears. He wipes his brow with his cambric handkerchief. He even knocks the dust from his knees, and advances towards Leo with exuberant friendliness. " Aren't you feeling well, Silberstein ? "

Leo, whose face is chalk-white with dark rings under the eyes, Leo, the hero of thirty knee-bends, the sole Jew and candidate for the Army Service Corps in the Quarta, smiles and replies almost gaily : " Please, sir, I'm all right ! " reeling as he speaks.

" Well, well," says Brosius. " Then it isn't half so bad. Next time tell me beforehand that you've a weak heart. . . . In any case," he adds, " that'll save you from the Army Service Corps."

Leo keeps his head rigidly at attention, gulps twice, and then says clearly and frankly in his teacher's smiling face : " Please, sir, I know I'm good for nothing."

Brosius laughs. " There's no need for everyone

to be a soldier. Perhaps you'll be a first-rate business man. Silberstein Limited. . . ." Leo's face flames; he cowers as if he had been struck.

At that Ferd raises his left arm. " Please, sir, Leo is trembling more and more."

" Then you must take him home," decides Dr. Brosius, waving me to join Ferd.

We lead Leo to the wall and take off his sandals. Ferd holds him up and I help him into his shoes.

"Oh, never mind," says Leo, but Ferd points out that he doesn't need to be shy of us if he's not feeling well.

Leo smiles at that and holds on to Ferd's strong hair. We support him and Ferd asks: "Shall we carry you?" " No," says Leo, but he staggers suddenly.

Just as we are going through the right-hand gate and Dr. Brosius' sharp orders come cutting unhindered through the air from the middle of the yard, and the responses of the Quarta being numbered off again rise with rattling precision, Leo abruptly doubles up and, just before the number thirteen, is twice violently sick over the outside fence of the Headmaster's front garden.

We bring him home. His mother presents each of us with a large Passover cake, and then telephones for the doctor.

. . . . . .

I went on with Ferd to his home. It was April, and the sun was quenched with mists. Peasants were driving their heavy teams across the black fields with loud cursing and cracking of whips. A sharp north-easter was whistling through the hazel-nut hedges, where the first catkins were showing. The air was sweet and reeked of the dung which the farm-girls were spreading with huge pitchforks out of steaming waggons.

At the poplar brook we called a halt. Ferd's shoelace had broken. He knotted it up provisionally. I took a bite out of the Passover cake.

The noise of hammers and the rattling of carts came echoing from the town ; and now and then the muffled hum of the spinning mills. The sky was low and heavy ; the clouds were greyish blue and swollen with rain. Columns of workmen going home on their bicycles jingled along the main road.

Ferd von K. stood facing me, his hands in the pockets of his leather breeches, and with his right foot kicked a white marble into the field.

" You know, what Brosius did was a shame." I nodded. The cake-crumbs were all over the breast of my jacket.

" Of course it's easy to make fun of poor Leo. He can't defend himself. Brosius knows that quite well. And even if he does tell his people, what can his father do ? Brosius is in the Head's good books, and is supposed to be a capital teacher ; my father says the Ministry are keeping an eye on him." Ferd sat down beside me. His small head drooped ; he crossed his legs and whistled to himself. I knew that he was thinking of a big scheme, for his right forefinger was on his nose.

Suddenly he got up and cut a switch from a willow tree. While he decapitated some dandelions whose golden heads gleamed poisonously in the young grass, he said : " We must protect Leo. . . ." He went on switching at the grass.

" Of course we must," I answered, enthusiastic at this proposal of his, " for Leo's always so decent. The other day he let me crib all my French homework from him because he knew I didn't understand about the subjunctive."

Ferd looked at me severely. " It has nothing to do
with his being decent. There's lots of decent fellows
I wouldn't lift a finger for. But he's absolutely
defenceless. They trip him up deliberately in the
football field every time and then abuse him for
limping. He's always up against it. He's always in
trouble. Everybody makes a butt of him because
there's no one to stick up for him. He can't say he
has a cousin in the Navy, and his father has no
decorations,—he hasn't even an uncle a doctor. He
has nothing to shelter behind, as we have, that isn't
made fun of. Of course, he thinks that his life
has got to be like that, and it depresses him. And
if Brosius goes on making a fool of him he'll end up
by being one."

Ferd assumed his grown-up face. He wrinkled
his brow deeply and contracted his nostrils, compress-
ing his mouth to a sharp line.

" My father told me the other day that it was my
duty to protect the weak, and that it was a dirty
thing to hit somebody who couldn't defend himself.
Brosius is a brute."

" He's conceited," I returned. " My cousin told
me that he talked about nothing but himself and the
Kaiser."

" He's a coward," laughed Ferd, " like all the
people who talk big."

He poked about with his switch in a puddle.

" But he'll get on. I heard the other day he was
bound to get into Parliament."

"Why not?" said Ferd. "There's lots there like him."

I was struck with admiration for Ferd. He had
no respect even for Parliament, the dream of my
father's life. All the things I had to take my hat off
to at home, or keep mum about while the grown-ups

talked, he held in contempt. He was so manly.
Nothing took him in. How I adored him !

" Yes," I cried, " we two will protect Leo ! "

He nodded. I put my arm round his neck. Then
we sang. In a pool covered with bubbles so
oily that they couldn't burst, Ferd found the first
spotted salamander. He tickled its head with his
switch. The creature winced and scuttled along the
edge of the pool on its clumsy feet which looked
like hands, disappearing finally among the reeds.
Across our path in perfect indolence a fat toad lay
sprawling ; dainty midges with opalescent wings
were walking over the grey bulges on its wrinkled
skin. We threw hard clods at some ravens who were
hunting for white grubs in the filthy straw of an
empty potato-pit.

The town lay behind us. A dazzling ray of light
broke through the heavy clouds and danced on the
dove-grey roofs which began to gleam. Then the
rain came on, and we took to our heels. . . .

The farm where Ferd lived lay about five hundred
yards from the main road, approached by a yellow,
smoothly rolled drive flanked by silver poplars. It
was a lovely drive to ride a bicycle on ; you hardly
heard the tyres. Ferd and I often practised doing
rings on it.

The yard was large and broad. The manor-house
stood on the right, an eighteenth-century building
covered with ivy. Next to it was the dairy, then the
barns and stables. On the other side was the servants'
cottage, and behind that the huts for the Polish
seasonal workers.

. . . . . .

Herr von K. had resigned from the Army a few
years after the fall of Bismarck. In doing this he had

followed the lead of his family, which agitated against everything Wilhelm II said or did. After his resignation the Major lived for three years in England, and from that retreat saw that his action was justified. His connections with the English aristocracy and the world of diplomacy soon made him sensible of Germany's growing isolation. He hated Wilhelm II as a traitor to the old Prussian tradition, which had always tried its mettle on the Continent, not, as now, wasting its strength in costly manœuvres with fleets and colonies. His conservative instincts turned against the loud aggressive style of the " new policy," which in his opinion was distorting the real image of Germany in the eyes of the world. In his letters he always contrasted the theatrical magniloquence of the Kaiser with the soldierly simplicity of his grandfather and the cosmopolitan liberalism of his father. He was convinced that a German-British understanding, based, of course, on a recognition of British supremacy in naval and colonial power, would guarantee the equilibrium of Europe for centuries. He wrote an essay to expound this point of view and sent it to the Foreign Office, including an account of the internal dangers to be feared should a war break out against a coalition led by England, and it was returned with marginal comments by the Kaiser of a tone and purport which horrified the Major and made him finally decide to retire into private life.

It was in England that the Major had found his wife. She was a member of the old aristocracy ; her father had been one of Bismarck's greatest admirers. With her the Major journeyed to India. His son Ferd was born in the Majestic Hotel in Calcutta.

Herr von K. spent three years globe-trotting and hunting, then his wife died of yellow fever during an expedition into the Himalayas. The Major rescued his son from the puritanic care of an English nurse and travelled with him to Japan. There, after his months of conventional mourning were over, he fell in with the daughter of a French Military Attaché. He succumbed to her Gascon temperament and lived with her for six months in a garden city of provincial Japan. These months the Major considered the happiest of all his life.

Ferd, meanwhile, had learned to walk and speak —he called Jaqueline Mamma, because she always kissed him when he was playing among the flowers in the garden. The affair was broken off by the intervention of the Attaché, who in spite of his liking for the Major foresaw that a scandal might arise which would ruin his public career. Jaqueline was enough of a Frenchwoman and a daughter to submit to her father's arguments. She bestowed a farewell on the Major which lasted for three days and nights, and which he had the strength to enjoy without sentimentality. A few days after Jaqueline had gone back to minister to her father's needs, he found a volume by Jean Paul Richter in a German bookshop in Tokio. After reading it he decided to return home.

He had forgotten the spirit of Wilhelm II.

He took the landward route over Russia. As an officer he was interested in the East Siberian Railway. In Vladivostok he caught typhus, and the name of Jaqueline ran through all his ravings. Ferd spent six weeks in the care of a taciturn Catholic sister. Then they journeyed through the monotonous days of Siberia. Ferd cried when he saw the steppes. His father comforted him with stories about Germany.

In Moscow the Major took his son to see the Kremlin at the very moment when the bells were being beaten with hammers. Ferd never forgot those bells. He called them later " God's oxen."

By the time they crossed the German frontier Ferd was four years old. He could lisp to his father in German, English and French.

When the Major got to Berlin he realised that he had been a victim of romanticism. That Germany no longer existed which had breathed upon him from Jean Paul's book and had spell-bound his heart in Tokio. It was being denied everywhere. Germany no longer lay in the mild glow of a fruitful and patient summer ; its thoughts no longer came stealing on the quiet feet of a great universal wisdom — they trumpeted, they screamed, they preened themselves as absolute — everything was loud, exaggerated and uncritical. The whole nation believed that it was marching in unison towards that place in the sun which its Kaiser was upholstering for it with fine phrases. Of the proletariat the Major knew nothing, nor of those people who lived retired in silent opposition. All he saw was the façade of a megalomaniac bourgeoisie and a Byzantine aristocracy. He saw Germany with the eyes of the world from which he came. At home and in society, at public assemblies and in the streets, in newspapers, railway carriages and parliamentary speeches he heard but the one note : our Army, our industries, our science, our art, our women, our character, our children, our good temper—everything that is ours is the best in all the world !

This refrain exasperated the Major to such a pitch
that he plunged into the composition of an out-
spoken article on naval and colonial problems,
which appeared in a well-known South German
Radical paper, accompanied by an editorial dis-
claimer. In that article the Major thrashed out his
idea of sacrificing root and branch an ambitious
overseas policy in favour of an understanding with
England, and lashed with contempt the unbounded
conceit of a Government which had apparently
quite forgotten to whose statesmanship it owed its
rank as a Great Power ; he warned the country that
it was politically unsound to under-estimate opponents,
pointed out that the colonies were of no value save
to stamp collectors, and described the policy of the
Navy as " a little child's game with a gigantic toy."
A result of this article was that he was expelled from
his aristocratic club and socially ostracised. Even
the Radical newspaper wrote to him that although his
warmth was humanly excusable he had all the same
gone a little too far.

From that day on the Major devoted himself
exclusively to the management of his estate and the
education of his son. He gave up the idea of telling
the truth to a nation which mistook the success of
its favourably placed industries for its own destiny.

He took refuge in the country. He became a
farmer. As a mere farmer he disclaimed all
responsibility.

· · · · · ·

I first met Ferd when he was six years old. In our
school his position was unique. His intellect,
precociously stimulated by his travels and his inter-
course with his father, assured him a superiority
which his silent habits helped him to maintain.

Within the range of our thought there was nothing Ferd did not know. It impressed us enormously when he marked out with a red pencil on his small school atlas the routes of his travels. Our imaginations surrounded him with all the glamour of strange lands. We saw him in adventures which we laboriously reconstructed in our games, and when in the geography class we had to learn by heart the dry details of foreign coast lines belonging to such and such a nation with such and such "chief products," it was in Ferd's eyes that we read all we dreamed of behind the names. He knew the world. He knew its wonders. Even the teachers used to ask him about what he had seen, questions which did not arise out of the lesson. Ferd could pronounce all the foreign words correctly at sight. He never blushed when confronted with a strange name.

Only in the Scripture lesson was he found wanting. For his father had omitted to instruct him at the right time in the empiric illogicality of Biblical events. So often Ferd would say, "I don't believe that." The miracle of the marriage at Cana, for example, or the Lord's injunction to Peter, "Put up thy sword. . . ." Once on a sultry afternoon when we were learning the Passion by heart and in bored weariness were adding moustaches to the pictures of Christ, he asked our asthmatic Scripture teacher "Why did Jesus go up to Heaven when he was resurrected? Why didn't he stay on earth? Everybody would have been glad if he had stayed . . .," and that earned him a black mark for insolence.

But in the gymnastic lesson he made up for his incapacity to believe things merely because the Scripture teacher said they were so. In gymnastics

Ferd was our ideal. He could do everything. He
was both strong and agile. His father improved
on the formal school gymnastics by giving him a
thorough training in sports. Every morning at seven
o'clock he gave Ferd a scientific boxing lesson on the
threshing floor, using as punch-ball a sack stuffed
with newspaper clippings from the Kaiser's speeches.
It was heavy enough for the boy's punches.

And while in our parents' dark sitting-rooms we
played at the Balkan war with tin soldiers or pasted
stamps, and were severely punished for going out in
cool weather without a scarf or a jacket, the Major
was riding with his son over the water meadows.
Ferd slept on a hard mattress, and in summer, to the
general indignation of the little town, often used to
bathe naked in the well-trough before his house. It
always made us turn red if we were there. We used
to steal glances at Ferd, whose brown body stood up
in the strong air of the fields and meadows as if it were
native to them. Once a small boy whose parents
forbade him to undress at night while the light was
on sprang at Ferd as he was stepping out of the trough
and I was holding the towel for him with my
hands trembling and my face averted, and bit
him in the back. Ferd, who was bleeding freely,
cuffed him soundly, and the small boy—he was
the son of S. the parson—burst into tears and ran
home.

Ferd was renowned throughout the school for his
boxing. Even the big boys in the top classes
respected him. He settled every difference with
sporting correctness. It always made him angry to
see unfair fighting. If anybody resorted to sneaking
tactics in a row, tripping up an opponent, for instance,
or hitting below the belt, Ferd always challenged

him to three rounds and laid him out to restore the
honour of the class.

Ferd never regarded the other fellow in a fight as
an enemy. He bore no resentment against those he
had beaten. His father had brought him up strictly
in the chivalrous tradition of the officers and gentlemen of the pre-bourgeois age.

. . . . . .

Feeling in our town was strong against the Major.
The first thing they noticed was his persistent absence
from celebrations of the Kaiser's birthday, and then
his abrupt refusal of every invitation to them ; after
that people got wind of his article about the colonies,
and many parents regarded with suspicion the way
he was bringing up his son. From certain hints
dropped by the District Commissioner, who had
received official memoranda about the Major,
people came to the conclusion that he was politically
suspect, a conclusion strengthened by the fact that he
often spoke English with his son. In people's houses
he was generally referred to as " The Red Major,"
although he might have been accused of anything
but an attachment to the proletariat. His feud with
the prevailing policy sprang simply from his love for
a past which he saw being threatened. He was
a conservative, and a man of culture. This in itself
would have sufficed to make him a firm opponent
of Wilhelm II, who, relying on a half-educated
bourgeoisie and the pedantic ideology of a few
professors, was promising world supremacy to a
people which lacked the taste even to dress well or
eat with discrimination. " What could they do
with the world," said the Major, " supposing it were
politically possible for them to get it ? Even in
Calcutta they would gorge on pork ribs."

The Major's wrath at the new policy had been already sublimated so far that he could give an æsthetic turn to his political ideas and prejudices. Nobody could call him a revolutionary.

In our town he was denounced as one. Brosius was responsible for the nickname, " The Red Major," and in the *salons* of the officials who were his spiritual brothers he industriously circulated versions of the Major's private life in which, of course, the affair with the French Attaché's daughter played a conspicuous part. In influential circles in Dr. Brosius' class the word French was synonymous with degenerate, syphilitic and perverse.

Under cover of moral indignation Dr. Brosius recounted all the details of that scandalous intrigue, details which he owed to a brother officer who was secretary at the German Legation in Tokio.

The mothers used to shriek when, with shocked prurience, Brosius touched up the story. Then they ran to their sons and forbade them to associate with the Red Major's son, hinting that nobody could be sure that Ferd was not the fruit of an illegal intrigue. They did this by saying that he couldn't pretend to an honourable name.

Their sons complied with their parents' instructions. They were glad of their moral superiority as a foil to Ferd's athletic superiority, which they reluctantly had to admit. Soon Ferd was known as a bastard —the very term of abuse we threw at the pupils from the elementary schools.

.   .   .   .   .   .

Ferd was perfectly indifferent to the boycott. He stood alone in the playground during the intervals, and ate his bread while the others conversed in groups. It bothered him little when they whispered

behind his back and occasionally flung at him the
word " bastard " or " red."

His father had explained to him the reason for
this isolation ; he accepted it as a distinction.

I was the only one in the class who succeeded in
breaking the boycott. This I could do because my
father left all questions concerning my education in
my mother's hands and devoted himself to his
official work and his stamp collecting. Besides, he
detested Brosius for his loose tongue. Brosius, who
liked to tell dubious stories when he was drunk, was
the complete negation of the strict Christian principles in which my father had been brought up.
True, he stigmatised all that he heard of the Major
as " immoral," but he was just enough to question
Brosius' ability to judge.

My mother loved Ferd. She often observed him
while we were playing, perhaps settling a dispute
or climbing up our nut tree with agile movements. She took great pleasure in him, for he
answered frankly and did not blush when a grown-up
spoke to him. When he bowed and took off his hat
it was not forced politeness as with other boys, it was
a free and winning gesture. She often spoke to him,
not in the ironically friendly tone grown-ups are
used to assume with other people's children, but
with serious attention. Even my father said, when
the boycott began—it was decided on in the academic
luncheon club a few days after the Kaiser's birthday—
" The boy has breeding ; a pity that his father has
such perverse opinions. Why can't he keep them to
himself ? "

" Everybody's not like you . . ." said my mother,
giving him a sharp look.

" Excuse me," cried my father, " that's putting it

a bit too strong. I admit that there's many things to-day I don't approve of either, and I hold my tongue. But I give the Kaiser his due. I do my duty. I'm a Government official. Let the world do what it pleases. . . ." With that he went off to his room, where he became absorbed in his stamp collection under the green lamp.

I sat anxiously at the table and knotted up the fringes of the cloth. As usual my father had left the decision to my mother. He trusted her instinct in everything connected with " the practical life," with which he wished to have as little concern as possible. That included even the correct knotting of his tie, a matter in which he was helplessly delivered into my mother's hands.

If she ever wanted to consult him about household questions, or the arrangement of the garden, or my education, he always said, " I am fundamentally in agreement with you, my dear ; do what you like." Then he went to his work with grave punctiliousness, and in the evening departed with quiet delight to his hobbies. These were stamps and commentaries on verdicts of the Supreme Court.

I glanced at my mother, who was beginning to embroider red and blue flowers on a coverlet. She was smiling, but I did not know whether at my father or at me.

" Well," she said suddenly, without looking up, " what about Ferd ? Will you stop playing with him ? "

" No ! " I cried. " No ! I'll stand by him. . . ."

" So you'll stand by him ? " repeated my mother. " But why do you want to do that ? "

" Because I like him awfully. . . . And now that he's alone, I like him ever so much more."

At that my mother looked up.

I turned very red, and did not know what to do with my hands.

" What makes you think you like Ferd so much ? "

I felt desperate.

" Oh, mother . . ." I cried.

But she sat there with a steady face, her eyes of a piercing blue.

" I could . . ."

" What could you do ? . . . Tell me all about it."

" I could kiss him . . . ! " And I was at her feet, seeking the forgiving warmth of her bosom. She clasped me very close when I began to cry.

" Have you ever kissed him ? "

" No, mother, he'd never stand that."

" But you like him very much ? "

" Yes, mother, nearly as much as you."

I knew she was smiling.

She picked up her embroidery and threw it on the sofa.

" If you like him you should stand by him."

" Mother ! " I cried, and kissed her hands.

" If anybody tries to interfere, you can just say that you have my permission. And, besides, that you know nothing about the things they accuse his father of. That these are things which concern only grown-ups, and that grown-ups should settle them among themselves. That you are only a boy, and Ferd is your friend."

" Yes, but," said I, foreseeing the consequences immediately, " Haugwitz, the Commissioner's son, has threatened to half-kill any boy who goes on playing with Ferd."

" He won't try that on while Ferd is with you. . . ."

I leapt up. She was right, as usual. Of course nothing could happen to me under Ferd's protection.

" Oh ! " I cried, " I'm not afraid ! Let them all come ! Ferd is the strongest, the handsomest, and the greatest of all of them ! "

" He's a clever boy, Ferd von K., and sterling through and through," smiled my mother. " There's a lot you can learn from him."

" I'll grow like him. Ferd is a hero ! "

In my wild enthusiasm I flung out my arms and knocked over with my left hand a half-filled tea-cup, which fell on the floor with a crash and broke.

The door of the next room opened and framed the figure of my father. Paralysed in the middle of my enthusiasm I stood there with rigid arms staring at the puddle of tea.

I heard the ominous voice of my father : " You've messed up the parquet flooring again ! "

" I was so excited . . ." I stammered. He made towards me. I knew a box on the ear was coming. That parquet floor was my father's pride ; it was the only one in our town. It had cost me many a box on the ear already.

But this evening my mother went up to my father, restrained his hand, and said softly : " Let him be. He really was excited. Only think, he's made up his mind to be a hero ! There's more than a tea-cup will get broken over that ! As for the floor, it's not too bad. I'll polish it up again. And all the floors are done on Saturday, anyhow. But your son seems to have inherited a temperament—from the distaff side . . ." And she dropped him a curtsey, smiling, but without malice. My father went back to his room shaking his head. " Well, please yourselves ! " I heard him say.

I ran to my mother, wanting to embrace her.

But she knelt for some time on the floor, gathering up the fragments, and wiping away the tea with a cloth.

" You must go to bed now," she said, " and to-morrow morning invite Ferd to come here for coffee on Sunday. There will be apple tarts."

I could not speak. I tiptoed gently beside her, knelt down, and kissed her on the cheek, where her hair began to grow.

That night I was very happy and took a long time to go to sleep.

.   .   .   .   .   .

Next morning in the main interval I went up to Ferd, who was standing alone by the north fence, and said to him : " Ferd, I want to go on being friends with you." " Oh . . ." he replied, " why ? " I turned red. " I don't know why, but you've to come to our house on Sunday for coffee. There will be apple tarts . . ." Ferd laughed at that and put his arm round my neck. We went through the play-ground. Whispers flew round us from the other groups. It was an exalted moment.

When the bell rang and all the boys fell into line, I seized Ferd by the sleeve and whispered in his ear : " All that I have is yours—even my life ! "

(That bit about " my life " I had read in a boys' story, where friendships were always cemented in that style.)

Ferd laughed. " Keep it to yourself ! But you can teach me to ride the bicycle." I was overjoyed. Riding the bicycle was the only thing I could do which he couldn't.

Eight days later he had mastered it.

Since then we had spent every day together. I was proud of our friendship, for we upheld it in face of the whole town, the veto of the parents, and everything that was respectable ; we were avoided, but feared ; we lorded it over the school grounds and playing-fields ; I soon learned to box, too, and everybody hated us, but could not lay a finger on us. On my suggestion we had organised the elementary scholars, who were strong enough but had never had a leader. Led by Ferd we beat the " gentry boys " three times in open combat, and since then the elementary scholars had never been called bastards. We were lords of the streets, and soon managed to get together a football team which was unbeatable. The elementary boys were devoted to Ferd. They called him " captain," and flung their caps in the air whenever he made them a speech. We carried little sticks as weapons, and a red strip of cloth on our arms as a badge. We called ourselves " The Red Guard." I was the trumpeter.

It was a beautiful friendship. For everybody talked about it.

It was considered a scandal.

Brosius said it was Socialist depravity.

But we were unbeatable.

Therefore it was no empty phrase when Ferd decided to take Leo under his protection. He could do it. The Red Guard was his to command.

. . . . . .

In these days, however, I was continually obsessed by a thought not concerned with the relationship between us boys. It turned on the thing, whatever it was, that all the grown-ups endeavoured to hide from us. I had often noticed that they broke off conversations suddenly and as if they had been

B

caught whenever they saw me or any other child
near them, that whenever I had to leave the room
their words changed at once in tone and colour, that
there was something between them only referred to
in whispers or winks, and that there was a corner in
their lives round which we were not supposed to see.
Of course, in school with the help of clumsy drawings
by older boys I had got an inkling of the existence
of hidden intimacies, but they were vague and, in
the way they were described, sordid. The girls I
saw bewildered me, for I knew they were different
from me, but I did not know why. This obsession
only became formulated after my stay on the farm.
I used to watch the animals there, and could not
believe that they were only playing as my mother
averred when I told her they jumped up on each
other. Since Ferd had very coolly and with an
expert air explained to me the difference between the
sexes, and I found proof of the same difference
among human beings, the question of how and why
they played like that interested me exceedingly.
" Playing," I called it, for the mystery would have
been still more of a torture if I had not found a word
for it. At first it was pure curiosity, an objective
desire for knowledge. Excitement, guilt and shame
were only associated with it after my first timid
attempt to get an explanation from my father, who
said that to ask such questions was indecent.

Ferd was very cool about these things. Girls
meant nothing to him, and the animals he took as
a matter of course.

CHAPTER II

WE ran up to the farm. Broad and solid it lay in the brooding expectancy of its black acres. Smoke was rising from the dairy. The shutters of the manor-house gleamed green and wet ; the spiders' webs in the ivy glittered with raindrops. In the bleaching-yard behind the kitchen garden shirts were fluttering on a line, ballooned into figures that were comic because they had no heads.

In the byre the cows were lowing. We could hear the horses pulling at their halters. From the fields came echoing the singing of the Polish land-girls, heavy and dark as their own hair. It was four o'clock, the break for coffee.

The first gnats were dancing in conical swarms above the midden, where a mongrel dog was hunting for mice. Under the projecting roof of a large barn a cock sprang upon a blue-grey hen, which went on patiently pecking on the ground.

I nudged Ferd.

" Do you see that cock ? "

Ferd turned round. I was very excited, and dared not look again. I edged close to him and whispered : " There it is again, the mystery ! "

" What mystery ? "

" There ! " I pointed and grew red, for it was the first time I had ever mentioned it to Ferd.

35

" But that isn't a mystery ! " laughed Ferd. " That happens every day. What's the cock there for ? "

" Oh, Ferd," I said, " it's not just the cock—it all hangs together, the fowls, the ducks, the horses . . . and people too. . . ."

" Well," said Ferd, with great indifference, " it does all hang together. I don't know exactly how it is with human beings, but it will be something the same. . . ." He moved off, and was not in the least excited.

I clutched at him.

" Ferd ! " I cried, " when do you think we'll know how it is with human beings ? "

Ferd stopped and thought it over.

" I don't suppose we'll ever know."

" Why ? "

" Because nobody's allowed to speak about it."

" But they do it all the same ! "

" Of course they do it, and you'll do it too some day. . . . But you won't talk about it, just like all the others. Not long ago I saw our foreman putting his arm round Kathinka, you know, the yellow-haired dairymaid, shortly after knocking-off time, and then they went sneaking into the cottage as if they had stolen something, so I slipped after them. When they got to the foreman's room he bolted the door. I listened. First they spoke in a low tone and Kathinka laughed, then it sounded as if something suddenly fell, and I heard the foreman panting as if he were lugging a sack : they groaned and they laughed, but it all sounded distressed—and then I heard Kathinka crying. Crying, you know, just as the wind does when it drives rain against the windows. The foreman came out afterwards and hit the cows viciously because they had bellowed at feeding time.

And Kathinka didn't look at him for days. . . . I think that it makes people afraid of each other."

" Do you think it's something wicked ? "

" Perhaps," said Ferd, " or else why should they try to hide it ? "

" But I will find out what it is," I cried, " let it be as wicked as anything ! "

" Not me," said Ferd, " I should feel like a criminal."

" But we'll have to know, when we get a girl."

" I don't want a girl."

His remark cut clean through the crystal air. He stood there immovable, his mouth screwed up and haughty.

" Ferd," I cried, " how can you say that ! A girl is the loveliest thing alive."

Ferd burst out laughing horribly, his body con-vulsed as if by an inward spasm ; he stood there on the sandstone step before the house laughing till he was beside himself, his face all broken up, with red patches on his temples, and his hair flying over his forehead ; his very tie was awry.

" Have you ever felt the kind of smell girls have ? " he asked.

" No," I said. " Do they have a smell ? "

" Yes," he cried, " I smelt it when my cousin was here the other day. She was given my room, I was turned out. In the morning I wanted to get a pencil for my drawing lesson, and when I knocked at the door she wasn't in. So I went in for the pencil. And when I got in the air was so thick it hit me in the face, sour and bitter and sweet all together. I was nearly sick, it was so close and stifling, not bad air but thick and strong ; I can't describe it, I had never smelt anything like it. Well, I ran out again, forgetting about my pencil. And in the corridor I met my cousin, looking sleek and friendly just as all girls do. I could have hit her, and when she tried to pat me I spat on her hand.

" In my drawing lesson I got a black mark, but I couldn't explain why I had forgotten my pencil. In the lunch hour I told my father all about it, and he said it was something quite natural to all girls. But I won't have anything to do with girls ! " concluded Ferd, jumping down beside me. " Do you see ? "

He put his arm round my shoulders.

" You mustn't ever kiss a girl either. Will you swear it ? "

I felt upset. I thought of my mother, and wanted to forget what Ferd had said. He stood waiting. I trembled, thinking of all the girls I knew. They seemed to have become different ; Ferd had taken away all their loveliness ; they were unclean.

I hated Ferd.

But I didn't want to hate him.

Slowly I lifted my hand and said : " Yes, I swear it."

Ferd grasped my hand and pressed it. Then I felt his cheek against mine. He was breathing very fast. It made me tremble, for Ferd had never been so close to me. I could see his eyes quite near ; they were like large berries ; their vivid pupils darkened, and in the white of the eyeballs ran a network of red veins.

His hand was lying on my shoulder. I felt helpless and dejected ; my head yielded to his winning pressure. His lips were before me ; I could see nothing but those red lips, which had a duskier gleam where they joined the white of his skin.

They were exactly like Hilde's lips, when I taught

her how to bicycle in the evenings on the boulevards,
the same lips that girls always have when they pass
you by and stare through you as if they knew much
more than you. And let Ferd say what he liked, the
mystery could never be solved without a girl. . . .
And suddenly I felt a stab of curiosity amid my
bewilderment ; what would happen if I were to
touch those lips ? Must lips be touched in order to
learn the mystery ? Were things only mysterious so
long as one had not touched them ?

I bent my head forward. Ferd's breath fanned
me. I saw nothing more ; the blood pulsed in my
ears. " Hilde," I thought, " Hilde ! " She was
before my eyes. Her black hair with the red ribbon,
her dark face—it leaned towards me, smiling. . . .
" The mystery ! " The thought pierced me, and
I kissed Ferd. I bit him in the lips, thinking to
myself all the time that he was a girl. . . .

The noise of carriage wheels turning in at the
gate ; it was the Major's coupé. My illusion shivered
into fragments beneath the regular beat of the
cream-coloured horses' hoofs, and I started back.
I was quite aware that what I had done must be
concealed. I let Ferd go. " Ow ! " he yelled,
" you've bitten me ! " He put his handkerchief to
his mouth, which was bleeding. " Hush ! " I
whispered, " don't give me away." He leaned up
against the wall of the house, his eyes tight shut ;
apparently he was in pain.

I had no time to feel ashamed, although I knew
that I had been false to him.

But perhaps he felt the power of the mystery too ?
For it was he who first laid his arm round me. Or
did he have a different kind of mystery ? I sprang
towards him and stroked his hand.

" Ferd," I begged, " if your father asks why you're
bleeding, tell him you fell and bit your lip. . . ."

" I won't tell a lie," said Ferd, turning away.

" But you must ! "

" I won't lie to my father. He's a gentleman ! "

" But the mystery ! " I cried. " We'll have to lie.
We'll have to lie often ! "

Ferd lowered his handkerchief, which was caked
with blood. His lips were blue.

" What mystery ? "

He stood by the wall tearing off ivy leaves, which
gave out a sharp smell something like the smell Ferd
said girls had.

He laughed.

" Do you mean the kiss ? "

I nodded in desperation, for I could already hear
the Major's firm military step coming across the
courtyard. And behind him the asthmatic wheezing
of fat Dr. Hoffmann.

" But there's no mystery about a kiss," laughed
Ferd. " You exaggerate everything. It's only with
girls that there's any mystery. But we have sworn
not to."

I felt very ashamed, for I knew I had been false
to him.

Ferd stood beside me and hit me twice sharply on
the calves with a trail of ivy.

" That's for biting me," he said.

I submitted to it.

The blows burned me as Ferd's lips had burned
mine. I felt like asking him to hit me again, but I
did not dare. I was trembling, filled with fear of
what was in myself. I wanted to forget it. For it
was wicked, because I could not speak of it to anybody.

The Major stopped beside us. He was wearing a tussore silk shirt under a coffee-coloured jacket, and no waistcoat. That shirt of his was my delight. It was the only tussore silk shirt in our town. The Major had brought it with him from India. An adventurous shirt !

" He looks like a play actor," people used to say, when the Major went out walking in the shirt. They were all for solid garments. Herr von K. was clean-shaven, too, which made it worse.

" Calls himself a man, does he ? " said the women, mincing proudly in their tight bodices.

" He's un-German," answered the men, twirling their moustaches fiercely. This was another habit they had caught from the Kaiser.

The Major held out his hand to me with a " Good morning." I looked away from him to the smiling Dr. Hoffmann, whose comfortable girth reassured me a little. Herr Hoffmann was wearing a cut-away and yellow shoes. His hat was pushed back off his forehead, for he sweated easily. He weighed 175 pounds. His fleshy hands were pink and soft. He was always smiling. His evenly rounded cheeks were creased with small merry wrinkles. He always had apples in his pockets for the children when he went out, and liked to be called Uncle. In his left hand he swung a cane with a silver knob on which his initials were engraved, and with which he emphasised his remarks, never letting it out of his hand even inside the house. These remarks of his were much feared, for Herr Dr. Hoffmann was a lawyer and a Social Democrat. He was a member of Parliament.

The Major had made his acquaintance when he found that all the other lawyers in town were

B *

unwilling to act on his behalf. The dead-set against
Herr von K. was so violent and so universal that
they were unwilling to incur social odium by having
anything to do with him. The Major was unpreju-
diced enough to turn to Dr. Hoffmann, and found
in him not only an able lawyer but a good friend.
Hoffmann was preserved from fanaticism by his
easy humour. He was assuredly a Socialist and
a revolutionary, but in measure, as he himself expressed it. He believed firmly and happily in the
ultimate victory of his ideas, which should not be
endangered by premature and precipitate action. {For
his faith he had given up his home life, the sweetheart of his youth, the possibility of becoming a
judge, and had suffered eight months' imprisonment.

In his own party he stood for moderation ; the
criterion of all his actions was plain common-sense,
according to which he forecast definitely a time when
the capitalist system would topple of itself and Socialism would bloodlessly take over the construction of a
new society.

" Violence is stupid," he used to say, " so if we
leave it to the others, we'll triumph all the sooner."

Through his influence the Major came to study
scientific Socialism, reading with arduous attention
all its literature and arguing it out afterwards with
Hoffmann.

The latter came twice a week to the manor-house
for supper. Although he and the Major were continually at loggerheads they were very good friends.

Dr. Hoffmann held out an apple to me. I shook
my head, and stole a glance at Ferd. He was standing beside his father with a serious face, the caked
blood on his lips glistening like bronze.

" What's the matter ? " said Dr. Hoffmann. " You

look as though the world had let you down ! " With
that he twirled on his toes and laughed happily.
" And what's wrong with you ? " he turned to
Ferd. " Your lips are covered with blood."
I trembled. If Ferd blurted out the truth, it
would be an end of our mystery.
" Dr. Hoffmann," I heard him say, " I've been in
a bad temper."
" And bitten your lip ? " Hoffmann laughed.
" That's true aristocratic behaviour ! "
" It's quite a serious matter, Dr. Hoffmann."
And Ferd buttonholed the doctor and related with
great exactness what had happened between Leo
Silberstein and Dr. Brosius.
Hoffmann listened earnestly, leaning on his cane.
The Major watched Ferd and nodded.
I thought : " It was a mystery after all, for Ferd
has told a lie."
" Hm," said Hoffmann suddenly, taking out his
note-book. He wrote down with great care what
Ferd was telling him. Now and then he laughed,
and cried, " That's capital ! "
" You won't surely bring it up before Parlia-
ment ? " asked the Major.
Hoffmann shook his head cheerfully. " No," he
said, " but in the newspapers. . . ."
" The boy will only suffer. . . ."
Hoffmann shut his note-book with a snap and eyed
the Major from head to foot. " My friend, when
will you appreciate the power of the Press ? Herr
Brosius won't be able to sleep for three nights after
suddenly finding himself in the *People's Guardian*."
" I regard such methods as unfair ! " cried the
Major.
" I know well enough that many Civil Servants

buy the *Guardian* on the sly whenever they know that
one of their colleagues is shown up. And they even
pass it on ! " roared Hoffmann.

" Oh, well ! " said the Major, turning away.

" When I attack a Minister in Parliament," went
on Dr. Hoffmann, " all his subordinates read about
it, and chuckle. . . . And what's more, I get fifty per
cent of my information from rigid supporters of the
Government ! "

" That's disgusting," said the Major.

" But it's effective," countered Hoffmann.

" So you think any weapon justified ? "

" If it's sharp enough, yes, I do."

" Then I don't understand why you condemn
violence."

" That's quite another thing."

" How so ? " cried the Major.

" I only undermine the system, in exposing what
is corrupt and humanly disgraceful in it. I only pick
out the details, my friend. I leave it to collapse of
itself ! "

Hoffmann swung his cane, and cocked a sly eye at
the Major, who burst out indignantly :

" You haven't a thought beyond party politics !
Your class war is just a primitive tribal concern.
Not one of you has a notion of what is happening in
Germany. And if it comes to war, you'll only see it
as something to be exploited for your party. You'll
simply salute and hold out your hands for what you
can get. . . ."

Hoffmann was highly amused.

" A war ? " He smiled.

" Yes indeed ! " cried the Major. " A war ! A
terrible war, which neither you nor the Kaiser will
survive."

" Hurrah ! " I yelled, prancing with inexplicable glee between the two men.

" There you are ! " said the Major.

" What are you cheering for ? " asked Hoffmann, somewhat taken aback.

" Because there's to be a war," I stammered, turning red.

The Major laughed, Ferd laughed, and I even laughed myself out of embarrassment.

" Stuff and nonsense ! " boomed Hoffmann. " The international solidarity of the proletariat will obviate any war."

He threw his arms wide, as if he were on the platform.

The Major went up to him, shaking his head.

" But you don't know the moral force of the working classes," persisted the doctor.

" Oh yes," said the Major, " but what about their leaders ? They'll do anything for the eight-hour day and universal suffrage."

" Never will a Social Democrat take up arms ! "

" Well, we'll see," smiled the Major, pushing Dr. Hoffmann in at the door.

Hoffmann swung his cane, and cried almost gaily, " Except against the Czar ! "

. " Aha ! " said the Major, going in after him.

.   .   .   .   .   .

Ferd and I stayed behind. He was close beside me. Kathinka crossed the yard carrying a brimming milk-pail.

" Shall we go and look at the horses ? " asked Ferd.

" Yes," said I, and we went into the stables.

The horses were in their stalls switching with their

tails at the first midges. A groom came along with
a steel brush, and told Ferd something in his ear.
Ferd stopped.

" There's a foal being born. Shall we go and
watch ? "

" No ! " said I.

" You don't need to be scared. Animals aren't
like people ; they don't mind being looked at."

We went along.

In front of the last stall but one stood a man in a
white overall, with two grooms beside him holding
towels.

" Frieda ! " cried Ferd, " it's Frieda who's getting
a foal." He ran forward.

At that very moment a whinny rose in the air,
which would have been called a scream had it been
human, the planks quivered, three hoofs drummed
against the plaster wall ; the man in the overall
rushed past with a bright pair of scissors, crying
" Look out ! " the grooms shook down straw and
one of them fetched water. " Don't let go ! " cried
the veterinary surgeon. Ferd was standing in front
of the stall, leaning on a pile of straw. He winced. . . .
I had sat down on a small cart near the door and
held my ears, for groans were suddenly coming
out of the stall, as if the mare were dying.

I could see that Ferd's face was grey, something
like the colour of the limewashed wall behind it. He
was plucking at the straw with his hands. I pressed
my hands tight till the blood sang in my ears. I
could see the other horses becoming uneasy, and
fretting their muzzles against the wooden bars. A
black stallion in a separate stall on my right lifted
its head, kicked out a little, tried to rear on its hind
legs, was jerked down again by its strong chain, and

neighed. It blew so strongly through its nostrils
that the oats in its manger scattered like dust. Its
eyes were red like peeled tomatoes, and there was a
yellow froth on its tongue, which came jerking out
every now and then. In all the stalls the horses were
now plunging at their chains, kicking their legs raw,
upsetting their mangers, and whinnying.

"Bring a piece of rope!" yelled the surgeon,
giving a groom a cuff on the ear with his excited hands.
The groom rushed off stumbling over a bucket full of
bran mash, which settled on the ground in a sticky
pool and was at once covered with midges. A mouse
scuttled out of a heap of straw and began to nibble at
the mess.

The air resounded with the neighing of the horses.
I took my hands away from my ears, for the noise
was so great that no single sound could be distinguished.

I kept looking at Ferd. He was standing before
the stall, staring with bulging eyes at the mystery it
enclosed.

Suddenly the surgeon clapped his hands, crying
"Bravo!" The groom with the rope came running
in at the door. "It's not needed now," said the
surgeon laughing. "A grand foal!"

"Yes?" cried the groom, dropping the rope.

"Hurrah!" shouted Ferd, flinging up his cap.

"Good old Frieda!" cried the groom, dancing
on the slippery floor.

"You'd do better to quieten the other beasts,"
growled the surgeon.

The groom ran with bright eyes to each of the
excited animals and soothed them. They gradually
quietened down, for no more screams came
from the stall where the foal had been born. Only

the surgeon stood there washing his hands. Ferd
beckoned to me. I went up on tiptoe. In the wide
stall lay Frieda, the mare, under yellow blankets and
straw. Her eyes were dull like spent bullets. There
was a reek of blood and sweat. To her right in a
nest of hay-straw and rugs the foal stirred.

I looked at its head, which was milky white ; its
eyelids were stuck together a little.

" That's my horse," whispered Ferd. " My father
promised it to me before it was born."

He laid his arm round my shoulders, and gazed
tenderly at the quivering little creature.

The surgeon said, " You must go away now."

" Yes, it needs to be left in peace," nodded Ferd,
with an understanding air. " I'll call it Hans."

Just as we were turning to go Frieda stirred. She
stretched out her neck, her forefeet struggled out of
the straw covering, and she felt for the foal and
began to lick it.

" Look at that, isn't it lovely ? " said Ferd. Even
the surgeon wore a benevolent expression.

We went through the stables into the yard. Ferd's
arm was still round my shoulders. The sun was very
low. We stood by the gate. Smoke was rising from
the fields in front of us. In their quarters the Polish
girls were singing.

" It's knocking-off time," said Ferd.

.   .   .   .   .   .

I went on my way home. The evening coolness
was spreading blue-white over the meadows. Birds
were darting out of the blossoming blackthorn hedges.

The grass by the roadside was wet ; it made one's
shoes shining black to paddle through it.

When we parted Ferd had charged me to go to

Leo that very evening and tell him of our resolve. In the name of the Red Guard he had ordered me firmly to refuse every gift of Frau Silberstein's, even if it were only an apple. He said it was a matter of honour.

But that was all he had said. Not a word about the mystery, nor why he had told the lie, nor any comment on the kiss or the birth of the foal, which had scared me very much. Nothing but an order and a prohibition.

In any case, I had played him false when I shut my eyes and pretended his lips were a girl's lips.

But perhaps it was the nature of the mystery to make one play false?

Ferd wouldn't admit the mystery. He had never hunted up certain words in the Encyclopædia as I had. He had never yet gone up to the bathing enclosure and peeped between the boards at the girls bathing, as I had. He had never yet taught a girl to ride the bicycle on the boulevard of an evening, like me, and held her firm on the saddle when the wind blew up her petticoats. Nor had Ferd wrestled with a girl for fun in the meadow, and noticed how the fun turned to earnest and how it was impossible to stop until the girl was thrown on her back.

Ferd did not know all that, and did not want to know it. He was a hero. An ideal. But he had no mystery. . . .

I decided to track down this mystery of which the air was full, even if all the grown-ups should conspire to hide it. It was certainly something wicked, but it would be more bearable to know the wickedness than to conjecture it.

CHAPTER III

THE house in which Leo Silberstein lived was in the market square. It was a large house with a bright spacious frontage painted yellow, and green folding shutters. Between the ground floor and the first storey ran a long white sign on which was painted in red letters with fine flourishes, " David Silberstein and Co., Wholesale and Retail Drapers."

Above the " David " hung a balcony with a moulded iron framework, from the parapet of which a flagstaff capped by a shining brass knob rose into the air. On festive occasions such as the Kaiser's birthday, the twenty-fifth jubilee of the Fire Brigade, celebrations of the glee club, or war commemorations like the anniversary of Sedan, Herr Silberstein hoisted on this staff an enormous black, white and red flag, which fluttered grandly in the wind and sometimes writhed complacently like a full-fed snake.

Herr Silberstein's enemies averred that he hoisted it only to vaunt the fine quality of its stuff, with an eye to business, so to speak. Now it was the finest and biggest flag in the town, but Herr Silberstein left it out even when the rain made it sodden and the wind flapped it like a stray rag against the telephone wires. " Aha ! " said his enemies, " he's only showing off the fastness of its dye."

So Herr Silberstein was in a difficult position. If

he hoisted his flag, people said, " The sly Jew, out
for business ! " and if he did not hoist it he could
not get to sleep at nights for the patriotic cat-calls
and howls of abuse, like " Red ! " and " Alien
trash ! " Finally he decided to hang it out. He
would rather be considered an unscrupulous business man than a Social Democrat.

David Silberstein's shop had eight plate-glass windows, with a different kind of material in every bay
of them. Checked, striped and flowered calico for
the aprons and working-dresses of the peasant women,
bales of linen, sheets, finely embroidered cushions,
table-covers, green aprons for saddlers and blue ones
for locksmiths, and workmen's overalls, ready-made,
too, for a year previously Herr Silberstein had added
to his flourishing business a new department for
making-up clothes. The most magnificent window
was number eight, which bore the inscription
" English " upon its glass, and showed a collection
of beautiful wax figures, some standing, some sitting
in small wicker chairs, and all advertising the fault-
lessly cut suits they wore. These dummies, whose
cheeks were painted *à la joie de vivre*—I wanted to
look exactly like them when I grew to be a man—
had caused great excitement on their first introduction. They were extolled, even although Herr Silberstein was in bad odour, as an achievement raising
the status of the town, and when Herr Silberstein
went still further and installed a ventilator in the
shape of a large propeller in his sale-rooms he aroused
genuine admiration.

" Novelties ! " said Herr Silberstein to himself at
that time. " It's only novelties that will give me a
leg up."

He published an announcement :

" Customers must insist on making their purchase only in hygienic shops which are in line with all the medical requirements of modern times, especially where textiles are concerned, considering how dust harbours bacilli.

Buy your goods from us !

David Silberstein & Co.

The most up-to-date house. Eight display windows !

Electric ventilation ! Ozone sprays ! "

Herr Silberstein himself manipulated the ozone spray. When he appeared in the showrooms spraying fresh air, all his customers who went in terror of microbes, a fear very common in those days, were convinced that Herr Silberstein was refreshing the atmosphere in the general interest, without distinction of creed or parties ; while at the same time printed testimonials, supplied by the makers of the ozone spray and endorsed by medical experts, which Herr Silberstein displayed in his windows, definitely allayed all suspicion of its being a commercial stunt.

So with five wax dummies, a ventilator and three testimonials to his ozone spray, Herr Silberstein disarmed the hostile feeling stirred up against him in the town, from a business point of view at least. And soon people were convinced of the fine quality of his goods, especially the English stuffs, which he got on commission from a kinsman in London and could sell, because of his smaller outlay in rent and wages, at a price considerably lower than the old-established firms in the neighbouring city. The Civil Servants' wives, of course, were forbidden by their husbands to buy anything but bare necessaries from Herr Silberstein, but they were clever and open-minded enough to get the cloth for their husbands' suits from

Herr Silberstein and to apply the difference in price to the relief of their scanty housekeeping allowances, while vaunting the stuffs to their husbands as the products of a solid and old-established firm, a vaunt to which the husbands complacently subscribed after a brief examination of their quality. In the end all Herr Silberstein's most bitter enemies were walking about in suits of his cloth. He was a secret adjutant of the women, and his business flourished more and more from day to day.

Leo was his youngest son. Leo's two brothers, one of whom was red-haired and unpleasant to look at, lived abroad. The red-haired one was the Paris representative of a German rubber factory, the other was studying law and philosophy in Geneva. He used often to write in our local paper short articles about the Lake of Geneva, delicate sketches, somewhat sentimental when he touched upon the free air from the mountains which an affliction in his foot kept him from climbing, but otherwise controlled and exact in observation. My father had made his acquaintance during the vacation, had even taken a few walks in his company, and commended him as a serious student of law who disdained casuistry and had what was rarely to be found, a natural feeling for the principles of moral philosophy on which law was based. He wrote to young Silberstein occasionally and was delighted to receive from him a set of the latest Swiss Jubilee stamps. So my mother was permitted to buy whatever she liked in Herr Silberstein's shop.

.   .   .   .   .   .

I came to a stop in front of Herr Silberstein's house under one of the thickest of the chestnut trees which threw their heavy shadows from the market-place

right up to the first storeys of the surrounding houses.
I ran over in my mind what I was to say to Leo.
" We have taken you under our protection from to-
day on," would be a fair statement of the truth, but
it did not sound impressive enough to me. " Ferd
von K., myself and the Red Guard send you greeting
and bid you welcome. We have decided to admit
you into our ranks. In pursuance of our high ideals
we summon you to raise your hand and swear fealty
to our statutes."

That would be much better, only we had no
statutes, which in that solemn moment seemed to
me a great disability.

So there was nothing for it but simply to state the
facts, and resign myself to doing without the exalted
sentiment of an impressive ritual. I went through
the paved courtyard, which was overshadowed by
two enormous lilac bushes. On my right stood a
large dilapidated crook-handled pump, an open shed
in which stood the little landau Herr Silberstein
drove in to visit his country customers, next to that
the lean-to which housed the one and only horse,
Johanna, who had shared the fortunes of the firm
from its very foundation, and finally the warehouse,
a flat building of hewn grey stone in which were
stored the great bales of cloth and where a naked
light was forbidden.

The entrance into the house smelt of beeswax.
The green linoleum on the stairs shone and the brass
stair-rods winked in a ray of the evening sun which
streamed through a clear pane in the corner of the
stained glass window. With the help of the banisters
I managed to take three steps at one bound, a feat
which enormously increased my confidence. I
needed confidence, for I was rather dashed by my

mission. In front of the door, which was curtained
with net, I took off my cap and then rang the bell.
Rolling footsteps came towards me, and I heard a
hasty whisper, " Lina, lay the cloth in the *salon*,"
then the door opened and Herr Silberstein stood
before me. He peered down at me over his glasses
with smiling reserve, as if he were astonished to find
me so small. " Good evening, Herr Silberstein," I
said, with a saucy upward inflection, " I want to
see Leo."

" Oh, it's you, it's you, is it ? "—Herr Silberstein
wagged his head, and curveted with his small fat
legs—" I nearly didn't recognise you, but come in,
come in." And he took hold of me and pushed me
into the lobby, which was dimly lit by a super-
annuated electric bulb and smelt of cooking meat
and damp rain-coats.

He held me by the hand and drew me on, wheezing with pleasure. " Lina ! " he called, " never mind
about that in the *salon*. This is a friend of Leo's."
With that he gave a laugh, which rang out as if he
were in some strange way delighted. I thought,
what on earth's the matter with Herr Silberstein
that he's snorting like an excited horse ! Has he
been waiting for me for ages ? Is he so glad to see
me coming of my own accord into his house, instead
of merely accompanying my mother into his shop ?
He hauled me through the long lobby straight towards the living-room, swinging my hand as if I were
a pump that brought up magic water. High over
me I could see his face lit up and red with joy, a
face which hitherto I had believed only shone with
kindliness when one had made a big purchase in his
shop, at the till, when he said " Many thanks,"
and dropped in the money.

"A friend," cried Herr Silberstein, "a friend to see Leo!" He paused at the door of the living-room. His face, on which the light through the door-curtain lay dappled in pink, green and lilac, bent down anxiously to my level, and he whispered : "Be nice to Leo, he's very ill."

"Has he had another attack?"

"No, but he's been spitting blood. To-day's the first time. Not much, but enough for me."

The little pouches under his eyes quivered.

"Herr Silberstein, I've come with good news for Leo."

"Come in!" he cried, "come in!"

He swung the door open, and with a deep bow pushed me into the room.

There in the spent light of the April evening sat Leo at the window, his feet wrapped in a heavy brown rug, a scarf round his throat, in a red arm-chair propped up with white cushions. Beside him was a small table, on which lay a board with black and white figures. His mother was sitting opposite him ; they were playing chess.

Leo had just picked up a pawn in his slender hand when the noise of our entry made him turn slowly round. He swung the pawn in his hand, bending his thin arm in a graceful curve through the air, which was thickening into dusk, and I saw him smile exactly as he had smiled on the morning when I put his shoes on—then Herr Silberstein clapped his hands and cried : "Leo, a friend to see you!"

"Oh, it's you," said Leo, "how nice! Have you brought me the home lessons for to-morrow?"

Gently and carefully he set his pawn on the board. His mother rose and said, "Leo is very pleased to see you."

Herr Silberstein spread his arms wide and cried,
"The young gentleman has some good news for you !"

The mother went over to the sideboard, which
was crowned by a carved gilt eagle straining forever
towards the sun, and surrounded by trumpeting
cherubs. Her red face smiled down anxiously from
over her yellow blouse. Leo half rose. " I'm glad
you've come, for it's a bore to be ill. I have to put
up with being fussed over ! " he said, with a wave
of his arm.

I edged past the sharp corner of the table towards
him, and gave him my hand. Then I stood by his
chair, gripped the back of it, took a deep breath and
began. " I've come to tell you that we are going to
protect you."

" Protect me ? " laughed Leo. He had a short fit
of coughing, then beat the air with his hand and
asked : " What for ? "

Herr Silberstein and his wife both came very close,
with their necks outstretched.

" Ferd von K. sends you the message, and the Red
Guard too."

" Why do you want to protect me ? " asked Leo.

" Because of Brosius, and all your other enemies,"
I replied.

" Oh—because of Brosius," said Leo, gazing very
quietly out of the window. I stood there beside him
wondering why he was not delighted. Then Herr
Silberstein came nearer, his wife clasping his arm.

" Do you want to protect Leo ? "

" Yes," I said.

" Against whom ? "

" Against anyone who insults him."

" Oh," said Herr Silberstein, " even if they cry
' Jew ' 'after him in the street ? "

" Yes," I said, " for that's an insult."

" Can you guarantee it ? " cried Herr Silberstein, turning his hands out inquiringly.

" Of course," said I, " for we'll thrash anyone who insults Leo." Leo sat still in his chair, looking away from his excited father. The mother fetched a bottle out of a wall cupboard and poured out Malaga for me into a cut crystal glass. Herr Silberstein waddled to a small table covered with porcelain dishes, mounted boars' teeth, little snuff-boxes and match-holders filled with red, green and blue-topped matches. " Where are my cigarettes ? Surely I had some cigarettes ? " His very voice sweated as he fussed about. " Thank you," I said, " I won't have anything."

The two Silbersteins stood rooted in astonishment to their own floor. From the glass which the mother had filled too full three drops of wine trickled on to the carefully preserved table cover, and spread in sad purple stains. Herr Silberstein, who had managed to find his packet of cigarettes, tore little strips off it, and played with them.

I forgot both of them in the thought that Malaga and cigarettes were at my disposal, and over against them Ferd's harsh prohibition. But harshness was the stuff of which heroes were made.

" No, thank you," I sighed in torment, with a courteous bow, " I won't take anything."

Very sadly Herr Silberstein put away his cigarettes and the mother poured the glass of wine back into the bottle.

They looked at me mistrustfully. Apparently they thought I despised their gifts.

Leo turned his head and said : " He's quite right."

His parents stared at him. " What ? " said Herr
Silberstein.

Leo shoved a cushion behind his neck. His face
stood out clearly against its unflattering white, and
his large eyes darkened. His hand on the arm of the
chair looked incredibly fine-drawn. " Yes," said
Leo, " he's quite right to refuse. You always want
to make some payment at once when anyone's nice
to me. Perhaps you're afraid no one will stick to
me unless he's paid for it. But I don't want friends
of that kind. I don't want what has to be paid for."

" Leo ! " cried Herr Silberstein, forgetting that I
was present, " you don't want what has to be paid
for ! But you're twelve years old. What idiotic
ideas ! "

" No," said Leo, very firmly. " I have no use for
what has to be bought."

Herr Silberstein walked wheezing up and down,
sweating, giving a little laugh to himself now and
then, and fastening and unfastening the lower button
of his waistcoat.

" Everything has its price," he shouted suddenly,
" everything in the world. From God in Heaven
down to the scrappiest bit o' cotton. All got to be
paid for. Pay nothing an' you get nothing. Got to
pay your way even into Heaven."

Leo said not a word. His mother ran to him and
stroked his hair. But his face did not relax.

When Herr Silberstein had stormed round the
table for the fifth time, she peeled an apple, cut it
into fine slices, and laid it anxiously on a painted
plate beside Leo.

" And believe you me," concluded Herr Silberstein, planting himself before the sideboard, having
suddenly remembered me and imposed a control on

himself which slowly dignified his language again,
" believe your father, we Jews above all must pay
for everything down to the smallest favour. We
can't risk being in anyone's debt, or we're done for.
Don't you ever take anything, Leo, without giving
something in exchange. That's your only security
for going to bed in peace when the day's done. For
the others only need to get their reward in the next
world, but we have to get ours in this one. Yes,"
he added, taking a deep breath, " that's the fate of
our people."

" A hard enough fate," I thought, secretly agree-
ing with Herr Silberstein as I remembered the tone
and manner in which the people of our town uttered
the word " Jew." Even my father, whose fanatical
passion for absolute justice I knew so well, had a
catch in his voice as if he had to overcome something whenever he said the word : it sounded like
" Hm, Jew."

I myself did not regard the Jews I knew—especially
the older men—as objects for derision, like most of
the other boys, who delighted in mimicking them, a
thing my mother would never have allowed (in any
case I had no talent in that direction) ; but they
didn't exactly rouse my sympathies, because as far
as I could tell from watching them in our town they
were so indiscriminately amiable to everyone, friend
and foe alike. According to my youthful conceptions
of honour, that was cowardice, although I could see
that it was a different brand of " cowardice " from
the usual. It seemed to me a cowardice which did
not run away but on the contrary compelled a man
to stop and endure the most difficult situations, but
not in the same way that a hero would endure them.
Ferd von K., with whom I often discussed it, once

told me of a paradoxical phrase his father used, the sense of which we did not comprehend, but which impressed us by its obscurity as being very clever, like everything the Major said. It was " courageous cowardice." Whereupon Ferd, who swore by his father's aphorisms, immediately concluded that there must also be a " cowardly courage."

Herr Silberstein was still planted by the sideboard, strongly moved. In his right hand he was swinging a blunt fruit-knife, which had been left there from dinner time, and making passes with it. He did not look at all heroic, but he appealed to me. He was like a man who was in the right without the requisite air to back it up.

" We have much less time than the others," he cried, " whatever we do has to be started from the very bottom. It's still the same as when the Temple was built ; while we build we have to fight, because no one will suffer us to sit down and be at home."

Herr Silberstein wept.

Leo smiled.

The mother jumped up and caught her husband by the sleeve, saying, " David, what are you thinking of ? "

I thought, why on earth should Herr Silberstein weep for a home. He had a house, a family and a good business.

" Perhaps," he went on again, " life is only a bad bargain. But everything we have got has been paid for twofold and threefold. We are in no man's debt. Whatever kindness we have received we have paid back over and over again. And when anyone treats us badly, we have behaved better than him. Our ledgers balance—yes, they do balance ! " Herr Silberstein raised his hand, as if he were accounting

to an invisible someone. Leo got up and walked
feebly across to his troubled father. He took his
hand, which was covered with black hairs, and
rubbed his cheek upon it. " Father," he said, " I
know what's upsetting you. But it's not so bad as
you think. The children who sometimes call names
after me don't really mean it. They call other names
after other boys. ' Jew ' is only my nickname ; there
are lots of nicknames. . . ."

" And Brosius ? " shouted Herr Silberstein. Even
I was startled when I heard the word. Leo dropped
his head as if patiently enduring a blow ; the mother
laid her right hand flat on her bosom ; Herr Silberstein stood with his mouth wide open like a fish and
repeated, " Brosius ! " Then they all fell silent, as
if they had no more breath left, standing rigid like
a group of statuary. I looked at them attentively ;
they made a group which was by no means ugly.
All that was ridiculous in Herr Silberstein's appearance had vanished ; I saw no longer his funny little
legs, and I forgot the unmanly crook of his shoulders ;
even the mother, whose blurred face always offended
me, had a fine air, and Leo, standing pale, thin and
weary between his anxious parents, looked as if he
were gazing into a tomb.

They were afraid, but their fear was not ugly.
Fear like that I had only seen among animals. . . .

" Here too," I thought, " there's a mystery. How
did such words come into the mouth of Herr Silberstein, who is a cute business man ? And Leo, who
was almost railing at his father, is caressing his hand
now. And the mother, who was running uneasily
between the two of them, is all at once dignified in
her sorrow. They must have a mystery in common,
for their faces are troubled."

Leo was the first to move. He shook his head, sat down in his chair and softly wrapped the rug round his legs. " Brosius," he said, " is a powerful man." Then he coughed.

Herr Silberstein leaned his arm on the sideboard, the veins swelling under the yellowish grey skin of his hand.

The mother took a dust-cloth and began to wipe the carved work.

" He's like the Kaiser," she sighed, rubbing the sharp beak of the carved eagle.

" A big man, Brosius," said Herr Silberstein. " He's wearing a suit of mine which his mother bought for him secretly, but he doesn't know it. . . ."

" It's always like that ! " cried Frau Silberstein. " They don't know that it's our stuff that they have on their backs."

She rubbed viciously at the bellies of the cherubs, who had dust in their navels.

Herr Silberstein played with his watch-chain.

Leo coughed.

The twigs of one of the chestnut trees were driven against the window.

.　　.　　.　　.　　.　　.

Leo beckoned to me, and I crossed to him. " Sit down," he said, " and let's play chess." He began to arrange the chess-men.

I decided to let him beat me.

While I was arranging my knights, Herr Silberstein came over to me and laid his hand on my shoulder.

" I thank you," he said, "for wanting to protect Leo."

I answered, " Please don't mention it : we're glad to do it, and especially against Brosius."

Herr Silberstein smiled sadly in the grey stillness of the oncoming evening.

"Against Brosius," he said, "nobody can do anything."

"Oho !" I cried, springing up so that the knights went tumbling over the pawns, "he'll soon stop bullying Leo when he sees that Ferd von K. and I and the Red Guard are behind him. Brosius only bullies those that he knows are alone."

"So Leo is no longer alone ?" asked Herr Silberstein, in a slow voice.

"No," I repeated, "he is no longer alone."

Then Herr Silberstein made me a profound bow, and again called me " Sie."

"You are a good fellow," he said.

I felt embarrassed and set up my knights again.

Herr Silberstein went to his wife and gave her a kiss.

"David," she said, laying her arm round his neck, "you must go down to the shop now, to do the accounts. It's seven o'clock."

They both went out, with their arms round each other.

    .   .   .   .   .   .

I played against Leo. His face was serene and resolute. I saw that he was determined to beat me, and was bending all his energies to work out the chances of his combinations. While I was still cautiously pushing my pawns forward his bishops and castles were already in action, and by a manœuvre with his queen he had my king twice in check. I dodged my king over the board, and finally entrenched him behind the pawns. Leo had captured all my knights. He played so rapidly and confidently that I had hardly time even to engineer a defeat. My queen, guarded by two of his bishops, was condemned to perpetual virginity. In ten minutes the game was his. He had wiped out my pawns, leaving the king alone and defenceless, and then chased him with a bishop over the board.

" I've won ! " cried Leo, clapping his hands.

" Yes," said I, " you've really beaten me, for I hadn't time to let myself be beaten ! "

Leo burst out laughing. " Did you think I didn't know what was in your mind ? That's why I was so quick, so that it should be a real win."

And he ate a slice of the peeled apple, which was already turning brown.

" You see," he said, " that's just as I wanted it. You and Ferd talk about protecting me because I can't defend myself against things you are better able to stand up to. While the others look on me as dirt and torment me when they can, you want to protect me. But it's fundamentally the same thing."

" But Leo ! " I cried, " we like you ! "

" You like me, and the others don't, but you both despise me. You protect me because I'm no good, and the others trample on me for the same reason."

And again I cried, " Leo, we want to help you ! "

" Yes," said Leo, " you only want to help me because you detest the others. I'm only an excuse."

I was scared by his penetration.

Leo settled himself in his chair and said in my very face : " You with your blue eyes and yellow hair will never need to know what it is to be trampled on or protected. You'll be either loved or hated. But we are never loved, not even by those who stand up for us. Can you understand that ? "

" No," said I, " I can't."

c

" Don't you understand, either, that Ferd protects me only because he hates Brosius ? "

" No," I answered.

" Why does he want to do it, then ? "

" Because he has a sense of justice."

" And you ? "

" I ? Oh, because I like you. I mean, you're decent, and much cleverer than the other chaps."

Leo stood up. His face was white, and his eyes brilliant.

" So you don't despise me ? "

" No," said I, horrified, " how can you think of such a thing ? "

" And do you believe we can be friends ? "

" Of course we can."

" Without your protecting me ? "

" I'll protect anybody who is my friend ! " Involuntarily I lifted my right arm.

Leo stood looking at me intently.

" Can you imagine being protected by me ? " I had to laugh hysterically. For I saw Leo's funny angular body, his timidity and his awkward legs.

" No, that I can't imagine ! "

At that Leo sat down quietly in his chair with a rigid face, and let his hands fall sorrowfully in front of him. Then he smiled as if he had lost something which had been his for only a short time.

I did not understand.

Leo began to cry.

Had I offended him ?

Slowly I went up to him, grasped his hand which hung relaxed from the arm of the chair, pressed it and said : " Leo, I really want to be your friend."

Leo nodded.

"Don't worry about anything. We'll look after you."

Leo shook his head.

" We don't despise you ! "

Leo smiled.

But he was quite rigid.

I beat my brains to think of how to move him.

Then I said in a low voice : " Will you let me copy the next French homework too ? "

At that he laughed, laid his arm round my neck, and said : " I'll write out all the subjunctives for you, and push them to you under the desk."

" Then I'll get my remove ! " I exulted (even though I should have got it in any case), and gave him my hand on it.

Leo escorted me into the hall. He was suddenly very gay.

" On Sunday we've to go to see Ferd on the farm."

" Yes," said Leo, " if I'm better."

" Oh, you'll be all right."

I put on my cap and went down the dimly lit stair, saying " Adieu ! " to Leo, and out through the yard into the street.

When I put my hand in the pocket of my cape to pull it closer round me I felt something strange —a soft package in tissue paper. I opened it under one of the street lamps which was just being lit. Three newly baked poppy-seed rolls glistened in my hand, still warm and fragrant. Behind me the shutters of the firm David Silberstein came rattling down.

CHAPTER IV

SABOTAGE

I WALKED slowly over the market-place, which was gloomy under the heavy foliage of the chestnut trees.

In front of the War Memorial, an obelisk of grey sandstone surrounded by a railing of gilt-bronzed lances, I came to a stop, and shielded by the thick shadow of that reverend monument drew the rolls out of my pocket.

They were still fragrant.

Twice I circled round the Memorial, twice I lifted a roll to my mouth, but I did not bite into it.

While I was leaning against the railing, my eyes fixed on the gilt inscription " Gravelotte," and my thoughts busy with these fatal rolls, August Kremmelbein came rushing down the street. He was not running with his usual confident alertness, timing his steps with that exactness which made him the most dangerous forward in our football team, but stumbling as he ran, his body leaving his legs behind.

I bounded from the Memorial right in front of him, and held out the rolls.

" August ! " I cried, delighted with this solution of my difficulty, " August—poppy-seed rolls ! "

But August went rushing past me without looking at them, his breath was hot in my face, his elbows punched me in the side. " August ! " I yelled, running after him, and overtaking him with difficulty. I had no breath to spare, and only gesticulated desperately with the rolls. But when I tried to stop him he nearly knocked me down.

So I went careering after August, not knowing what was making him run.

At the third cross-street I managed to get a few yards ahead of him, and turning round did a desperate quick-step backwards in front of him. I put all the coaxing of which I was still capable into my voice, " August. . . . Poppy rolls. . . ." But August shook his head.

His face was red, his eyes swollen. His cheeks were smeared with dust and sweat and tears. His mouth was wide open, his lips blue.

" August, what's the matter ? " I yelled, twisting up the rolls.

" My father ! " he shrieked, giving me a push, so that I could not stop him, and flying round the next corner into the street where his parents' house stood.

I was left alone again with my rolls. I could hear the clatter of August's hob-nailed shoes echoing between the house walls.

" There must have been an accident," I said out loud, and was startled at the sound of my own voice. Perhaps August's father, who was a stoker in the sugar factory, had fallen into one of the great cauldrons, and was lying dead and sodden in an outhouse, or even already brought home in state and laid down in the best room.

Cautiously I began to run, on tiptoe. For I had never yet seen a corpse.

The poppy-seed rolls I stowed heedlessly into my pocket.

. . . . . .

The Kremmelbeins lived in the tenement " barracks," as it was contemptuously called by all the people who had houses of their own. This tenement, built two years ago by the sugar factory, had been deliberately set on the very outskirts of the town, and housed eighteen families. On each ground-floor there were two flats with a separate hall, reserved for superior workmen ; the families on all the other floors had to be content with two rooms apiece. There were swarms of children in the tenement. They squatted in gangs on the staircase, and hooted at any stranger who came in. Most of the time they fought among themselves. They stuck out their tongues at every woman except their mothers. They nearly always clutched a hard piece of bread smeared with black treacle, and when they bit into it the treacle got mixed up with the slime from their noses. They played often round a pool of stagnant milky water which had a vile smell. There was some wretched grass beside the pool, and a lilac bush. When the scent of the lilac blossom mingled with the stench from the pool the air was fetid and heavy.

The inhabitants of the tenement called this part of the yard their park, for the directors of the sugar factory had provided seats there for use when work was over, two pine benches with inscriptions on them : " Commit no nuisance." The use of these benches was apportioned in turn to the different floors ; and the relays kept a strict eye on each other to see that the seats were vacated at the proper time. As caretaker the factory had installed a retired sergeant-major, who was addicted to brandy and enjoyed thrashing the children. He used to call them bastards and often shut them into the cellar without apparent reason—perhaps because they had put out their tongues at him.

The popular name for the tenement was " the gipsies' doss-house," because in the upper floors the factory usually quartered seasonal workers who came from the south-eastern corner of Europe. They shared beds with the various families and helped to swell their numbers, providing many of the women with a change from the matrimonial boredom of over-worked husbands. Black-headed children swarmed in the tenement. They were mostly sharper than the others and dominated them at play. The mothers favoured them too, giving them better clothes and extra pieces of bread and butter.

They were called the " cuckoos," and made splashes of gay colour against the grey walls of the house. They could sing beautifully, and often began to dance in the middle of a game. Their fair-haired brothers used to stand round in wonderment at their nimble movements, which spoke of a strange wild blood. While the " cuckoos " danced not a foul word was heard in the yard, even the sergeant-major sat still with a dazed smile in his fuddled eyes. Many a " cuckoo " wore a brilliantly coloured Southern scarf, the one thing left him by his father. And even that had only been an oversight.

The " cuckoos " were usually full of wiles. They were clever at stealing sweets and small coins out of the shops, and were adepts at putting on innocent faces and diverting suspicion to their slower-witted comrades, even planting the stolen wares in the latter's pockets if they thought themselves under suspicion, so that if the theft were found out they could winningly protest their innocence, and if not, could recover their booty again at home.

In all quarrels the " cuckoos " were the arbiters.
They were given little work to do, and their mothers,
who had almost nothing but abuse for their legal
offspring, reserved for them names which were
drawn from long-forgotten romances. They were
never beaten. Even the men whose name they bore
refrained from bullying them after an orgy of drink
on pay-night. They were treated like foundlings of
mysterious origin, although they were merely the
bastards of Southern vagabonds.

The Kremmelbeins lived on the ground floor, for
August's father had been fifteen years in the factory,
and was one of its permanent staff. He was a quiet,
taciturn man. In his spare time he busied himself
with carving and fretwork, or with the study of books
from the local lending library. He sacrificed many
an evening to his desire for " education." The books
he read were mostly scientific treatises on medicine,
technology and political economy. After a close and
laborious study of Marx, Engels and Bebel he joined
the Social Democratic party. He was unlike many
of his comrades in having a scientific basis for his
convictions, as he pointed out, for he had thoroughly
tested the cause he was fighting for before adopting
it. His was a solid character. He organised with
great skill the works movement in our town, founding
a working-men's sports club and choral society, and
out of the scanty funds at his disposal creating a small
library which contained only scientific volumes and
works by the founders and leaders of the party. He
refused to admit books of a lighter nature, for they
only diverted people from the main subject and put
ideas into their heads which had nothing to do with
the class-war. For that war was an economic war.
Statistics on housing, on infant mortality among the

working classes and on the proportion of accidents in mines and factories, the soaring curves of the tuberculosis graphs, the figures which told the normal expectation of life in various occupations such as mining, chemical industry and weaving, the balances of firms, dividends of shareholders and salaries of directors, the variations in the Stock Exchanges ; in short, the statistics of the whole social system excited Kremmelbein the stoker much more than any novel could have done.

" Figures tell the truth," he said once, at a session of his party's Committee on Education.

With the zeal of a preceptor he devoted himself to the enlightenment of his comrades. He relied on nothing but facts ; where others drew rhetorical conclusions he confined himself to a statement of the position. He was a revolutionary by example. Instead of providing slogans he handed out statistics ; instead of metaphors he gave figures. The evening classes he held were as dry and exacting as mathematical lectures. With fanatical sobriety he expounded his views by means of large placards on which he had neatly tabulated his statistics in Chinese ink, views which the middle classes in our town never accepted as valid because Herr Kremmelbein lacked an academic education. But the workers revered him, for he could produce a proof for every statement he made. He was a solid revolutionary, with a passion for truth.

It was with growing concern that the directors of the sugar factory followed the development of this dependable worker. His avoidance of all rhetoric baffled them. They had several times conveyed to his wife the information that only his political activity stood in the way of his promotion to a foreman's job.

c *

But Kremmelbein remained firm, and even organised a model strike which he won because on his
summons every worker in the local factories immediately downed tools out of sympathy. The directors' sole hope of bringing their refractory employé
to his senses was his wife. She was a Bavarian and
attended church regularly. But Herr Kremmelbein's
statistics withstood even the gentle admonitions of
the confessional. When his wife spoke of God and
of what he had ordained, Kremmelbein produced
his statistics from a drawer and declared that if they
represented God's will he was against God. His wife
vacillated between the telling force of his arguments and the power of her traditional faith. She
could never make up her mind. She was a good
mother.

All this had been told to me by August, who loved
his father as if he were of a higher species, grounded
in immortality.

.   .   .   .   .   .

While I ran towards the tenement I realised that
August's father couldn't have had an accident in the
factory, since there had been another strike for the
last five days. The safety appliances for the vats
and machinery in the factory were extremely inadequate, and the workmen had demanded an im-
provement. This was refused by the directors, at
the bidding of the shareholders, who were mostly
large farmers. So the workmen had gone on strike.

August's father, as usual, was the leader. The
directors had countered this move by importing a
gang of foreign workers to act as strike-breakers. The
strike leaders had immediately posted pickets to prevent by force anyone entering the factory.

So the accident which had befallen August's father must be of another kind ; perhaps he had been run over by a train.

When I got close to the house I could see dark and uneasy knots of men. They could only be workmen, for they were all wearing caps. They were whispering, and some of them shook their fists at the brilliantly lit façade of the house over which played the uneasy blue shadows of the neighbouring trees. The main door was wide open, the entry lit by a bleak gas lamp, under which stood a gendarme. The scent of the first lilac blossom stole through the air ; under the oily bubbles in the pond a solitary frog was croaking. The gendarme took off his helmet and produced a red handkerchief to wipe his brow, which was marked by a searing line.

He sighed as he did so, sweating. The street was seething with people ; new workmen kept pouring in, usually in groups. They spoke in undertones, but their boots clattered loudly. All the windows in the tenement were open, except the three on the ground floor belonging to the Kremmelbeins. These were even curtained.

All the men who lived in the tenement were standing in the street. Their wives were hanging out of the windows, talking in low voices to their neighbours. One or two children rejoicing in their immunity from attention were playing football on the pavement with an old tin can.

While I ran about among the knots of men, trying in vain to find some means of getting at the Kremmelbeins' house, I heard the same word repeated again and again : Sabotage. Because I had no idea what it meant it excited me terribly. The poppy rolls in my pocket began to crumble, but I could not risk throwing them away among so many working men. For my mother had told me only recently that one should never provoke poor people unnecessarily.

Suddenly a ripple went through the dense crowd in the street. I felt it unmistakably.

It began among the men nearest the town, and spread towards where I was standing by the main entry. It was the same kind of movement that runs through a class when the teacher comes into the room, that kind of involuntary springing to attention which finds its supreme expression in prayer. I felt it surge through everybody, and I was affected too. Although I did not know what was afoot I was identified with those who gave that startled jump.

Steps resounded on the pavement from the right, steps that rang out with a sharp, firm elegance. They belonged to a man who was certainly energetic. Beneath the faint halo of the gas lamp I saw two white blotches, hanging in the dusk of the stale evening like two little clots of melting snow or two lumps of dough. They were the white gloves of Dr. Persius, the Chief of Police.

He had another policeman with him.

He went through the dark ranks of the workmen, the gendarme beside him crying, " Make way."

The workmen made way, but in retreating before him they became a solid wall through which he had to advance without seeing where he was going. He had room enough, but no clear way. Behind him the sabre of the gendarme rattled on the paving-stones like a defective piece of machinery.

. . . . . .

Herr Dr. Persius was one of my acquaintances.

While he was still an unpaid junior in my father's office he had often come to see us, bringing bouquets for my mother. As a matter of fact, she disliked him because he always laughed so immoderately at any joke made by one of his official superiors, but my father felt in duty bound to befriend him, for he himself had been a junior in the office of old Persius, who in his day was a most respected lawyer in our town. Persius senior was more addicted to the pleasures of this world than his income permitted, and so when he was in the fifties he was forced to save himself from impending bankruptcy by marrying the rich and somewhat feeble-minded daughter of one of the numerous rich farmers in the district.

His son's deficient intelligence was the result of this marriage. Persius senior was soon happily released from it by an apoplectic stroke, and his son was sent to school in a little country town of upper Hesse, where the standard of work had been lowered to accommodate the half-witted sons of the local ruling princes. When he had struggled through that school his mother decided to enter him for the Civil Service, since he was too dull for commerce. With the help of crammers he managed to pass the first entrance test, and he got through the state examination by dint of learning by heart his father's old college lectures. He even passed the examination with credit, for like all stupid people he had an excellent memory, and since he had no thoughts of his own he retained everything he had read twenty times. His head was like an empty store-house in which others could pile up their products. As long as Persius still had an examination to surmount he was very modest.

To everything he was asked he responded, " Cer-

tainly, sir," and before he asked anything himself he
made a bow. His politeness even went the length of
letting the voluble wives of officials talk to their
hearts' content, and following with amiable attention their irrelevant tirades. When other men spoke
he held his tongue. He learned their opinions by
heart, and whenever his was asked for he always
reproduced the exact words of his questioner, a
characteristic which greatly endeared him to all. It
was generally believed that he would make an excellent official. When he had passed his final examination he was appointed Assessor in the District Office
of our town, and put in charge of the police. But he
had become quite another man. Since he had no
more examinations to fear and seemed to be in an
assured position for life, he threw his modesty over-
board and joined arrogance to his native stupidity.
He snubbed people and put on airs, as if he were in
command of the town. Although he could not ride
he carried a riding-switch, and adopted a monocle
and white gloves in imitation of the officers in the
neighbouring garrison. An old magistrate who made
no secret of his radical views he abused as " a swine
of an internationalist." He cut in the street a Jewish
lawyer who had coached him in the principles of
common law shortly before his finals. All the people
whose views differed from his own he set down as
stupid. The French in his eyes were a degenerate
crew, and Germany was the land of the poets and
thinkers. He knew by heart all the poems of Theodor
Körner, and whenever he came on a piano he played
a potpourri of German national airs. When he was
drunk he always sang : " They'll never, never get
it." As for the workers, he called them the rabble.
Even Bismarck, according to him, was not entirely

pure and undefiled. He never travelled abroad, but
spent his holidays attending the Imperial manœuvres.
He was the District Commissioner's right hand. As
Chief of Police he devoted himself mainly to rooting
out " the enemy within the gate."

The last thing he had learned like a parrot was
the phrase about " alien trash." His stupidity saved
him from any contact with Socialist ideas. He
was fighting opponents of whom he knew nothing,
and that gave him an incredible assurance in attack.
My father had followed with a smile the development of his deferential junior. He was enough of a
National Liberal to find it understandable, and besides Persius still showed him the same respect. He
paid us a visit every month, and whenever he met
me on the street he said, " Well, my friend, and how
are you ? " I thought he really meant it.

So when, escorted by his gendarme, he reached the
entry I cried, " Good evening, Herr Doctor ! " He
stopped and screwed up his eyes to survey the cold
wall of workmen. I burst through them, and sprang
into the light of the gas-lamp, crying again, " Herr
Doctor ! "

Persius wrinkled up his nose haughtily and asked,
" What is it ? "

" Oh, Herr Doctor," said I, thinking of the time
when he was my father's humble junior and accepted
instruction in his study, " dear Herr Doctor . . ."

I stood there bowing, and he raised his eyebrows
and asked, " What are you doing here ? "

His eyes, which were as cold as those of a stuffed
eagle, regarded me with exasperation.

" Herr Doctor," I said, " I want to see August
Kremmelbein."

" You should be ashamed of yourself ! " shouted

Dr. Persius, and left me alone under the bluish white
gleam of the swinging lamp.

A few seconds later he raised his right glove stiffly
to his flecked grey hat, acknowledging the salute of
the gendarme who stood by the house door. Then
he went up the steps.

The workmen stood silent. Faces peered from the
windows. Nobody said a word. The steps of the
gendarme accompanying Persius clattered loudly on
the frail staircase.

The workmen drew together. One of them said,
" Now he's being arrested."

Behind the curtains of the Kremmelbeins' flat
stumpy shadows were seen. Then there was a stillness, as if a light had been turned off.

The gendarme at the entry buckled on his sword
more firmly.

I could smell the lilac, and through it the fetid
pool.

Two of the " cuckoos " pranced across the courtyard with enormous slices of bread and butter.

I climbed up on a wall and from there surveyed
the street ; the men seemed hardly to be breathing ;
they were avoiding each other's eyes, as people do
at a funeral just before the coffin is carried out.

All that was happening was being conducted
according to prescribed rules, a kind of ritual, so
that even the face of the gendarme was ceremonious.
The workmen were silent. Apparently this cere-
monial reduced them to speechlessness ; it was a
process they were not equal to ; it embarrassed
them.

Suddenly there was a rush towards the entry.
Not a word was said. There was no sound but the
dull impact of pushing bodies. Persius was standing

on the steps. He was striving to assume that severe
official expression which was the fashion then among
the men of his class. Lips compressed, eyes screwed
up sharply, nose slightly curled, head rigidly on high.
He gave an order to the fat gendarme beside him,
whose good-natured moustache hung under his nose
like a bunch of sauerkraut. He tucked his sword
under his arm, stumbled down the steps, and shouted
at the silent throng, " Move on there ! Move on !
Make way for the escort ! "

Herr Dr. Persius stood on the lower flight of steps
and pulled on his soft gloves.

Framed in the house door appeared the figure of
Kremmelbein the stoker, handcuffed, and with a
policeman on either side. He had no collar on, only
a scarf.

" Make way ! " shouted the fat gendarme, beating
the workmen back with the flat of his scabbard.

" Out of the way,—or I'll have the street cleared ! "
Persius lifted his left hand, as if giving a signal.

At that moment a sound began, a kind of laugh in
chorus, and keeping time : Hahaha—Hahaha—a
dry, clear sound as if bones were being clashed
together.

Dr. Persius' thin legs made a comical picture.
There he stood behind the sweating gendarme (who
was raging like a lion against the contemptuously
passive resistance of the workmen) with every trace
of self-control wiped from his face, which was as red
as a lobster, and after stammering twice before getting
it out he screamed : " Any man who obstructs us
will be arrested !—On the spot ! " he added, with
another shout, which the hoarseness of his voice
made incomprehensible.

The workmen whistled shrilly through their fingers

—whistles like football signals. Whistles as sharp and clear as glass. And whistles resounded from every storey in the tenement. The women leaning out of the windows whistled somewhat less shrilly, and many of them who could not whistle shrieked with a sound like the splintering of enamel ware.

" Swine ! " they shrieked. " Swine ! "

The tenement rocked. From the corner window over the entry a bucket was emptied.

" Damnation ! " yelled the gendarme with the huge sabre, springing out of the way.

" Do your duty ! " shouted Persius, catching him by the sleeve.

The gendarme drew his sword.

Out of the basement emerged the sergeant-major, drunk as usual, and holding a revolver, which his position as concierge empowered him to carry.

One of the two gendarmes beside Kremmelbein also drew out his dagger in readiness.

They closed up, Persius behind them.

He lifted his arm.

The handcuffed stoker Kremmelbein smiled down from the steps.

" Out of the way ! " ordered Persius.

A burst of laughter answered him.

I sat still on my wall. " Now the row's going to begin," I thought, and shivered with excitement.

" Attention ! " yelled Persius.

His troop prepared to charge.

There was a sudden breathless silence.

It was broken by a mellow bass voice that rang out like an organ, free of all heat or passion.

" Out of the way, comrades ! "

" Silence ! " cried Persius, giving his men the order to charge.

But before they reached the enemy the way was cleared. The workmen had silently fallen back against the wall on which I was sitting. Their eyes were fixed on Kremmelbein, who was smiling between his gendarmes.

" Thank you, comrades."

He lifted his bound hands in a simple greeting.

Persius was furious. He stamped his foot and went raging up to Kremmelbein, raising his hand as if to strike him.

" Hold your tongue there ! "

" We can go now," said Kremmelbein, " the way's clear."

" March him off ! "

Persius waved his hand, and one of the gendarmes beside Kremmelbein gave the order " March ! " " March ! " repeated the second gendarme, closing up on Kremmelbein's left. Kremmelbein descended the steps. He walked quietly and firmly, and even the policemen beside him seemed to be drawing their strength from him. Behind him at about three yards' distance marched Persius, attended by the fat gendarme.

The drunken sergeant-major leaned against the entry surveying with a melancholy eye the steel-blue barrel of his revolver.

The escort swung into the street. I noticed the workmen quietly massing themselves. There was no sound but the hobnailed tramp of the gendarmes' feet on the pavement.

All at once, when the escort were not more than ten yards from our wall, the outburst came.

At first only a single voice, young, shy and soft, but as if they had all been waiting for a lead the other voices joined in after the first few bars in per-

fect harmony, the deep basses of men in the fifties,
the lyric baritones of the thirties, and then from the
window of the tenement the clear soprano of a young
girl.

They sang their Party's song ; they sang it in
honour of Kremmelbein.

And keeping time to their voices they formed
themselves into a column and marched.

They marched behind the escort, overwhelming it
with their song.

I heard Persius shouting, but no one could tell
what he said.

Everything was drowned in the refrain : " The
Internationale unites the human race."

I jumped down from my little wall and ran after
the crowd.

I could see all the faces. How incomprehensibly
jubilant they were ! And Kremmelbein, handcuffed
and guarded by two gendarmes, was marching at
the head of the procession as if he were leading it
with Persius captive in his train.

Persius, hemmed in by the throng, was gesticulating nervously to his gendarme, who had his hand
curved to his ear to help his hearing, but answered
all questions only with an obsequious shrug.

So they marched to the rhythm of the song, which
even the gendarmes could not resist following,—only
Persius marched awkwardly because he was doing
his best to keep different time.

And suddenly all the workmen linked arms, and
shoulder to shoulder sang :

" The dawn brings in a brighter day."

At that Kremmelbein, handcuffed as he was,
nodded quietly. The workmen's faces shone.

I halted. This jubilation baffled me.

I must find August : he would explain it all.

The procession surged past me. I could no longer distinguish individual faces ; I was dazed by that strange song, which rose as if from one mouth and was marked by one united step. Persius was the only man I recognised for a brief minute ; he had left the procession and was disappearing down a dimly lit side street with quick, short steps, attended by the gendarme.

" Who is being driven off, Kremmelbein or Persius ? " I thought to myself, and while the song surged up with new strength between the houses of the Inner Town I ran back on tiptoe to the tenement.

.   .   .   .   .   .

In the courtyard the sergeant-major was sitting on the bench beside the pool. His left hand was clutching a flask of corn brandy, and his revolver was esconced in his right hand like a private toy cannon built into its own small castle. He was singing " The Internationale," hiccuping from time to time into the blue evening air, drenched with lilac. The stairway was empty. The people in every storey were at supper ; there was a smell of potatoes and hot meat sausages. Only a pretty little " cuckoo " was sitting on a window-sill tinkling the " Lorelei " out of a musical box. When he caught sight of me he stuck out his tongue. At the Kremmelbeins' door I listened at the keyhole. I could hear a voice inside which I knew, but had never heard there before. A laughing voice, one would call it. Soft and flowing in the range of its tones : such a voice as only our red-headed evangelical parson owned—or Dr. Hoffmann.

It was Dr. Hoffmann in the flat.

I could clearly hear him saying, " My dear comrade "—it sounded exactly as if it might have been " my dear congregation."

" Condescending kindness," the Red Major was wont to call that manner of his friend's.

The air in the lobby was heavy with the exhalations from Herr Kremmelbein's working clothes, a clinging smell of oil and sweat. That was how August's father smelt when he came home in the evening. Wherever he went the smell of his engine stuck to him closer than a brother. Even in the small hours, when he was his own man, the smell of his " duty " never left him.

The door into the living-room was ajar, and I heard Hoffmann saying, " My dear comrade, please don't worry ! I'll bring it up in Parliament next week. The Government will fight shy of leaving us such a fine piece of propaganda for the elections. They're not keen on martyrs. I think the local authorities have over-reached themselves, that's all. . . ."

" He'll be out again in four weeks." Although I could not see him, I was sure that Hoffmann was switching the air with his cane.

" In four weeks ! " Frau Kremmelbein's voice rose hysterically.

" The Party will look after you meanwhile."

" And what about the disgrace ? " A chair was upset. Hoffmann cleared his throat delicately.

" Yes, the disgrace ! " shrieked Frau Kremmelbein. " Jail ! I'm an honest woman. What's he treated me like that for ? "

She whimpered.

" Comrade——" said Hoffmann, walking up and down.

" I'm none of your comrades ! I come from a
respectable family. And he knew that well enough
when he married me. And he wasn't like that then.
He wanted to get on. He might have been a foreman to-day if it hadn't been for those books. And
the Party. Everything's been neglected for that—
me too ! And we're none the better for it. We're
still in the gutter. I have to go out washing to make
both ends meet. The Party's got everything. . . .
And now there's this disgrace ! " Frau Kremmelbein jumped to her feet. " It's prison you've brought
him to ! . . . And you've driven him out of the
church ! He has no God left ! And he could have
been a foreman. . . ."

" We must all suffer for our ideals," brought out
Hoffmann, with an asthmatic wheeze.

" You've enough money," screamed Frau Kremmelbein, " you've enough money to afford that kind
of nonsense. But what about us ? "

" Prison ! Disgrace. . . ." I heard her collapsing
in a chair and weeping.

Hoffmann was walking up and down.

I did not dare move.

Then I heard August's voice. " Mother," he said,
" my father is a hero."

Frau Kremmelbein laughed. So wildly that I was
terrified she might see me.

" A fine hero, who doesn't do his duty by his
family."

" He certainly should have been more prudent,"
agreed Hoffmann.

" He was right," cried August, " in keeping the
Slovaks and Italians out of the factory. They were
strike-breakers ! "

" Hold your tongue ! " raged his mother, " he's

in prison, and if you're in jail you're a criminal ! "

" At any rate," put in Dr. Hoffmann, " I'll get him out again."

" But the disgrace will be left ! " Frau Kremmelbein had risen again, and was trudging up and down the room with her heavy countrywoman's tread.

" On the one hand I can understand your distress, but on the other hand you must not forget that your husband is fighting for a great cause."

Through the crack of the door I saw Hoffmann swinging his cane.

" Yes," cried August, " I'm proud of my father ! "

With a violent jerk his mother halted, and in the sudden stillness a box resounded on August's ear which made me jump and nearly lose my balance.

The door swung open. August stood there, his left cheek red and swollen, but not a tear in his eyes. He stood holding on to the handle, and said as if he had an appointment, " Well, I'm going out now."

I could see his mother's convulsed face ; it was grey and haggard, the wreck of a face. She threw her head back and screamed, " Go where you like ! You'll soon land beside your father ! In jail ! And I'll be pointed at in the church and in the street, and none of the best people will give me any more washing because of you, you . . . you. . . ."

With a sudden convulsive movement she collapsed. Her face was purple, her breath laboured, as if she were choking. August's sisters, two golden-haired little girls of six and eight, came running out of the kitchen with blubbered faces. " Have they come for Mamma too ? " asked the six-year-old, catching sight of me among the clothes in spite of the darkness in the lobby.

Hoffmann was the first to collect himself. " A heart attack," he cried, " eau de Cologne ! "—" We haven't any—only vinegar," said August, running to the kitchen. Hoffmann laid Frau Kremmelbein on the sofa and undid her bodice.

I blushed.

August came back with a large bottle of vinegar. They wetted Hoffmann's handkerchief and laid it on her brow, rubbing the vinegar on her cheeks too.

" Does your mother often have these attacks ? " asked Hoffmann, as Frau Kremmelbein began to breathe quietly again.

" Yes," said August very coolly, " every time my father doesn't do what she wants." Then they both gazed at her. Hoffmann had taken out his watch and was holding her pulse. August's face looked as if he had lost a football match because of an unfair decision.

" Do they tend to recur ? " Hoffmann replaced the sleeper's hand gently on her bosom.

" Sometimes, but not so bad."

" Then we'd better get a nurse in for the night." August put on his cap. " Shall I go for one ? "

" Yes, but go to the Catholic Sisters ; they don't mind what politics their patients have."

August stood in the lobby and put on his cape, a faded blue cape which had been given him by the Commissioner's wife, whose pavement he swept every Sunday.

I touched him gently on the shoulder. He signed to me to come with him, and we went out.

On the stairs he said : " I knew you had run after me." In the courtyard I answered : " August, your father is a hero."

At that he put his arm round my shoulder and so we went out at the gate.

The sergeant-major was still sprawling on the bench by the pool with his bottle and his unused revolver.

" Did you hear how they sang ? " asked August, when we were in the street.

" Yes, that was lovely."

Then we went a long way without exchanging a word. At the house of the Catholic Sisters August remarked : " It's a pity you're one of the gentry boys. You don't need to sweep the street for any-one, but then your father can never be such a hero as mine."

" Well," said I, " my mother wouldn't hit me if my father were a hero."

August shut up at that, and took his hand from my shoulder.

He stared fixedly at the enamelled plate on the yellow house, which had " Night Bell " written on it in a flourishing script.

I wanted to ask him why his father had been arrested, but I was afraid he might really have done something wrong.

So I asked instead when our next football match was to come off.

" Next Friday."

" At Ferd's farm ? "

" Yes," said August, " a friendly among the Red Guards." Then he held out his hand.

" August ! " I cried, " so you're not going to run away ? "

" No," said he, " I must wait till my father comes back."

He ascended the red sandstone steps, and put his right forefinger on the push-button.

I stood below and said quietly, " Good night." August pressed the bell. A delicate tinkle answered him, sweet as a bell at Mass.

Just as I was turning away to run home I remembered the poppy rolls. They were the cause of all my adventures ; but for them I should never have discovered that August's father was a hero ; I owed my evening to them, and they must be handed over. " August," I called, " here ! " and I sprang up the steps. The door opened at that moment, and a Sister stood there like a large swallow. " My mother . . ." stammered August. I was holding out the poppy rolls. " God bless you," said the Sister, taking them. Then she let August in. " And you ? " she asked me. I shook my head. " God bless you," she said again, and shut the door with kindly firmness.

When I got home my father was in high spirits. At noon he had received the grand ducal decree appointing him a Commissioner of the Lower Court.

In the drawing-room the crystal chandelier was lit. The grey covers protecting the chairs had been taken off, and the finest glasses were set out on a yellow damask cloth. My mother was sitting in a green frock with bare arms playing a minuet of Mozart at the piano. I could see her gleaming back reflected in the Venetian mirror.

My father met me in the lobby, as he was coming out of the cellar with three fat bottles of champagne under his arm.

" I'll let you off for being so late to-night," he smiled. I was astounded by such amiability. He waved me on. " Come along, you can have some wine with us for once, and clink glasses. I've been made a Commissioner of the Lower Court."

Two of his colleagues were sitting in the drawing-room, Judge Galopp, a short-legged bachelor, who tried all the criminal cases in our town and was very much feared for his severity, which was the result of chronic dyspepsia ; and beside him one of the Assessors, whose wife was very rich and addicted to picking her nose.

I made a correct bow and shook hands with each of them. Herr Galopp patted me on the shoulder, the Assessor said, " Well, well. . . ." After they had all given me a brief smile they composed their faces again into the frame of their conversation. " Here," cried my father, handing me a glass of champagne. I set it on the window-ledge and retreated behind my mother. She was leaning back with her eyes half closed as she struck the yellowed keys. I turned the music for her. She nodded. Her fair hair, which was softly waved, gave out a mysterious fragrance. I stood beside her feeling very sad, for I could not help thinking of Ferd and what he had said about girls.

At the table they were all on their feet. " Hallo," cried my father, " come and clink glasses."

" The Ladies ! " fluted the Assessor, and everybody laughed as if at a good joke. My mother's playing broke off. Her face was bright and happy again. She went up to the table and took her glass. They all crowded round her. " The Frau Commissioner . . ." said Herr Galopp, touching her glass. " The Frau Commissioner . . ." the Assessor clicked his heels together. " The Frau Commissioner . . ." said my father impishly, looking into her eyes with patriarchal benevolence. I felt scared by the room, the people, and what they said, and when I tried to clink glasses with my mother a splash of champagne

tippled over the edge of my glass on to the parquet
flooring. They all behaved as if they had not seen
it ; even my father on that evening forgot his duty
to his parquet flooring. My uneasiness grew.

Quietly I replaced my glass on the window-ledge.
I heard Herr Galopp saying, " Yes, so I ordered the
fellow to be arrested. I'm sorry for his wife's sake ;
she's a decent woman ; but unfortunately she has
no influence over him. Still, an example has to be
made. It won't do to have that rabble keeping the
machinery idle and hindering the willing ones from
working."

" The workmen made a demonstration to-night,"
said my mother.

" I should have turned a good volley on to them
instead of a hose-pipe. We're much too lenient,"
spluttered the Assessor.

My father regarded the parquet gloomily. " Yes,"
he sighed, " the world's in a bad way. Manners and
morals are relaxing everywhere. In all ranks of life.
There's a big punishment needed."

" Tut, the law alone will never manage it . . ."
Herr Galopp washed his hands of it.

Then the Assessor bent towards my father. " What
kind of punishment were you thinking of, sir ? "

" Perhaps a war," said my father.

The Assessor sprang to his feet. " That would be
magnificent ! " he cried. " That would be a gor-
geous refresher after the sluggish rottenness of
peace ! "

And forgetting his manners he waved his glass on
high shouting " Hurrah ! " and drained it at one gulp.

" The spirits of youth ! " smiled my father, picking up his own glass. They all raised their glasses
as if they were saluting a happy prospect. . . .

Ten minutes later they sent me to bed. I kissed my mother on the left cheek and shook my father's hand.

" To-morrow's Sunday, and for once you needn't go to church," he said. " You can take a long sleep."

" Thank you," said I, and bowed myself out backwards. Then while I was quietly undressing in my room and finding myself suddenly weeping with an incomprehensible sense of trouble, the powerful rhythms of the " Wacht am Rhein " came rolling up from the drawing-room. But on that evening my mother did not come to say good night to me in bed. I lay awake for a long time and was afraid to think.

CHAPTER V

FOR some time nothing happened. The impressions of that bewildering day survived merely as pictures, and even these faded more and more. They obliterated each other, their contours became blurred and all that remained was a painful distrust of anything that grown-ups said or did. I avoided them as if contact with them might hurt me, for it seemed to me they had no other aim in life but to wound each other as much as possible.

My mother paid little attention to me during that time. She was reading Maeterlinck's *Life of the Bee*. A young doctor with a poetic temperament had lent it to her, and had aroused her passion for literature by his conversation, full of sensibility. Hofmannsthal's *Death of Titian* was her favourite book. She had it bound in silk. The young doctor came to see her once a week with a bundle of new books. Then they spent the afternoon in the garden under the pleasant dappled shade of our nut tree reading poetry to each other. These poems were of a beautiful melancholy. They sang of Southern groves. Somebody was always dead in them or just dying, and then he was bewailed by men, animals and trees in very high-flown phrases. It was usually evening in these elegies, and there were a great many gods in them, gods who lived in grottoes or in winds, and

95

were visible to men. The men conversed with them in language I had never heard any man use. My mother knew them all by name, and once when I was sitting beside her in the garden in the sultry heat of a June day which stifled every sound, kept every leaf motionless, and even made the birds in the sky look as if they were nailed there, she said with an intense expression, " Pan is asleep." I hardly dared to touch my coffee-cup for fear a movement might annoy her. Then she read me a poem in the high-flown style. I marvelled at the author, for I had found in school it was not easy to keep all these gods' names distinct. Otherwise I had no interest at all in Pan. I would much rather have talked to my mother about August Kremmelbein and Leo Silberstein. But the light in her eye, the smiling melancholy of her mouth, the tones of her voice which she had borrowed from the poetry, scared me away to a hopeless distance. I worshipped her, but I no longer dared to talk to her.

The reason for this change in her I could not then account for. Besides, I was much too troubled to look for reasons. To-day I can see that like many women of her time my mother was escaping from the monotonous atmosphere of her daily existence into a world of beauty and exalted sorrow, where the hideous echoes of reality could not reach her. She continued to look after the house with the same energy as before, in the regular round of family life, but it often seemed to me that it was only her body which was there.

My father noticed nothing. He did his duty. In between times he collected stamps. It was only rarely now that he championed his theory about war as a divine punishment, but then he did it with such zeal that he would probably have felt it as an insult had the war not duly arrived. He was waiting for it, as Noah waited for the Flood, with the grim cheerfulness of a righteous man.

I often went down to the farm. Leo Silberstein was made very welcome there. Ferd's protection had freed him from any further tyranny in the school ; even Brosius had of his own accord excused him from gymnastics, and set him instead to help with the apparatus. He was not well. In the evening he often had two burning spots on his cheeks and a feeble shaky cough. His parents were very proud of his friendship with Ferd. I had told Ferd about Leo's suspiciousness, and he allayed it by treating Leo exactly like August and myself. While Ferd and I went riding Leo did our homework in the bright living-room, and drank a glass of rich milk. He was passionately fond of cows, and used to lean his head against the beasts' warm bodies. Horses he did not care for so much. He played a lot at chess with the Major. Ferd was attached to Leo, for his father had told him that Leo would die young, and Ferd had decided to be very good to him so long as he lived.

I had told Ferd about my adventure with August Kremmelbein. After the friendly match among the Red Guards he mentioned it to his father, who sent Frau Kremmelbein a sack of flour and a smoked ham. August was taken on at the farm to help in preparing the fodder. When his work was done he had supper in the dining-room with Ferd, Leo and me. His mother was not doing badly. She had soon recovered from her heart attack, and attended early Mass every morning with ostentatious punctuality. The priest, delighted with his faithful

D

follower, saw to it that the God-fearing wife should not have the sins of her refractory husband chalked up against her, and by his influence enabled her to go on washing in all the best families. She was even welcomed there as an acceptable martyr, and had many old clothes bestowed on her for the children. Besides, the Party was supporting her. She was doing well. In spite of Hoffmann's cleverness her husband had been condemned to a month's imprisonment. She was even able to buy herself a china cabinet from the proceeds of all the sympathy showered on her. August hated his mother, but he went on living with her.

The Red Major in these days had become very taciturn. Political events of which I understood nothing—occasioned by a speech of the Kaiser's in the officers' mess of a large liner—had finally convinced him of the blind conceit in responsible quarters. He received news from London of the critical imminence of an upheaval, and he did not dispose of it, like my father, with an easy phrase about a " divine punishment," but recognised it as the consequence of human stupidity ; and he was distressed, for he felt himself responsible for that stupidity. Through his connections in England he had precise knowledge of the many ways in which it was possible for Germany and England to come to an understanding, and he staked his last hope on the German Ambassador in London, whose acquaintance he had made abroad and whose sober knowledge of the world he trusted.

At that time the Major was the sole grown-up person in whom I had any confidence. I had often listened to his arguments with Hoffmann, which grew more and more vehement, and I admired his clear and manly language, which was not smothered under a rank growth of ideology. Everything that others said—whether they were in the right or not—was too verbose, pompous, and obscured by phrases ; but the Major never used a word more than was needed to say what he thought.

The war which my father prophesied did not interest me in the least, but the war the Major spoke of seemed to me a practical possibility. For it was to be made by men, and not declared by God for reasons I did not know. That men should turn to rend each other and try to destroy each other I could very well believe after all I had so recently seen in our own town.

Hoffmann always laughed the Major to scorn.

" It'll never get so far as that ! " he used to cry. " We'll stop the war by sabotage."—" Then you'll be put in jail like Kremmelbein," was the Major's reply to the optimistic Doctor.—" Oh, Kremmelbein," smiled Hoffmann, " Kremmelbein was a little too hasty. But if things turn out as you expect, the liberation of the proletariat will be proclaimed over all the world and will rouse an echo everywhere that will guarantee peace."—" And what about the Czar ? " asked the Major shortly.—" Oh well, the Czar is a different matter ; if war is declared against him all the good old Socialists will shoulder their pop-guns."—" Then the Czar will be stuck in the forefront of the war." The Major cut the argument short with a brusque gesture.—" You're incurable," returned Dr. Hoffmann. I have quoted this conversation, which recurred frequently, to illustrate the Major's scepticism. He felt that he was quite alone in his convictions, since they were based on a knowledge of the real situation, and at that time in Germany there was no visible body of well-informed opinion.   Only a few people had remarked the trend of events, but they had no influence because they were not organised.

My interest in these arguments soon flagged.   For I decided that it was impossible for grown-ups to understand each other.   They all saw the world as they wished to see it ;   even Hoffmann lived in accordance with a programme.   And in discussing war they were only projecting further their civilian disagreements, which did not concern me.

I began to feel bored, and had recourse to what naturally absorbed my childish interest.

That talk about the mystery had destroyed something between Ferd and me.   I still loved him, but it was a love full of reservations.   During these days when, through my curiosity, I was getting hopelessly entangled in the web of society, he was of an exasperating simplicity.   He had his father to love, and his own strength to protect him from attack.   He knew exactly where he stood : by his father's side, even though that were against the whole world.   August Kremmelbein had his father, too.   Even Leo. They all knew where they belonged, what they had to do and to suffer.   I did not.

So I was compelled to be a seeker and a spectator, while the others simply lived.   But I kicked against it.

CHAPTER VI

HILDE, 1914

IT was one of my father's habits to go for a walk every Sunday shortly after coffee if the weather were fine. He loved to walk through the cornfields along narrow winding paths, and to run the waving stalks through his finger with a low, sweet whistle as if he were testing the yield of the crop. In his right hand he swung his stick and cut off the golden heads of the dandelions with its sharp ferrule. His hat was secured to his coat by a small clip. Behind him walked my mother and I in single file. If ever I stole into the waving corn to pluck a shining red poppy for my mother, who liked to wear one in the belt of her white frock, my father used to scold me and accuse me of sinning against the noblest gift of God. Besides, poppies were poisonous ; in China they were used for making that pernicious opium.

He himself never plucked anything save a small cornflower flaunting on the edge of the path, which he used to fasten in his right lapel with a pin taken from under the left one. He wore that buttonhole with pride, because it had been the old Kaiser's favourite flower and symbolised the simple nature of the man who found his sole reward in the quiet pleasure of duty fulfilled. He said this with obvious scorn for the present generation, which had lost all sense of simplicity. Many a criticism of his time escaped him during his botanical digressions, but even so, it was only in the bosom of his family.

These walks through the sprouting fields would have been lovely if my father's prohibitions had not hedged me in with their prickles. I could not run into the mysterious cornfields, through which lovers in the evening had left broad trails without reflecting that they had "sinned against the noblest gift of God." I was forbidden to run my stick along the tall stalks as I loved to run it along the iron railings of the front garden ; I was forbidden to throw clods at the crows, for the crows were useful birds, and ate up the noxious grubs ; besides I had to take care of my Sunday suit and my best shoes, and in general keep to the path, walking quietly behind my father whose broad back often cut off the sun. Sometimes my father stopped, taking a deep breath, and cried, " Ah, Nature is too beautiful ! " and then I had to nod assent and look pleasant. I had to sing, too, when my father bade me. His favourite song was, " I shoot the deer in the wild forest."

The time I had spent playing on the farm had accustomed me to running through the fields, not quickly, but at a gentle trot. I used to run even when I had plenty of time. I could never understand how people could keep walking slowly when once they were beyond the houses. Walking did not seem to go with the motion running through every blade and bush, and rippling in waves over the corn-fields. I hated people who walked. I hated Sundays when the countryside was treated like a large garden in which one had to keep to confined paths, and walk at that horrible pace which was so obviously a determined attempt at recreation.

This disciplined Nature-worship was sometimes

interrupted by a hare. Startled from its sleep in the
sun by our tramping feet and the echoing sound of
our singing, a hare would often spring in blind fear
from the safety of its form right across our path.
" Ho ! " my father would shout, " hoho ! A hare !
Halloo ! Puss, puss ! " We would take up the hunt,
not because we expected to catch the hare, but because it was fun to chase it. Had the creature only
known the nature of the German official, it would
have left the path at once and made for the security
of the open field. If ever it did so my father stopped
immediately, held me back and said very seriously,
" Halt ; walking over the fields is forbidden. I can't
allow my son to break the law." The hare was safe,
and we went on again slowly.

Once, however, after an incident of this kind my
mother said, " But the hare is breaking the law ! "
My father parried her thrust. " The beasts aren't
German subjects." My mother, who would never
admit defeat, smiled and repeated one of the current
psychological phrases which were supposed to be
very modern in those days, " But the beast in man ? "
With the remark " To-day's Sunday," my father
cut short any further discussion and devoted himself
anew to his enjoyment of Nature. That was the
first time I was conscious of hearing an expression
which later provoked me to scorn and disgust, the
expression " German subject." Exactly four years
later, in the pallid days of November, 1918, many a
man who was seized by the throat stammered it out
as a justification, and was believed.

Whenever we came into the forest, which was
separated from the fields by a high wooden fence,
since it was a sporting preserve for the Grand Duke
and his guests, my father always said, " Breathe

deeply ! " That was because of a pine plantation, which stood out in a sharply cut black mass against the light foliage of the beeches.

On these Sundays the forest was alive. There was yodelling everywhere. A young student whose father had sent him for two terms to Munich to sow his wild oats had imported yodelling into our town and made it so fashionable that everybody succumbed to it, from the Academic Club to the Wednesday Artisans' Union ; even the " Free Gymnasts " yodelled their greeting through the Sunday forest. Then there were the dun herds of the fallow deer, which were so tame that even the Grand Duke managed to shoot them. Sometimes we caught sight of a white buck, and then my father would tell me the legend of Hubertus.

The forest re-echoed with songs, mostly " Schna-dahüpferl," * which were in great favour because everybody could join in, whether musical or not.

The young fellows from the shopkeeping classes in the town—whom my father dismissed briefly as " hooligans "—came singing, " Red are tomatoes, and girls when they're kissed, but redder the tie of the Socialist."

Sometimes a gymnastic club went marching in their white shorts round a clearing, singing with deadly seriousness, " Gymnasts up and conquer, march into the lists," while a working-men's cycling club overtook them, filling the patient forest with the strains of " The Internationale," punctuated by the flapping of their little red flag. But however they might be at variance with each other in their songs, it was the same goal they were all making for, the inn of " The Green Huntsman " beside the blue

* Topical extempore songs.

basalt of the main road, which was run by a forester's wife.

Her speciality was cider with cream cheese.

After enjoying Nature everybody assembled there at red-painted tables to the accompaniment of an electric piano. For " the better classes " there was a reserved room, a dark sitting-room bedecked with antlers and chromolithographs in which poachers were shot or hares leapt in comical death-throes. Here my father always ordered fried eggs with bacon and green salad. The cider he drank was scored on his pasteboard table mat, which advertised in vain the delights of Munich beer.

I always got a small bottle of seltzer ; when my father was in a specially good mood he let me sip his cider.

Outside in the yard the hooligans sang their " Schnadahüpferl," which got more and more obscene as the cider mounted to their heads. Their girls shrieked as if someone were pinching them.

Meanwhile the " Song of the Navy " was reeled off the cylinder of the electric piano. A young druggist whose ambition to join the Marines had been defeated by his defective chest-measurement scrambled with ape-like nimbleness up a stable ladder, unfurled a small paper flag and yelled " Hurrah ! " three times to the applause of the whole courtyard. Some who were drunk burst into tears.

The forester's wife stood solidly behind her counter reckoning up with a motherly smile the day's profits on the cider, the cheese and the electric piano. What she made on this side-line went to pay her son's fees in the Department of Forestry.

The academic families met in the reserved room. Regularly at ten minutes past five Judge Galopp

D *

made his way through the heavy reek of cheese and tobacco smoke. He spent his spare time in imagining himself sick of various diseases, which he then cured by some method of his own. He always carried his stick pressed firmly across his back and when he was in the forest he took deep breaths. For fifteen years he had walked every evening to " The Green Huntsman " and back ; it took him, he assured people, three thousand two hundred and thirteen steps from the outskirts of the town. He was often accompanied by Brosius.

At our table three chairs were reserved for the family of J. the apothecary. They were usually later in arriving than we, for Herr J. liked a long sleep on Sundays. He often worked late into the night to save the expense of an assistant, which he could not afford because of his wife's extravagance. He had made her acquaintance in a Garmisch hotel on the one grand tour of his life, and her Southern beauty had so captivated him that after one night of gallantry he had immediately offered her his hand, threatening to commit suicide if she refused him. The flight of her latest lover, a young Austrian officer, had left Isabella at the end of her resources, and she knew well enough from experience what was to be gained from a solid income and the possibility of queening it over a sheepishly devoted bourgeois husband ; so after a coquettish hesitation, which robbed the apothecary of his last remnant of sanity, she accepted him on condition that he asked no questions about her past. The real story of her past life was that she had run away at an early age from home, where a drunken father, a captain cashiered for gambling debts, raged through the house and a careworn Jewish mother was always

weeping. After that there came the usual series of
affairs with wealthy bachelors or capitalists bored
with their wives, who gave her money enough, but
treated her brutally. Finally she had taken to hiring
herself out in the better hotels, where she made the
time pass pleasantly for elderly gentlemen travelling
alone. The arrival of the lovesick apothecary
rescued her from this life, which was already dis-
closing behind its glittering exterior the spectre of
an existence on the streets. She reckoned up that
she was still young, beautiful and versed enough in
amorous arts—unlike the ordinary citizens' wives—
to make matrimony interesting for a man of assured
position and respectable morals, and that such a
match would mean for her a secure old age in solid
comfort. The apothecary's determination clinched
the matter. He renounced all claim on her past out
of fear that she would again deprive him of the possession of such a lovely and experienced woman,
which was more than he had ever dreamed of. He
married Isabella on the spot. She swore eternal
fidelity to him—and kept to it. She deceived him
only in one thing ; she concealed the Jewish ancestry
of her mother, and gave it out as Italian. In our
town this background was never suspected, and
everybody believed the apothecary's story that his
wife was the daughter of an officer of high rank and
of a respectable lady from Southern Italy. Italy
belonged to the Triple Alliance, and moreover the
apothecary had a secret deposit of his own which he
now produced with many flourishes as the dowry
his wife had brought with her. Isabella retained
only a taste for expensive Paris clothes and model
hats, for costly jewellery, fine cooking and horses.
She ran through a lot of money in this way, but with

a perfectly clear conscience, for in his madness the apothecary had pretended to her that his income was more than it really was, and so he had to compensate for his wife's extravagance by working into the night. This he did without any bitterness, almost as a voluntary tribute to the beauty which was his to embrace with an untroubled sense of exclusive possession later in the night.

In the second year of this happy marriage Isabella bore a child in terrible agony. Wild with the joy of fatherhood the apothecary swore to her that she should never bear another, for he did not want her to undergo such suffering again on his behalf. From that day on Isabella loved this simple man with a graciousness and tenderness that made him envied by the whole town. They called the child Hilde, for Isabella confessed to her husband that that was her real name, and that she had only chosen the name Isabella to make herself more interesting. " It was as Isabella that I first loved you," smiled the apothecary, " and you must go on being Isabella,—for the town's sake, too. But we'll call the child Hilde, and then that puts it all right."

So without realising it the apothecary gave back her innocence to his beloved, the physical proof of which he had never missed. A few years later during his night work in the laboratory he invented a nerve tonic called " Nervalux," which brought him in so much profit that he was able to satisfy every wish of his wife and keep an assistant for himself. . . . The only curious thing was that his wife always refused to go travelling with him ; she loathed hotels ; nor would she ever visit Garmisch again.

· · · · · ·

It was about this time, shortly after the discovery of " Nervalux," that I began to observe Hilde. True, I had known her for a long time already—a long friendship, founded on postage stamps, existed between the apothecary and my father, and our mothers too were great friends—but I had never regarded her before as I began to regard her now.

Before my talk with Ferd about the mystery, Hilde had been for me one of those girls whom one was compelled to accept as a playmate because one's parents used to go as a general rule with hers for their Sunday walk. One had to be friendly with her, had to be polite to her at table while the grown-ups talked loudly and importantly about their affairs, and when they rose had to go into the yard with her and play at tag. When she expressed a wish one had to fulfil it at once, do everything that she desired, pluck flowers, wipe the strawberries for her, knock down nuts for her and tie her shoe-laces when they became undone. When Hilde's family entered the reserved room at " The Green Huntsman " I had at my mother's command to rise up and help Hilde to take off her coat. After that if we ventured into the yard— " fine for playing "—our fathers would smile across at us. Hilde would sit down on the swing and I would have to push her, or collect a few pine cones which she would throw at me. I obeyed, full of rage, and hated her just as I hated those Sundays.

That changed when Hilde begged me once to teach her to ride the bicycle. She was fourteen then and had been given a bicycle at Easter as a present. I replied importantly that I would think it over, but I was flattered by her request. On the way home from " The Green Huntsman " Hilde asked her father if he would give his permission, which he did smilingly, while my father expressed doubts. That decided me. I cried : " None of the boys is so safe with the bicycle as me, not even Ferd. Everybody admits that." Hilde smiled. She knew it ; that was the very reason, of course, why she had chosen me. My father, actually a little impressed by the reputation of his son, concurred.

Every evening shortly after supper I taught Hilde to ride the bicycle on the main road until it was dark.

With the zeal of an instructor I dedicated myself to this task.

It was during these days that I had the talk with Ferd and the other experiences which confused me so much. And what confused me most of all was that I thought of Hilde when I kissed Ferd.

Surreptitiously I began to observe her.

Her breasts had already developed.

I carefully concealed these exercises on the main road from Ferd.

Once, when I had kept Hilde waiting because I had returned late from the farm, she said in a piqued voice : " Oh, this Ferd of yours is your darling, is he ? "

I blushed and was afraid of her.

True, August had seen us. But I succeeded in buying his secrecy, as far as Ferd was concerned, with fifty pfennigs. He laughed, pocketed the unasked money, and said : " You be on your guard with her. She knows a thing or two." I was filled with excitement, for I hoped to get behind the mystery through Hilde, the mystery that the grown-ups kept so close that we could not reach it. Only when I knew the mystery would I be able to understand their world which bewildered me so much. The mystery seemed to me the cement which held their world together.

I wanted to know at last why people hated one another so much.

In contradistinction to Ferd I struggled to find an explanation.

When Hilde was sitting in the saddle I had to hold her. I took a grip of the saddle spring, and the back of my hand came into contact with the soft curves of her body. I ran fast behind her, Hilde's blue pleated skirt billowing high in the wind. Sometimes above the tops of her stockings appeared a strip of smooth skin. Her breasts were tossed upwards when she passed over a rut in the road. Sometimes she laughed into the head-wind ; then it was as if her hair sang. I could not have looked away, for if I had looked away she would have fallen.

We always went on until we came to the poplars. There I had to help Hilde down by taking her under the arms, for she could not yet dismount by herself.

" Ooh ! " Hilde would shriek then, " you're like a bear ! " I felt the presence of her little breasts.

Hilde seated herself beneath the poplars. The fields were empty. Her skirt was spread wide like a forsaken fan. She was breathing hard, for she did not care for free-wheeling.

I had often noticed that in a dip in the road where any sensible cyclist would have free-wheeled, she pedalled with particular vigour, so as to put me out of breath. It was a great pleasure to her to hear me panting. From that I decided that she was attracted to me.

.   .   .   .   .   .

The educational theories of grown-ups about children are ruled by the belief in their " primitiveness "—a devastating prejudice. People cannot even imagine that children can think and reason purely speculatively, that they can proceed systematically according to plan towards an end resolved upon, weigh things in accordance with an inner logic, observe, draw conclusions, and that they are no longer " innocent," but in their methods very early adult and subtle. The " innocence " of the child consists only in this, that in contradistinction to the grown-up he does not morally drape and hide his actions and feelings, but rather carries through his meannesses and cruelties without hypocrisy. He is more defenceless because he cannot yet avail himself of that aid which is permitted to the grown-up ; to find fine names even for his worst actions.

. . . . . .

I acted in accordance with a plan. That plan was diabolical. During these days, in other words, I had observed that between men and women who were married, especially among the younger, but also between those who were only engaged and used to walk in the park, and yes, even among the boys in the highest class who always met the girls out of the Lyceum at lunch-time and carried their portfolios for them—that between these people there were certain forms of behaviour, which were very clearly distinguished from the usual ones. Men whom I had known to be loud and self-important, mighty men of impressive appearance and confident step, men set over perhaps twenty others, of whom each again was a superior over other men, officers before whom

companies sprang to attention, teachers under whose
eye classes competed for favour and distinction, sixth
form boys who beat us if we did not salute them ;
all these, who were power incarnate, altered their
bearing and their expression in the presence of certain women. Their movements lost their stiffness,
from their voices vanished the tone of command,
they said " Thank you " when the lady gave them
anything, they stood ever in readiness to do the lady
a favour, to pluck a flower, to put up an umbrella,
to procure a theatre ticket, to turn over a sheet of
music, to post a letter, to carry a bag ; they were
transfigured so much that I sometimes believed they
were good. But they were only " in love. . . ."

So this state was called, and, moreover, it did not
last once they had been married for any time.   I
could not imagine these people doing anything for
nothing ; they must have expected something in
return, then, for this alteration in their nature. For
if this was their true nature, why did they not treat
everybody else in just the same way ?

.   .   .   .   .   .

So I resolved to fall in love with Hilde, for that
seemed to me the best way of getting the mystery
out of her.

I had soon noticed that Hilde loved white lilac.
I surreptitiously stole a few sprays from our garden
and laid the bunch in her arms. Hilde was terribly
fond of digestive biscuits. I stole twenty pfennigs
from my mother's household cash-box and bought
Hilde an enormous bag of digestive biscuits.   I
owned a silver pencil, which she admired very much.
I gave it to her. Her music portfolio was heavy. I
carried it. She wanted a propeller mounted on her

bicycle. I made one for her. She had a pebble in her shoe. I took it out.

I did everything she wanted, and she wanted a great deal.

But I never forgot my goal. I proceeded quite consciously and systematically, for love never came into my head. I wanted to know. . .

Once when my father saw me presenting a rose to Hilde he threatened me playfully with a finger and said : " Now, you little cavalier. . . ."

From that I decided that I was on the right way.

My visits to the farm became imperceptibly shorter. Only Ferd noticed it. He said nothing and devoted himself entirely to looking after Leo Silberstein, who often spent whole days at the farm. I became jealous and suffered the deepest anguish of my bewildered childhood whenever Ferd put his arm round Leo's shoulder when we were walking through the stables, or said when we were running across the fields : " Not so fast, Leo must take care of himself." At the same time Ferd remained outwardly the same to me ; only once he said as he led his foal into the stall : " Time's up. You must go. Hilde's waiting." I went home as if I had been beaten. For I knew I was betraying him. Perhaps because he was the only one I loved. . . .

That evening Hilde awaited me in great excitement. " I can't cycle to-night," she said, " my parents are away at the military ball (mine were there too), we'll go and sit in the garden. The air's still lovely." And she took me tenderly by the hand and bent her head until I could feel her breath.

Her eyes were slightly moist, her lips a little parted.

" You'll come with me into the garden, won't you ? " she smiled.

I considered carefully why Hilde should want me to go into the garden. Did she want me perhaps to pump up the tyres, or make a new propeller, or help her with her lessons—or ?

Her parents were not at home : why, just this evening, did she not want to ride the bicycle ?

I went with her into the garden.

When we were in the front yard I put my arm round Hilde's waist, exactly as I had seen the grown-ups do when they walked in the park of an evening. Hilde made no objection. We did not speak.

" I mustn't make any mistake now," I thought, " that's it, no mistakes ! Just behave as if you knew everything, be very kind, speak as if you were in love."

" Oh, Hilde," I said, " what a lovely evening ! Not a cloud in the sky. The first stars are coming out." (I had heard my cousin talking like this once as he walked with his sweetheart in our garden.) Moreover there had not been a single star visible that evening, any more than now.

" Yes," I heard Hilde saying, " the air is so still."

" You've said that more than once before," I thought, but I replied : " Yes, wonderfully still."

As we went through the wrought-iron gate, which hung between two red-stone pillars on which cherubs stood blowing trumpets, I laid my hand under Hilde's breast.

" Now you must speak softly," the thought shot through my head, " then pause for a little and sigh."

The apothecary's garden was among the finest in our town.

From the black wrought-iron gate a white path,

bordered with yew, and flanked by espaliers, led in
elegant windings to a pavilion of compact Baroque.
It was white, almost windowless, and most of its
figures lacked a nose or an ear. Left and right of
the pavilion luxuriated a confusion of bushes, lilac,
hazel and red may. An ash stood there too, and
overshadowing everything a copper beech. It was
very old. It was said that the Landgrave to whom
this pavilion had belonged had planted the tree with
his own hand for his sweetheart ; for before it fell
into the hands of the municipality, the apothecary's
shop had been the country seat of a lady whom a
ruling prince of the eighteenth century had ennobled
in order to legitimise her charms. The family of the
apothecary used the pavilion as a store for their
garden implements. The garden itself was protected
as a public monument. None of the trees were
allowed to be felled.

We went towards a seat which stood under the
copper beech near the pavilion. Hilde's head rested
softly on my shoulder, we fell into step. We sat
down on the seat. The air was really very still. Only
under the eaves of a shed close by the sleepy croon
of a few pigeons could be heard.

" Hilde," I asked, " do your parents know that
I'm here in the garden with you to-night ? "

" But of course," replied Hilde, " my mother even
telephoned to your father first, asking if you could
keep me company until I went to bed."

" And what did he say ? "

" That he trusted to his son's upbringing."

I sat beside Hilde, held her soft hand, and thought
that my father trusted in his son's upbringing, as a
business man trusted in the efficient running of his
branch establishments.

We sat still for a long time, not a leaf stirred, the evening sky gradually took on the hues of a jam tart.

Oh, I thought, everything is as it should be, we're sitting on a seat concealed by bushes and uncannily still trees, nobody sees us, we're breathing very softly, there's a scent of flowers (that it also smelt of stagnant water, which was going bad in the fountain basin, I would not admit to myself). Sometimes Hilde quivered or a strand of her hair tickled my ear, the dark was falling and in the sky the first star had already appeared. Everything concurred, everything I could think of was there in readiness ; now I must give Hilde a kiss, then I could ask her about the mystery.

" The evening star ! " cried Hilde, and pointed ecstatically at the sky.

I sprang up. " Yes, the evening star," I shouted, " but it's called Venus as well, and in Greek Aphrodite."

" Oh, how clever you are," cried Hilde, and lay with closed eyes against my shoulder.

Actually I had put my arms round her so that she should not fall, but as her face sank as if accidentally nearer and nearer to mine and she began to sigh, I kissed her very hastily on the mouth, so that part of my kiss was spent on her chin.

" Darling ! " whispered Hilde, flung her arms round me and embraced me closely. And she planted a kiss on the right side of my nose. I had to summon up all my strength to keep us from falling off the seat. Hilde, who noticed it, hinted that it would be more comfortable on the grass.

We lay down on the grass.

Hardly had I lain down beside her before she

began to pull my hair playfully and say that I was
her idol. I resolved to see the thing through, and I
kissed Hilde again. The mystery no longer seemed
remote.

.   .   .   .   .   .

Suddenly I felt that Hilde was about to do something, I heard her moving, she was rolling over the
grass, her pleated skirt rose in dark waves, but I
could scarcely see her, for darkness had fallen. Then
her hand seized me by the shoulder, and she snuggled
close to me while I lay rigid, my fingers convulsively
clutching some blades of grass. " Now, now," the
only thought I had was " now."

Hilde put her mouth to my ear and whispered :
" I know what it is. . . ."

My body was as if paralysed, I could only listen.

" My cousin who's a medical student in Heidelberg told me all about it. He talked to me about
things that the grown-ups only talk about when
we're out of the room', and he didn't turn a hair. I
know now where children come from."

I asked, lowering my voice : " What has the mystery to do with children ? "

Hilde tittered.

" Go on ! " I cried, " go on, Hilde ! " She lay
quite close in to me, she was sweating, at first I
imagined she was crying.

She pulled me on top of her, her skirt flew wide,
I saw nothing more, everything was gone, Hilde's
name, the garden, the house.

She sighed. " The mystery ! " I shouted. " The
mystery ! " In that moment I seemed to see everything, my father, my mother, Ferd, Leo, August,
Hilde, the whole town.—" The mystery ! "

I felt Hilde's arm round my neck. " Do you love me ? "

" The mystery ! "

Very gently Hilde laid her cheek against mine. " I don't know it."

" Hilde ! " I pushed her away. My face was lying against the ground. I cried out into the dark grass stalks which got into my mouth : " You don't know it ? "—" No," said Hilde, and sat up.

For a long time I lay without speaking. Hilde too had lied to me. Then I felt her pressing against me.—" But you must know it surely. You're a man." I did not stir. Hilde leant against me and said : " I would let *you* show me, for you're my sweet-heart. . . ."—" Oh, Hilde," I replied, " I don't know it either. I thought you would tell me." Then Hilde clapped her hands and laughed.—" Stupid, stupid ! " she laughed, and pulled my nose, " You cheat, you cheat ! "—I sprang to my feet. I shouted, furious : " You don't know it either ! " and I seized her by the wrist.—" But you call yourself a man ; you must know it ! "

She tore herself free and began to dance round me.

Suddenly I felt very tired. As if I had been wakened too soon.

And Hilde flung herself upon me, she pulled my face down to hers and cried : " My cousin's coming in August ; then I'll know, yes, then, in August. . . ."

" Oh ! " I said, and felt that I was crying, " he knows nothing either, nobody knows anything. Everybody tells lies. . . ." and without shaking hands I walked through the garden, past the yard to the gate.

There Hilde caught me up. She jeered. " What ! " she cried, " my cousin doesn't know ? But he's studied it at Heidelberg. He knows it all scientifically, so there. You're only jealous."

Then she shut the gate. I heard her singing as she ran up the front-door steps. I made for home and suddenly for no cause began to limp.

The tallowy moon hung over the grey roofs. Pianos were being played in many of the houses. 'Cellos in a few.

Before the house Kathinka, our maid, was standing with her sweetheart, a cobbler. When I approached the cobbler walked a little distance along the street, as if he had nothing to do with Kathinka. She opened the door for me and said that I would find something she had left for me on the sideboard. There I ate what I found. Three slices of cold roast beef, cream cheese, and some cucumber and tomato salad. Without knife or fork, all with my hands. With a little wooden spoon I plastered on a layer of mustard. I had a sudden desire for sharp condiments. Then I went through the sitting-room with its stale smells to my bedroom, and undressed in the dark.

CHAPTER VII

THE REVELATION

NEXT morning I refused to get up. Kathinka knocked three times on my door, but I did not answer. I did not want to go to school, for I was afraid of meeting Ferd. Besides, a mathematics lesson was due that day in which I would be sure to do badly, for, no matter how hard I racked my brains, I could not remember a single formula. I had forgotten everything.

After knocking three times Kathinka went to my parents' bedroom door and reported her lack of success. I turned on my back at once, lay motionless, made all my limbs rigid, and held my breath. For cases like this I possessed a certain technique, for I often managed to evade unpleasant situations by a sickness ; and soon my face had become white, and drops of sweat appeared on my forehead. The sudden stoppage of my breathing quickened my heart-beat, and its irregular, violent thumping raised my temperature. Next I rumpled the sheets so that the red mattresses half showed, scattered the blankets, and kneaded the pillow into lumps, so that my mother might think that I had had a bad night. When she came in I pretended that I was still asleep, and only woke up out of a troubled slumber when she took hold of my hand. I held my breath as long as I could, forcing out sweat on my forehead ; and when

my mother laid her hand upon it she was convinced
that I was ill. I spun a tale to her that I had had
frightful dreams all night, and seen hosts of men all
red ; then she stuck the thermometer under my arm
and went into the kitchen to make me some pepper-
mint tea. I employed her absence in sending the
thermometer up by breathing on it and rubbing it.
When it stood at 37.8 I stopped. On these occasions I would complain of pains in the chest, the
stomach or the throat, whichever came into my
mind. This morning I announced that I had pains
in my head and chest. My mother decided that it
was a feverish cold. I did my best to round off the
picture by coughing and wheezing. By ten o'clock
my bronchial tubes were so irritated that I coughed
in earnest ; my mother rolled me in a wet sheet,
gave me lime tea and said that I would have to
sweat. Soon I broke out into a profuse perspiration
and by midday it had weakened me so much that
my father could write with a good conscience a card
to the school excusing my absence on account of a
bad cold, and send it to Brosius' house by
Kathinka.

I had attained what I wanted. Peace !

By midday I was naturally rid of my fever ; my
cough too had slackened, which my mother attributed
to her own prompt intervention. She declared that
she had nipped the illness in the bud. I could ask
now for the things I liked best to eat. Veal cutlet
with white sauce and mashed potatoes. The appetite with which I devoured this appeared to my
mother the clearest proof of my recovery. Often
I have invented illnesses like this simply to win my
mother's affection and to be given some particular
dish of which I was very fond. For that I would

even go through two hours' sweating, for it seemed to me that parents were really good to a child only when he was ill. I have often malingered that I might be petted by my mother. . . .

But on this day I only wanted to be left alone. For many children illness is the only way to win solitude, for as long as they are in good health they must do what their elders tell them. This midday I lay in bed, my mother had prescribed quiet, the thick gleaming leaves of the walnut tree brushed against the window, whose muslined curtains deadened the rays of the sun. I meditated what I should do ; my plan with Hilde had miscarried, there was no point in being in love. Should I renounce all hope of a solution of the mystery ? It was the thing I would have liked best, to go back to Ferd at the farm where one could live so securely among the cattle and under the Major's eye. If I had followed Ferd's lead that time and kept the oath, I would never have been so humiliated by Hilde as I had been the evening before. True, I comforted myself by saying, Hilde was a stupid goose ; like lots of girls she behaved as if she knew God knows what, and afterwards, when you held her to the point, it was nothing ; but she had called me a cheat, and doubted my manhood ; it was clear that I must revenge myself on her. And the only revenge possible was to discover the mystery sooner than she, before her cousin arrived. . . .

Besides, it seemed to me a sign of cowardice to give up all my attempts to solve the mystery now, simply because my first attempt had miscarried. I had just lately been made to write out fifty times " Fortes fortuna adiuvat ! " for inattention in the Latin class. " Fortune favours the brave ! " But what other favour could there be than the mystery ?

My strategy had been wrong, I knew, but the
goal had lost none of its seductiveness. In addition
there was the private obligation to revenge myself
on Hilde.

.   .   .   .   .   .

Towards six o'clock my father appeared and sat
down on my bed. He talked enthusiastically about
the military ball. The *tableaux vivants* had been the
best feature of all—the old-time officers, the con-
secration of the recruits, Blucher's crossing of the
Rhine at Caub, the Kaiser Hill during the battle of
Leipzig ; after that they had all danced till four in
the morning. Young D. had made a very good
impression. He had kept on his fancy dress—he
was the Czar of Russia—and had led out Queen
Louise, the cheese manufacturer Bloch's daughter,
to dance the polonaise.

Young D. was the Kalmuck ; at least we called
him that because of his prominent cheek-bones and
his dirty-grey pimply complexion. His father was a
butcher, a fair-skinned, robust man, very brutal ;
his mother was from East Prussia, where Herr D.,
then a journeyman butcher, had promptly married
her for her money. She was ugly and spoke little.
In quick succession she had presented the butcher
with eight children ; since her last confinement she
had been paralysed. The Kalmuck inherited his
looks from his mother, his character from his father.
He liked to torment animals, cats in particular,
which he would bind together in pairs by the hind-
legs and then hound them on by pouring water over
them. In our school—he was in the Untersecunda*
— he was little liked, for he evaded every oppor-

* Class corresponding to Lower Fifth.

tunity of fighting with boys of his own age, and
secretly thrashed the younger scholars. All the same
I had thought it strange that some of the younger
boys, whom I knew that he often thrashed, were
always going about with him. They always went
to bathe together in out-of-the-way places, in the
canal where the reeds grew very close together and
there was a thicket of willows. Here the Kalmuck
always thrashed them, especially when they had
nothing on, after which they had to do something
for him that was very exciting. When I asked what
it was of the Pastor S.'s son, who had told me all this,
he replied that they had sworn never to reveal it.
They had a secret pledge. . . . But if I could hold my
tongue, I had only to go with them some time ; the
Kalmuck was always glad when new ones came ;
there were eighteen of them now from all the classes.
I asked Ferd at the time whether I should do it, and
Ferd asked his father, who forbade us. In spite of
this the mysterious assignation of the boys with the
Kalmuck held a secret allurement for me, especially
when I noticed that more and more boys attached
themselves to him. But when I learned that he
extorted part of their pocket-money from some of
them by menaces, because his father gave him none,
I avoided him.

All this came back into my mind as my father was
describing the military ball that afternoon. I decided
to be well again from next morning on, and to seek
out the Kalmuck at once, for it seemed to me that
he knew something of the things I wanted to know.
I had often seen him with Polish workgirls on my
way home in the evening from the farm. They sat
mostly in a sand-pit which was hidden from the road
by a thick hawthorn hedge. The workgirls screamed

in a foreign tongue when the Kalmuck flung them
down on the sand and tied them up with straw ropes.
I always ran away at that point.

.　　.　　.　　.　　.　　.

Next evening, my parents being reassured of my
quick recovery, I offered voluntarily to go to D. the
butcher, to get sausages. The Kalmuck was standing in the white-tiled shop with a blood-stained apron
tied round him. Although he was not allowed yet
to help in killing the cattle, he liked to wear this
blood-stained apron. He was cutting up beef
sausages, and I bought a half-pound, although my
mother had expressly told me to get liver sausage.
The Kalmuck sliced off a length for me, and I winced
slightly as I saw the knife almost grazing his nails
and finger-tips.

" I say," I whispered, as he weighed the sausage,
" I say, I want to ask you something." The Kalmuck gave me a furtive side-look. I grew very red
in the face. When he noticed that he nodded and
wrapped up the sausages.

I was standing between two slaughtered calves,
whose hind legs depended from sharp hooks. Little
runnels of blood, ending in mere threads, showed on
their brown hides flecked with white ; their heads
had been sawn off. Behind the counter stood the
butcher bringing a little axe down among bones
and flesh still warm. Sometimes a gobbet flew up
and with a tiny smack stuck fast to the wall. The
Kalmuck wiped his hands and came towards me.
Under his apron he was wearing a pair of brown
breeches, his boots were spotted with blood. I stood
between the calves, the sausages under my arm ; the
Kalmuck said, " The shop will be shut in five min-

utes. Wait for me at the monument."—" All right,"
I whispered, " it's something very important, I don't
want anybody to overhear us." Thereupon the
Kalmuck smiled, and his mouth stretched until it
watered.—" I know what you want. Little S. told
me what you asked him about the other day."—
" No, no, it isn't that ; it's something else I want to
know."—" All right, wait outside." I went away,
and waited beside the monument. Again as I stood
there I began to be troubled about what I should
really do. For I had noticed that the Kalmuck
thought I wanted to go bathing with him.

In five minutes he arrived. He was still wearing
the apron. He led me behind the monument, where
there was a row of firs which hid us from the street.
Then he took me round the neck, I smelt the blood
on his apron, he forced me down on a bench, his
nails clawing into my arm. " I always thought you
were in with the little major, but if you come with
me I'll teach you far more."

" No," I said, " I don't want to go bathing with
your crowd."

He put his face quite close to mine, and I had
great difficulty in avoiding his breath. His hands
pressed me firmly to him, he was already beginning
to caress me, when, fighting down the smell of his
apron, I whispered in his ear : " I say, I would like
to look on sometime when you play with the Polish
girls in the sand-pit."

The Kalmuck laughed and let me go. " You call
that playing ? But it's real . . ." And he pronounced
a disreputable word.

" Yes," I said, " I want to see that sometime."

" Do you want to do it yourself ? I can arrange
it for you."

" No," I whispered, " only see it. . . ."

" So that's it," said the Kalmuck, leaning back importantly ; then after a pause I heard him again : " That'll cost two marks." I started in fear.

" And over and above that you must give me something for myself. Do you think I would just let you look on for nothing ? Two marks for the girl, and one mark will do for me."

" I haven't any money," I whimpered, " why do you need money for it ? "

" Do you think the girls would do it for nothing ? They earn too little to be respectable."

" But seeing it's you that does it ? "

" It costs two marks and it's cheap at that ; in the big towns you must pay five."

" And that's why you thrash the boys and take their pocket-money from them ? "

" Yes, that's one of the reasons," said the Kalmuck calmly, getting up. " Well, how about it ? Do you have any money ? "

" Not just now," I stuttered. " All right," said the Kalmuck, " if you have it by Friday, meet me in the school and we'll go to the sand-pit in the evening and there you can look on." Then still wearing his apron he went back to his father's house, in the front of which in golden letters could be read : " Butcher, Electrical Fittings. Speciality : Sirloin."

I clutched my sausages and ran as fast as I could to my parents' house. I felt very dejected. Where was I to get three marks ? That was as much as my pocket-money for six months. The contents of my savings-bank, a green apple made of earthenware, I had used up last Christmas for presents. Three marks ! The mystery was expensive, and my revenge on Hilde was beyond my means. I had not known till now that one needed money to discover the truth.

.   .   .   .   .   .

After I had handed the sausages to my mother and sworn to her that there was no liver sausage to be had, I noticed that she stuck the change into a drawer in the kitchen table which she did not lock afterwards. Among the copper and nickel coins glittered a three-mark piece. Then we had supper. I could not keep from thinking of the three-mark piece. Sometimes, when my mother looked at me, I blushed.

After supper I announced that I was tired. My father thought that very probable, for I was convalescent. I went to bed and lay there for two hours awake, until I heard my parents talking in their bedroom and my father beating the eiderdown until it lay to his satisfaction. A quarter of an hour later I heard their regular breathing. My father was snoring.

I got up. Silently, by minute-long degrees, I opened and closed the door. I stood in the passage in my night-shirt. The moon was shining, and the branches of the walnut tree cast restless shadows on the window. I crept on. From my room to the kitchen took me ten minutes. When the clock struck in the dining-room I gave myself up for lost. But the noise did not bring anyone. Some cats were miauling in the yard. The door of the kitchen stood open, the window as well. There was a draught, my night-shirt billowed up. Pale in the full rays of the moon the table stood in the middle of the room. When I reached it I found courage. The drawer opened easily. From among the small coins I picked up the three-mark piece. A few pfennig coins clinked

E

as I picked it up. I ran back very fast, my hand
where the coin lay was sweating. I put the money
in my satchel between the leaves of the manual of
German history.

Then I went to sleep.

In the school next morning I made a sign to the
Kalmuck. When I showed him the three-mark piece
he nodded and said : " Right. Then Friday at six
by the poplars." They were the same poplars which
Hilde loved.

.   .   .   .   .   .

That Friday I went to see Ferd at the farm ; Leo
was there with him, August was working in the dairy.
Ferd had got a riding suit with leather insets in the
breeches. Leo was feverish, so we stayed in the
sitting-room, though Ferd would have liked to go
riding. The Major was sitting in his study with Dr.
Hoffmann. They were arguing violently. Once I
heard the word " war," but I was not in the least
interested. About five I took my leave ; we had
visitors at home, I said. Ferd saw me to the gate.
He said, " Leo will die soon ; yesterday he spat
blood again." I gave him my hand, with the other
I held the three-mark piece fast in my pocket.

" Why are you crying ? " I heard Ferd saying.

" Oh," I lied, " because Leo is dying." Actually
I was in the grip of an intense jealousy, of Leo, of
Ferd, of Leo's approaching death, which only bound
him closer to Ferd, of Ferd's riding suit, of his foals,
of his father——

Then Ferd put his arm very tenderly round me,
went with me for a little along the drive, and wiped
the tears from my cheeks with his handkerchief.
" Go on," he said, " I know why you're crying. I'm

not angry with you for breaking your word, for you're more inquisitive than I am, and so you'll have more to cry about too. . . ."

" Ferd," I cried, " I'll tell you everything." But he shook his head.

" But that wouldn't help you. You're still my friend as things are."

" Ferd ! " I wanted to clasp his hand, but I did not dare to lose hold of the three-mark piece.

And while I held it and ceaselessly rubbed its cold smoothness between my fingers, and while like a happy refrain Ferd's words ran through my head, " You're still my friend as things are," I asked him : " I say, have you any money on you ? "

" Yes," said Ferd, " shall I lend you some ? "

" No, change some. . . ."

" How much ? "

" Three marks."

He drew a blue leather case out of his pocket and counted three single mark pieces into my hand. I gave him my taler. At that moment I flattered myself that I was no longer a thief. Then we parted.

I kept to the path leading to the town till Ferd was out of sight. Then I ran so as to make up for the time spent in going out of my road. When I reached the poplars the Kalmuck was already there. He was wearing his brown suit.

" Have you the money ? " I rattled my new mark pieces in my pocket.

" Give it here ! " I retreated.

" What, you want to have it now ? But I haven't seen anything yet ! "

" Don't you play with me ! Out with the cash ! " He seized my arm.

" Where's the girl then ? I must see the girl first ! "

The Kalmuck led me to a hawthorn hedge and pushed aside some twigs ; beneath in the sand-pit sat one of the Polish workgirls, very fat, in a blue blouse of flowered cotton. " That's the one," whispered the Kalmuck.

" Does she know I'm looking on ? "

" No, you just stay here quietly, and you're not to move till everything's over."

" How long will it last ? "

" Three minutes."

" What ! Three minutes ! " I whispered. " Three minutes for the whole mystery. . . ."

" So, fork out the money ! " The Kalmuck made a grab at my pocket.

I defended myself desperately.

We fought. Among the bushes the Kalmuck could not take advantage of his full strength. Besides that I got in two shrewd blows on his thighs.

" Why won't you give me the money ? " His voice was less gruff already. " I must see it first," I panted. " Then I'll give it you."

" That's impossible." The Kalmuck leant back with an important air. I crouched in the undergrowth among thorns and snake-like branches ; through a gap I saw the Polish girl : she had top boots on, and was picking her nose in boredom. In her other hand she held a handful of yarrow. She stuck it into her bosom. Then she began to tidy her hair with a broken comb. Meanwhile she sang.

" Well, what is it to be ? Are you going to give me the money ? "

" Yes," I said. " Does she do it really, like all the grown-ups ? "

" Of course," grinned the Kalmuck, " they're all the same in that."

" And is it the real mystery ? "

" You can try it yourself."

" No, no. I only want to know about it."

Then the Kalmuck laughed, " Don't you know anything about it at all ? "

I shook my head. The Kalmuck leant very confidentially towards me.

" Oh, you want to know exactly, so that you can show your girl ? "

" Yes," I lied.—" Right," said the Kalmuck. " If you promise to go bathing with me sometime. . . . "

I gave my promise. He stood up. " But I need the money first." I held out two marks to him. He examined them carefully and then said : " And the other mark ? "—" I'll give it to you afterwards."— " You don't trust me ? "—" Of course," I said, " but I want to see first if it's the real mystery. . . ."

" Mystery ! " snorted the Kalmuck. " You do have some funny ideas."

I sat motionless among the undergrowth. " All right, if you don't believe me, give me the mark afterwards."—" If it's the real mystery," I answered.

" Taken," said the Kalmuck and crept out from the bushes.

I looked towards the Polish girl. She was squatting on the sand and began to unbutton her blouse as soon as she saw the Kalmuck standing before her. In his hand he held my money. He sat down beside her, the girl lay back. Then the Kalmuck gave her my mark pieces. She stuck them in a bag of crochet work. The Kalmuck took off her skirt. She said nothing. I looked through the branches. Suddenly the girl began to laugh, she seized the Kalmuck and drew him down on her. Then it was as if they fought. I sat in the bush, held my mark piece in

my hand and regarded the scene, whose silent fury
I did not understand. Suddenly the Polish girl
screamed. I held my hand before my face and only
heard her scream. I sprang out of the bush. With
the impact of my body a bird's warm nest fell to
the ground. I was in a field. The path ran on, a
brown stretch. The sun gleamed on the sand. On
the leaves of the poplars lay the soft glow of evening.
I ran. I flew. I believed I had seen the greatest of
crimes. I felt I was an accomplice in the guilt of
the world. " The mystery is murder," I thought.
" That's why she screamed for help." I ran as if I
were bound to rescue all manhood from the mystery.
I ran towards the farm that I might see Ferd. I
wanted to beg him to forgive me for everything. I
had seen it all. I could not understand it—the picture was too dreadful—and for that reason I cannot
describe it even now. The greatest human agonies
cannot be put into words ; I was a child who had
seen what reality was—I could not comprehend it.
I could only cry for help.

I wanted to be with Ferd, with August, with the
Major, and with the foals as well.

I ran and ever again the cry of the Polish girl rang
in my ears : " Hi-i-iau ! " I held my hands before
my face and stumbled over the knotted roots which
grew on the path.

When I came in sight of the farm, suddenly I felt
the mark piece in my pocket which belonged to the
Kalmuck. It was rolled up in my handkerchief. I
crouched in a rye-field and realised that I was
delivered into the Kalmuck's hands. If he were to
run to my father and tell him all, and my father
seized me and found the mark in my pocket—then
how was I to explain how I happened to have a

mark ? All would be revealed, my theft, and why
I had done it. And the Kalmuck could say that I
had bribed him to go to the sand-pit ; actually I
would be the guilty party, because I had had the
money. And it was because of my money that the
girl had had to cry for help.

My father would be sure to believe the Kalmuck,
for the Kalmuck had been dressed as the Czar at
the military ball.

As I looked round I saw the figure of the Kalmuck
running fast towards the town. The Polish girl was
walking in broad silhouette towards the red out-
buildings of the farm. In the uncertain light of
early evening she looked superhumanly big.

.   .   .   .   .   .

I had to catch up the Kalmuck, I had to cut
him off. I had to reach the house before him. I
would post myself at our gate and defend it against
him. And if everything else failed, then, yes, I would
give him the mark if he would keep his mouth shut.
Nobody must know that I knew the mystery, nobody ; I too wanted to forget it, to spit out the very
memory of it, for it seemed to me as if I had seen
the most terrible crime. I was convinced that they
would kill me if the Kalmuck gave me away, for I
had been the cause of it, yes, I bore the guilt, and
then there was the theft, too. . . .

The Kalmuck had a lead of half a mile at least.
He was not a good runner, but it seemed almost out
of the question to catch him up before he reached
my parents' house. Yet if I avoided the field path
which wound in yellow turnings to the town, and
cut straight across the fields, then through the
meadow and struck the path again where the gardens
began, I would have a better chance of catching the

Kalmuck in time. I ran. Over the fields lay the
first mists of evening ; gradually the dew began to
wet the leaves and grasses. From the hedges came
the muffled twitterings of sleepy birds ; in soundless
arcs the swallows shot over the pools, from which
clouds of gnats and midges rose in smoky columns.
The potatoes were in flower. A field of maize,
whose stalks were as tall as a man, the knobbly
ears covered with thick, white bristles, like those in
a horse's tail, cut off my view ; I could not see the
Kalmuck any longer. I plunged into the jungle of
maize stalks, a sweet greenish fragrance stupefied
me, the sharp leaves cut my cheeks, the tall stems
swished about my head. I fell, struggled up again,
stumbled out of my way and lost in my battle with
the jungle of maize all that I had made up before.
When at last I had fought my way through, the
Kalmuck had disappeared. My cheeks were bleeding.
I kept on running simply because I was afraid of
standing still.

.   .   .   .   .   .

I am lost, I told myself, I have seen the mystery,
they will arrest me. My father will drive me from
the house, all the grown-ups will point at me, they
will put me in chains, for I have laid a blasphemous
hand on something that they all wished to hide.

Dog-tired I ran along the road. I had given up
trying to follow the Kalmuck. He was with my
father now, that was certain. Should I turn back
and hide myself in the fields ? Should I take my
life ? I was too tired.

So I simply ran home, though I knew what awaited
me there. It could not be worse than those last
moments behind the bush at the sand-pit. Every-

where along the street groups of men were standing.
They were talking in great excitement, their faces
were flushed, they were gesticulating with their
hands. Sometimes their eyes raked me, furious and
full of hatred. " Oh," I told myself, " they know it
already, the Kalmuck has told them." I lowered
my head and ran on. If anyone was to thrash me,
then at least it would be my own father.

As I raced in full career across the market-place
my eye fell on Herr D. the butcher's shop. And
there was the Kalmuck, standing in his white apron
behind the counter, slicing sausages. But in front
of the shop, on the sandstone steps, I noticed the
butcher himself in the middle of a big crowd of men.
They were all shouting at the same time, the butcher
loudest of all. I held on to a tree. With the last of
my failing strength I thought it over : " The Kalmuck has blabbed it all and perhaps he has added
something on to it, saying that I did what he did
himself. My father is the only one he hasn't told,
because he is too cowardly. If the town knows it,
my father will learn it soon enough : that's what the
Kalmuck has reckoned on. For it's impossible that
in this short time he could have been to our house.
My father would have been certain to keep him
there until I came." For my father was so just. . . .

In front of all the houses the people were gathering
and talking together excitedly. Neighbours who had
hated one another for years were exchanging words
for the first time. They must all feel themselves in
great peril because I knew the mystery.

There was only one chance of salvation for me ;
to run home, throw myself at my father's feet, and
confess everything. He was a man whom everybody
respected, and nobody would dare to do anything to

E *

me if he forgave me. I would fall at his feet and
cry : " Father, forgive me, I only wanted to know
. . . forgive me, I made a mistake. I didn't know
that it made people almost kill each other. . . ."
And if he only showed a single sign of relenting then
I would swear to forget all that I had seen, to be
again without curiosity, gentle and docile as before,
and never to grow up. Never to grow up ; I would
pay that price gladly if he forgave me.

Like fire in dry straw hope leapt up in me. I ran
across the market-place towards the street where my
parents lived. And everywhere people were standing talking about my crime. " Run," something
cried within me, " run, before it is too late. . . ."
And I ran as if I had to save my soul. I flew up the
drive, I clattered up the steps, I stood in the hall,
which was dreadfully empty, and only illuminated
by a dim light held by a stuffed owl. Then behind
the door of his room I heard my father's voice. He
was speaking at the telephone. I could not understand what he was saying, for he was shouting.
" Too late ! " I thought, " he is being told over the
telephone. . . ." I sank down beside the umbrella
stand and awaited the blow. With a sudden bang
the telephone receiver was put back on its hook.
Three steps behind the door. It sprang open. My
father stood in the doorway. His collar was awry,
his moustache was quivering, his coat-tails flew, his
face was one exclamation mark. . . . " Father ! " I
whimpered, " Father . . ." and I covered the back
of my head with my hands. He'll strike me, I
thought, my father will strike me . . . and I prayed
suddenly quite beyond myself, " Dear Lord Jesus,
be our guest. . . ."

Then his fist seized me, he heaved me up to my

feet, my legs failed me, I was only a wretched bundle
of clothes, long since dead ; and my father bellowed
till the air in the hall reeled, while he shook me to
and fro : " The Austrian Crown Prince has been
shot. . . . ! "

I hung in his grip and stuttered : " Who has been
shot ? "

" The Crown Prince of Austria ! To-day at one
o'clock in Serajevo. . . ."

" Thank God ! " I said, breathed deeply and felt
the blood flowing back into my veins again in a
blessed tide.

But my father had long since released me, and
was stumping down the steps to the garden to tell
my mother, who was reading Hugo von Hofmannsthal under the walnut tree.

I went into the kitchen and washed my hands with
scented soap.

" Serajevo . . ." I smiled, " Serajevo. . . ."

CHAPTER VIII

GASTON

THE crime at Serajevo had shielded me from the attention of the grown-ups. Nor did the Kalmuck even come to get his mark. In his free hours he had to be in the shop to serve customers, because his father these days spent all his time in the public-house, debating the political situation with his acquaintances. Suddenly everybody discovered that they had brothers in Austria. An innkeeper with an eye to business actually hung out an Austrian flag. When the men had a little drink in them they sang and shouted that we must keep faith with Austria. I was for keeping faith too, for I had once broken it with Ferd. So I was also for Austria. . . .

I decided to forget the mystery. Ferd had gained the day. One should not trouble oneself about such things. They were ugly and evil. With childish ardour I took an oath never to grow up. I destroyed radically everything that reminded me of that horrible day. Next Sunday during the service I threw the mark into the collection. It was destined for home missions.

Then I told Ferd that I had seen the mystery. He asked me if I was any happier now. " No," I said, " it was better just to be curious." We did not talk any more about it. Soon I was his friend again. My jealousy of Leo Silberstein disappeared. I for-

got the mystery. Now that I could live again carefree at the farm with nothing to hide it all vanished
like a horrible dream. Yet if my father had learned
of it that evening and had thrashed me, I would
never have got rid of the impression of that picture
in the sand-pit. Those who know how children can
forget if they are not punished will understand this
sudden revulsion. It all came right of itself, as a
sound body conquers infection.

Soon I was every day at the farm again riding with
Ferd, while Leo finished our school exercises in the
sitting-room and drank milk.

I was not troubled much because Hilde looked at
me scornfully when she passed. I knew what was
in store for her and felt myself revenged for everything.

In these days the Major was very troubled. He
closed himself often in his room and wrote letters.
Once after he had returned from a visit to Berlin
very silent and gloomy, Ferd told me in secrecy next
day that his father had made his will during the
night. There was going to be a war. I believed
this, for at supper every evening my father too maintained that Austria could not possibly put up with
such doings. My mother laughed him to scorn.
She said people were far too civilised to start a war.
But my father shook his head ; he was of the opinion
that nothing was more needed than a war to raise
men up and lead them back to God. My mother
retorted that only art could do that. " Oh, art ! "
said my father, " art is only for exceptional people ;
the masses need sharper measures to bring them to
their senses. Besides," he went on, " if it comes to
it, we're sure to win, for we have the best army, the
best generals, and in comparison with the others the

best morale. Just look at the birth-rate statistics of
the French. That speaks volumes ! And then "—
he drew himself up to his full height like a monument—" God will certainly be on our side. For the
others have fired the first shot."

My mother smiled and went quietly into the
drawing-room to read Hugo von Hofmannsthal.
My father repaired to his table at the club, where
he discussed the war prospects with his friends.

The Major was continually wrangling with Dr.
Hoffmann during these days. Hoffmann maintained
that in the event of a war every wheel would stand
still, the proletariat, and their leaders in particular,
would put a stop to any advance of the troops ; it
was simply insane to think of such a medieval institution as war nowadays. The programme of the Party
put a veto on war. " And what if we are attacked ? "
cried the Major. Hoffmann stood up with a very
serious and impressive air, and said that that was
a different matter ; they would defend the Fatherland as one man. " Then we'll be attacked, you'll
see ! " laughed the Major. " Every nation will say
it is attacked, and they'll all begin to let fly at each
other in the most noble way." Hoffmann smiled
again. " You forget the International. Our brothers
in France and everywhere will know how to hinder
them from attacking us, just as we will put a stop to
all plans for attacking them." Then the Major
laughed as if somebody had told him the best joke
in the world. But Hoffmann was seriously offended,
he switched his silver-headed stick elegantly three
times in the air and shouted that the Major was only
embittered, he wanted the war just to prove himself
in the right ; besides, these things were all a baga-
telle, they would solve themselves ; the Party had

something else to think about, equal franchise for
men and women and the eight-hour day ; these
were ideals which demanded real work, and day by
day they were pressing nearer to their difficult goal ;
the Grand Duke, for instance, had already recognised the Socialist town-councillors of Offenbach.

" Offenbach . . ." smiled the Major, and ran his
fingers through his hair as if he did not know at the
moment where Offenbach was situated. Then with
a friendly gesture he invited Dr. Hoffmann in to
supper ; Hoffmann accepted and was soon restored
to his good humour.

But Leo Silberstein said that evening as we went
home that there was not another man like the Major
in all Germany, which I could not verify, but believed.

August, whose father was to be released from
prison in a fortnight, thought it was a shame that
the Major was not a workman ; then he would have
far more friends. Actually he said comrades.

But I involuntarily translated the term into my
own language, because I could not suffer Dr. Hoffmann, who used it so often.

I did not bother my head over the war, although
at the time almost everybody was talking of it. It
seemed to me to be an affair of the grown-ups which
they could manage among themselves, just like the
mystery. I did not want to entangle myself a second
time in their hateful affairs. I only listened when
the Major spoke of war, for it awoke the same resistance in me as the mystery did in Ferd. I hated war
before I knew it. I was sure that war, too, would
make people cry for help and fight each other as if
they wanted to kill, like the Kalmuck and the Polish
girl in the sand-pit.

.   .   .   .   .   .

It was the beginning of July, and in our town there was very little further talk of war, for in addition to the reassurance created by the declarations of the diplomats, the war had lost some of its importance in the preparations for the great rifle carnival, which was to take place at the end of the month. —At this time my aunt from Weimar came to pay us a visit. She was a kind of generalissimo in our family. Her imposing figure qualified her for this part ; moreover her husband was a ministerial councillor, who in a short time would be nominated as minister. She had made a tour round the world with him, and since then had posed as an authority in our family, none of whose members had ever been further than Venice at most. Her letters were ukases ; she claimed that she knew life. She considered that her opinions on everything, but especially on the education of children, were the last word. Of course they were, for she had no children. She possessed the original of a letter of Goethe's, and with that she impressed my mother ; my father did not dare to contradict her, for her husband was a ministerial councillor. In her leisure hours she collected porcelain. In four great glass cabinets in her drawing-room stood Chinese cups, old Meissner statuettes and French tabatières. That was where she wrote her letters. They were army commands. Everything was provided for in them, down to the most minute details. Side by side with cucumber recipes were commands that the children should have sunbaths. When my cousin August had a cough he was compelled at my aunt's command to have little bags containing hot potatoes applied to his chest. If it snowed my aunt wrote : every day boots must be changed twice. If it was March weather and the

air sharp, the command came from Weimar : in
this weather the children must keep their mouths
shut when they are in the streets. . . .

My aunt's chief interest was travel. Like an in-
specting officer she appeared unannounced in our
families, let loose a crisis at once, dismissed servant
girls at a moment's notice, tore pictures which did
not please her from the walls, cleared away plush
hangings, and, indeed, everything in the room on
which dust could gather, for in spite of all her
acquaintance with life my aunt had an *idée fixe*, a
fear of germs. Yet wherever she found a medica-
ment, in bedroom or bathroom, she flung it with a
loud crash into the yard. She would say that people
nowadays were all effeminate, and that illness was
only an effect of their effeminacy, and an invention
of doctors keen for business. She herself was never
ill, her robust constitution resisted all sorts of weather.
The one remedy that she swore by was Haarlem
drops. She always carried ten bottles of them with
her in her suit-case. With them she cured every
sickness, and it was really remarkable how, if she
came and stood by my bed when I was pretending
to be sick, I never succeeded in resisting her command to get well. To be sure, the hot potatoes which
she put in a woollen stocking and laid on my chest
were partly responsible for that. When they got me
up double quick from my bed, my aunt would laugh
loudly, give me a slap on the bottom and shout :
" Well, little man, we've managed it again ! " Then
I would have to take fifteen Haarlem drops—to prevent a recurrence of the illness. She was a terrible
aunt. . . .

When I was greeting her in the hall on her arrival
about this time, she pulled me at once under the

fan-light and shouted while she felt my cheeks :
" Good God, how white the boy is ! No colour !
Where are the dimples he had last year ? " Then
she pushed me in front of her, rushed in her hat and
coat into the drawing-room, seated herself under
the Venetian mirror, threw one leg over the other,
so that her enormous black boots, which were too
large for her, stuck out like small cannon, and bawled
at my disconcerted father : " Something must be
done ! " (Something always had to be done when
my aunt came—we had grown used to that.) " Certainly," replied my father, very embarrassed because
in her agitation my aunt had kicked up her skirt so
high that one could see her garters. My mother
thought I was growing too fast. I had no idea what
they wanted with me. " Papperlapapp ! " cried my
aunt, pinching my cheeks and drawing her finger
under my eyes. She asked an intimate question.

The ash fell from my father's cigar. " Out you
go ! " he shouted at me. " Out ! " I went out.

Leo Silberstein was waiting for me below in the
yard. I asked him if he knew what my aunt's
question meant.

" Oh," said Leo wearily, " if I told you and it
were to come out, they would say again that the
Jews were to blame. . . ."

Then we sang " Free is the life of a gypsy," but
after the second verse we had to stop because Leo
was coughing terribly. When the coughing fit was
over we went up to the farm.

.   .   .   .   .   .

That evening, my aunt taking the chair, it was
decided that I should go with my mother in the
appoaching summer holidays to a high mountain

resort in Switzerland. The mountain was to be as
high as possible ; my aunt would admit nothing
under 3000 feet. True, my father had scruples on
account of the political situation, but my aunt told
him bluntly that a father's business was to consider
the health of his child and not the political situation.
Besides, all this talk about war was twaddle. On
her travels she had met many French people, and
they were human beings just like us. The war that
we were talking about so much was nothing but
eyewash. In reality there simply could not be a war,
because she—my aunt—had so many friends in
every country who would soon see to it that it was
stopped. Her friends in Paris had sent her only
the other day a post-card with the warmest greetings.
There would be the devil and all to pay if she had
to look upon these friends to-morrow as enemies.

My aunt was like that. Nobody dared to contradict her. In her absurd optimism was mirrored the
blindness of those intellectuals who scornfully over-
looked the real tension in Europe because they kept
up a cordial private post-card correspondence with
other countries. I did not understand that at the
time ; but I remembered later that my aunt from
Weimar declared there could be no war because of
a post-card she had received.

Her belief seemed to me to have no relation to the
fact on which she based it.

In a week's time splendid prospectuses were to
hand, printed on glazed paper, with illustrations and
assurances of the goodness of the air, the spaciousness
of the view, and the health-giving properties of the
forest. Words which for their absolute dogmatism
were only paralleled in my experience by the manual
of German history. My father was most impressed

by the views. " Look ! " he cried, pronouncing a
name I did not know, " from here you can see Mont
Blanc on certain days in clear weather, 14,400 feet
high ! " Even the mountains during these days were
a ground for boasting. I noticed this clearly when
my father, in reply to a friend's inquiry where we
we were going in summer, answered, " My son is
going in the neighbourhood of Mont Blanc." It
sounded just as if he had said that the Kaiser had
shaken hands with him.

On the 12th of July I said good-bye to Ferd. He
promised to write often and to tell me about Leo
as well, who had suddenly grown much worse and
was confined to his bed with fever. August Kremmelbein was not there, for this was the day on which
his father was to be released from prison.

The Red Major smiled as he shook hands with
me. Dr. Hoffmann said Switzerland was his ideal ;
not only because of its natural beauty, but also
politically.

.   .   .   .   .   .

A splendid sailor suit was bought for me, of course
with an anchor on the sleeves ; round the cap,
which was embroidered with silver and gold, there
was a band with the words " H.M.S. Iltis." My
mother was wearing a large, soft straw hat like a
cowboy's. Kathinka pushed our luggage to the train
in a small hand-barrow. My father had seen to the
tickets. For the first time in my life I was travelling
second class. My aunt had left to put some other
family to rights.

When we reached the little railway station we were
the only people from our town waiting for the train.
The porter bowed to us as he punched our tickets.

Even the man in the red cap gave us a military salute. There was still five minutes before the train would come in. I was holding a big posy of field flowers in one hand, which Kathinka had plucked in the early morning. The stalks were wrapped in silver paper, which she collected. The flowers smelt of hay, their colours changed in the glare of the sun. They were a trial to me, for I could scarcely get my fingers round the stalks, the posy was so big. At least I gave that out as a reason for getting rid of them ; in reality I was ashamed to go into the elegant second class compartment carrying such ordinary flowers, which anybody could pluck. My father said : " Just do it to please Kathinka. At the next station you can throw them away. . . ." And he smiled at me as if we had both made up a little plot.

As my mother was dabbing her forehead with eau de Cologne, I saw the train coming. My father promptly gathered up the luggage, as if in such a critical moment as this, when we were going away in an express train, he did not credit Kathinka with sufficient strength.—" Quick ! Quick ! " he cried, " the train only stops for two minutes ! " But the train was not there yet. My mother declared, it was true, that the train would have to wait until we got in, but my father held that the only thing that mattered to it was the time-table. I was filled with fear of the train, which came rushing in like a hostile law. The name of that law was " Two minutes." On these two minutes everything depended ; foreign travel, Switzerland, Mont Blanc, second class, the bunch of flowers. . . . I trembled as if in the space of these two minutes I must pass an examination for which I was not prepared. " The time-table ! " something cried within me. " Look out for the time-

table ! Look out ! the time-table takes first place
here ! " All that I had experienced and still wanted
to experience was concentrated in these two decisive
minutes. The time-table was law. The time-table
had dominion over everything which would happen
in the next two minutes. I myself, my mother,
even my all-powerful father, any one at all with
a name—all the people who stood there, were
delivered over to the time-table, even the man in
the red cap ; for the first time I felt the power of
impersonal organisation. In these agonised seconds,
which I shall never forget, because in them was
consummated unconsciously, and on that very
account with great pain, the destruction of my faith
in the power of personality—for could my father,
nay, could even the Red Major have altered the
time-table ?—in these few seconds I can find the
source of my later scepticism regarding any kind of
personal free will. . . .

A hand pulled me back. It was my mother's.
The train ran in. The brakes screeched. Steam
was belching from the engine. My father had disappeared in a cloud with the luggage. We could
only hear his voice : " Here ! Here ! "

A door is torn open. Some one pushes me on
to the foot-board. I clutch a brass rod from which
shoot rays of light. I am in a corridor. A window
is let down. Outside stands my father laughing. He
lifts the travelling bags inside. I help to take them
from him. It all goes with uncanny rapidity, for
behind us stands the time-table. Its laws shout
from the faces of the guards. The passengers consult
their watches. Two minutes. Quick ! Quick !
Outside my father is laughing, Kathinka too shows
her satisfaction at a respectful distance, we are all

gratified, for we have got the better of the time-table. There is still a minute left.

I hung out of the window and kept on repeating " yes " whenever my father said anything. It seemed unreal to think that we did not need to hurry any longer. And while my father, just to fill up the interval, addressed words to my mother which he had already said to her before, on the opposite side of the platform a local train rolled in. As it came from the other direction the fourth class carriages stopped just across from us.

August sprang out of one of the compartments. He flung the door back with a bang and reached his hand inside. Now his father appears holding on to it. He climbs out somewhat helplessly. Probably he is not yet used to walking freely. He is wearing his best clothes, as if he were coming back from a confirmation. In one hand he carries a little grey canvas portmanteau. His face looks pale. His suit is too wide for him, and there are great folds between the shoulders. August is radiant. He keeps his eyes fixed on his father, as if he had wrested him from death. Three workmen from our town who have waited for the train shake the stoker Kremmelbein by the hand. They are all wearing red carnations in their buttonholes ; one of them takes his carnation and sticks it into the buttonhole of August's father. Meanwhile August holds the portmanteau. His face is as bright and happy as if this were a Sedan anniversary. A whistle goes. The last door in our train is banged to. My father stretches his hand through the window. " Now, get well quick and be good ! " To my mother he says, " You'll be in Bâle at 8.19 according to the time-table." With a jerk the brakes are released. At the very moment when the hand of the clock reaches the minute the man in the red cap raises his arm. " On the second," observes my father, radiant. Then, as the train slowly draws out, a sudden anxiety seizes me.

" August ! " I cry, and wave the flowers desperately.

" August ! " He does not hear me, for he does not realise that I am here.

My father, who has begun to run cumbrously alongside the train, barks at me : " Don't make a scene ! " My mother has put her hand over my mouth. I cry to August still, but my shout is smothered under her fingers. My father is running a few yards behind the window. He waves his hat, my mother flutters her flimsy handkerchief, I mechanically raise and lower my bunch of flowers. Kathinka signals with her apron. As we pass the last platform sign and the train gathers speed, I see, far away, that August has turned round and is waving his red handkerchief, but I know that he has not recognised me. Then suddenly he gives a start. He begins to sprint. He has seen my father. He flies after the train, the engine has already crossed the first points. I tear myself free from my mother. August makes a desperate spurt. He is not the fastest player in the football team for nothing. He reaches the last carriage, and while my father is shouting : " Come back with red cheeks ! " I shriek till all the passengers look out from their compartments. " August ! August ! Last lap ! " And August keeps it up. He catches up the last carriage, he catches up my father, he manages to get within shouting distance . . . then with a supreme effort I throw my bunch of flowers towards him, he picks it up and waves back to me with the same bunch with which I had waved to him so long in vain. " Hurrah ! " I cry. And August makes a hand-spring. In the middle of the platform he makes a hand-spring. Far behind him stands my father wiping the perspiration from his brow—quite far away gleam the red carnations of Kremmelbein and his comrades. I have no more anxiety, for a friend has waved to me. . . .

.   .   .   .   .   .

Our compartment was empty. I let myself down reverentially on the green plush seat. My mother began to peel an orange. After that she read *Jugend*, to which she subscribed. The train was going so fast that the cornfields seemed one great yellow expanse. Even the forests shrank to mere masses of green. We were going along the left bank of the Rhine. The first passengers came into our compartment at Strassburg. They talked without stopping and in French. I was uneasy in front of them, for I was afraid that they might suddenly begin to put my French to the test. As I was helping a lady who was vainly attempting to close the window (my mother had made me a sign) she said : " Merci bien, mon cher. . . ." I blushed and stuttered : " Oui, oui, madame. . . ." She laughed and gave me a sweet. Then she talked in German with my mother.

My uncle met us at Bâle. He ran a confectioner's shop and was moreover a good singer. Whenever there was a celebration at any of his societies—he belonged to a countless number of them—he was called on to sing. The proudest day of his life had been the one on which he had sung " Figaro " before the King of Italy. The King had shaken hands with him afterwards, a fact of which he was just as proud

as another uncle of mine, who while master-at-arms
in Frankfort-on-Main had been accorded the same
honour by Prince Heinrich at a public celebration
and before all the people.

My " Figaro " uncle began to curse Richard
Wagner, and later the Kaiser. After he had drunk
some wine he began to praise up France. " The
Germans," he shouted, " always behave as if they
were the only people in the world. And hardly a
single one of them has seen the world either. . . ."
—" Oh, Alfonse," said my mother, " why excite
yourself about nothing ? It's only politics, all that."
And she made a gesture as if she were waving aside
something unclean. " Why, in God's name," cried
my uncle, gripping his wine glass firmly, which was
balanced precariously on the table, " do you Swabians take no interest in politics ? "—" No," answered
my mother, and turned her face away as if my uncle
had insulted her. He sat there with bulging eyes
and chewed his cigar to a pulp. " I say, what do
you do, then, all day ? " He stared at my mother
as if he put her down as an idler. She smiled. " I
perform my duties as a housewife and a mother and
in my spare time I devote myself to art. . . ."

My " Figaro " uncle rose to his feet. " Art," said
he, " art, that's all very fine—I sing a bit myself—
but what I say is that you can't simply go about in
the world without knowing what's up. And especially
you people in Germany who are always blowing. . . ."
—" I don't bother myself with such prosaic things,"
said my mother. " In my leisure hours I live in a
more beautiful world. My books make me forget
everything." My uncle stood rigid. He began suddenly to pick his nose. " More beautiful world," he
muttered. " Hm, what can that be ? A kind of pri-

vate paradise that can only be opened with one key
. . . art ; everything else is dirt to you, and when
your Kaiser opens his mouth as if he wanted to eat
up everybody that doesn't stand at attention before
him, then you think that's only prosaic rubbish. . . .
Herrgott Sakrament, have you never heard how
people talk about you Swabians in other countries,
or that you're only judged by what you do and say
every day and not by your art ? After I sang to the
King of Italy I said to myself : ' Alfonse, that was
a credit to the whole of Switzerland, and if you had
sung badly it would have been a disgrace to the whole
of Switzerland.' But you talk as if there was some
kind of art standing all by itself, and as if you could
simply set it apart from other things. . . ." " Why
do you get so excited about it ? " asked my mother,
quite astonished. " I only said that politics don't
interest me. And besides, I think it's a queer thing
to make me answerable for anything the Kaiser says
that you don't like."—" Of course I make you answerable ! " shouted my uncle. " In this country
nobody could talk like that without having his mouth
shut for him after the first word. But then we belong
to Switzerland." He stretched himself to his full
length, took a gulp of wine, and then sat down at
the piano and played his own accompaniment to
an aria out of " Rigoletto." " He's come to his
senses at last," my mother said to me, as if I were a
grown person. I thought of the Red Major, but I
did not trust myself to say anything, for I was in a
foreign country.

We went early to bed. I was to sleep with my
uncle in his room. While I was undressing he opened
a wardrobe and took out a rifle and a sabre from
among underclothes and stockings. He tenderly

stroked the barrel of his rifle and said, that was a
dependable weapon. The sabre belonged to him as
lieutenant. They had lovely sham fights every year.
In the mountains. Then he took off all his clothes
and washed himself. The water splashed as far as the
very coverlet under which I lay. I was filled with
wonder, for I had never seen a lieutenant like this
one before.

At noon next day my uncle left the bakery to look
after itself and accompanied us to the train. There
on the platform he said to my mother : " Anna,
things look bad in Europe. Have you seen the
morning papers ? There's going to be a fine tug-of-
war."—" I make a point of never reading a paper,"
my mother smiled. My uncle shrugged his shoulders.
" I only mean that there may be a general dust-up
soon. Still, with us you're safe." Then he vigorously stowed our luggage on the rack. We promised
him to break our journey at Bâle on the way back.
As the train drew out he gave us a short but friendly
yodel.

On the journey I asked my mother what my uncle
had meant by a general dust-up. " Oh," she replied
in irritation, without looking up from her book,
" this tedious war that they're all talking about. . . ."

Then I was allowed to stand at the window and
look at the scenery. We were going to Solothurn.

It was a lovely day. All along the carriages the
windows were let down, the air streamed in glittering
cascades through the narrow corridors, the sunlight
played hide and seek with the pale yellow curtains.
Many people were singing.

And my mother was very good to me. At one of
the stations among the many little towns we stopped
at she bought me a tablet of chocolate. Gala Peter.

Two hours later she pointed out a blue chain of mountains with a very delicate silhouette softened by gauzy blue clouds.

" There," said my mother, who was standing beside me and had put her arm round me, for it was evening, " we're going there." She pointed towards the mountains, which were gradually coming nearer and nearer and changing their contours.

I was disappointed, although all I saw was very beautiful. The little towns with their green, too tightly packed gardens, the meadows misted with blue, the bright yellow roads, the signal-boxes gay with pots of flowers, the glittering, singing wires which ran alongside the embankment and sometimes quivered as if a thought had struck them ; the bright painted barriers and the people who stood behind them waving as if they were all our good friends. I was disappointed because the mountain was not so high as I had imagined it.

" It looks much the same as the Melibokus," I said to my mother, " and it's nothing like 3000 feet." —" Ah," she replied, " you must not look at it like that. You must count the number of feet above the sea-level. Where we are it's 900 feet at least." I looked on that as a quibble, for how could anybody hold that a mountain was 3000 feet high when it was 2100 at most when one stood before it ?

The grown-ups measured everything with a secret measure. One had to be on one's guard.

When we drew up at Solothurn the mountains had come quite near. Amid their wooded slopes gleamed a white dot. The sanatorium where it would be my duty to acquire red cheeks. Its glass verandah caught the parting rays of the sun.

On the platform my mother shouted the name of

the sanatorium. Immediately a man in uniform rushed up and lifted our luggage. We followed him in silence across the lines. Beyond a white wooden trellis I saw the private garden of the station-master, a riot of sweet peas.

The man who had rushed away with our luggage halted in the square before the station. With a great deal of talk he flung the bags on the roof of a coach, then he tore open the door, let down a little stair and told us to get in. The seat inside the coach was upholstered in red, and studded with brass nails. Beside the door hung a bunch of strange flowers. My mother whispered to me that they were mountain cyclamens. Thereupon the man in the uniform addressed a few short, but it seemed to me energetic words to the horses, swung himself up to the seat and cracked the whip, and the horses set off at a mild trot, and the coach rolled through Solothurn. Before the cathedral stood a very lugubrious image of Christ in stone ; the figure hung with outstretched arms, and the face, filled with pain, was turned upwards. I asked my mother softly whether everybody here was Catholic. She nodded and dabbed her forehead with eau de Cologne.

We were not alone in the coach. On the plush-covered seat opposite a very stout lady with a hand covered with rings sat fanning air vigorously down into the cleft of her bosom, and a man in a black cap of dull silk without a peak was reading a newspaper ; and beside them was a boy of my own age, apparently their son, for the lady struck him over the knuckles once when he aimed at my gold-embroidered cap with a ball attached to an elastic band. His mother scolded him in French. I had never yet seen a boy of that age who could speak

French as well as a sixth form pupil. He put his arm quite unabashed round his mother and whispered endearments into her ear until she nodded and said, " Eh bien." These were the only words I understood. It meant " Very well," I had learnt in school, and " alors," which was the boy's reply, was translated as " all right." I admired him, for he could speak better French than any of my teachers, of whom I stood in awe.

When we came to the woods which grew on the mountain sides, the boy, whose name, Gaston, I had caught at last, drew a tiny rubber ball out of his left trouser pocket. He threw it to me with a laugh. The ball hit me on the nose and rolled under the seat. " Hélas ! " cried Gaston, and slipped under the seat ; but my mother held me back firmly when I tried to help him, for I was wearing my good clothes. I was ashamed in front of Gaston.

Then he threw me the ball from where he was on the floor and I caught it. I threw it back, he caught it ; so we tossed it between our mothers, who regarded each other with mistrust, because they did not understand each other's language.

When the coach stopped in front of the sanatorium, Gaston sprang out on to the spacious drive, tossed his ball high in the air, clapped his hands like a tight-rope dancer, and caught it again. My mother ordered me to go in with her. But in the evening at supper-time I saw Gaston again. We ate at a little table in the huge dining-room. Gaston and his parents sat opposite us. While I was enjoying for the first time the revelations of French cookery, Gaston laughed over to me and I nodded back to him. He reminded me of Ferd. Only he was darker, and his eyes were more lively.

Out of the soft inside of a roll which his father had discarded he was kneading comical little human figures, which he set on the upturned wine-glasses and speared with tooth-picks. One fell in his mother's soup. After his father had pulled his ears, he kept on talking in French until his father was placated again. After supper we met on the terrace. Gaston flung his ball so high that for seconds it seemed to hang like a blue sphere in the soft evening light. As soon as it fell on the gravel of the front garden I cried " J'aussi ! " which was supposed to mean " I also." Gaston understood me, we climbed over the wall and retrieved the ball from among the bushes. I threw it. It disappeared among the tree-tops which were lost in darkness. I was confounded. " Ça ne fait rien," cried Gaston. The first sentence of French that I understood easily, although it was not taught until the Untertertia.*

After that evening I played with Gaston every day. We were not very successful in making ourselves comprehended, but we understood each other without needing to translate our wishes into words.

My mother had raised no objection to this friendship. She had soon noticed that I would never have endured the life of the sanatorium without Gaston. There was no other child there, only a girl with swollen glands who came from Bruchsal.

.   .   .   .   .   .

The sanatorium was not a real sanatorium at all, only a hotel which exploited its mountain air, 3000 feet above sea-level. The only cure it provided was the woods, which were very stunted, but thick. Sometimes cows with bells tinkling were driven past

* Lower Fourth.

the hotel to show that we were in the country and
in Switzerland. The hotel's special attraction was
the alpine glow. As soon as it began, that is, as
soon as the distant mountain chain whose culminating
point was the Jungfrau began to grow red like an
overheated stove, a man in livery blew a horn to
assemble the guests and gave a short address on this
rare treat provided by nature. We had run three
times to see the spectacle, then we stopped going, for
the Jungfrau always glowed in the same way and
the man in livery always declared in several languages that never yet had it been so beautiful as on
this evening. Gaston began to laugh helplessly when
he heard these words the second time. Only a few
English married couples continued to go into raptures before the Jungfrau. They even came provided
with field-glasses so as to see it better.

We preferred to wander among the mountain
pastures. There were oxen there which one could
tease till they went off in a comical gallop, and an
aged donkey on which Gaston loved to ride.

About that time my father sent a letter from the
plains which lay almost 3000 feet below us saying that
the political situation was absolutely safe, for the
Kaiser had set off the day before on his northern tour.
My mother smiled and began to strike up a friendship with a Russian lady. I played with Gaston.

.   .   .   .   .   .

Gradually I began to recover from my encounter
with the world of the grown-ups. What strength I
had patched up immediately after my experience at
the sand-pit through an effort of will and Ferd's
calm superiority, now grew in these days along with
Gaston into a serene and unperturbed recovery.

F

There was no need of speech, with its malice and ambiguity which so often put human beings at variance ; there was none of the vanity of disputation nor any disruptive struggle to " be in the right " with words. We did not need to translate our desires ; we understood each other through our eyes, through our senses, and all that we did was honest. If we quarrelled over a ball, a stick, a curiously shaped stone, the combat was silent and incisive and not inundated with the spate of words about being in the right, about morality and duty, with which men are accustomed to veil their real intentions. I could never make it clear to Gaston that a particular stone which we both wanted belonged to me because I had seen it first, or because he had already eight fossil shells and I had only five ; we fought for the stone until one of us was the victor and the stone belonged to him. There were no words exchanged, no misunderstandings or lies ; it was an honest fight. Sometimes Gaston won because of his agility, sometimes I won because of my boxing. So we divided in fraternal battle whatever pleased us.

For the first time life became clear, simple, without danger to me, troubled by no snare, no misleading words, no lies. Grass was grass, earth was earth, an animal was an animal ; and life was a fact. I recovered splendidly. My mother wrote to my father saying that the air of Switzerland was working wonders.

As I was all the time with Gaston I hardly noticed how the atmosphere in the hotel began to change about the end of July. While before that the people from the different countries had sat together in picturesque confusion, gone on excursions and danced at evening on the terrace, there now began a sorting

out of the guests according to the colours which the
flags of their country bore. The English drew away
from the Germans, with whom they had liked so
much before to share the alpine glow ; the French
separated from the Austrians, although they had
enjoyed so much dancing together ; and instead the
French joined forces with the English, whose idio-
syncrasies only a few days before had awakened
their friendly ridicule, and the Austrians attached
themselves to the Germans, whose women were much
stiffer to dance with than the French women. People
were sorted out, rearranged according to an unknown
law ; each of them was an article which belonged to
a stated department. The Russians resisted longest.
In spite of energetic representations by several
Englishmen, they chose rather to go walking with
three pretty Viennese women, whose husbands had
already gone away, than to converse in the lounge
with the flat-breasted English ladies. As one of these
Russians was leaving the room of one of the Viennese
ladies on a hot afternoon, he found round the corner
an elderly Frenchman lying in ambush, who overwhelmed him with abuse, as if he had been stealing.

I noticed these changes, but I did not think much
about them, for I was all day long with Gaston, and
we were only in the hotel at meal-times ; but later,
when things came to a head, I understood their
meaning. Nobody troubled about Gaston and me ;
we were for the time only children.

In these days when the sorting out was beginning
(telegrams were put up in the hall telling of an
Austrian ultimatum) a letter came from my father.
An express letter.

He wrote of grave clouds on the horizon, of the
postponement of the Kaiser's northern tour, of

waxing enthusiasm and of our brothers in Austria.
He thought it best that we should return home as
soon as possible ; all his friends were betting ten to
one on a war ; and he too was convinced that it
must be the will of God, who had great things in
store for the German people. My mother laid the
letter aside among her others, and said she wished they
would leave her in peace with their fatuous politics ;
a new book by Hofmannsthal had appeared, and
she was more interested in that. Besides, if they
absolutely must have a war, we still had plenty of
time to take the train home. I was entirely of her
mind. What did I care about war ? What did I
care about the affairs of the grown-ups ? It was
their war, and I had had enough of it. It is true, I
thought for a brief moment of the Red Major, also
of my earlier plighted faith to Austria ; of Ferd too,
who believed what his father said—but Gaston's
whistle under my window was enough to shatter the
picture, and I ran from my room, sticking two balls
into my pocket, and as soon as I bounced one of
them just before Gaston's nose on the terrace, off
he went after it with a laugh. Then we ran towards
the meadows. Here we threw ourselves down on
the warm grass, Gaston took off his shoes so as to
run about bare-foot, while below us in the misty
blue plain the hard light was reflected from the lake
as from a silver shield, and the heavy warmth of the
cattle cropping lulled us to peace ; and I forgot
everything that lay 3000 feet beneath me. I was in
sound health and consequently without any interest
for what was not before my eyes. But in the evening
I found a letter beside my place at the table. It
was from Ferd. He wrote : " Leo is very ill. He
cannot live much longer. I see him daily, he sends

his greetings and hopes you will have a quick recovery. When are you coming back ? Austria has
declared war on Serbia. My Father says that
nothing can stop it now. If you were sensible you
would stay in Switzerland. All passports from Germany have been already stopped."

" Mother ! " I cried, " Austria has declared war
on Serbia ! "

" I know," smiled my mother, with great adroitness
carving a roast chicken. " The telegram has been
put up in the hall. But what is Serbia to me ? "

I looked over at Gaston. As he was nodding to
me his mother shouted at him and pulled his ears.
He bowed his head very sadly over his plate. I
looked anxiously round the dining hall. Everywhere
I looked I encountered scornful glances. The
Englishmen were clinking glasses with the French.
With the Russians they made up the majority in the
hotel. The Austrians had gone. Also the family
from Bruchsal. We were the only Germans.

Then, during the dessert, a young Frenchman got
up, sat down at the piano, and played a melody I
did not know. It was very beautiful. It was the
Marseillaise. . . . Everybody in the room sprang to
his feet and sang. All—French, English, Russian.
And Gaston. He stood squeezed between his parents
and sang with his serviette round his neck. He
gazed at me as if he had never seen me before. But
when his parents glanced aside to look at the setting
sun he nodded to me as if he wanted me to help him.
The singing grew louder and louder. Everybody
was looking at us. My mother went on calmly
eating, and behaved as if she heard nothing. I
could not eat. I felt them looking at me hatefully,
at me and my mother, as if we were bad people.

" Mother ! " I cried, pushing away my dessert,
" Mother, what have we done ? "

Then approached, his steps unsteady with wine,
an elderly gentleman who looked somewhat like
Napoleon III. His face was as red as the rosette in
his buttonhole. He swung a little cane in his hand
and planted himself by our table. " Levez-vous ! "
he shouted at my mother, " Levez-vous ! "

I trembled, for his voice was the same as that of
Brosius.

My mother gazed at him as if she had seen him
for the first time. She raised her eye-brows and
surveyed his deranged appearance. " Prussien ! "
screamed the Frenchman, and brought his cane down
on our table. My mother stood up (she was a head
taller than he), she tore the cane from his hand and
flung it violently into the middle of the room. Nobody spoke. Two waiters seized the Frenchman and
held him fast. My mother signed to me. We walked
straight across the room, which was quite silent, to
the door. As we closed it the man who looked like
Napoleon III cried, " Vive la revanche ! " A storm
of applause broke out behind us.

My mother said he was drunk.

We went to our room. The porter handed us a
telegram from my father : " Come at once."

My mother curled her hair. I stood at the window
and looked for Gaston.

Beneath us they were singing. Probably Gaston
would have to sing too.

Next morning we ordered our breakfast to be
served in our room.

My mother telegraphed back to my father that
we would leave in two days.

I looked for Gaston. I stole past his room, but

when I saw the man with the Napoleonic face coming round the corner I ran away.

I ran to the meadows. The cows were cropping quietly as before. And the grass too was just the same. I looked for Gaston. I wanted to play with him. I wanted to beg him to come away with me. We would go away by ourselves and let the grown-ups do what they liked. Everything had gone wrong again. I did not think of the war, I did not think of the insult to my mother, although that was reason enough for declaring war on France : I only thought of Gaston, the friend of whom I was to be robbed because the grown-ups were angry with one another.

As I was lying behind a little bush and thinking of his name I saw him coming out of the hotel and beginning to run towards the meadows. He kept turning round as if he were afraid someone might see him, then he began to run as if he wanted to escape. I spread out my handkerchief as a flag over the bush. It was a white flag. . . .

Soon Gaston was within shouting distance. He panted up the slope, sometimes he stumbled over rocks. I did not dare to call to him, for I did not trust the peace around me ; perhaps in a moment the cows too would unmask themselves as German, French or English and lift us on their horns. . . .

Gaston had certainly noticed my flag. He made straight for the bush, in two minutes he must reach me. Then we would hide ourselves away. Gaston approached. I watched him through the network of twigs. He was wearing a beret and on his tweed suit was a strip of ribbon with the tricolor. " He's going away," I thought. " He's wearing his good clothes. He's come to say good-bye." Then I heard Gaston cry, " Mon ami ? "—" Mon ami ? " he cried,

and looked round him. I burst out from behind the
bush. " Mon ami ! " cried Gaston, and flung himself into my arms. Then we sat down. The grass
was long. The sun was straight overhead.

Gaston was sweating. I wiped his face with my
white handkerchief. Below there lay the hotel.
Heavy and full, as if nothing mattered to it, the
banner of Switzerland billowed on its façade.

.   .   .   .   .   .

" Nous partons," said Gaston, after a while.
" Aujourd'hui ? " I asked. " Oui, le soir." I held
out my hand. " C'est defendu," he laughed, " la
guerre. . . ." Then when he noticed how I shrank
at the word, which is one of the first that is learnt
in all the schools in the world, he put his arm round
my shoulders, and while his wide and defenceless
eyes took in all the deceitfully peaceful scene, he said
in his singing voice those unforgettable words of my
boyhood : " La guerre, ce sont nos parents,—mon
ami. . . ."

Then something broke inside me, for I knew that
in a few minutes I should lose him. Everything that
I knew about the grown-ups I told him, all of it ;
their fighting with each other, the mystery—things
which I had long forgotten, I told them : the
life on the farm, Ferd's great friendship, Leo's suffer-
ings, August's bravery, the Red Major's isolation,
my breaking my promise and why it had happened,
Hilde's corrupt virginity ; I told him of the Kalmuck
and the police, of Brosius and Herr Silberstein, of
the apothecary J. and my father, of Persius and the
stoker Kremmelbein ; I concealed nothing, I ad-
mitted all my meannesses, but the undertone which
ran through this outpouring of myself, which came

over me like a hysterical fit, was : " La guerre, ce
sont nos parents ! "

Gaston did not understand one word that I said,
for I spoke in German ; but he nodded and listened
attentively. Then he gave me one of his best balls
and I gave him my pocket-knife inset with mother-
of-pearl. Gaston stood up. " Adieu ! " he said, and
held out his hand. I knew that he must say good-
bye to me here behind the bush, so that his parents
might not see us. I took his hand. " Adieu," I
replied, " adieu. . . ."

At that moment we heard the sound of horses'
hoofs. Out of a hollow a cavalcade appeared, some
fifty horsemen in brilliant uniforms. They were
Swiss officers. They rode at a smart gallop towards
the hotel. We could only hear the sharp beat of
hoofs on the gravel and·see the light gleaming on the
gold-embroidered helmets of the officers. " Hélas ! "
cried Gaston. We set off at once behind the horsemen. We had forgotten everything, we saw nothing
but the beautiful horses and the brilliant officers
on their backs.

Although we ran fast we could not make up on
them. But they kept the road towards the hotel.
Gaston clapped his hands in delight and waved to
me as he ran, and I too had thrown away all caution.
The horses were standing in front of the hotel on the
broad approach. We ran straight in among them
and stood admiring their silky skins and their beautiful leather trappings. The officers had gathered
round an elderly grey-haired man who was in conversation with the proprietor of the hotel. We were
enraptured by the riot of colours, for every officer
had a different uniform. We planted ourselves beside
a horse, a powerful black one. Gaston wanted to

F *

get on its back.   There was nobody near paying
any attention to us.   The horse sniffed at us
benevolently.   The officers were standing in a circle
staring at one point in the centre, the mouth of their
commander.

Gaston nodded to me.   I caught hold of the stir-
rup.   Gaston, who was short, got up on my shoulders,
and from there prepared to climb on to the back of
the horse.

At that moment a hand seized him from behind.
It dragged him back.   I fell on the ground.   The
black horse plunged.   And as I lay on the ground
I saw Gaston's father give him two resounding slaps
on the side of the face and point at me, saying : " Fi
donc, un prussien ! "

When I stumbled to my feet Gaston had disappeared.   I ran between the horses on to the
terrace ; in the hall a crowd was assembled in front
of a telegram which was nailed there ; as I ran
along the corridor towards my mother's room I
heard Gaston's voice for the last time ; he was
sobbing.   His father was beating him.

A strange man was standing with my mother.   It
was my fancy-bread uncle.   He was in uniform.   I
had not recognised him.

" Well," he cried, thumping triumphantly on the
table, " was I right ? "—" Yes," said my mother,
" humanity has gone mad.   We'll leave this very
evening."

Down below in the hall the news was tacked up
that Russia had declared war on Austria and that
the German army was being mobilised.

People were singing everywhere. . . .

CHAPTER IX

WE left by train that very night. My uncle the confectioner booked a compartment for us and accompanied us to Solothurn. On the way he told us that everything had come very unexpectedly ; nobody knew who was really to blame. Probably whoever lost the war ; that was always the way. My mother was silent. I thought of Gaston and closed my eyes.

At Solothurn my uncle took his leave. He had to go back into the mountains, along with the rest of the officers, to see that the frontiers were secured. He was in great spirits at the prospect. He was an enthusiastic mountaineer and an ardent nature-lover.

As we got into the train the porter, who had received a substantial tip from my mother, declared that Germany would certainly win. On the platform were standing a group of Austrians who had worked as waiters in west Switzerland and now, burning with ardour, were returning to their fatherland to take revenge on the Serbs. They sang " God maintain our Franz the Emperor," and had taken off their jackets. At last it had come, they shouted. They did not mean the train, which had just come in, but the war.

An elderly gentleman was sitting in our compartment. He began to talk to us at once, as if we were intimate acquaintances. On the back of his hotel bill he had added up the numerical strength of the European armies, and balanced them against each other. He compared the two totals and assured my mother that the spiritual qualities of the German troops compensated for the numerical superiority of the Russians. For in this war spiritual qualities alone would decide the day, and Germany's spiritual qualities were the best in Europe. As a university professor he knew that our youth were ready for the fray, and full of ideals. At last the hour had come when our people could enter on its great world mission. He himself had been almost cast into despair by the crass materialism of the last few years—particularly in the lower classes ; but at last life had regained an ideal significance. The great virtues of humanity, which had found their last refuge in Germany—fidelity, patriotism, readiness to die for an idea—these were triumphing now over the trading and shop-keeping spirit. This war was the providential lightning flash that would clear the air ; after it a new German people would arise, whose victory would save the world from mediocrity, brutalising materialism, western democracy and false humanitarianism. He could see a new world, ruled and directed by a race of aristocrats, who would root out all signs of degeneracy and lead humanity back again to the deserted peaks of the eternal ideals. Those who were too weak must perish by the wayside. The war would cleanse mankind from all its impurities. The future belonged to Siegfried ; in this war Hagen would be slain.

The professor talked very gently ; the light was reflected from his glasses. My mother, sitting opposite him, listened attentively. With her lips she silently repeated many of his phrases after him. For

the first time she began to take some interest in the
war.   Perhaps because the man was a professor,
perhaps because all that he said sounded so clever,
perhaps because it had nothing to do with politics—
at any rate when, as we neared Bâle, the professor
foretold that the war would give a mighty impetus
to art, she capitulated to his logic.   She believed in
the war as she would have believed in a new poet.
As we got out at Bâle station she said to me that a
great time was before us.

The professor walked beside us.   His face was grey
and covered with an irregular stubble of hair.   His
shoulders looked feeble and were drawn up.   Every
now and then he sucked at his teeth with his tongue,
as if he were dislodging decayed scraps of food that
stuck between them.   He limped.   I did not understand his enthusiasm for Siegfried.

When he made his name known to my mother,
she whispered to me that he was a famous man.   I
must carry his bag.

The waiting-room was crammed.   A telegram flew
from hand to hand telling that Germany had declared war on Russia.   On account of our brothers
in Austria.

The " Wacht am Rhein " was sung and the " Song
of the Flags."   The professor joined in the singing,
my mother as well.   I was afraid of so much joy, for
I could not help thinking of Gaston.   If Gaston had
been there I would gladly have sung too.

" Do you see the people," said the professor to my
mother, " how uplifted they are and how united ?
Does not that in itself justify the war ? "   He pointed
to the waiting-room, which rang with songs and
shouting.   The men were shouting " brother " across
to one another and went about shaking hands,

although few of them were acquainted. Many of
them were workmen. One could recognise them by
their caps. They had come from Switzerland, from
Italy, from France, where they had been working
on machines. They went from table to table and
fraternised with rich townspeople who had just come
from holidaying in the mountains. In a corner sat a
man of Jewish appearance along with two frightened
daughters ; he kept on treating the workmen to beer,
and when they sang he sang too. " We're all
brothers ! " shouted the workmen ; the gentleman
nodded rapturously and paid.

" Is it not wonderful ? " said the professor. " All
our social divisions have vanished."

My mother nodded. She said something about
" mass emotion."

" This war," answered the professor, " is an un-
paralleled æsthetic experience. For the first time I
have seen the soul of the people laid bare." I sat
with my lemonade in front of me and still thought
of Gaston. Would he be singing too . . . ?

It was three o'clock in the morning when someone sprang on to a table and shouted that the frontier
was closed. A howl, as if they all felt betrayed, was
the answer. " We must get home ! We must join
our brothers ! " Then they sang again. The professor said that he would march over the frontier on
foot, if no more trains were going. What should he
do here in Switzerland ? It was only a neutral
country.

When towards six o'clock a Swiss official announced
that they had managed to get together a train which,
as the absolutely last one, would leave in twenty
minutes, the whole station broke into jubilation, as
if we were all going to a festival.

The train was rushed. We lost the professor in the confusion. We sat down on our bags in the corridor. My mother said it did not matter ; we should have to make sacrifices now. Shortly after leaving Bâle we came in sight of the Rhine. Everybody rushed to the windows. The men uncovered their heads, the women leaned tenderly on their husbands' shoulders. They sang solemnly and gravely, as if they were in church. Many had tears in their eyes. And the children, who stood apart by themselves in the corridors, gazed in silent wonder at the strange solemnity of the grown-ups.

At Müllheim we saw the first German soldiers. They wore new uniforms of grey-green cloth, and over their helmets was a protective covering of the same material. The railway embankment was guarded by soldiers. Every hundred yards there was a sentry, and on the bridges there were patrols. They were greeted with storms of cheering. " Die Wacht am Rhein," cried the women, and threw them fruit, cigarettes and chocolate. The soldiers waved their rifles, some kissed their hands. These were officers. . . .

Flags fluttered over the roofs of the villages. The colours of harvest, the yellow and red, gleamed heavy and languid in the soft morning light as we passed through Brandenburg. They fluttered over the huts in the vineyards, they billowed from the belfries of churches and the chimneys of farm-houses, they filled the stations with colour, they almost covered the schools, and the children waved them as they stood behind the barriers and shouted " Hurrah ! " Yellow and red. Wheat and poppies. The air smelt of them.

As we neared Freiburg the whole train was singing.

We all knew one another. Strangers shared their food together, exchanged cigarettes, presented the children with chocolate. The children were a little afraid, for they had never seen so many good people before.

I stood beside my mother at the window and did not dare to move. I thought I was dreaming. A single movement, I thought, might destroy this dream, and the people would become as indifferent or as hostile to one another as before. I held my breath and implored God to keep the miracle from coming to an end.

I did not think any longer of Gaston. The flags and the singing closed me in. My mother kissed me, strange men lifted me on their shoulders, strange ladies gave me chocolate and stroked my hair, young girls talked to me as if I were their brother—I was giddy with this incomprehensible human love.

When we drew into Freiburg the platform was thronged with shouting people. Students in fantastic jackets sprang into the train singing. Through the open windows they kissed girls, who showered flowers upon them. Elderly gentlemen had fastened little flags to their canes, and carried them over their shoulders. Presents were being showered on soldiers (whose rifles were trimmed with sprays of roses) as if they were all celebrating their birthday. Even the waiters in the station restaurant looked cheerful, and the porters springing from the carriages laughed like benevolent uncles.

On the opposite side of the platform stood a long red transport train. In the wide-open door of the cattle trucks the laughing round faces of the soldiers hung like clusters of brown fruit. The carriages waved with banners and sprays of foliage, their sides

being covered with drawings in chalk. Gay groups
of white-clad girls ran up to the soldiers and stuck
flowers in their tunics. Before a second class carriage in the middle of the train, where the officers
walked up and down in their fine uniforms and
shining leather gaiters, a military band was playing
light marches and cheerful folk-songs. When a handsome soldier seized one of the white-clad girls round
the waist and gave her a resounding kiss clean on
the mouth, the whole station roared " Hurrah ! "
New military transports kept rolling in. Even the
cannons on the flat goods trucks were adorned with
flowers and green branches. On the officers' carriage were stuck complete little birch trees hung
with brilliant ribbons, and sometimes with sausages.
Everybody was laughing, the soldiers loudest of all.

Were they going on a holiday or to a festival ?

As our train drew out and slowly left the station
behind the military band struck up " Deutschland,
Deutschland über alles." Deep-throated the crowd
joined in ; like a choral the song mounted in the
clear, sunny air fluttering with banners ; all took
their hats off, the officers saluted elegantly, the
soldiers presented arms, the young girls sang in
voices as clear as their white frocks, the students
took hands, the women laid their arms tenderly
round the shoulders of their husbands, and the faster
the train went the louder and higher rose the singing.
I was swallowed up, submerged in the singing. I
could not distinguish things any longer. It was to
me as if I had a thousand mothers and a thousand
fathers. . . .

Then my mother bent over me, her hair brushed
my cheek, and she whispered in my ear, her voice
choked with emotion : " Is it not wonderful ? " I

flung my arms round her. She drew me to her.
" Yes," she said, and nodded towards the people in
the corridors standing close together like lovers,
serene and happy. " Our dear German people,
how terribly we have misunderstood their real
nature." She was crying. A little in front of us
beside the lavatory the students were singing : " No
better death in all the world, than on the field to
perish. . . ."

The train rolled between the rich pastures of
Baden, heavy with grain. From all the towns and
villages rose shouts of rejoicing.

I was as if dazzled. The world lay transfigured.
The war had made everything beautiful.

.   .   .   .   .   .

In Offenburg the train remained standing until
late in the afternoon. The line was blocked by
military transports. I saw hussars, uhlans and heavy
artillery passing. My mother ran along the trains
distributing books which she had bought at the
station bookstall. Unfortunately she could only get
light popular stories, but the officers assured her that
for serious reading they had all brought *Faust* in
their haversacks.

When five hours later we neared our town, mortars
were crashing and a rocket tore crackling up into
the sky. It was the third day of the rifle carnival
and the evening on which the carnival king was to
be crowned. My father was standing on the platform. He waved to us with a little flag. " Hurrah ! "
he cried, as he saw us. " Hurrah ! " roared the
people on the train as we got out. " Hurrah ! "
cried Kathinka, laughing, as she took over our luggage. " So," said my father, " you're here at last."

" Yes," we cried, " we're here at last." Then we went, arm in arm, he, my mother and I, towards the exit. Behind us Kathinka panted happily with the luggage.

As we turned into the Bahnhofstrasse my father indicated the flags which waved everywhere, almost covering the fronts of the houses. " Only a few of these were put up in honour of the rifle carnival, by the members, of course—we've to thank the events of the past few days for this great forest of flags. We're counting on the French declaring war every hour. Everybody is waiting for that as for a deliverance."

For the last time the name of Gaston shot through my head. But soon it was lost amid the confusion of banners, the laughter of the people who went about the streets in their Sunday clothes, and the confused scraps of music which came to us from the field where the carnival was being held. I forgot Gaston, as a child forgets his best friend, standing before the booths of a fair.

The windows of Silberstein's shop in the market-place were blazing. From the balcony over the golden lettering of the shop-sign a new banner hung to the very ground. My father praised it up, saying it was the biggest flag in our town. In shop-window number eight the dummies were standing holding in their yellowish waxen hands little paper flags with the black, white and red colours. The female dummies, all in white, wore the colours in sashes round their waists. Besides this Herr Silberstein had provided them all without exception with blonde wigs. But all of them were dominated by a dummy which stood on a pedestal and wore a field-grey uniform. It represented an officer, who with his

right hand was preparing the draw a sword from
its sheath, as if he were about to run the other
dummies through the body. On the glass panes
stood written in flourishing script : " Am prepared
to deliver the latest uniforms from lieutenant upwards, made to measure. Best quality, dependable
material."—" On parle français " and " English
spoken " were scratched out.

I thought of Leo. In the house above the shop
there was only a faint light. My father said that
the evening before Leo had had a violent hemorrhage
and had remained unconscious until this morning.
" He's dying, there's no doubt of it," he added. " It's
a great misfortune, just at this glorious time. . . ."
I looked up at the windows ; the curtains were
swaying a little.

We ate our supper as quickly as possible. My
father rushed away to the carnival ; at eight o'clock
the prizes were to be given out. Besides, the latest
telegrams were announced there ; every half-hour
the master-at-arms rang up a news agency in Frank-
fort. Half an hour later we were in the carnival
enclosure. It was a spreading meadow ; in the
middle a large marquee was set up ; on the right
were the rifle butts. Two bands played alternately
in the marquee. On a huge buffet towered five
hogsheads of beer. The waitresses had been specially
sent from Bavaria ; they were very fat.

I found August in front of the marquee. " Hurrah ! " he cried, when he saw me. He was wearing
the black, white and red colours. " Well, my boy ? "
my father addressed him. " Come," cried August,
" my father's here too." . . . My mother nodded
permission. I ran away with August.

At a big table near one of the bands sat the stoker

Kremmelbein with a crowd of his comrades. They
all wore black, white and red rosettes in their coats,
where the red carnations had been before. August
pushed a stool towards me and got me a glass of
beer. As he set it down the stoker thumped on the
table. " Comrades ! " he cried, " Germany is being
attacked, that is evident. You know I'm not easily
taken in, but we must defend our fatherland."—
" Hear ! Hear ! " said the comrades, lifting their
beer glasses. " From a purely objective point of
view, this is how we stand," Kremmelbein went on.
" If the ruling classes need us now, so that we—the
real workers—may turn aside the attack of the enemy,
which is also directed against us, then of course we're
not going to do that for nothing."—"Hear ! Hear ! "
said the comrades, lifting their glasses. " What I
mean is that when Germany has won we'll put
forward certain demands, the eight-hour day, the
right to vote and the right to go on strike."—" Hurrah ! " shouted the comrades, raising their glasses a
third time. " For us the war is a good proposition ;
the *bourgeoisie* need us, we'll see that our services
are amply recompensed." The comrades smirked.
" And then you're not to forget that in France
they've shot our comrade Jaurès, and we as Socialists are in duty bound to revenge him—that's what
the war is for ! "—" Down with France ! " shouted
the comrades, and the cry was taken up and pro-
longed by the respectable burghers. " Down with
France ! " roared the whole marquee.

Then Kremmelbein sprang on to the table and
shouted : " Every German worker will fight for the
safety of his fatherland to the last drop of his blood.
German people, you will see that in the hour of
danger your poorest son was also your truest one ! "

The marquee howled. The bands gave a flourish of trumpets in unison. At every table the people sprang to their feet. " Here's to Kremmelbein ! To Kremmelbein ! " And as the shouting passed over into the German national anthem, Persius, already in uniform, approached our table and held out his hand to Kremmelbein. " Let bygones be bygones. Let us stand as one man. In the hour of danger we know no parties." Kremmelbein smiled and took his hand. " Everybody has his own opinions, doctor. Your opinions had the police behind them last time. But now, when the father-land is in danger, we'll forget everything. When peace comes we'll have another talk."—" Yes," said Persius, and involuntarily drew himself up, " when we've won. . . ."

They shook hands. The bands played another flourish. Kremmelbein and Persius were surrounded, and while the whole marquee all at once broke into the " Wacht am Rhein," Persius shouted to the Bavarian waitress : " All the beer that's drunk at this table goes on to my bill ! "

At this moment I saw Dr. Hoffmann and Brosius burst into the marquee. They were waving their arms. My father had stationed himself behind me and from there had ordered pork chops for Kremmel-bein and his comrades. A trumpeter blew the German army charge. On the platform Hoffmann was standing waving his cane. Beside him Brosius. Hoff-mann held an extra edition in his hand. " Silence ! " he cried—then after a calculated pause he said in a devout voice, as if he were intoning a prayer : " France has just declared war on us. . . ."

" Hurrah ! " roared the marquee. The people flung their arms above their heads and leapt up on their stools, as if from there it was easier to see a better future.

My father clapped me on the shoulder and laughed. Two members of the corps let off their rifles. Many people embraced each other. And while Kremmelbein leapt on the table again and shouted, " Revenge for Jaurès ! " while his comrades took up the cry and the name of Jaurès, shouted by everybody, echoed round the marquee, as if Jaurès were a national German hero—Dr. Hoffmann and Brosius stood on the platform and shook hands.

" Fellow-countrymen ! " cried Hoffmann, " in the hour of danger let us forget all our petty quarrels. Let us reach out hands to one another—the worker to the employer, the peasant to the worker. Let us be worthy of the words of our Kaiser, who desired peace to the last and only drew the sword at the last minute, because we were attacked—let us swear to remain true to the most noble words of these stormy days : ' Party is swept away ; from this hour we are only Germans ! ' "

A forest of upraised hands surrounded me. I too raised my hand.

Deep-throated the words boomed through the marquee, as if a giant were speaking : " We swear ! " It was said as if by all collectively, the individual was submerged. How festive the world was. . . .

.   .   .   .   .   .

While one of the bands played the first verse of the Netherland hymn of thanksgiving our hands remained uplifted. Only when the second band struck into the German national anthem did we snatch up our beer glasses, raise them on high, laugh across at one another and begin singing. At the beginning of the third verse, which hardly anybody knew by heart, Brosius shouted, " Silence ! His Majesty the Kaiser, our most gracious prince of peace and supreme lord of battle—long may he live ! "—" Long may he live ! "

" His Majesty ! " cried Brosius. We set our glasses to our mouths and emptied them at one draught. Some of mine went down the wrong way. The beer soaked through the jacket of my sailor suit and trickled down my legs. Brosius put his arm round Hoffmann's shoulders and they both descended from the platform. They were overwhelmed with ovations. At the buffet five new hogsheads were being set up by burly tapsters.

Gradually I slipped down on my stool. Round my head a soft cloud was swaying. August was sitting beside me. His voice was very far away. My eyelids seemed difficult to keep open. At the buffet Kremmelbein was drinking schnapps with Persius. My father had also invited one of the comrades over, whom he was treating.

The bitter taste of beer rose into my mouth. Sometimes the tables turned round, and the people sitting at them rose and sank like corks in a heaving sea. Just beside me August said : " All men are the same now. There are no differences any longer." " Yes," I stammered, trying in vain to distinguish one face from another, " I can't see any difference either."

Everything went round. All the faces were lost in a blur.

Slowly I sank back. It wasn't only the beer. . . . My mother brought me coffee and began to laugh gaily when my tongue stumbled over words. Other voices at the table laughed too. August supported

me. The coffee woke me up. Suddenly I saw
Brosius. He was standing before me, mighty as a
new law. He smiled at me. He laid his hand on
my shoulder. For the first time in my life he smiled
at me. For the first time he laid his hand on my
shoulder. " Hm ! " said he, " a German lad can
surely stand a glass of beer ! "

I sprang up. I swayed. But as soon as I caught
his eye I stood at attention and cried : " Here,
sir ! "

" Bravo ! " I heard him saying, then he passed
on. I sank happily back on to my stool. For the
first time Brosius, my teacher, had praised me.

Before me lay the world of the grown-ups whose
hatred and evil had bewildered me once, whose mystery had led me to treachery, to theft, to my first
terror of death and at last to an oath never to grow
up—before me lay this world of pain in a new light.
Wherever I looked people were falling into each
other's arms. All were good now just as they had
been bad before. Persius and Kremmelbein, Brosius
and Hoffmann—none of them hated the other.
They drank together, they sang in unison, their eyes
had the same light. The world had grown young.
The war had made everybody good.

" Oh, mother," I stammered, sinking blissfully
against her, " how lovely war is."

She and August led me out of the tent. Turning
round I saw through a mist of rapturous faces Brosius
and Hoffman hobnobbing at the buffet over two
huge mugs of beer.

In the fresh air I began to reel. August led me.
Passing the blue, red and green illuminated front of
a shop which showed scenes out of the Wars of
Freedom we sang into the patriotic tumult of this

night of rejoicing : " We march in prayer to God
the just."

It was the second of August. It was my first
experience of being drunk.

.   .   .   .   .   .

Leo Silberstein died during that night.

Ferd von K. called on us about nine o'clock next
morning and told Kathinka. I was still asleep. Ferd
came again at eleven. I was cleaning my teeth, to
which the taste of the beer still clung like sour wool.
Drums were thudding outside in the street. The
door of the bathroom was flung open. My father
stood in the doorway. He was radiant. Behind him
I saw Ferd. He was very pale. From the street
came the thud-thud of the drums.

" The Landsturm is called up ! " shouted my
father. He belonged to the Landsturm. Then he
hurried away to the kitchen to tell my mother of
his good fortune. I washed out my mouth. Ferd
came in.

" Leo is dead." Then he gave me his hand. In
the street the drums were still thudding.

" He died this morning at twenty minutes past
three. I went to ask how he was, and they told me
he was dead. . . ."

I sat down on my bed. Then I began to dress
quickly. For I was ashamed to talk half-naked with
Ferd about Leo, who was dead.

" If you want to see him for the last time, then
I'll call for you this afternoon at four. He's to be
coffined at seven, and buried to-morrow afternoon
at three. It must be done quickly, because there's
a war now and the rabbi hasn't much time to spare
for burials. The day after to-morrow he must give

an address in the synagogue to the men who are
going to the front. Besides, all the horses will be
requisitioned ; nobody knows whether there will be
any horses left to pull the hearse the day after to-
morrow."

"Yes," said I to Ferd, " call for me. I would like
to see Leo once more."

"He was always asking for you. He was fond of
you, because you did everything that came into your
head at the moment. We've often spoken about you.
Leo said he admired your curiosity about things.
You could be both nice and unpleasant, too, and he
liked that. Besides, he made over his chess board to
you in case he should die before you came back.
Herr Silberstein will give it you."

I trembled so much that I could not finish dressing. "Leo is dead," I thought, " and yet here he
is giving me something. And I can't thank him for
it."

Then Ferd said as if to comfort me : " It's a good
thing that Leo died. My father says he oughtn't to
have lived any longer. He's one of those people who
die at the right time. He would have been too sensi-
tive for the war."

"Oh," I replied, " but it is a pity that Leo has
died just now, when everybody is so kind, and he
wouldn't need to be afraid of Brosius."

"Kind ? " Ferd laughed harshly. " You mean
because they put their arms round one another and
sing the same songs ? I thought that too at first.
But my father explained to me why they behave as
if they loved each other and were united. *Because
they need their hatred for the other peoples.* Don't you
see that ? Before this it was individuals who hated
each other, now it's the peoples. It was Brosius and

Silberstein, or Persius and Kremmelbein that used
to fight with each other—now it's the Russians and
the Austrians, and the Germans and the French.
It's the same thing."

I stared at him. I could not understand. What
he said was certainly clever, for his father had explained it to him. But what had the French to do
with Kremmelbein, or the Russians with Herr Silberstein ? I was a German. My greatest experience
had been the oneness of all Germans. What were
the other peoples to me ? I had experienced the
wickedness of the grown-ups in Germany, and in
Germany everybody had suddenly become good
again. For me Germany was the world. For as
far as I could see there was only—Germany.

" Ferd," I said, " I don't understand what you
say."

Ferd smiled. " You have a different kind of
father." Then he came up to me and laid his hand
on my knee. " I don't reproach you in the least
for liking the war. Everybody likes it. You're in
with the rest of them, you can be glad when you're
father's glad. But all the time I must be sorry
because my father's sorry, for he always thinks the
opposite from others. I would like to be just like
you . . . if my father were not there." He was crying.

All at once his hand lay slack and lifeless on my
knee.

" Ferd," I cried, " what's wrong with you ? "

" Oh," he answered quietly, and with dry eyes,
" my father's in the right—but you others can get
something out of life. . . ."

I did not understand him, but I loved him. For
a long time we sat together on my bed. The drums
were still beating in the street.

" Ferd," I said after a while, hoping to comfort him, " why are you so sad ? Everybody is kind now ! "

Then he lifted his small head and smiled. " They're only bad in a different way. My father has explained it all to me."

I wanted to contradict him, but Ferd stood up.

" I'll call for you at four o'clock. Then we'll go to see Leo."

He held out his hand. Standing in the door he said casually, as if he had forgotten it : " Last night they requisitioned all our horses."

Then he went. I knew at last why he had cried.

. . . . . .

I finished dressing. My father entered and said that to-day we were to have soldiers billeted on us.

Our town was to have two regiments quartered in it. They came from Bavaria. They sang even more loudly than the civilians. They were Life-Guards. Five men were sitting in the kitchen with Kathinka. In our drawing-room a captain was playing the piano. My mother turned the pages for him. My father brought him wine. The captain sat before the piano ; his sword got stuck between the pedals. He was a very cultured officer. He played Bach. On the bedside-table in the spare room where he was lodged a copy of *Faust* lay beside a handsome steel-blue revolver. My mother gave him Hofmannsthal's *Little Dramas* as a present. The captain ran through them with fine discrimination. Almost tenderly he repeated the lines which my mother had underlined with her pencil. When Ferd came for me the captain was entirely of my father's opinion, who praised the war because it had united and deepened the German people. The earlier theory that the war was a judgment of God he applied now to Germany's enemies.

" Yes," the captain said, with quiet conviction, " when we come back after we've won, everything will be different. The war has made us brothers, and we'll cherish our brotherhood." Then he played Bach again.

I stole out on tiptoe to Ferd, who was waiting below. I felt very solemn. To the grave strains of a Bach cantata I went out with Ferd into the street under the waving banners to see Leo for the last time. I had put on my best clothes. My mother had covered up the gold embroidery on my sailor's cap with crape, and had cut a bunch of white carnations in the garden, which I had to take with me. " Your poor dear friend," my father had called Leo, and Ferd told me that Brosius had sent a bouquet of freshly cut flowers with a note of condolence, over which Herr Silberstein had wept with joy. Everybody was suddenly kind to Leo, because he was dead. Or had the war worked this miracle too ? I believed it had, and once more I thought as I went beside Ferd through the gay streets : " How beautiful war is. . . ."

Troops were continually marching in. They came from the railway station. Round their helmets the soldiers wore garlands of green leaves, their rifles were decked with flowers. A band was playing in the market-place. From Herr Silberstein's house waved the great banner. The shop was full of people buying flags and garlands in a newly opened department. Herr Silberstein stood at the cash till. With his right hand he turned the handle, with his left he counted the money. He smiled at every customer. He smiled like the dummies in show-window

number eight. In the house above one window was
darkened with red curtains. " That's where Leo is
lying," said Ferd. I followed his hand as he pointed.
It was the window to the left of the splendid, wide
waving banner.

We were trying to cut straight across the market-
place, which was crammed as at a fair, when from
the Bahnhofstrasse rang out a quick march. A new
kind of tune that almost made one want to dance.
Fanfares. We were crushed back to the pavement ;
we could see horses looming up in a cloud of dust.
From the dust cloud lances emerged which the sun
turned to silver. " Cavalry ! " someone shouted.
" Uhlans ! " replied a knowing voice. Above it all
blared the fanfares. We were held fast in a wall of
people. It was impossible to get across to Leo. I
held my bouquet fast against my breast ; a few
flowers were broken off.

As the head of the company turned into the market-
place and the clear brazen blare of the trumpets flew
over us and the horses brought their riders nearer
and nearer at a dainty trot, the crowd broke out into
an endless hurrah. Handkerchiefs waved, flowers
flew into the road, the windows sprouted a countless
array of flags. The riders bowed from their horses
and sank their lances, at whose keen points fluttered
coloured pennons. The officers lowered their swords.

At that moment somebody snatched at my bouquet.
A small hand tore the carnations from my arms and
flung them in handfuls towards the soldiers, whose
horses trampled them. I tried to save my bouquet
by sticking it into the blouse of my sailor's suit, but
the hand snatched at them there, seized the whole
bouquet and flung it with a shrill hurrah to an officer,
who neatly caught it and stuck it between the ears

of his horse. Then he threw a kiss in my direction.
I turned round. Behind me stood Hilde.

"Hurrah !" she cried, and waved to the officer.
I seized her by the shoulder. "You've stolen my
flowers ! "—"Well," laughed Hilde, "why didn't
you throw them yourself? "—"They were for Leo !"
I cried. "Him? Oh, he's dead !" said Hilde, tore
herself free, and ran after the officer, flinging him a
kiss in return.

"Let her go," said Ferd, holding me back. "Leo
does not need the flowers so terribly."

"But he does !" I cried, and I rushed into the
street and hastily gathered together the flowers over
which the Uhlans had ridden. Many were still
undamaged. There were actually roses among them.

Then we went to see Leo. We had to go through
the private entrance.

There was a crush of people in the shop. Herr
Silberstein stood smiling at the till ; beside him stood
his red-haired son, who had got out of Paris in time
and was selling flags and garlands.

Frieda, the servant-girl, answered our ring. She
conducted us to the sitting-room with that subdued
smile which all employees put on for sad occasions.
Frau Silberstein was sitting in a chair. When she
saw us she nodded. Then she invited us to sit down.
She rang. Frieda appeared bearing on a tray a bottle
of Malaga and a plate of sandwiches. Frau Silberstein poured out two glasses ; we drank. At last I
had got my Malaga which at Ferd's command I had
refused a few months before. Frau Silberstein said
that her husband sent his excuses, he had so much to
do in the shop. On account of the war he had had
to open a new department.

I kept my dusty bouquet concealed under my

chair. Frau Silberstein suddenly began to cry. " He died very peacefully," she said, amid sobs. " The last thing he understood clearly was the declaration of war on Russia. My husband told him about it five minutes before the hemorrhage."

She wiped away her tears. Ferd and I sat listening very attentively.

" He was alone when he died. We had so many business matters to attend to during the night. When the hemorrhage stopped we thought it was the end. But after lying unconscious for two hours he suddenly wakened and wanted to eat, and his eyes were very bright. He didn't answer our questions. He only said : ' Veal cutlet and mashed potatoes.' That was his favourite dish. We thought he was recovering. That was early in the morning. Where was I to get a veal cutlet ? Frieda knocked up a butcher. He gave her a cutlet. While we waited I sorted out the latest batch of flags and garlands with my husband. Then I grilled the cutlet. Frieda mashed the potatoes. When we brought the food to him he was lying there very white. I cried : ' Leo, here's your cutlet ! ' But he didn't reply. Frieda cried out and let the mashed potatoes fall. My husband came running in from the office. Leo was dead. . . ."

" Yes," said Ferd. " Can we see him once more ? "

Frau Silberstein stood up. She went into Leo's room. She put her fingers to her lips. We stole in on tiptoe.

" Here he is," said Frau Silberstein suddenly, and switched the light on.

The body of Leo lay on a high bed. At his feet flowers were heaped up. We stood by the door. Ferd held me by the hand. We looked at Leo.

His face was serene and smiling. His eyes were open. They were turned up a little. One could

G

only see the whites, which had become almost yellow.
Under the lid of the right eye there gleamed a
little arc of the dark blue iris. Over the forehead,
which was white and stretched taut like silk, fell in
soft disorder Leo's dark curls. There was a scent of
different flowers.

" This here was sent by Dr. Brosius." Frau Silberstein lifted a bouquet of blue asters. From the
street came the sound of military music and the
hurrahs of the crowd. Frau Silberstein cried. I laid
my flowers softly on the green coverlet under which
Leo was lying.

As Ferd went up to the bed and took the hand of
the dead boy in his, from below rose the thud of the
feet of a battalion marching out. The band played
a light, cheerful tune. The soldiers sang : " Must
I then—must I then leave my little home. . . ."
Rapturously the crowd joined in, and a desire ran
through me too to rush out and wave to the soldiers,
who were marching to the station. I was suddenly
afraid of Leo. " Out of this ! Out of this ! " I
thought. " Hilde was right—Leo is dead. Why is
he so uncannily still ? Why, why is he dead ? "

Then Ferd made me a sign. Trembling I approached the bed. Ferd took Leo's hand and laid it
in mine. " Bid him good-bye ! " Gathering all my
strength I held the cold, strangely soft hand, and
while Frau Silberstein sobbed quietly, I stuttered
twice, shaken by a hysterical shudder : " Good-
bye. . . ." In the street the music suddenly broke off.
In a harsh tattoo the drums began.

When at last we were in the bright sitting-room
again, Frau Silberstein invited us to have another
glass of Malaga. We took up our caps and politely
declined. Ferd said we would accompany Leo on

his last journey. " To-morrow at two o'clock," replied Frau Silberstein. Ferd kissed her hand on
leaving. Then we went.

When we reached the street Herr Silberstein suddenly saw us. He left his till to look after itself and
ran out on his short legs. Under his right arm he
was carrying the chess board. " You were seeing
Leo ? "—" Yes," replied Ferd, " we have said good-
bye to him."—" Oh ! " cried Herr Silberstein—
nothing more than that—" Oh . . . oh ! " The little
pouches under his eyes trembled. The tears ran
down on to his neck-tie. With his left hand he held
on to Ferd. His lips were quite beyond his control.
Spittle ran from them.

Then he murmured almost tonelessly and with
absent eyes : " He's dead—he has died—why did
he not wait, for only another month ? For the war's
here—and nobody looks down on us any longer—
everybody recognises us now. . . . Leo, my son, ' the
Jews are Germans too,'—the Commissioner said that
to me this morning when he was ordering a new
uniform. . . . And I can't sit beside you and hold
your hand and cry like other fathers—I must stand
in the shop—behind the till and give a smile to all
these kind people who are not in the least ashamed
now of buying at your father's shop. . . . Little Leo,
don't be angry with me because I have so little time
to give you—it's the shop—I can't do anything
against the shop. If I closed it they would say at
once that I was against the war, and that the Jews
were not Germans at all. . . . Little Leo, don't be
angry with your father. . . ."

At that moment a gust of wind caught the great
banner which hung from the balcony of the house
almost to the ground, and after billowing it a few

times in the air flung it over Herr Silberstein's head.
He reeled. Ferd extricated him.

"Thank you," said Herr Silberstein, with the
smile which he wore behind the cash desk. Then
he took hold of the chess board and handed it to
me. "Leo left that to you." I took the board
trembling. On the brown varnished top Leo had
written in coloured chalk, "For my friend E. In
remembrance of his first intentional defeat."

Herr Silberstein went back to his cash desk. We
promised to be in time for the funeral.

As we turned the corner of Herr Silberstein's shop,
Leo's red-haired brother was standing in the main
entrance screwing to the door a celluloid placard
which bore the German colours and announced in
beautiful German script:

"Don't use the foreign phrase, 'adieu.'—Good
Germans say 'Auf Wiedersehen!'"

.   .   .   .   .   .

I parted from Ferd. When I returned home my
mother was triumphantly waving the latest edition:
Richard Dehmel* had volunteered for active service...

We had a disturbed night. Troops were continually marching in. Towards morning, after an urgent
summons, the Bavarians left. A little after three
o'clock Kathinka made coffee. The captain left a
gracious letter of thanks. Beside it lay his photograph with an inscription in writing: "In remembrance of the great time—Edgar von P., Captain,
2nd Royal Bavarian Rifles." My father stuck the
photograph in the family album. As the sun rose
and the first birds began to chirp, our town was taken
over by Thüringians. . . .

* A well-known German poet, somewhat elderly at that
time, since deceased.

CHAPTER X

NEXT morning I went to see August. In the tenement the Cuckoos were playing at war. They were formed up in little columns, shouldering arms with sticks for rifles, and sang in their deepest voices : " Three lilies, three lilies shall bloom on my grave." They kept on marching round in a circle.

When I reached August's flat, Frau Kremmelbein was packing a box. August's father had been called up, and he was to leave immediately after lunch. I asked August if he was coming with us to the funeral. " Yes," he said, " I'll come."

At two o'clock we gathered in front of Silberstein's house. The coffin was already in the hearse. Behind it, in a carriage, sat Herr Silberstein with his redhaired son. We walked along the pavement beside the hearse. As we turned into the Bahnhofstrasse, five batteries of heavy artillery came along it, with two riders at their head, and the trumpets blaring. The street echoed with the rumbling of the howitzers ; on the gun-carriages the gunners sat in pairs and sang. They overhauled our procession at a gallop. The hearse had to pull in to the side ; from the windows the people cheered.

" Hurrah ! " cried August, and he threw his cap in the air. Even Herr Silberstein raised his tophat.

The gunners waved back with flowers and green

branches. The hearse with Leo in it was backed into a side street ; the horses in their black trappings nibbled at the grass which grew there between the cobbles.

As the third battery was galloping past us the pole of a gun-carriage snapped. · Two horses leapt clean into the air, and as the driver pulled them back fell prone on the ground. At once the whole column halted. The gunners sprang from the gun-carriages. The street was blocked with artillery. The hearse bearing Leo's dead body had to back a few yards further into the side street. Leo's father spoke a few words with an officer. The officer shrugged his shoulders. He could not clear the street until the damage was repaired. There was a war on, and the Army must take first place. " Of course, of course," Herr Silberstein smiled, " my son can wait, sir."

For a quarter of an hour the funeral procession remained standing in the street. When the pole was repaired, and the fallen horses were yoked again, we all cried, " Hurrah ! " The horses drawing the hearse neighed. The batteries rolled past us. The gunners sang " Saint Barbara. . . ."

Then there was nothing to be seen but a cloud of dust, pierced occasionally by the massive mouth of a howitzer.

We went on slowly behind with the hearse. Step by step.

At the gate of the cemetery we saw that a great many people were turning back. We thought it must be the usual custom among Jews and we went back too into the town. Everywhere flags were waving. The air was filled with colour. On the way August said we should have buried Leo on the farm. In the meadow, where he liked so much to go with us to see the foals. Then Ferd laughed and said quite softly as if he did not want to disturb our thoughts : " Don't you know that ? Even when one's dead one is only the son of one's father. . . ." Then we parted. When I got home a newspaper was lying on my father's desk with the news that England had declared war on Germany. . . .

In the kitchen Kathinka was sitting with the Thüringian soldiers. In the streets there was very little singing now.

.   .   .   .   .   .

Nobody had expected such outrageous conduct from England. " The more enemies, the more honour," said my father, when towards four he came home, but his voice sounded as if he were thinking of secret creditors.

That evening we had to attend at the school. The Head had decreed a service of thanksgiving. As captain in the Reserve he had to join his regiment next day. The ceremony began with a Te Deum in the hall. Then the Kalmuck recited a poem : " Germania to her children " by H. von Kleist. With unction his voice rose to the lines : " Strike them dead ! For human laws ask you not for ground or cause. . . ." After the school orchestra had played a flourish the Head made a speech. One passage has stuck in my mind. " At last the ignoble peace is ended. The iron age begins. Our thanks must go up to our Creator that we are considered worthy of experiencing it."

The janitor came in from the left, and handed up a note to the Head. As if possessed the latter jumped about on the platform and waved the note like a flag. " Hurrah ! " he shouted, " our first victory."

Liège had fallen. By forced marches the German armies were pouring into Belgium.

The Head commanded silence. "What does it say in the beautiful poem which you learned by heart last year for the Sedan anniversary?"

Brosius acting as conductor, 250 clear boyish voices answered: "Where is Paris? Here, you say? Follow my finger, that's our way!"

The orchestra played a flourish, then slowly changed over into the German national anthem. We took hands and sang.

After the second verse the Scripture teacher stepped forward and read a speech from a sheet of paper. The issue was decided: God, the Lord of Battles, was with our flag. We must pray every evening that He should remain with it. We belonged body and soul to the Fatherland—that was the highest command of the God of Germany. In these stormy days He had manifested Himself to our people. We must never become of little faith. The more numerous our enemies, the nearer God would be to us. He said nothing about Jesus. I was struck by that.

After the choral, "Do not lose courage, little band . . ." and Luther's hymn, in which the Catholics joined as well, we were dismissed. The school was to be closed for the next fortnight. Recruits were to be drilled in the play-ground. We were in raptures and gave thanks for the war.

．　　　．　　　．　　　．　　　．　　　．

The English declaration of war had come as a complete surprise. Nobody in our town had expected it. My father had declared that the English were really Germans, and I recollected as well a

pronouncement of the famous professor in the
waiting-room at Bâle, according to which the English
as representatives of the blonde race were our natural
allies ; in them too existed the Siegfried spirit ; and
if they betrayed it, there was always Japan, who
would straightway, with its army officered by Germans, attack the English in India.

I found this pronouncement very puzzling at the
time—for what had Japan to do with Siegfried ?

But the professor was a famous man ; he must
know.

I was walking with Ferd through the town. The
flags hung limp. The air was sultry and as if stagnant. In the western sky towered thunder-clouds.

Ferd smiled. " It is all coming out as my father
said. We'll lose the war."

I was so horrified that I stood still. " It's a lie,"
I cried, " for then all this would have happened for
nothing."

" That's just what my father says, all this will lead
to nothing. . . ."

" England has betrayed us," said I, to comfort
myself, " it will be punished for that."

" How stupid you are," Ferd replied. " England
has never lost a war yet."

I walked beside him and noticed that I was gradually beginning to hate him. Again he wanted to
forbid me something. My faith in Germany, my
faith in the new purified world of the grown-ups.
For without victory what sense had all this brotherhood, all this unity ? And was not God on our side ?
Had Liège not fallen ? Could God lie ? . . . Yes,
earlier, while the grown-ups were still bad, I had
believed the Red Major ; but now when even Kremmelbein had shaken hands with Dr. Persius, now

G *

that the war had revealed itself as the great unifier and regenerator of mankind, I was bound to praise and love it.

Everything in me rose in resistance to Ferd, and as I slowly drew back from him, as if he were carrying a dangerous pestilence about with him, I spat at him : " You yourself are half English. . . ."

Ferd did not say a word. He only bowed his head. Then, after a horrible pause, I heard him saying : " My father reports to his regiment this evening." We walked on in silence. I did not understand why he was crying. I would have been proud if my father could have helped, as a major, to beat the enemy. My father was only a sergeant in the Landsturm. . . . Really *I* should have been the one to cry.

On a red-carpeted balcony in front of the town-hall the pastor S. was standing giving an address. He was known as a fiery orator. His voice had an astounding resonance. After every sentence the people even in the farthest outskirts of the crowd cheered.

" England has betrayed us ! " he bellowed, swinging his arms as if he wanted to buffet the clouds : " Down with England ! "

From the market-place rose a single shout : " Down with England ! "

The pastor drew a deep breath, his right hand clenched itself, and while he brought it down with a thunderous blow, from his mouth came in a bellow the mighty words : " God, who sees all sins, the Avenger and Ruler—*God punish England !* "

In a harsh and resolute chorus the crowd repeated his words. I saw women praying ; the men raised their hands and swore ; above stood the stalwart form of the pastor giving us his blessing. We all took off our hats, the soldiers raised their helmets. Ferd had disappeared.

August had climbed on to a lamp-post. When he saw me he slid down. " I say, my father has gone to D. to the barracks there. In a fortnight he'll be on active service. He must drill recruits first ; he's a sergeant. And who do you think is in his section as a private ? Galopp, the Judge." August's face was radiant. " The war ! " he cried, " the war's making everything right again ! "

As we were making our way with great difficulty through the excited crowd, I saw my father coming out of a public-house with J. the apothecary. They were carrying rifles and had white bands with badges round their right arms. " We've registered as special constables," said my father, showing his rifle proudly. " We're going to post ourselves on the outskirts and hold up all the cars with civilians in them. For there's news come that the French are trying to smuggle millions of gold through to Russia in motor cars. Besides, the whole neighbourhood's swarming with spies. We've power to arrest anybody that looks suspicious, and shoot if they don't stop after we've called ' Halt ! ' three times. You go home and ask mother to tell Kathinka to bring me some coffee about midnight ; we'll be stationed at the bridge with the poplars until sunrise."

" Father ! " I cried, " Father, I'll bring the coffee at midnight ! "

And August begged to be allowed to come too.

" Good," said my father, visibly moved, patting our heads, " good, my lads—the password is ' Count Haeseler.' "

Then they shouldered their rifles and marched to-

wards the outskirts of the town. In the middle of
the street, not on the pavement. As if they were
vehicles.

I invited August to supper.

As we neared the park behind which my parents'
house lay, we saw a band of boys jumping excitedly
round a tree to which they had bound somebody.
August, who had keen sight, suddenly cried out :
"They've got hold of Ferd ! " And at once he set
off at a run. I ran after him. All my anger against
Ferd vanished before the fact that they had set on
him. He stood alone against a superior force of
enemies. That turned the scale. " Of course Haugwitz and the whole of his precious crew ! " cried
August, gaining three yards on me. We took a short
cut, leapt over the rose-beds and flung ourselves with
wild howls among the enemy, who were just then
taking council what they should do to Ferd. They
had bound him to an ash with their book-straps and
left two " men " to guard him. The Kalmuck was
just proposing : " Each of us will walk up to him
and give him one on the ear, and spit in his face,"
when with a noiseless spring August was among
them, dealt the Kalmuck a kick in the belly, so that
he rolled on the ground with his face turning green,
and seized young Haugwitz by his tartan scarf, shook
him three times backwards and forwards, and then
gave him a buffet on the nose, so that the blood
streamed.

" You swine ! " he cried, and his eyes were blood-
shot with rage, " ten against one ! " Then he rushed
almost howling to the tree and with his pocket-knife
cut the straps and set Ferd free. Meantime I had
settled the guard and landed a blow on the bread-
basket of a third. " Captain ! " cried August, stand-

ing beside the ash wiping Ferd's bloody face with his handkerchief. Then he rubbed Ferd's wrists, which were blue and swollen.

Then Haugwitz, his nose still running blood, stepped forward and said to August : " We didn't set on him because he's your captain. But because he said that Germany would lose the war. . . ."

" Yes," cried another, " he did say it. We offered him friendship first because there's a war, and we all want to be allies. But he laughed at us and then said that the English, the traitors, would win. He's a spy ! "

" Yes," they screamed in chorus, gaining courage again, " his mother was English, and that's why he wants the English to win."

Ferd stood beside August and wiped the mud from his shoes with wisps of grass. His face was scornful. He behaved as if all this had nothing to do with him. " You set of liars ! " cried August, flourishing his pocket-knife, " Ferd never said that ! " —" Then ask him yourself ! " jeered the others. And the Kalmuck sprang forward, seized Ferd by the wrist and demanded : " What did you say ? " Ferd shook him off, then he lifted his small head and said into the fading dusk : " Yes, Germany will lose the war. . . ."

We were all struck dumb. I too felt as if some-one had knocked me on the head, although I was hearing the words for the second time. " Spy ! " screamed the boys. Then August went up to Ferd, gripped him by the shoulders, and while he kept on shaking him as if he were trying to waken him he cried, " Captain ! Captain ! " He was crying.

" I believe my father," replied Ferd, and with a proud step walked past us towards the street. August broke into loud sobbing. " He's betrayed us," he said to me. " He's English." I felt as sad as August.

Then behind a bush we saw the Kalmuck lifting a stone and throwing it at Ferd. It hit him. Ferd tottered. Then he fell in a heap on a pile of sand which lay by the side of the road. We ran to him, even young Haugwitz ran. Ferd was bleeding from the back of his head. In soft runnels the blood flowed down to the nape of his neck. August supported him. Young Haugwitz said : " Even if he is English, that was a rotten thing to do." We bound Ferd's head with our handkerchiefs. The wound was not dangerous, for the Kalmuck had happened to lift a blunt stone. " I want to go home," murmured Ferd, and began to walk on alone. August held him fast. " We'll go with you." We led him. When we reached the last houses, the Kalmuck sprang from behind some bushes and shouted " Spy ! "

I thought, why isn't the Kalmuck English ?

We made for the farm. August spoke to Ferd coaxingly ; he must come to his senses, Germany couldn't possibly lose the war, all the comrades were of the same opinion—but if in spite of everything he didn't believe it, then he should only talk about it to us two, and not to the others. August said it would be a hard job always having to rescue him again.

Ferd only smiled. Then he was sick. We carried him for a bit. He vomited. I could not help think-of Leo, and that time when we had led him home from the school. Suddenly Ferd asked what time it was. " Five minutes to eight," August answered proudly. His father had given him a nickel watch as a parting present. " My father is leaving for his regiment at nine," said Ferd. He laid his arms over our shoulders. We went on at a run. "For his regiment?" said August. "Then he *does* believe that we'll win."

"No, he's only doing his duty as an officer." Then August was piqued.

"Our fathers are doing their duty too!"

"But they don't know that it's no use."

"He must be ill, that's it," whispered August to me. I nodded. It seemed the likeliest explanation to me.

We were nearing the farm. From the town the bugles sounded the evening roll call. Thunder crashed.

We were perhaps about three hundred yards from the farm when we became aware of a huge crowd assembled there. "Stop," said August, "something's happening here." We heard shouts. Three gendarmes, pushing hard at their bicycles, over-hauled us. As we drew nearer we could make out the shout: "Spy! Spy!"

"That's meant for my father," said Ferd. "I must go to him."

We held him back, but he tore himself free and ran on.

A little before he reached the gate we caught him up. It was surrounded by a crowd of a hundred or so. "Englander!" they screamed. "Spy!"

Some of them were lifting stones and throwing them at the windows. At their head stood the fore-man. The gendarmes drew their swords and tried to force their way through the crowd. They were greeted by showers of clods. Then the crowd sang the "Song of the Flags." At that moment we saw Ferd breaking through the outer ring of the crowd and running towards the gate. "Stop! Stop!" a

few of them cried at his back, and began to throw
stones. " That's his little English cub ! "—" Stop
there, stop ! " Ferd fell. Someone had tripped him
up with a cane. The gendarmes formed a ring
round him. " Hoho ! " yelled the crowd, beginning to crush forward and making for Ferd. August
was crying. I was too. We loved Ferd still. In
spite of the war. Against our convictions. . . .

Just as the crowd had forced the gendarmes and
Ferd back against the outer walls under a hail of
stones, and were rushing for the gate, the gate
opened. In the courtyard stood Herr von K.'s
carriage with the two cream-coloured horses in readiness. Slowly, as if he were recollecting something, the
Major began to descend the lighted steps from his
door. He was in the uniform of his regiment. Round
his waist he wore a silver-coloured sash. Nobody
stirred. The gendarmes saluted. The crowd stood in
silence. The uniform dazzled them.

Herr von K. walked past the horses, through the
gate, straight towards the crowd. It retreated before
him. Slowly the people dispersed and scattered into
the next field. Unnaturally tall in the light of the
setting sun the Major stood in front of his house.

His uniform glittered. Nobody cried " Spy ! "
now. The Major smiled and pulled off his gloves.
The gendarmes were still standing at attention.

" I think we've misunderstood him," whispered
August, and pointed towards Ferd, who with his
head bound was crawling slowly towards his father.

" Ferd ! " cried the Major, and caught up his son.
" Ferd ! "

" They all fell on me ! " Ferd broke down and
clung to his father's knees.

Then the Major lifted his son in his arms and

walking carefully carried him back into the house.
The gendarmes stationed themselves before the gate
with swords drawn. We lay down behind a bush
and waited.

Half an hour later the Major's carriage left the
farm at a sharp trot and with the blinds drawn. In
Ferd's room the light went out. August decided that
we must beg Ferd's pardon next day. He had only
said what he had heard his father saying, and besides
the war with England had burst on us so quickly that
the Major hadn't learned about it soon enough to
correct Ferd in his opinion. I wondered at August.
His ideas always came so pat.

Shortly before we reached the town the thunder-
storm broke. We ran through the streets. It was
pitch dark. We only saw each other when the
lightning flashed. The flashes came fast. When
we reached the house after an exciting sprint my
father was already there. On the advice of J. the
apothecary, he had deserted his post at the poplar
bridge. The rifle barrels would attract the lightning.
Besides, no cars would be arriving in weather like
this. . . .

As the storm was growing worse, August was
allowed to sleep with me.

.   .   .   .   .   .

Next morning we set out to visit Ferd. When we
reached the streets the bells were ringing. The flags,
drenched during the night with rain, were dry again ;
they fluttered gaily and festively, only in some—the
cheap ones—the colours had run. In front of the
town-hall thronged a crowd waving sticks and hats,
and someone, who, sweating profusely, was being
carried on the shoulders of two other men through

the crowd, was reading out a telegram. A new fortress had fallen, Namur I think it was.

We forgot our visit to Ferd ; we ran home, got out my atlas and drew a thick red line under the word Namur. We put off our visit till next day, but one victory came on the heels of another, our marks in the atlas could hardly keep pace with them. August added up the numbers of the prisoners reported captured, and when the result overtopped the population of our town we were exultant. The names of the fallen fortresses were continually changing and August called this " victory by wholesale." We followed the onward march of our armies as if we were reading an exciting romance. An adventurous story of travel, which was couched in the curt language of the Army Command. Sometimes it gave us nothing but figures, and these inflamed our imagination most of all. Eight generals, 15,000 men, 10 banners . . . that was enough for us. August soon lived in an orgy of statistics. God was on our side—before the roar of Big Bertha the first outworks of Antwerp were falling.

We did not.live at home now, we lived in a strange land ; the road to Paris seemed nearer to us than the road to Ferd at the farm.

.   .   .   .   .   .

Ten days later August's father left for active service. On the station platform at D. the Kremmelbein family turned up in full force ; the mother was very proud of her husband's rank ; he had every prospect of being made a sergeant-major. When, after an address by the colonel, the signal for departure was given, and the prematurely aged woman embraced her sergeant, she blushed shyly as he took her

round the thin waist and kissed her before everybody.

" No tears, Mother," he said, pinching her cheek
playfully. " By Christmas we'll be home again."
Frau Kremmelbein smiled. For she was, oh, so
proud ! that her husband was respectable at last.
August was allowed to hold his father's rifle. He
told me later that the proudest moment of his life
was when Galopp, the Judge, stood at attention
before his father and reported that all belt buckles
were polished. As amid the cheerful strains of
" Must I then, must I then leave my little home,"
the soldiers' singing, and the endless cheers of those
left behind, the train with studied slowness drew out
of the station, the tears came to Frau Kremmelbein's
eyes too—but not tears of sorrow, as she maintained,
but of joy at so much honour and solemnity. It was
only August's little sisters who sobbed when their
father went away. But when a young Red Cross
sister gave them two tablets of chocolate, they gaily
waved their hands, into which August had stuck little
paper flags.

At this time my father too received at last a command to report himself. He came back from D. a
sergeant. He looked very well in his uniform. It
made him younger. Brosius and Persius had been
sent long before to the front ; on account of his
delicate health Dr. Hoffmann was given a post as
regimental clerk.

The German armies had pushed far into France ;
August reckoned on the fall of Paris in fourteen days
at the latest.

I discovered that Ferd was ill. He had been seized
by an unaccountable fever the day after his father
left. We were not allowed to see him. He lay in

delirium behind the red curtains. Often he cried
out for his father. A distant relation—an old aunt
from Pomerania—had come to nurse him. August
thought that the war would be over before Ferd
recovered ; then we would go to him and behave
as if we had forgotten everything. He must have
been very ill that time, obviously. I agreed with
August. I was very glad that we could put off
our visit, for now the first war prisoners were
arriving.

They were mostly Belgians in shoddy uniforms.
" Garman," they would say, " bom, bom . . . o . . .
o . . ." and they would give themselves a shake and
raise their hands. We begged uniform buttons from
them ; August actually acquired a blue képi for ten
cigarettes. Soon the French preponderated. Their
uniforms were more soldierlike, also they refrained
from any attempt at communication ; they often
smiled mockingly when we showed them the advance
of the Germans marked on a map. Nor would they
consent to sell any of their buttons ; on the other
hand they obeyed the commands of their guards to
the letter. When with the help of a phrase-book I
prophesied to one of the prisoners the imminent capture of Paris, he laughed and replied with a knowing
look : " Et les Russes . . . ? "

I became silent and ran away to August. The
man was right. It could not be denied. The
Russians were fighting on German soil.

It was at this fact that everybody in our town was
indignant. Though it was only a little strip of East
Prussia of no importance compared with our conquered territory in the West—everybody held that
this state of things was unendurable ; not one hand's-
breadth of German soil should be in the enemy's

possession. Great meetings were held in the public-houses ; it was a shame that we were retreating before the Russians ; and the comrades in particular, at least those who were still left, shouted that we should put back the capture of Paris for a month or so, and crush the Czar first. Resolutions were carried demanding the speedy defeat of the Russians. Dr. Hoffmann had them sent to the proper authorities. We had become used to victories in France.

We wanted something new.

During these days August and I were never away from the station. We helped to load the military transports, we waved when the trains rolled out again, towards the west—often too we went into the church, when volunteers were being consecrated.

We had made peace with Haugwitz's band. We could not lag behind the grown-ups.

Soon we noticed that the direction of the transport trains began to alter. The result of the resolutions. . . . Huge trains passed through the stations day and night, without stopping. They came from France. The last remaining regiment marched out of our town—to the north-east front. The victories in France continued. They were received enthusiastically, but as a matter of course. All eyes were turned towards Russia. German territory was invaded. The Kaiser should intervene. We could easily settle with the French afterwards. They were running just like hares. East Prussia must be delivered. This was shouted in the public-houses, thundered from club tables, and even preached from the pulpit, if somewhat less incisively. Perpetually the red transport trains went rolling from the west to the east. August's father, who had been last heard of at Namur, wrote a postcard telling of his night journey through Osnabrück. The Kaiser had intervened. Everybody awaited a great stroke.

I bought a good map of Russia, and August and I began to sharpen our red pencils.

The victories in France became fewer. We considered that a good sign.

    ·   ·   ·   ·   ·   ·

One of those days—we had been waiting for a week already for the great stroke—I decided at last to visit Ferd. His fever had left him ; Kathinka, who was often sent to the farm by my mother to ask after Ferd, reported that he had been up for the first time two days before, and that his aunt pushed him through the park in a bath-chair every afternoon between three and four. He was still very feeble. I walked slowly through the town. At many houses the flags had been taken down again ; the dust and rain combined damaged them too much—besides, a silent understanding had been come to among the people only to put out flags when there were " great victories." Except at Herr Silberstein's and the office of the military command, no flags were now to be seen. It was very quiet in the town ; most people who were not in the Army had returned to their usual occupations.

My mother too had begun to make jellies and preserves. After all, one could not neglect necessary work on account of the war, even though it had brought so much joy and inspiration.

I went through the suburbs and passed close by the tenement—August hed gone with his mother to stay with his grandfather in Bavaria—and I considered what I should say to Ferd. Although I felt myself borne out fully by the events of the past few weeks—God was on our side, He granted us victory after victory, at St. Quentin an English army had actually been annihilated—although all this told against Ferd—the blow directed at the Russians would conquer his last doubts—although, like Germany, I was in the right, I could not quite rid myself of a feeling of uncertainty at the thought of meeting him. In an uncanny way his illness had withdrawn him from all that was happening. Perhaps too I was afraid of meeting him because it was at his house-door that the great impulse of brotherhood among men had come to an end ; yes, it was because of him and his father that their hatred and evil had flamed up for the last time. Ferd was uncanny to me because he stood apart.

I came upon him in the garden. Wrapped in brown blankets, he sat in his chair under the jasmine leaves. His face was white, his chin pointed, his lips colourless. He waved to me. I went over to him and gave him my hand. " Hullo, Ferd—how do you feel now ? " He nodded. I sat down beside him on a red garden-chair. " Do you know," he said suddenly, gripping the arms of his chair, " in eight days I'll be all right. I've written to my father to-day telling him ! "—" Yes," I said, struck by the sharpness of his voice, " of course you will. But where is your father now ? "—" They've given him a Landwehr battalion, all old men, so as to humiliate him, because they know what his views are ; and they've sent him to East Prussia—to that second-rate front where he has to retreat all the time because there are no reserves."

His face was quivering. " Second-rate front ? " I ventured to put in.—" Of course ! The war will be decided in the west, if anything can be saved still, that is. But the generals in command there are all stupid and jealous." I was silent, Ferd's fingers plucked at the blanket. " I could show you a letter of my father's, where all that's made quite clear. We could have safely let them come as far as the Weichsel. Instead of that, on some stupid question of prestige, they're interrupting the campaign in the western front to fling indispensable troops across to East Prussia. They've given the Schlieffen advance a blow from behind."

I did not understand him. What did I know about Schlieffen ? I only saw that his father had set him on again. I did not contradict him. Even when he said that the war would last for several years I held my tongue. He was still very ill, it was clear. . . .

We sat on under the jasmine leaves ; it seemed to me as if I were seeing him for the last time.

Then suddenly from the town there came a dull, heavy boom. Mortars roared. Faint, but distinct, the wind carried to us the sound of singing and pro-longed cheering.

I leapt up and ran to the gate. With radiant faces the maids rushed out from the dairy. High up, in magnificent folds, two huge flags waved from the steeple of the church.

" Victory ! Victory ! " the cry came from the fields, where the harvest was being gathered in by the last remaining labourers. " Victory ! Victory ! " shouted a man who was racing along the poplar boulevard on a bicycle, waving a newspaper. We rushed over to him. We pulled him from his bicycle. He laughed as if he were drunk. " One hundred thousand Russians ! " he cried, " one hundred thou-sand Russians captured—eight hundred cannons, a

dozen generals—two armies done for ! Driven into
the marshes.—Victory ! Victory ! "—then he tore
himself free and ran waving his arms towards the
labourers, who were rushing from the fields in
crowds.

Almost reeling I went back to Ferd. The maids
had linked their arms and were dancing in a ring
on the meadow. They sang. The bells pealed.
Ferd sat without moving in his chair. I seized him
by the shoulder. " Victory ! " I said softly. " Victory ! " I stammered, " one hundred thousand Russians captured—two armies in the marshes."

Vaguely through the tears of joy which rose to my
eyes, I saw Ferd rise up, fling aside the blankets with
a sharp movement, and march straight as an arrow
for the gate. There stood the Major's carriage.
Bent double, cautiously supporting herself on her
crutch, Ferd's aunt got out. When she saw Ferd
she cried, " My child ! My child ! " Then she
whimpered. Ferd marched up to her ; his legs
moved as if on hinges. Then, a little way from his
aunt, who was hobbling towards him stretching out
her free hand in anxious tenderness, he remained
standing and asked in a clear, carrying voice :
" What has happened to my father ? ".

His aunt put her arm round his neck, weeping ;
two servants sprang forward and supported him ;
the cream horses became restless standing in the
carriage, and while the bells rang heavily over the
land and the hurrahs of the labourers echoed from
the fields, Ferd screamed into the rejoicing landscape
in a voice that cut the air like a knife : " The
truth ! . . ."

Then his aunt broke down and handed him the
telegram. He read it, and every one drew back from

him as suddenly with a horrible laugh he crushed it in his hand and flung it on the ground. Then strangely upright he went into his father's house. Behind him his aunt hobbled on her crutch. " My child ! My child ! " she whimpered, and she kept her free hand outstretched as if she were looking for another crutch.

One of the servants unfolded the telegram. He read it out. I ran as fast as I could back towards the town, and while through my head ran the words " The Red Major has fallen in action," to kill the fear and horror that lay upon the farm I rushed with a deliberately loud " hurrah " into the rejoicing crowd in the streets, which kept me from thinking.

PART TWO

THE WAR

Since the beginning of human thought the two world-conceptions " War " and " Peace " have fought for the palm of victory. Which motto shall prevail? The classical " Pleasant and honourable it is to die for one's country," or the motto of our day : " No more war " ?

From a film announcement of the year 1928. (Pola Negri : " Wire Entanglements.")

CHAPTER XI

THE BREAK-UP

EIGHT days after the battle of Tannenberg my father
was sent with his battalion to the fortress of Thorn.
We gave him a very cordial send-off. As his was a
Landsturm battalion, and was not going to the front,
this send-off was less solemn and more private.
Nevertheless my mother was glad of the reprieve ;
people of that age, she said, were not fitted for the
front lines ; the most that could be required of them
was to cover the rear.

I did not know at the time that her words gave
voice to a secret apprehension which had been started
in our town—and especially among the women—by
the Red Major's death. Already many women were
beginning to ask half in jest whether after all we had
not won enough as it was.

I myself was glad that my father was gone, for I
would have felt embarrassed before my friends, whose
fathers were all at the front, if he had remained
behind any longer.

August and I became more and more close friends
with Haugwitz's gang. We fraternised as we had
seen the grown-ups doing. The Red Guard was
disbanded.

I tried with all my strength not to think of Ferd.
I knew that I had lost my best friend, but I offered
him up to the war with the same exaltation as

Kremmelbein and Dr. Hoffmann had offered up their Socialist programme in those wonderful days. I heard nothing more of Ferd. A few days after his father's death his aunt had taken him away with her to Pomerania.

After our fathers went away life became quieter in our town. The jubilation of the first days cooled down into a settled solemnity.

Behind the ramparts of the front we felt ourselves sheltered like a faithful community under the roof of their church and safeguarded by the promise of their Lord. God was on our side, our fathers were His instruments, we, His people.

The faces of the grown-ups gradually acquired that expression of inward certainty which may be seen in the faces of Seventh Day Adventists.

They all felt themselves elected. " We Germans," they said, and made great eyes as if they were posing for a religious picture.

They were perpetually emphasising their brother-hood, as if to live without quarrelling were a great virtue.

Their voices were full of unction ; they were careful never to raise their voices, or to speak an angry word. The " poor people," as they called the proletariat, were kindly treated ; nobody found it beneath his dignity any longer to speak a few words more than was absolutely necessary to a small shopkeeper or a workman. The term " Socialist " lost its disreputable ring. We were a united people, the war had bridged all social divisions. I marked this with particular joy in the case of August. Wherever he went he was pampered by everybody and overwhelmed with little presents, and his mother had daily remembrances in the form of presents of money or food. Gradually August acquired the habits of a son of a well-to-do family. He even spoke in High German. The war had made him refined.

In these days our only thought was for our fathers. They had become heroes overnight. We regretted our youth, for it kept us from being heroes. We loved our fathers with a new, exalted love. As ideals. And as in former days we had often given expression to our admiration for the heroes of Homer or of the War of Freedom by slight modifications of our clothes aided by Greek helmets of gold paper or Lützower caps, so now we began, but with far more intensity, to transform ourselves symbolically into the ideal figures of our fathers. We had our hair cropped. Bare. Smooth. To the eighth of an inch. For we had seen our fathers' hair cut like that when they left for the front. They had no hair to part in the middle now.

One evening in late September fifteen of us boys went resolutely to the barber's. We formed up according to height, and let the clipper pass over our heads. When after an hour's time the barber was sweeping the hair up with a broom, he said : " There ! Now you look just like recruits. . . ."

We were very proud of this distinction and paid enthusiastically forty pfennigs per head.

The girls too altered their frisures about that time. They combed their hair straight back, and fastened their plaits in a roll on the tops of their heads. And even if their hair was curly they oiled it until it would lie flat on their heads. They all looked the same. The patriotic standardisation was taken up more intensely by the girls even than by us. People called this way of dressing the hair, " German style."

Some of the girls, among them Hilde, whose father had been sent with mine to Thorn, had even had their hair cut and sent it to some Government department, though nobody knew what could be done with plaits of hair. But the girls said that the same thing had happened in the War of Freedom. Then they had had to have their hair cut. The girls demanded receipts and had them framed.

But at that time the women's enthusiasm for sacrifice in all sorts of things was very great. They put away their jewellery and dressed very simply. They lost in charm, but they rose in estimation. My aunt from Weimar actually sold her original letter of Goethe and gave the proceeds to the Red Cross. She was suddenly very bitter against France. She declared that her Paris friends had swindled her horribly. It was a scandal to send one an effusive post-card and a fortnight later to stab one in the back. She had broken off all connection with France —inwardly as well. I thought that very right, for a few days before my mother had proudly shown me a public appeal in the newspaper, in which ninety-three writers and men of science had said the same thing as my aunt. All my mother's favourite poets were among them, as well as the professor in the Bâle waiting-room.

By the end of October the general opinion had grown that the war would last longer than Christmas. The western front was stationary ; August himself did not reckon on the capture of Paris now before Easter.

The letters which our fathers wrote were full of confidence and hope, but they kept putting us off. Every Wednesday evening we went to the military church service. Pastor S. stood in the pulpit and praised in resounding and beautiful periods the deeds of our fathers. He declared they were immortal and pleasing to God.

We were not to be of little faith, for the work which God had in view for our people could not be accomplished in a day. I was struck again by the fact that in all his sermons he never spoke of Jesus. Even in school our Scripture lessons had very soon been changed. Instead of the New Testament we were taken through the conquest of Canaan and the wars with the Philistines.

The pastor's sermons inspirited us. We were very proud of our fathers, and soon realised that they needed time in order to accomplish immortal deeds. Nevertheless when a precocious Jewish boy remarked that even Hercules had required ten years for his labours, we beat him, for to us that seemed too long.

We had, of course, sworn to remain exactly as we had been when our fathers left. We wanted to greet them with the same voice which had cheered them on their departure for the front. We did not want to be changed. Just as the position of a picture on the wall, when they had last seen it, or the bed on which they had slept on their last night at home dared not be changed.

Such was our psychology. It sprang from fidelity and admiration.

We did not dare to disturb the exalted destiny of our fathers by any independent action of our own. This feeling went so far that August, for example, wrote long letters to his father at the front, asking whether he could venture to buy a new suit with the money he had saved, or whether he should make his old one last until the war was over. I myself sent a letter to my father at Thorn, asking if

H

he would mind if I put up a new table in my room
instead of my old desk which was falling to pieces.
Young Haugwitz even refused to give up his old
greasy cap, because his father had sewn a flag with
the colours on it. We no longer signed our letters
with our Christian names, but with " Your German
boy." Even in that we were standardised.

As it became clear that the war would not be
ended that winter we saw our mothers returning
quietly and unobtrusively to their daily round of
work. They washed, they baked, they made up
parcels for their husbands, they knitted socks, ear-
pads and comforters. They organised meetings—
they were very eager. The war became part of their
daily calculations. It meant no longer for them a
new and miraculous brotherhood, a new heroic myth
before which one had to prostrate oneself dumb and
motionless—the war had widened their sphere of
operations and provided new opportunities for their
desire to have something to look after. It became a
part of their day's work. That gave us the first
shock.

Meanwhile the school had opened again. We had
to take our studies up where we had left them off
before the war. We had to fetch out our school-
books which had for long been gathering dust in our
bags ; we had to open them again at the same pages,
on which the ink stains of a vanished age were slowly
fading. Every morning for five hours we had to
give our attention to subjects which seemed dead to
us, because in them nothing spoke of the time. Our
time. Our great time.

We did not understand, but finally we were forced
to understand. Vaguely we felt that the war was
losing its sacred character. With astonishment we

heard people talking of it as if it were part of their daily round. They still praised it, but no longer as a miracle, only as good business. Already the first annexation programmes were appearing. Many people began to make money out of the war. It became a sort of industry. Their representatives spoke very glowingly of war. But for other grounds than we. . . .

The war had become a work-a-day matter. People had grown accustomed to it.

Life in our town went on its own way. Soon people thought of the men at the front as of dear relatives who were away on a long business tour which was not without danger. They were judged according to the successes they had.

Already elderly gentlemen in high positions, who had stayed at home, were beginning to estimate the probable winnings. They wanted to gain Poland and Belgium. They wanted to become rich in the war. Our fathers had said nothing to us about that. They had gone out because they had imagined they were being attacked. That, too, was why they had become united. They did not want to gain anything. They wanted to protect us.

We had experienced the war as a great impulse to brotherhood ; now we saw it suddenly declared to be a business proposition. Germany, it was said, must become richer ; it needed this or that coal-field, this or that road to the sea.

We did not understand. Had Germany become a firm and the war a commercial undertaking, and were our fathers travellers for this firm, whose board of directors stayed in their homes ? Since when had heroes.been transformed into commercial travellers ?

Nor did our mothers understand this contradiction, but they did not consider it deeply, for the war had increased their household duties.

We felt very clearly this alteration in the war at that time. We only lacked words to express it. We wondered darkly what God had to do with the iron mines of Briey, with the annexation of Belgium and the suzerainty of Poland. For in school that was declared to be the object of the war. In every history hour. In the geography hour as well.

During these days we standardised our games. We fraternised perpetually. We took hands and sang. We called each other " German brother." We swore eternal fidelity. We embraced. We played over again our fathers' great hour.

But soon we were bored too by all this unity. We did not know what to do with it. We needed an *enemy*.

August hunted him out. He was called Pfeiffer. A year before, on the strength of good marks in the elementary school, he had been entered in my class. As he was very shy nobody paid any attention to him.

I have to thank this thin, pale boy for my first acquaintance with war as it is in reality. For that reason I shall relate his story.

CHAPTER XII

PFEIFFER had red hair. He wore it short as all the
rest of us had done since the beginning of the war.
In the middle of his grey, freckled face, which was
always sweating a little, was planted a broad snub
nose. His mouth was usually open. His lips were
dry and colourless and sometimes peeling.

In nothing was Pfeiffer a specimen of the true
German boy of the year 1914. He did not even wear
a sailor's suit with an anchor stitched in red or gold ;
only a grey woollen sweater coming up to his neck.
Pfeiffer was ugly. He blinked when you talked to
him.

He offered his services to everybody. He only felt
sure of himself when he was doing something. He
tried to make up for his looks by his humility. He
had been given a free place in our school.

His father, a tailor in a small way, who was only
employed by peasants already in his debt, had been
on active service since the beginning of the war. He
left behind him a family of five, which the mother
supported by selling newspapers and taking in washing. Pfeiffer flung himself on any job that was going.
The scraps of paper which fluttered about the play-
ground and the school corridors he collected and
put in the dust bins. He procured cockchafers and
any other insect required for the professor of zoology.

At one o'clock punctually he presented himself at the staff-room and carried the teachers' exercise books for correction home for them. Pfeiffer went for stamps, delivered invitations, collected money at the house doors for all the charities, fetched from the post-office the latest telegram telling of a victory, took small children out walking, and if it was autumn made them necklaces of fallen chestnuts, and if it was spring when the elders are still full of sap, cut whistles for them. The boy was ugly and was aware of it. He tried to serve people.

In our games Pfeiffer was given the rôle of enemy. That meant that he was fallen upon by all of us together and beaten. According to the offensive which was actually taking place at the moment, he would be Russian or French. On his back, which we sometimes thrashed black and blue, we celebrated our fathers' victories. Pfeiffer was perpetually being knocked about.

Whenever the grown-ups saw us at this game— the teachers in the playground, clergymen in the streets, old peasants in their fields,—they would chuckle and give us advice how to bring our game still nearer to the reality. Pfeiffer endured everything patiently. He was the scapegoat of our patrotism.

Pfeiffer was shot, cut off, buried, taken prisoner. Pfeiffer was caught trying to escape, followed, and in the subsequent pursuit killed. Sometimes we forced him to station himself behind a hill, where we bombarded him with clods, then we stormed the position and flung ourselves upon him, so that often he would roll down the grassy slope as if he were dead, and lie motionless with his crumpled soldier's cap among the meadow saffron. As a prisoner we conveyed him from the fields to the town, as a spy he was pulled out of cellars and shot in front of stable-doors. We compelled him to flee, hunted him with loud halloos through the whole town, and then dragged him in chains to a sand-pit, where a court-martial sentenced him to death. A handkerchief was tied over Pfeiffer's eyes and he had to beg for his life. He whimpered, flopped down on his knees before the Lieutenant, and if, as a subtle modification of the game, the latter spared him his life, Pfeiffer had to kiss his hand.

Haugwitz was Lieutenant ; August had got as far as sergeant-major.

The supreme point of this game was reached when Pfeiffer was shot.

This idea we owed to Sachs, the son of a subordinate governmental clerk who was fighting on the Somme. Every week his father wrote him a long account of the fighting, describing the nightly patrols, the shooting of enemy sentries by moonlight, surprise attacks, encounters with skirmishing parties, a fight for a farm, the burning of villages, the humours of trench life, the cheerful, confident spirit at the front.

We modelled our games on the descriptions in those letters. Unhappily we only learned half a year later that the writer was in charge of a clothing depôt twelve miles behind the front, and that he owed his knowledge of the heroic fighting of our soldiers to the columns of an Army newspaper.

Pfeiffer was shot in the woods. First he had to climb a tree as high as possible and hold in readiness a stick, which served as a rifle. We formed up into a column, and in peaceful marching order, singing a harmless song, defiled past this tree. As soon as

Pfeiffer saw us he had to let out a sound like " boom !
boom ! " and make a motion with his forefinger as
if he were pulling a trigger.   Immediately two soldiers at the head of our column would fall, the others
would scatter among the bushes, and one, who had
a trumpet, would sound it.

Thus all the conditions of a treacherous surprise
were provided, and the decision was : " No quarter."
The tree was surrounded.   Pfeiffer sat up in it and
let off his " boom ! boom ! "   We lay in the undergrowth, sticks at the ready ;   three of us had toy
rifles with percussion caps.   " Look out there !
Take cover ! " cried Lieutenant Haugwitz.   August
sounded the alarm on his whistle.   " Advance
slowly, under cover ! "   We crawled on.

Pfeiffer's shots were sounding feebler and feebler.
His mouth must be dry and his breath exhausted.
Suddenly someone cried out beside me : " Comrade ! "   He declared he was wounded.   " Shot
through the calf," the Lieutenant decided ; " go back
to the dressing station."   He hobbled along the glade
to a bank where two girls were sitting, who attended
our battles as Red Cross sisters.   They carried a
supply of old handkerchiefs with which they bandaged the alleged wounds in the most approved
manner.   Often while doing so their hair would
brush the hair of the wounded, sometimes even touch
their lips.   For many of us these girls were the real
cause why we took part in this game.   It was lovely
to be wounded.   But the loveliest of all was to be
killed.   For then one of the girls would throw herself
on the top of the " dead man " and kiss him and
break out into lamentation.

These girls—they were almost fully developed
already—could never get enough dead soldiers to

throw themselves on. Matters went so far that we began to draw lots for " a hero's death." But if one of the fallen, excited excusably enough by the girl's embraces, kissed her back, she would spring up red with shame and cry " Cad ! " They were German girls. . . .

Taught wisdom by my experience with Hilde, I steered clear of a hero's death.

(Hilde herself did not take part in this game. As she was two years older than we, she was already taking an active part in the town's work. At knitting parties where the women made all sorts of woollen things for the soldiers. All the same she no longer scornfully looked me up and down, for her cousin had been sent to the front and could not come now to see Hilde during his holidays. The war procured me this satisfaction too.)

Meanwhile operations against Pfeiffer proceeded. The " boom ! boom ! " became more irregular. " His ammunition is giving out ! " the Lieutenant smiled knowingly. Then he sprang out intrepidly from behind a hazel hedge and cried : " Do you surrender ? "

" Never ! " Pfeiffer had to cry, then he must repeat " boom ! boom ! " three times more, then stop. At that moment, led by August, we burst out from the undergrowth. We surrounded the tree, and one who had been chosen beforehand was given the honour of dispatching the spy.

He stationed himself beneath the tree and levelled his rifle at Pfeiffer, who crouched among the leaves and now had to whimper for mercy. Then he let his stick fall and raised his arms. His body was bent forward, his legs clamped round the branch ; swaying and stuttering, he was allowed to beg for mercy

H *

for a minute or so ; thereupon the marksman had
to lower his rifle and glance at the Lieutenant
questioningly. The tension of that moment was
terrible and always new.

The Lieutenant put his left hand on his hip, held
his breath for an instant, then said : " Fire ! No
quarter ! "

Every time I heard these words " No quarter " I
began to tremble. I felt secretly drawn to Pfeiffer
and was afraid for his life. For the first time the war
appeared to me in a different light. I had to say to
myself fiercely : " It's only a game," but my body
refused to answer to this thought. It grew chill with
fear.

Once when I could not keep command over my
feelings any longer I actually ran back to the girls
and declared I was wounded. In answer to their
eager question, " Where ? " I did not know what to
say. They jeered at me, called me a coward, smashed
my wooden sword and reported me to Lieutenant
Haugwitz as a deserter ; but Haugwitz took no
serious steps against me because I used to help him
with his German composition.

All this time Pfeiffer sat in the tree, held up his
hands and whined, and turned up his eyes so that
we could only see the whites. He held his head a
little to the side and his whining reminded me of the
noise a fly makes when its wings are torn off.

At the Lieutenant's words the marksman turned
away, shrugged his shoulders, levelled his rifle,
lowered it again, ran his fingers tenderly along the
barrel, then brought it quick as lightning to his
shoulder, screwed up his eyes—and shot. He made
a sound like " pin-n-g," not " boom."

Pfeiffer gave a strangled cry, somewhat like a

pheasant's, fell forward and crashed with outstretched arms, limp as a wet sack, through the branches. He was very clever at that. . . .

Lying on the ground he had to remain motionless for a while with eyes closed, and scarcely breathing. (Pfeiffer could hold his breath while you counted up to sixty-three.) Then the Lieutenant went over to him, kicked him with the toe of his boot, rolled him over and remarked : " Dead."

Only then could Pfeiffer get up and dust his clothes.

In close formation, singing " A Frenchman went to hunt a chamois silver grey," we marched to the dressing station. The wounded had recovered again. With the handkerchiefs, no longer in use, the girls waved us a warm greeting. " Hail ! " They shook hands with all of us. Pfeiffer, who had limped along with us, for he was always straining a sinew in his daring plunge from the tree, was laid flat on the bank and his wound examined. One of the girls, a daughter of the second parson in our town, who in his capacity as army chaplain wrote weekly for a newspaper in the nearest big town a brazen column praising up " the iron life " at the front, a column in which he indulged in that pious facetiousness which was perhaps the most loathsome thing in the war (I can still recollect quite clearly one of his later sermons in the town at the time when the submarine warfare was made unconditional ; it began with the shattering Christian phrase : " 70,000 tons sent to the bottom. . . ."), well, the daughter of this ruddy-faced field chaplain bent over Pfeiffer now and opened the shirt at his neck. Pfeiffer kept his eyes shut and lay rigid. On his forehead stood a few drops of sweat, like tiny lamps lit by fear ; the girl uncovered his left breast, squeezed the skin over his heart into a fold between her forefinger and thumb, and said in a voice full of admiration to the marksman who had come up with a smirk : " Well aimed, comrade ! " The marksman bowed. The girl shook him by the hand. . . . As I was walking home across the fields alone with Pfeiffer, he said : " I say, if that was intended to be a shot through the heart, I should have made my right leg twitch before I fell. That is how one does if one is shot through the heart."

I asked him how he knew that.

" My father said so in his last letter ; there were three in one day in his company just lately. . . ."

.   .   .   .   .   .

These fights were Pfeiffer's only connection with the war. He let himself be beaten.

It was as if in this ugly, red-haired boy a more than human endurance were allowing itself to be humiliated. For his capacity to bear our beatings was greater than our persistence in beating him. He conquered us by the readiness with which he offered his back to our blows. Our victories bored us. We conquered him until we were tired of conquest. All the same, we continued to beat him. For the eager seriousness with which he carried out his daily tasks, his mania for lifting and carrying things, were looked upon by us at that time, when we ourselves were patriotically shirking our lessons at school, as undignified and effeminate. For us nothing existed but the front. Life in our town seemed second-rate to us, and whoever bothered about it was a traitor. And Pfeiffer bothered about it, so we beat him. True, his father was at the front, but that wasn't a unique distinction when almost every father was at the front. If he were asked where his father was he would say, " Out there " ; if we were asked, the proud answer would come, " In the neighbourhood of Warsaw," " Sixty miles from Paris " or " Cruising along the English coast."

Pfeiffer neither collected shrapnel splinters nor did he gum portraits of generals on bottles. Nor had Pfeiffer a map on which he pinned off the fronts, no, not even a rosette with our colours or a stamp with " God punish England." Instead he ran messages, swept the streets before well-to-do houses on Saturdays, and earned 3.50 marks each month, which he gave in full to his mother. This boy of twelve was a civilian ; we felt it without being able to formulate it—and so we beat him. He rose superior to our beatings by enduring them.

.   .   .   .   .   .

On a bright, fresh February day in 1915 I was standing in the market-place looking on at an inspection of horses. Beneath the naked branches of the chestnut trees some hundred horses, brown and black, were rubbing sides. The smell that went out from them exhilarated me. A sergeant went about among the horses, whose neighing and stamping rang through the chilly air. The sergeant had a large note-book. Behind him went a private carrying a red-hot iron. The sergeant looked the horses over, examined their teeth and their hoofs, then he made a sign to the private. The latter went up to the horse, and while the sergeant wrote in his note-book pressed the glowing iron against its flank. The horse reared, screamed, stamped, and was immediately pulled back by two other soldiers who held the bridle. On the brown hide, which smoked slightly

and gave out a smell of burning, slowly appeared
the mark : " XVIII. A.K." The farmer was given
his voucher, the sergeant passed on. Behind him the
man with the glowing iron.

While the peasants were trying to quieten their
horses, and the square was filled with neighing and
stamping, I saw Pfeiffer coming round a corner with
his father. The little tailor—his white face was
adorned now by a pointed beard—was carrying a
heavy haversack and a rifle slung over his shoulder.
They were running at a trot. Three days before
Pfeiffer's mother had fallen when she was out selling
newspapers. The streets were slippery with ice and
very dark, and Frau Pfeiffer, who had only kept on
moaning quietly to herself, had not been discovered
for a long time, and had at last been brought to the
house in an unconscious state by a passer-by. The
doctor diagnosed grave internal injuries and serious
loss of blood. This was the reason why Pfeiffer's
father was home on leave. This was why they were
running at a trot, for the doctor had said there was
no hope of recovery. Just as I saw Pfeiffer and his
father disappearing through the street door of their
narrow house, a great tumult arose in the square.
A team of horses, which were just about to be
branded, had torn themselves free and were now,
amid a deafening hubbub, galloping down the street
which led to the fields. In front was a black stallion
which had apparently given the signal to break away.
The horses' eyes were wide open, the breath which
they blew from their nostrils had a yellowish tinge.
There were about eight of them, but it was as if all
the horses standing in the square had suddenly begun
to stampede. The people all shouted at the same
time with a sound as if the whole front wall of a

great building had caved in. The peasants ran blindly about in circles, cracking their whips and colliding with one another.

His moustache twitching with rage the sergeant sprang over the enclosure. Behind him the man who had been carrying the glowing iron. Instead of it he had a rifle in his hands now. " Fire ! " cried the sergeant. The man fired. A clear, sharp report split the cold air.

The peasants shrank together. The people rushed from the houses. The women dragged their children in from the street ; barrows were upset with all their contents. Becoming frantic the black stallion flew along the pavement, knocking over an aged post-man, from whose black bag a shower of different coloured letters fell on the ground. The fall of the postman had the advantage of clearing the street, for the women, who had been running about in confusion screaming, now gathered round him. From the houses appeared men with bicycles ; the sergeant had dashed into a doctor's house, fetched a motor-cycle out of a shed, and set off with a great clatter after the horses. I fetched my bicycle too, and soon found myself past the last houses amid a crowd of cyclists.

Although we pedalled smartly, the distance between us and the horses lengthened steadily. The sergeant was the only one who must be on their heels, for from the cloud of dust which they raised there spurted pale blue puffs of petrol gas.

Our column was sweeping noiselessly down the gradient of the road when someone said :

" Stupid beasts, these horses. Why do they keep to the road all the time ? If they turned off into the fields we would never get them again."

" Don't you talk," I heard someone replying;
" none of us would take the risk these horses have
taken. . . ."

I turned round to look at the speaker. But every
man sat silently bent over the handle-bars, looking
straight ahead ; only their feet were moving

We had gone on for perhaps another five hundred
yards when suddenly we saw a flash in front of us.
It was as if something had exploded, or a lamp had
been overturned. We pedalled harder.

The dust cloud had come to a standstill. Its edges
contracted. It became smaller. It seemed to melt.
Here and there flashes of light burst through it. We
watched it breaking up, and now saw between its
folds the horses' bodies looming unnaturally large.
" I hope nothing's happened," said the man next
me, scratching his head. We redoubled our speed.

When a few minutes later we came to the place
where the horses were standing, we began to go
quite slowly as if we were in a procession. There we
dismounted softly, kept our hands on our bells, so
that they might not make any noise, and laid our
bicycles on the stiff, frozen grass. The picture that
we saw paralysed us.

On the stone parapet of a little bridge, which led
across a ditch cut to drain the fields, lay the sergeant
in a heap, his broad face resting on the ground, on
which a palish red pool was beginning to coagulate.
From his breast were sticking a few broken-off spokes
of the bicycle wheel. About ten yards away the half-
charred remains of the motor-cycle were smoking ;
it had run on by itself, and was lying under a
poplar. There was a sweet, nauseating stench of
burning rubber.

We were advancing very softly on tiptoe when we

heard something groaning. Behind the poplar, where the embankment of the road fell down into a field, a horse was lying. It was the black stallion. His legs were doubled under him, and he was rubbing his head without stopping against the ground. His forehead was splintered, and he was bleeding too on the flank. The other horses were standing round him in silence, staring at him. Sometimes one would lick him, but only for a second.

" Was it the stallion ? " someone asked.—" He must have ridden into the middle of them and been knocked off," a man said. " Maybe the black horse attacked him, stallions can often be nasty when they bear a grudge."—" We must shoot the poor beast, he's still alive. . . ."—" What with ? "—" Has anybody a revolver ? "—" There's one ! " A man pointed towards the dead sergeant. At his light yellow belt hung a Browning. Two men lifted the dead man, with a faint crunch his face detached itself from the frozen crust of blood on the grass, his forehead was shattered.

I saw the face of my first dead soldier. It was not the face of a hero ; it was an indistinguishable trampled mass.

" He looks just as if he had been killed in the front lines," said a man who had come from France three days before on leave. " A real front line dial," he kept growling, then he loosened the belt and leant the shattered form of the sergeant against the wall. " Has anybody something to lay over him ? " Nobody had anything. " You stay-at-home heroes aren't much good in an emergency." The soldier was very irritable. At last an old saddler, who had come with us, took off his green apron and laid it fearfully over the dead man's face.

The soldier on leave took the revolver and went up to the black horse. " Now, my beauty," he said, and he put the Browning to its ear. The horse laid its head almost tenderly against his shoulder. " Now then," the soldier said, then he shot. There was a muffled report. Twice the black horse flung out its hoofs, then it collapsed. The horses which were standing around reared a few yards back, then let their heads sink and tried to find something to nibble in the frozen grass.

" We need a cart."

I promised to see about one, took my bicycle and made for the town.

.   .   .   .   .   .

It was evening before I reached home. I was very upset and could not eat anything. My mother was at a meeting of some charitable organisation for " our brave soldiers on the eastern front " ; I sat alone and did not know how I was to get through my mathematics exercise for next day. The encounter with the dead soldier had robbed me of all my confidence. I saw his face with the drawn mouth, and suddenly I could not help thinking of Pfeiffer. I decided to go to see him and tell him the story of the horses and the sergeant. The voice of the soldier on leave was always in my ears : " He looks just as if he had been killed in the front lines." Did they all look like that, those who were killed there ? Was this what " a hero's death " looked like ? Till now I had thought of it as something beautiful.

Apart from that there was the fact that Pfeiffer was good at mathematics. He would be sure to let me copy off him. I had forgotten about his mother's illness.

It was dark when I stood before Pfeiffer's house. I knocked. A shutter was flung open. Pfeiffer's ugly face appeared.

" Oh, it's you ? I'll open in a minute." Shortly afterwards I heard steps inside. When Pfeiffer stood before me I noticed that he was very pale. " Just come in," he said, " that is. . . ." And he swallowed something. He was crying.

" What is it, Pfeiffer ? "

" Oh, it's only my mother—she's dying. . . ."

I could not go away. I could not think of a suitable word to say. I stood there and stuttered : " The mathematics lesson. . . ."

Pfeiffer had taken my arm and pushed me in. " You don't need to worry, just come along."

In the sitting-room, which swam faintly in the reddish light of a worn-out electric bulb, the table was set. Pfeiffer's father was sitting there eating, Pfeiffer's young brothers and sisters beside him. Children with red hair and wide, astonished eyes. The room was quiet. One could hear nothing but the sounds of eating, and in the next room, whose door was slightly ajar, someone moving about. " Good evening," I said. Pfeiffer's father nodded. It was half-past eight.

Pfeiffer pushed forward a chair for me at the other end of the table, fetched his exercise book and said : " There, take it down ! " He disappeared into the next room. I sat with the munching family and scarcely dared to stir. The figures danced before my eyes. The geometrical diagrams were like shapes in a nightmare.

Suddenly Pfeiffer's father stopped chewing and listened ; in the next room there was a short groan, twice repeated ; I heard a noise, whispering, then all was quiet again. The tailor kept looking at his watch. With his left hand he crumbled a piece of bread.

" You didn't know that Mother was dying ? "

" No," I replied, looking away.

" Nor me either. Two days ago they sent a telegram saying I was to come. The major gave me three days' leave including train journeys here and back ; it was a special favour, for they need every man. I must leave again to-night, the 10.10."

He said this in a voice which sounded as if he were reading out of a book. Then, after a pause, in a quite different voice : " If it were only over . . . if it would only stop now, in time. . . ."

I shivered. I could not get up and go away, for the tailor's eyes were looking into mine. If Pfeiffer had been there I would have shaken hands with him quickly and run away.

" Will you have something to eat ? " asked the tailor. He pushed potatoes in gravy towards me. And I actually ate. I stuck the slices of potato into my mouth and chewed just to have something to do.

At a quarter past nine the doctor came out of the next room and asked for warm water. The tailor looked at him questioningly and pointed to the clock. The doctor said : " I can't promise anything. Death may come at any moment, or she may linger on for two or three hours."

" My train goes at 10.10," the tailor wailed.

The doctor shrugged his shoulders : " In any case the end will come to-night." Then he went into the other room again.

The tailor unfastened his broad-banded wrist-watch and laid it before him. It was quite still in the room. I could hear the watch ticking. At half-

past nine the tailor began to walk up and down.
Pfeiffer's young brothers and sisters had huddled
into a corner beside the stove and were playing with
dominoes.

At twenty minutes to ten the door of the next
room was opened. The tailor got to his feet with a
jerk. In the doorway stood his son.

" It's time now, Father."

" Is she just dying ? "

" No, you must go."

The tailor swayed. He gripped the table. His
eyes protruded. His face was stuck like a staring
mask on his shoulders, as if it did not belong to him.
" I'm not going ! "

" Yes, you're going ! "

" Not until she's dead."

" That may be for hours yet."

" Tell the doctor he must hurry it up . . . he must
. . . he must. . . . But I'm not going like this ! No ! "
he said once more, and sat down on his chair.

Pfeiffer went close up to him. He bent down and
said in his ear : " The 10.10."

And then in an almost coaxing tone : " You know
you promised the major not to take any extra leave.
You know what'll happen to you if you arrive late."

The tailor seemed to collapse ; Pfeiffer lifted him
up, fetched the haversack, fastened it on, slung the
rifle over his father's shoulder, put the helmet on his
head, and then pushed him, ready for the field, towards the next room, opened the door a little and
said : " Give her a wave ! "

Whether the tailor waved or not I cannot tell any
longer. I can only see him standing in the room,
kissing the children and shaking Pfeiffer by the hand.
Pfeiffer said : " Don't you worry, I'll look after

everything here." The tailor nodded, then he went out. The stock of his rifle struck with a loud clatter against the door-post. Outside I heard him running.

Pfeiffer came back and sat down beside me. He was breathing fast. I heard him saying : " The thing that matters most is for me to keep things going here." Then turning to me : " What sense would it have been for my father to stay till to-morrow ? They would have searched him out . . . and he would have had to talk himself blue in the face before they believed him. Yes, that's what this war's like, run to a time-table—or else it could never have happened, or would have been over long ago. . . ."

I did not understand what he said, but it remained in my memory.

" Pfeiffer," I said, " what will you do when your mother's dead ? "

He looked at me in astonishment. I believe he laughed. " Work—what else is there ? " I felt ashamed. He seemed to notice it. " Look here," he said, taking my hand, " you don't understand that yet, because you're too young."

" But we're the same age ! "

" No "—and now his voice was sharp—" you've had an easier time."

" Pfeiffer," I stuttered, " Pfeiffer, I'll see to it that nobody hits you after this." Pfeiffer smiled. " I'll have no time, in any case, to play with you now. And perhaps we'll not be able to play like that any more, for the war is quite different from what we thought. My father said to-day that there were far more dead men than heroes."

" Pfeiffer," I wailed, " I've seen my first dead soldier to-day."

But he took up my exercise book and showed me

the geometrical diagrams. When he had finished he looked at the clock. It was ten minutes past ten. . . . I felt suddenly afraid, took up my book and shook hands. At that moment the door of the other room opened. A nurse in a blue cotton uniform made a sign, Pfeiffer nodded and went into the room without looking at me.

Furtively, as if I were stealing something, I stuck my book into my overcoat pocket and felt my way down the dark stairs. The street was white. Snow had fallen. My footsteps were noiseless.

.   .   .   .   .   .

Pfeiffer, whose mother died during that night, soon won great respect in our town. His work secured his young brothers and sisters a tolerable livelihood. We did not beat him any longer. For he was the first of us who, in the pastor's words, had " taken his place in life."

CHAPTER XIII

" A HERO'S DEATH "

I TOLD August of my experience with Pfeiffer. He put on a look of importance. " Yes," he said, " my father wrote me about something of the same kind three days ago. A real big one came in among his company—eight dead. And besides, their enthusiasm is wearing thin now. The officers get far more leave, he said, and the safest dug-outs." August was out of humour at that time, too, for other reasons. His father had not yet been made a sergeant-major. Gradually he began to regard Haugwitz and the other boys, whose fathers were all officers and were oftener on leave, with the same old look. He drew away from them and struck up with Pfeiffer, who was employed at the district office as an errand-boy. Pfeiffer was allowed his afternoons off by the school authorities, a Red Cross sister cooked meals daily for him and his brothers and sisters ; their needs were covered by Pfeiffer's wages, what the tailor could save out of his pay for them, and contributions from the Red Cross. Their needs were small.

The war went on. It had become an everyday matter to us all. In our fathers' letters we detected the first signs of home-sickness. They made no talk now of heroism, they said they would do their duty. To the utmost. By which they meant to the death.

248

Suddenly the parsons began to preach about death.
To die fighting, they declared, was the noblest of
sacrifices. The German soldier was dying for an
ideal. A death like this was pleasing to God. All
at once there were a great number of women in our
town who cried during the service. When they left
the church they held their children fast by the hand.
Very often they were seen running along the street.
They had caught sight of the postman.

These women, whose numbers grew steadily,
altered the appearance of the war. They made it
a serious matter.

By the end of 1915 the women were the secret
rulers in our town. It was true, they still prayed,
" May God crown our arms with victory," but by
that they meant, " May God send peace." They
were thrown together at their gatherings, at " Help
the Wounded " meetings, at Bible circles ; they
understood one another at once ; only a look was
needed, and if they only talked about little household affairs, still in all their voices there was the
same ring. Death, which was gradually settling
down in our town, was the secret password in all
their conversations.

At that time the parsons were the messengers of
death, and when one of them turned the corner in
the course of his pastoral circuit, the heart of the
whole street stood still for a few minutes, to resume
its beat again in tumultuous relief as soon as one saw
that it was one's neighbour's door behind which he
disappeared. I had often watched him going in and
then with other boys pressed my ear against the
door, listening breathlessly until my lips were dry ;
and always I heard the same thing ; an outcry, a
heavy noise as if a table had been overturned or a

picture had fallen from the wall, then a whimpering, and through it all the monotonous voice of the parson, which sounded like the dripping of oil.

In these last days, however, we had often heard, instead of the usual outcry, a laugh, sometimes even a curse, and then we would see the parson rushing out of the house with his lips set tight.

Once actually (it was in the working quarter), shortly after a visit from the parson, who had had to convey the news of the death of her only son, a mother had poured paraffin over the floor of her room and set fire to the miserable hovel. Against her will and after a violent resistance the woman was rescued by a handful of men over sixty. She bit and scratched. An old gendarme had carried her by main force out of the burning room, and afterwards, down in the yard, she had kicked him in the belly with unsuspected force ; and for this, four weeks after her compulsory rescue, she was sentenced by a legal court, the ages of whose judge and clerks together totalled almost two hundred years, to five months' imprisonment for resisting the authority of the law. There she succeeded at last in hanging herself. Her neighbours said she must have been out of her mind, for she would have received a good pension, now that her son was dead.

That happened in 1916 ; a German army was fighting in front of Verdun, the list of killed and wounded mounted overnight, it went up by leaps and bounds, it reached a dizzy height, the printers could hardly keep pace with the figures—so monstrously did death pile itself up. We knew from letters smuggled through from the front that this battle was very murderous and made little or no headway, but it seemed to us, all the same, that our

small town was particularly badly struck ; the deaths
reported reached the total of twenty-two in one
week. Every day when I returned from school in
the afternoon my mother ran out to meet me at the
gate and would say in a hurried, apprehensive voice
that this one or that had been killed. When I asked
where, the reply would come, " At Verdun." Always at Verdun ; that name was just then the refrain
of death.

My mother behaved very strangely during those
weeks. After she had told me in this way of the death
of someone I knew, she would pull me hastily into
the house, as if in the open I might be hit any moment by something, make me sit down at the table,
where the food was steaming, and overwhelm me
with caresses and a tenderness which bewildered me.
She picked out the best morsels for me, she almost
pushed them into my mouth, and could not take
her eyes off me if I ate with appetite and relish.
Then she sat down at the piano and sang in her
soft voice little folk songs which she knew I liked.
I whistled the air and roasted an apple at the fire.
In these hours I forgot the war, whose real nature
by that time I could no longer understand. The
things it brought and, still more, those it took away
—all these were outside the gate there, settled, done
with, finished ; we had closed the door against them,
and the door had a secure lock. We breathed in
relief and looked at each other as if we were the only
people alive. We did not talk.

Once, just as my mother was striking up the sentimental refrain of a folk song, I suddenly stopped
whistling, for before me I saw the last page of the
local paper lying open. It looked quite black, divided
up into little squares, and each square was marked by

an Iron Cross. There were fifteen names. Fifteen names recorded for the last time—a newspaper cemetery of fifteen names.

A great dark sheet, a plain geometrically divided by death ; they had actually had to leave out the church announcements to get enough space.

I sat over this page, my head in my hands,—everything that I had thought about the war until then died in front of this cemetery of names. The grown-ups were dying a death whose rapidity I could not understand, just as earlier I could not understand their lives. To me it was as if all the doors had sprung open and the roof flown away. My mother turned round, tore the paper out of my hand, flung her arms round my neck, and while she pushed a basket of fruit towards me with her left hand, she cried almost in a voice of despair : " Eat something ! Eat something ! "

I ate to oblige her, and when I noticed that it made her happy, I went on eating. Then she sat down at the piano and began to play with all the skill at her command a Viennese waltz, provocative, pert, with the technique of an entertainer. While she was playing she threw me kisses, at which I blushed, although she was my mother. All day she hardly let me out of her sight, she would not let me go out, she looked after me with exaggerated solicitude and gave orders to Kathinka to close the outside gate and the shutters, as if she feared that any minute I might stand up and go out into the street or even take a walk in the woods.

Although I knew that my father's battalion, in 'spite of the age of its personnel, had been for days under fire on the eastern front, I could hardly understand her anxiety.

I no longer understood the war. Why had the
men laughed like that when they went away and
why did the women cry now whenever they thought
of their men ? Pfeiffer's words, " There are more
dead men than heroes," still rang in my ears ; and
when I stole a glance at the newspaper that lay in
torn pieces on the floor, my mother turned my head
round the other way and allowed me to smoke my
first cigarette.

The day passed without my leaving the house, but
indeed I had no desire to do so, for during these
weeks the streets were generally empty. People only
went past their doorsteps when their affairs compelled them ; the rest of their time they remained
fast in their houses as in prison cells ; they seemed
to be afraid of the open air, in which death, all
powerful, hung like a great pestilence.

And to accentuate this feeling one could hear any
day in favourable atmospheric conditions the sound
of the guns before Verdun. I knew very well the
place where it could be heard most distinctly—in a
signalman's shed on the outskirts ; and there we
often stood and listened, straining our ears for the
reports which sounded as if a heavy harvest waggon
were passing over a wooden bridge.

The old signalman—he was in the seventies, and
had already lost two sons—would always say : " Do
you hear it ? That's a whole lot of men's heads
rolling there . . . a whole lot of men's heads." Then
he would laugh with a sound as of a blunt knife
cutting through tin : " They'll all come to it . . . all
of them . . . these ones too . . ." and he would point
towards a transport train full of pale recruits which
with blinds drawn was flying westwards. We were
afraid then and ran home. Over the town the sky

hung like a vault of whitened bones. The moon illumined it. We could do nothing.

"Oh," I said on the way to August, "they've cheated us with their war." He laughed and shook his head. "They'll find out soon what my father said in his letter yesterday ; we were all a bit drunk at that time. . . ."

. . . . .

One day a hospital train stopped at our town. It deposited a few seriously wounded, whose condition was critical. I had sneaked through to the platform, so as to have a peep behind the mysterious curtained windows. In the most up-to-date carriages the windows were of frosted glass. I stole along the train ; sometimes a nurse or a doctor in a white coat would silently cross the narrow gangway between the carriages. A few of the slightly wounded had hobbled down from the foot-board ; their formless bandages exuded the sweetish smell of carbolic. A scurf-like stubble covered the faces of some ; the younger ones all had inflamed eyes. They talked very softly, as if they did not trust the peacefulness of the summer day.

Suddenly a hand held me fast by the shoulder. I thought I was going to be punished now for sneaking in. Before me stood a Red Cross sergeant.

"Here ! " he said, and held out a haversack to me.

I took it ; it was very heavy and the straps were almost worn through at the shoulder-pieces.

"To give you something to do, my lad," said the sergeant, and he pushed me in the direction of a stretcher which was just being lifted carefully out of the train by four soldiers.

On the stretcher lay a man, motionless, his face

staring upwards with a strange rigidity. His head was almost covered with thick white bandages, his eyes were invisible, all that could be seen were the sharp, white nose and the bloodless, closed lips.

The man seemed to be asleep ; sometimes his lips twitched as if he were dreaming of something horrible.

" Quick ! " I heard a doctor's voice ; the soldiers lifted the stretcher, fixed it on a trolley, and after a signal had been given and the slightly wounded helped on to the footboard and the big train had slowly drawn out of the station, an old Landsturm man softly pushed the trolley with the stretcher on it along the platform and into the street. I walked beside him carrying the haversack. After a while— we were in the middle of the town and the streets were deserted, for it was very hot—I heard the old man saying : " I don't think he's long for this world —he's curiously still in front there."

He cast his eye apprehensively over the form on the stretcher. The sun beat down on the bandaged face of the soldier. The trolley bumped over the uneven road—its wheels squeaked and complained. They had not been oiled for a long time.

Five minutes later the old man suddenly whispered : " There's a big fly settled on his face . . ." then he halted and stole on tiptoe to the end of the stretcher where the man's head lay. I let the haversack fall on the ground in exhaustion. Its weight, the heat and the smell of carbolic had made me dizzy.

Indistinctly through the over-heated, shimmering air I saw the Landsturm man gesticulating. " He's not moving at all now," he called softly to me. " I pulled his nose, I wet my finger and held it to his mouth. He's stopped breathing. . . ."

I tottered to the end where his head lay. We stood dumbly looking at his face. It was greenish. More and more flies were settling on it.

And suddenly, as if seized by an evil fear, the old man ran to the back of the trolley and began to push it at a sharp trot down the street.

" Quick ! Quick ! " he cried, and accelerated his speed as much as his age and his load allowed him. The stretcher swayed on the screeching trolley like a coffin flung into tossing waters.

The Landsturm man threw all caution to the winds. He flew.

I ran on behind him. The haversack kept knocking against my legs. When in a few minutes we turned into the cool yard of the hospital, the bandages over the soldier's eyes were hanging loose. An open gash, half an inch wide, yawned on his forehead. There was clotted blood in his eye-sockets. I had to take the haversack to a sergeant-major who was stationed on the ground floor. The corpse was to be laid there provisionally too, for the hospital was already overcrowded with wounded.

Half an hour later a doctor certified that the soldier was dead. He wrote the certificate on a scrap of paper, which he handed to the sergeant-major. The latter made up a paper, which the Landsturm man and I had to sign. Then the sergeant-major and I emptied the haversack. We found two pairs of woollen drawers, a novel by Paul Höcker, a bundle of letters, eighty cigarettes, some handkerchiefs and grey socks. A dried-up piece of cake, which had been cut into. And aspirin. The sergeant-major drew up an inventory. He confiscated the iron ration, two sausages and a packet of biscuits. Then we put the papers in order.

The most difficult business was the letter to the widow. As the sergeant-major had no given formula for the case, we had to think one out. We tried to remember all the catchwords of the time, which, as the sergeant-major said, were suitable for such cases, but none of them was convincing, for beside us lay the dead soldier.

Finally the sergeant-major made me a gift of ten cigarettes and told me I must draft it out. He went into the canteen, where I saw him slapping the backs of the fair-haired Red Cross nurses with much noise and great good humour. I sat beneath the light of a candle, outside the evening sky was reddening, beside me lay the dead man, and I wrote : " Dear Frau K. I am sorry to say your husband died to-day while being conveyed to the hospital in G. I am deeply sorry. Along with this I am sending the things I found on your dead husband. If you have any wishes relating to the funeral, we beg to request you to telegraph as soon as possible. Otherwise your husband will be buried in the cemetery here with military honours. Yours sincerely. . . ."

When I had finished it the sergeant-major entered, clapped me gaily on the shoulder and signed his name under the letter with a great flourish worthy of a general. Then he stamped it and gave it to me to post. The dead man on the bed made no objection. . . .

When I got home that evening my mother told me Brosius had been killed. I hung my head.

.   .   .   .   .   .

A few weeks later—on the fields outside the town the first bonfires of potato shaws were smoking—an event took place in our school which in addition to

I

us boys set the whole town in a turmoil and at last caused the authorities to step in.

When, as captain in the Reserve, our Headmaster had left gaily and confidently for the front in 1914, his position had been provisionally entrusted to the professor of botany, a quiet retiring man, who had been rejected as unsuitable for the Army on account of his hump. This man, who by virtue of his absorption in minute scientific studies was not peculiarly fitted for the carrying out of administrative work, and was not even a member of any association where he could have learned its first rudiments, had now in addition to his purely administrative functions as Head to carry out public duties as well—that meant just then making a speech after every new victory.

As he was never inwardly prepared for these victories and was more concerned with filling up his herbarium than with marking off advances of the German army on maps, noting the position of battles, or adding up the number of prisoners and captured artillery, every victory irritated him as an interruption of his work ; and he usually got over the compulsory celebrations by having a choral sung in the hall and giving us an afternoon off. Without family connections and himself outside the whole business, he felt the war at first merely as a hindrance to his studies ; nevertheless the frequency of the reported victories which were always dragging him out of his retirement and forcing him on to the platform to expatiate on a matter of which he knew nothing, soon drove him, at first out of sheer exasperation, to occupy his mind with the phenomenon of the war ; by which means he very soon, in accordance with his nature and temper, began to adopt opinions

which diametrically contradicted those officially dic-
tated by the authorities.

Already in 1915 this quiet man of whom one could
say nothing, not even that he was a democrat, had
become one of the most resolute opponents of war.

At the professional clubs in our town, which at
that time were occupied only by simple sixty-year-
old country doctors and " indispensable " die-hards,
his name was very soon hated. For while the others
almost went off their heads in their ecstasy over the
capture of some Russian position or the storming of
some five hundred yards of trenches in France, he
added up with that exactitude which his profession
had taught him the figures of the latest list of losses,
and presented them to the victory-intoxicated gentlemen with the hope that God might settle the bill.
These called him a defeatist, the strongest term of
abuse at that time. He left them with a smile, and
with an uncanny conscientiousness went on with his
computation of the totals of the dead. Thereupon
at a secret and solemn meeting of the professional
men's club he was expelled and declared free game
for all patriots. Very soon he had the sympathy of
the women and the poor people. We loved him
because he let us off school when our fathers were
home on leave.

The authorities had him secretly watched, and
every month received a report on his doings, composed by one of his colleagues.

Soon this man, whose existence before the war had
passed almost without notice, so deeply was he buried
in his scientific studies, became the storm centre of
the feeble life of our town—hated by his caste,
secretly admired as their champion by the women.
The life of our town was indeed a feeble one now,

for there were scarcely any men left except those over fifty, and only women who lacked their husbands.

The Professor had followed the beginning of the fighting round Verdun with particular bitterness. As the pastor one Sunday evening was celebrating in his sonorous voice the capture of an enemy trench as a new proof of God's partiality for our side, the Professor in his great Inverness cape got up in the middle of the sermon and, not content with that emphatic gesture, threw into the collection box as he was going out a sharp little splinter of shrapnel, such as circulated in thousands at the time as souvenirs.

From that day he was lost, for now the pastor too went openly over to his enemies.

The authorities lay in watch and only awaited a favourable opportunity. It came.

The losses which our town suffered mounted from day to day. We thought of ourselves as a number which was continually being lessened. In these days many people thought no longer of winning the war, but only of stopping it, and while only a few months before the women were still praying " Lord, preserve our heroes," now almost past hope, they clasped their hands and said : " Lord, preserve our husbands."

Nobody bothered about us boys. We had to come to terms with the war as it was. Before, we had had to rejoice, now we had to mourn. Every eye was turned towards the front. Our fathers were no longer heroes. We knew no longer why they were away. People talked of them as if they might die any day. Nor were they fighting any longer to capture Briey. They were simply holding on.

Only the Government buildings hung out flags

now when there was a victory. The women sat in their houses and congratulated themselves if their husbands hadn't taken part in the victory. Soon they were utilising our maps to find out how far away our fathers were from the seat of victory. They were overjoyed at every extra mile. They measured the distances very carefully. At this time Herr Silberstein opened a new department : mournings.

. . . . . .

The first words that struck home to us and brought us out of our isolation almost into line with the times came from the hump-backed Professor.

It was about eleven in the morning during the botany lesson, while the Professor was holding up a labiate flower and ecstatically expounding the mysteries of its fertilisation—even Becker was listening, though his father had been killed only three days before—that there came a sudden knock at the door, and the face of our aged janitor appeared. He handed a paper to the startled Professor, who read it. It was a small piece of paper, but he took a long time to read it. Then he said in a hoarse voice : "The whole school is to assemble in the hall," and to the janitor : "Hang out the flags."

The flower had fallen on the floor, I picked it up and laid it on his desk. He sat there, our hump-backed acting Headmaster, and staring at the soiled flower, said to Kaiser : "Play the Largo."—"Händel's Largo?" asked Kaiser, who conducted our school quartet. He was the son of an office manager killed in the war. It seemed to me that it was with his hump that the Professor nodded assent.

In the corridor I heard the news that Fort Vaux had been taken.

Ten minutes later we were all standing in the

chilly hall, numbered off in rows, in that state of
silent constraint which youngsters fall into when they
are ordered by their elders to attend an official celebration. Behind the large laurel trees in their heavy
tubs the notes of the Largo resounded. We stood
there quietly, looking neither to the right nor the
left, in the horrible embarrassment of boys who don't
know what to do with their hands. The Largo died
away, and I realised that without noticing it I had
been staring for some minutes at "Blücher crossing
the Rhine near Caub," a life-size chromo-lithograph
on the opposite wall.

The staff was gathered on the platform, looking
like a row of Swedish turnips. The Professor emerged
between the laurel trees. He walked hunched up,
and gave me the feeling that his back was bowed
under a heavy burden. He took up his stand at the
lectern, which was draped in a black, white and red
flag, and let his eyes run over the room. Beneath
him the singing-master, a red-haired consumptive
student from the theological college, intoned "Praise
ye the Lord," and with his thin finger gave the
signal after the first few bars for all of us two hundred
boys to sing the usual anthem.

Becker was standing beside me crying. His confirmation was still six months off, and his dead father
had promised him a gold watch which had been left
in the mud in some trench before Verdun a few
hours after its owner's death. Becker had been
boasting to us about that gold watch for a long time,
and now it was gone like his father. "Gather together . . ." and I saw in a flash Becker's father lying
on a heap of dead, with his watch dangling disconso-
lately from his smashed body, swinging on a chain
which reached out in vain towards his son.

The Head stood by the lectern, his eyes wide and embracing all of us. We noticed that, and waited. Close behind him was the gymnastic instructor, a bouncing fellow with hair parted in the middle, the only member of the staff excused from army service as being indispensable for the military training of the young. He widened his mouth into a red circle, singing with great enthusiasm, but out of tune, " Praise ye the Lawd. . . ." I shivered. It was impossible for me to sing.

Suddenly I noticed that the Professor was shaking his head continuously. The last strains of the anthem lapped us round like honey, but we stood staring at the Professor's head, which turned from side to side as if goaded by an evil thought whispering first in one ear and then in the other. " Raise ye the hymn of praise," resounded about us, the singing-master's thin finger dropped abruptly, silence fell, and we waited for the speech.

I can still see him lifting his crooked back, thrusting forward his head, and stabbing fiercely in the air with his finger as if at a huge slimy lie in front of him. His face was beautiful, and hung over us as if crowned by a thousand sorrows. His voice, which I had always liked, had the firm ring of passionate conviction ; it went soaring above our heads like a strong wind before the sail heels over.

" We have won a victory ! " cried the Professor, and it was as if he were crying for help. " Vaux has fallen. . . . What is Vaux ?—A word, a hill, a wart on the earth's face. . . . We have won a victory ! . . . Out with the flags ! . . . Jubilate ! "

The consumptive singing-master played a trumpet-like flourish.

At that moment the Professor drew a large docu-

ment from his tail-coat pocket, and waved it over
our heads like a sacrificial fillet. And read it out.
And read it out. And went on reading it out.

Dead . . . dead . . . dead. The names of all those
whom our little town had lost during the past weeks
in the siege of Verdun. A long procession.

Suddenly there was a shriek beside me. It was
Becker. His father's name had been read out. I
saw a large golden watch steadily ticking backwards
instead of forwards. " Vaux," came rolling from
the lectern. " Vaux . . ." and then like a groan,
" We have won a victory. . . . For this ! " and he
read out the list of the dead once more.

I saw the staff growing pale, and there was whispering among us. The Professor was now beside
himself, his voice kept breaking as he went on to
say that he was done with all victories, that one only
needed to walk through the town to perceive the
harmful, destructive effects of the war which he was
now expected to glorify before young people entrusted
to his care.

" No ! No ! " he cried, " that I will never do !
I have counted a hundred thousand dead before
Verdun up to this day." And he waved the list.

Suddenly he jumped down from the platform,
upsetting the lectern behind him so that the glass of
water ran over the boards. He ran through our
ranks, crying nothing but " Children ! . . . Children ! " Then in the middle of the hall, with a
noble sweep of the arm that embraced us as if with
a magic circle : " Not you ! Not you ! "

We hung our heads. " Promise me that ! "

We lifted our heads and looked at each other.

At that moment the gymnastic instructor bore
down from the right. His face was scarlet and puffy

with fury. He seized the Head by the arm from behind, jerked him round, and pushed him in short rushes towards the door, past all of us, so that we shrank back. " Get out ! You're not in your senses ! " he hissed, giving the Professor two more blows between his hump and his neck.

The Head made a brief resistance, but at the sight of the other's face he collapsed. A little way from the door he fell down, and the instructor picked him up and carried him out like a bundle. It all happened so quickly that we hardly grasped it.

From the platform came the nasal voice of the Scripture teacher. " Silence ! " The Headmaster unfortunately had had a nervous breakdown, and we were to go home quietly. He would take over the Head's duties for the present. The victory would be celebrated later.

But the victory was never celebrated. For two days later, when the acting Headmaster had been hastily dismissed from office and was under observation as a mental case in a sanatorium, Vaux was again in the hands of the French.

I *

CHAPTER XIV

HUNGER

IN his letters during those weeks my father no longer
said that these were great times ; he called them
grave times. He was glad to be kept in Russia. On
his sector of the front in Lithuania days often passed
without a shot being fired. The Landwehr men
didn't want to shoot, and only did so when they
were ordered. And the Russians had grown lazy ;
they lay in the trenches and sang the whole day.
No one had suspected that the war would last
so long. They were filled with admiration for
the fight their comrades were putting up on the
western front, and only hoped it would soon lead
to a decisive action and an honourable peace. We
were very glad that my father was in Russia, and
when he was detailed a few months later to serve
with the civil authorities in Kovno we breathed
freely.

In our town people were combed out more and
more rigorously. The few men under fifty who were
still left were inspected nearly every month in the
Town Hall by a surgeon-major. They feared him
as if he were a surly teacher. They did all they
could to evade him. People with money enough got
some doctor or other to certify that they had serious
disabilities, suddenly becoming short-sighted or asthmatic or subject to periodic heart attacks. One

manufacturer left no stone unturned until he actually got himself confined in an asylum, on the ground that he had fits of frenzy in which he smashed his drawing-room furniture. He was safe there, for he had had the good luck to discover a case of dementia praecox in some distant branch of his family.

Those who had not money enough tried other means. Just before the inspection they would race three times up and down the stairs of their houses until their hearts were beating irregularly, or they would secretly undergo systematic fasts, and when even that ceased to be of any avail the most desperate among them took to stealing, and did everything they could to be arrested, for prison would give them the same temporary respite from the war that it gave to poor tramps in winter from hunger and frost. Not a hint of such incidents appeared in the newspapers. These still conveyed the impression that the war had only broken out a day or two before, but they could not prevent the notices of deaths from accumulating in their columns. In public the war was still commended, but we soon began to notice that people's words had ceased to correspond to their thoughts.

Most people were still able to screw some phrase or other from the inflexible orations of ministers and generals so firmly into their heads that they could put up a show of conviction, yet their actions belied it.

What they really thought came out when they were called up for inspection. How relieved they were to be let off again, and how they beamed when they succeeded by means of money, good luck or influence, in being appointed to an office at the base !

The surgeon-major was soon the despot of our town, like any tyrant of old. He was treated as if he were lord of life and death. He was fawned upon and hated. Many of the women sent him wine when he allotted their husbands to home garrisons to peel potatoes. In that case they recapitulated with unction the glittering phrases of the generals. But it was fear that made everybody express the proper sentiments. For anyone who protested aloud against the war was sacrificed to it at the next comb-out. The very soldiers who came back grimmer than ever from the front confined themselves to hints —their leave depended on it. What they really thought only came out sometimes in their jokes. " Shut your mug and sing the ' Wacht am Rhein,' " laughed my cousin, who had been slightly wounded, when I asked him about the war as he was passing through the town. He had just come from the Somme. . . .

.   .   .   .   .   .

" This is going to be a hard winter," sighed my mother on one of those days as Kathinka set dinner on the table. Dinner consisted of a few slices of sausage without any fat, shavings of turnips held together by a thin sauce, and three potatoes per head. The bread was very good for modelling figures in ; it was like clay.

We sat waiting before this meal almost in prayer. Perhaps we thought that a miracle might happen and transform it to our desires. While I unfolded my napkin apathetically,—for we had had the same dinner nearly every day for months—my mother caressed the back of my neck and almost timidly stroked my hair, saying in a low, broken voice : " I

can't help it . . . perhaps I'll get some eggs and a
little meat to-morrow . . . don't be so unhappy . . .
I might get some white flour too. . . ." She burst
into tears.

" But, Mother ! " I lied bravely, " I like it quite
well, only of course a change would be still better."
Then I grabbed my spoon and plunged it with a
flourish into the pale turnips.

At that Kathinka, who had been allowed to eat
with us ever since the war began, seized my arm,
looked at me sternly and folded her hands.

We sat up rigidly in our chairs, and while a company of new recruits marched past outside singing
to order on their way to the shooting-ranges, I prayed
in a loud defiant voice : " For what we have received,
O Lord, make us truly thankful."

The motto of that year, " Better K-bread than nae
bread," winked at me in red letters on the bread
plate. . . .

Then we bent our heads quietly over the food.

Kathinka gave me her potatoes, and my mother
two small slices of sausage. Then I was made to lie
down after dinner so that it should agree with me.

But Kathinka was implored to visit her parents,
who were peasants in Upper Franconia, next Sunday
and bring back some butter. In return my mother
gave her one of her best blouses, and for her old
father, who was fond of reading, Felix Dahn's *The
Fight for Rome*, in three volumes.

" Thank you, mem," said Kathinka, so delighted
that she twisted her hands in her apron, which had
a little black, white and red flag sewn on its pocket.
" I'll bring the loaves of butter home all right—
they'll not catch me ! " She meant the field gendarmes, who had been posted for the last month at

the stations to search arriving passengers for forbidden foodstuffs. We trusted Kathinka, for we knew where she hid the butter—in her woollen bloomers. The shamelessness of the war had not yet gone to such lengths that the gendarmes would look for it there.

And it was a hard winter right to the end. The war now got past the various fronts and pressed home upon the people. Hunger destroyed our solidarity ; the very children stole each other's rations. August's mother went twice to church every day, she prayed and grew thinner and thinner : all the food she could get was divided down to the last crumb among August and his sisters. Soon the women who stood in pallid queues before the shops spoke more about their children's hunger than about the death of their husbands. The war had shifted its emphasis.

A new front was created. It was held by the women, against an *entente* of field gendarmes and controllers. Every smuggled pound of butter, every sack of potatoes successfully spirited in by night was celebrated in their homes with the same enthusiasm as the victories of the armies two years before.

Soon most of the fathers who happened to be in fertile districts where they had powers of requisition over the enemy inhabitants, began to entrust packets of food for their families to men going on leave. Managers of food depôts, town clerks who gave out bread cards, farmers with sound cattle and rich acres, became supreme authorities whom one courted as if they were wealthy and influential relations. Whenever we went into a farm kitchen where new milk was standing in great basins or a ham swung in the smoke of the chimney, we felt the same awkwardness that August and his proletarian comrades

had used to feel years before at the sight of a genteel
drawing-room or a piano.

This change in the situation really delighted us
because of its scope for adventure. It was thrillingly
dangerous to steal out of a farmyard with forbidden
eggs, to fling oneself down in the grass whenever a
gendarme appeared and to tell off the minutes by
the loud beating of one's heart. It was wonderful and
uplifting to outwit these same gendarmes, and after
triumphantly running the gauntlet to be welcomed
by one's mother as a hero.

.   .   .   .   .   .

August had invented tactics all his own. Whenever a gendarme hove into sight he used to transfer
the contraband he was carrying into my bag, cram
his own bag full of grass, and with a careless air
walk down the road alone towards the gendarme
carrying this suspiciously bulging parcel. Then
just before he met the gendarme he would start as if
terrified, and when the gendarme held him up he
would put on a guilty air. Meanwhile I raced at full
speed across the fields and got the food safely into
the shelter of our house. The gendarme couldn't
say a word when August pointed out that it was
only grass for his rabbits.

Incidents like these delighted us. We nearly forgot the war. We grew accustomed to the high death
rate ; it became matter of fact.

Soon a looted ham thrilled us more than the fall
of Bucharest. And a bushel of potatoes seemed
much more important than the capture of a whole
English army in Mesopotamia.

Death still beset our town, and the parson went
on singing its praises ; we got used to seeing so many

widows ; we bowed profoundly to them, shivered at their growing numbers, and walked with quiet solemnity behind the hearse whenever a woman succeeded in getting her husband's corpse home for burial in the local cemetery. With the same zeal we went collecting the last pennies from the various houses and distributed appeals for contributions to a new War Loan, which many women subscribed to because it made leave easier for their men. Nobody asked us what we thought of it all. The war concerned the grown-ups, and we were left isolated in the middle of it. We believed in nothing, but we did everything. We had realised for a long time that the war was an evil affliction, for we saw everybody trying to escape it. Even the soldiers at the front were glad when they were wounded. There was no more common unity, hunger had annihilated it. Every man spied on his neighbour to see whether he had more than himself. People who tried by every means to evade being sent to the front were called shirkers, and yet they only wanted to save their lives. We thought that very natural.

.   .   .   .   .   .

In the spring of 1917 I was lying with August behind a hedge. With infinite caution we had managed to get a small bag of flour as far as that ; the eighteen pounds it contained were to be used by our mothers for our confirmation feast. It was the week before Easter. August lay on his stomach and peered along the road, chewing at a blade of grass. I had thrust the bag deep into the bushes, and covered it with brushwood. We knew that a gendarme usually came down the road at about this time, the last patrol of the evening. We intended to wait till he was past, and then smuggle our flour into the town in the twilight. August had again undertaken to draw his attention, and it was my job to deliver the flour.

Suddenly August pulled his cap over his eyes and said with a grave face : " My father won't be coming to my confirmation."

" Why not ? "

" Because he said to the captain, quite loud, so that all the others could hear it, that the war was a capitalistic swindle."

" And what did the captain say ? "

" Oh, that was the funny thing. At first he made a frightful row, but then two hours after roll-call he called my father into his dug-out and told him confidentially that as man to man he agreed with him, but as his superior he could not permit such expressions. He told my father to be sensible and not make unnecessary trouble, for one man could do nothing against it by himself. And the whole show would collapse some day of its own accord. And that the French were in the same way, for so he had been informed by one of the captured officers. . . . That captain, I must tell you," added August importantly, " has been at the front since the war began. So he has had his eyes opened at last."

" Well, but why can't your father come to your confirmation ? "

" Because Judge Galopp, who is doing his best to be made a lieutenant, reported it to the regimental authorities. So my father's leave has been stopped for the present, and he won't get the Iron Cross either, which the captain recommended him for long ago."

I lay there beside August and thought that it was

all just the same as it had always been before the war. I could not help thinking of Persius and of that evening when Herr Kremmelbein was arrested. It was clear that the grown-ups had played us false with their enthusiasms, even with their God, who had not even yet fulfilled His promises. Or was it the parsons who had misunderstood Him?

I tried to grasp it, and asked August in a low voice, waiting for his answer with excitement, as if he could explain the mystery of the war to me, " What does that mean, capitalistic? " He thought it over for a minute or two. Then he said : " It means when the few grow rich at the expense of the many."

I did not understand him. " Who are the few? What people are they ? "

Instead of answering, August extracted a letter of his father's from his left pocket. It was written with a copying pencil, and was addressed to " Dear Everybody." August held it up solemnly, close to his eyes, as if it were an official document. He believed in his father as in a medical expert. In a weighty manner and in his best accent he began : " These few are :

1. The generals, for the war is their handiwork.

2. The ministers, for they want to annex Belgium and Poland.

3. The large manufacturers, for they make millions out of munitions.

" These three types are to be found in every country. That is why the war goes on. They have ever so many servants who cajole the people with fine speeches and a philosophy of idealism. These servants of theirs are the parsons, the teachers, most editors and those *bourgeois* writers who are too stupid or too lazy to tell the truth. Of course, one must remember that they all stand or fall together, and that they are not likely to take the privations of the proletariat on themselves merely for the sake of truth. Besides, they are the victims of their class ; from childhood they have heard nothing else but what they are now repeating, and presumably they believe in it. You know what it means for one of them to oppose the thought current in his circle—think of the Red Major ! But I notice already, that many of them are beginning to question things—the war speaks too clearly. My captain is an example. I admit that in 1914 they managed to cajole me too. It is the worst reproach of my life that I stopped thinking scientifically then ; but now when there's a quiet day and I read my old books again, for which I thank August most particularly (nobody has discovered them yet, and the other comrades in the regiment read them eagerly), now I can see clearly again. I realise that this carnage would never have happened had we all seen as clearly then that no war could ever arise were it not for the powder and shells that are manufactured beforehand. Everything has to fulfil its nature, and gunpowder must explode. I am writing this in the dug-out, it is Sunday and very peaceful at the moment. Keep your hearts up. It won't last much longer. For his confirmation present August is to have my walking-stick with the silver knob and two pounds of bacon-fat which I gave yesterday to a man going on leave."

" Isn't my father clever ? " asked August, folding up the letter with tender pride.

" Yes," said I, " but I think he exaggerates."

" How ? "

" My own father and many others I know don't

make anything out of the war, and yet they don't say things like that about it. In any case, the French attacked us first, and even though my father will be glad to have it soon over he certainly wouldn't write like that."

" Oh well, he's one of the capitalists' servants ! " laughed August, springing up and cramming his bag full of grass.

The field gendarme came into sight on the road, and while August skilfully attracted his attention I made with great strides for the town with the eighteen pounds of flour.

.   .   .   .   .   .

After our confirmation, which passed off simply and uneventfully (the parson for the first time did not preach about the war, but spoke of our future, which he hoped would soon lie in the mild afterglow of peace, even venturing to say to our mothers : " Christian sisters, in your sorrow for your husbands do not forget the tender souls of the children God has entrusted to you. Keep them from all the evils of the time. The impressions of youth determine the whole course of life." This was a new parson, a very old man ; our own pastor S. was a chaplain at the base)—a few weeks after this gentle and unlooked-for sermon three classes of boys from our town were detailed for work on the land. We were to help the farmers. August and I went together.

My mother was delighted, for the authorities had announced that in return for the work the farmers would give us board and lodging.

We were sent to the Spessart district and divided among five villages. We slept on straw sacks in a big room in the parish institute, and washed ourselves in the morning at a pump in the yard ; then we marched off to our work. The Scripture teacher, who had wangled himself this country holiday, was in charge of us. While we worked he played skat with the village parson and an old schoolmaster.

At five o'clock in the morning we rode on the cumbrous grey waggons, packed full of implements, to the fields, which ran over the hillside like shining ribbons. A cow lazily pulled our turn-out over the yellow field paths, and the farmer's wife sat in front keeping the blue flies off its lean back with a whip of plaited string. The air was soft that morning ; the June sun had not yet topped the mountains, and we could see the village below dark and fresh in the warm hollow.

August and I leaned against the side of the waggon ; we had to get out sometimes and lead the cow when the path was rough or broken.

In front of us walked the grandfather, an old farmer well over seventy, carrying the scythe. He walked quickly, much faster than the cow, and he rarely said anything to us, preferring to talk to himself. That was why he always went in front. We sometimes saw him standing on the crown of a rising slope, clearly cut and enormous against the lonely fields, with the young light of the morning turning his bent figure into a spectral silhouette.

The farmer's wife crossed herself whenever we passed one of the stone crucifixes which stood at the forks in the road. Her husband, who was in Galicia, had been granted no harvest leave this year.

She was nearly as taciturn as the grandfather, but she was good to us, especially to August, who had the same kind of hair as her husband. She often stroked it right down to his neck.

When we reached the meadow the grandfather
was already there mowing. Every time he swung
his arm he muttered a curse which we did not understand. Later the farmer's wife told us he was cursing
the gendarmes and the food-controllers, who confiscated the harvest and the cattle. She said he wasn't
quite right in the top storey, for not so long ago
when he was slicing turnips he suddenly cried that
the fat ones were gendarmes, and he chopped them
into little pieces with a wild laugh and threw them
to the pigs. Then for a few days he was quiet and
happy. But at the next visit of the controllers he
flew at the gendarmes like a madman with the
turnip knife. They pushed him into the empty
stable, and he had sung hymns all that evening and
the whole night through, only coming to himself in
the morning, and since then he had not spoken a
word.

We looked at him. When he swung back the
scythe we could see the corded veins standing out
on his arm up to the elbow.

Then we took our rakes and turned the grass.

A soft sweet scent hung in the sparkling air. The
clover was in blossom.

At midday Mienchen came from the village bringing us new milk in earthenware jugs, soft cheese, and
a loaf of bread made of pure, unadulterated flour.
The farmer's wife held it to her bosom and cut off
three huge slices for each of us. The grandfather
had his bread broken into his milk, and the brown
crusts he could not chew fell to August and me.
Every third day there was ham.

Soon I noticed that the farmer's wife was secretly
giving August extra delicacies. Eggs and blood
sausage with thick chunks of fat in it. She stroked

his hair more than ever, and made him always sit next to her.

In a fortnight I had gained five pounds in weight. I wrote and told my mother.

She came at once to see me. She presented the farmer's wife with a lovely dress, so thickly embroidered with beads and gold thread that she was embarrassed by it, and there was also a new pipe for the grandfather. When she went away she had arranged that I was to stay there for the summer holidays too. August announced that he was going to do that in any case, for he did not want to go back to the town where the war pressed so closely.

I went to the station with my mother. She was looking very pale. On the way she told me that Kathinka was in hospital with dysentery. This disease had attacked many people violently, for out of sheer hunger they had fallen on the green half-ripe fruit and swallowed it raw. Not an apple was left to ripen ; the children were ranging over the country knocking the green fruit down from the trees. She was so glad that I was safe in this secluded valley where the war could not penetrate easily, only she felt lonely in the evenings ; she found no further pleasure in reading the writers she used to like. They were a luxury, she understood that now, and her sole comfort was the Bible, especially the Gospel according to St. John. The whole war was prophesied in that ; perhaps it was the end of the world. Many women believed that, even Frau Apothecary J., whose husband had been killed.

I stood stock still. " Herr J. ?" I said, " Herr J. ? "

My mother went on with her news very calmly, without a sign of emotion. " Yes, and only fancy, Hilde has got engaged in spite of it, to a flying officer

she met in D. She was a temporary nurse in a
hospital, and they say she couldn't leave the officers
alone, and even went off to Brussels with some of
them. She wasn't affected at all by her father's
death, and at the moment she is in Berlin with her
present fiancé, dancing at charity balls. Frau J. is
not to be comforted ; Hilde is her only child and
not eighteen yet."

Then the train came in, and I shook my mother's
hand ; she kissed me and begged me not to eat any
raw fruit, and so went back to the town. But in her
handbag she had a large chunk of ham, and a roll
of butter under her blouse.

I went to the village. August was sitting in front
of the farmhouse with the farmer's wife ; they were
singing.

August's voice had been breaking for some weeks,
and his shoulders had broadened. The farmer's wife
had noticed it. She caressed his hair.

I said : " J. the apothecary has been killed."

" Oh ? " said August. " Hilde's father." He did
not seemed surprised. Suddenly he bent towards
the farmer's wife and giggled in her ear : " That
was his sweetheart."

The woman leaned forward eagerly. " Has he
had one already ? "—" Yes," laughed August, " he
wanted to know what it was like."

At this she burst out laughing, her mouth wide
open and her breast heaving, and while she grabbed
August round the head she shouted, " And does he
know ? Does he ? " I made off. To our sleeping
quarters. What were they after ? On the way there
I caught sight of our Scripture teacher in the inn
behind a row of beer-bottles. He was sharing a
newspaper with the parson. They were speculating

on the consequences of a victory in Macedonia.
" Monastir ! " I heard him call, " a victory at
Monastir ! " Then they turned again to playing
skat.

It took me a long time to remember where
Monastir was.

. . . . . .

It was very late when August came to bed. I saw
him climb through the window and heard him snore
a few minutes later. Once, in the middle of the
night, he cried out, " Bacon-fat ! " then he fell to
snoring vigorously and soon passed over into a deep
sleep.

I lay awake until the morning. I was shivering
when the sky began slowly to turn lilac and my comrades were tumbling over each other like young
kittens. I did not think of anything, I only kept on
hearing the voice of the farmer's wife. When we
were summoned by an old parish beadle with a bell
and the first boys were running into the cold yard
I said out aloud into the pale air : " August, what
was she laughing at ? " .

" Here ! " he cried, coming up to me. He had
only heard his name. I was taken aback and stag-
gered up, my eyes all reddened. August steadied
me. " Come along, we'll have a wash down." We
went to the pump. The first waggons were already
leaving the village.

Suddenly there came the roll of a drum.

. . . . . .

The drum taps were short and shrill, as if beaten
on a toy tin drum. We slung our towels over our
bare shoulders and ran into the street. In front of
the humble little church overgrown with moss, and

right under the War Memorial of 1870, the grandfather was standing in his shirt, with a small toy drum hung on his trembling belly, beating furiously upon it with two little wooden sticks. People came tumbling out of all the houses; they were only women and old men.

There stood the grandfather before the memorial, drumming, a white figure in the pallid light of the early morning. The more people crowded up the more joyously he drummed. Everybody was excited; even the priest came rushing out of his door in his dressing-gown. The cattle grew uneasy in the byres; the little calves lowed as if they were in a slaughter-house.

Suddenly the grandfather raised his arm for silence. The dawn wind blew out his shirt. His white hair fluttered. An owl came swooping with a startled cry out of the left loophole of the church tower.

" County folk and brothers ! " screamed the old man. " The next time the gendarmes come to take away all we have, let us take our scythes and turnip-knives and kill them dead ! We own the fields, we own the corn, we own the pigs, and if the towns and the Prussians want to go on making war let them do it without us. We'll keep what is ours ! Hallelujah, hallelujah, farmers and brothers. . . ."

He reeled, but recovered himself and went on drumming. A wave ran through the crowd. The women screamed and wept; the old men cried in their shrill voices : " Yes, Gaffer Anthes, yes, yes, yes ! "

Gaffer Anthes went on drumming, and suddenly began to dance, singing, " Holy Mother of God, holy Mother of God. . . ."

" He's gone mad," whispered August, " but he's right."

The priest had run back into his house and returned in a few minutes in his full robes. " Anthes ! " he cried, " you are heaping the wrath of God upon your head. Is it not written, ' Render unto Cæsar the things that are Cæsar's ' ? "

" No, no," returned Anthes, almost gaily. " ' Put up thy sword,' and, ' Thou shalt not steal.' "

The priest drew himself up to his full height, and bore down on the dancing grandfather. " Begone ! " he shouted, " begone ! Is it not written, ' Servants, be obedient to them that are your masters ' ? "

At that Anthes the grandfather went crouching stealthily up to the priest on his bare toes, like an animal, and after a rapid muttering banged him on the head with the toy drum, shrieking : " Blasphemer ! Gendarme ! . . ."

Then he collapsed. All around the peasants fell on their knees and prayed in an undertone : " Holy Mary, Mother of God, holy Mary. . . ."

After a penetrating glance at his kneeling parishioners the priest called for the village policeman and the sexton, who carried the grandfather into the fire-station. Next day he was taken in a closed cart to the prison in the nearest county town, where he died two days later without regaining consciousness. The priest was only slightly injured ; he had merely lost a little more hair round his tonsure.

When we arrived at the farm the farmer's wife said that the grandfather had been raving away the previous evening and she had locked him for the night in his room. But in the morning she was wakened by the crashing of glass, and had heard him getting his knife from the kitchen, but she did not dare to try to stop him. Afterwards when she heard the drumming she was too ashamed to come

out of the house. The whole cause of it all was
a letter from an old friend of his in Upper Bavaria,
telling him of the oppression of the farmers there by
the gendarmes.

She went to the Mayor's office and made a statement to that effect. When she came back she said
to us : " Now you'll have to stay on longer. For
now I'll have to do the reaping."

We promised to do so. She put her arm round
August. I remembered how they had sat together
by the door in the evening. August laughed.

We went off to the fields.

.   .   .   .   .   .

Eight days later the school classes went back to
the town in charge of the Scripture teacher. The
summer holidays had begun. August and I shifted
into the farm. We slept in what had been the
grandfather's room, sharing one bed. That was a
hot July. We had to work hard. The crops had to
be got in and threshed as quickly as possible, for the
starvation in the towns was increasing. My mother
wrote : " Yesterday there was a riot before the district office, mostly women from the working classes.
It was terrible to see them, with their children hanging on to them, lifting their thin arms in the air and
crying all the time, ' Bread ! Bread ! ' Many of
them fainted in the heat ; Frau Kremmelbein was
one. But don't say anything to August about it. I
have seen to it that she gets a pint of skim milk daily
on a doctor's certificate, but I am afraid she gives it
all to the children too. Kathinka is getting better.
I shall be glad when she's well again. For she hasn't
been able to visit her parents since she fell ill, and I
have been reduced to the official rations. My head
sometimes goes round, and I sleep a great deal.

Your father is getting on comparatively well ; but he too is depressed about the war. Nobody knows when it's going to end. Surely before the winter comes, for there's scarcely a bit of coal to be had. Who would have imagined it ? . . ."

I hid that letter from August, but two days later his mother wrote to him, telling him everything. " Dear August," she wrote, " when are you coming to see us again and bring us something from the country ? I had a bad turn last Friday. We had all gone to the district office to ask for more bread-cards, but the Commissioner didn't show himself, and so after standing for about twenty minutes in the hot sun we shouted for him. Still there was no sign of him, and so we shouted louder. Then we yelled. Then two gendarmes came out against us, and I was suddenly terrified and wanted to run away, but I fell down and saw nothing more ; everything went black before my eyes, and they carried me home, but I knew nothing about it. Your friend's mother has got milk for me, and I am glad to have something at last for the children. Little Erni is tired all the time and has a bad rash on her body ; the doctor says she's under-nourished. Your father writes often. He is so clever in his letters that I can hardly understand them. I beg and pray him only to be careful and do what his captain tells him. We must all be quiet and thankful to have anything to eat. Only I'm so worried about the children. Can't you bring us something soon ? Perhaps some eggs. That would mean something decent to eat on Sundays at least. God only knows what is going to happen. They want to start a new offensive in Russia, I don't know why they should do that. Your affectionate Mother."

August spoke to the farmer's wife at once. He let her stroke his hair and sat so close to her that his legs almost crossed hers. Then at night he went off on the farm bicycle taking eggs and potatoes and bacon for his mother which the farmer's wife had given him. He did that regularly every Saturday from then on.

When he came back he sat in the garden with the farmer's wife, and they drank blackcurrant wine and sang a song I had heard Kathinka sing :

> " The dearest spot on earth I have,
> Is the turf above my parent's grave."

I played dominoes with Mienchen, her fifteen-year-old daughter, and cards, with a pack on which the likenesses of the most famous generals were printed. In gay colours. . . .

August was changing. His voice was growing deeper and deeper, and he ate enormously. That pleased the farmer's wife. Once when he got up from supper and out of sheer high spirits did a few gymnastic turns on the edge of the table she said to him, running her eye over his youthful body : " If you go on like this you'll make a fine sweetheart one of these days."

Mienchen, who was sitting beside me, grasped my hand, pressed it, and then nodded to me. When August went off with her mother into the garden she put her mouth to my ear and whispered : " You'll make a fine sweetheart too. . . ." I was startled. What was she after ? Was it the mystery again, which had been so pleasantly ousted by the war ? Was the war all in vain ?

Mienchen had already laid hold of me, and pulling my face close to her freckled one with her rough

hands, she kissed me on the mouth. " No ! No ! " I
shouted, pushing her away. But she held me fast
in her strong firm arms, then she seized my nose,
pulled back my bent head, and with her light blue
eyes suddenly quite dark she said to me, holding on
to my hair, " You're my sweetheart ! "

" But I don't want. . . ."

" Yes, yes ! " she protested. " I want to have
someone too. Every girl in the village has one of
your crowd for a sweetheart. And now that they've
all gone home they send them parcels of eggs and
sausage to the town, as they used to do to soldiers
at the front. I want a town sweetheart too ! "

She spoke very petulantly, thumping on the table.
" I don't want any of the stupid country boys, I want
one of the swell town boys that speak with a fine
accent." Then she laid her head on my shoulder,
gazed at me with parted lips, and rubbed her hair
on my cheek, saying, " When you've gone I'll send
you parcels too."

The faint dusk of the late evening filled the kitchen.
In the garden I could hear August laughing loudly
with the farmer's wife. My mother's letter was in
my pocket. I could see the sentence, " My head
sometimes goes round, and I sleep a great deal." I
could see Frau Kremmelbein swooning. I could see
little Erni's rash. I could see my mother's pale face,
and the other boys who often came out on Sundays
to see the village girls and went into the woods with
them ; I could hear Frau Kremmelbein saying, " We
must all be quiet " . . . and when Mienchen asked :
" Will you be my sweetheart ? " I pulled her slowly
towards me, nodded, and gave her a kiss. " Eggs—"
I thought, while I did so, " eggs and bacon. . . ."

Then the mother came in and lit the petroleum

lamp. August's hair was all rumpled. He had two
bottles of currant wine under his arm. The farmer's
wife brought out ham. We drank and ate a second
supper. Mienchen took my hand in her lap and kept
it warm. Her mother whispered all the time to
August. He was laughing excitedly. It was very
late when we went to bed. August, who was a little
elevated, stripped to the skin, and then lying down
stemmed his left leg, which was already very hairy,
against the grey wall and said : " You know, a
woman like that is a fine thing after all."

I did not contradict him, for when I had kissed
Mienchen for the second time a wave of heat had
gone through my body such as I had never felt
before.

.   .   .   .   .   .

Next day—it was raining and the farmer's wife
had gone to the mill to get bran for the cattle—
Mienchen showed me her blue apron full of eggs
and laughed ingenuously : " Send them to your
mother." We packed them carefully in a box, and
I laid my socks on top with a note saying, " From
your affectionate son."

August, who was bicycling home again that night,
took them with him. I gave Mienchen lots of kisses.
" Oh, my sweetheart," she sighed.

Soon I found out that Mienchen wanted only
kisses. The other thing, the mystery, she called
" getting married." We agreed to put it off until
later, after the war. . . .

The grain was gathered in, the old peasants waver-
ing along by the side of the heavy yawing waggons,
and in the yard of the parish institute we could hear
the muffled whirr of the threshing machine.

I stayed at the farm with Mienchen and tended the cattle, bringing fodder or clover from the meadows in a small barrow. August and the farmer's wife took the grain to be threshed. Two gendarmes were posted beside the threshing machine at the institute to check the quantities. They confiscated all the harvest. The farmers hated them as much as they had hated the French in 1914 ; even more, for they weren't able to shoot them.

The word " enemy " now meant the gendarmes. Even Mienchen clenched her fist if one of them came into the yard to inspect the granary. August discovered the most out-of-the-way places for hiding grain and sausage in. By night the old farmers secretly buried sackfuls of smoked sausage in their fields, and killed pigs in the woods. The people were traitors to the " authorities," or rather had these not betrayed the people with their war ? My mother went on staying in the town with Kathinka, and with the aid of Mienchen I was able to help her. Every Saturday August set off on his intrepid bicycle run ; he had to travel nearly thirty-two miles during the night.

We hardly mentioned the war, all our talk was of lack of food.

Our mothers were nearer to us than our fathers.

The holidays were coming to an end, but August and I never thought of that. We belonged to the village, we did not want to go back to the town. At night when the gendarmes were not to be seen the farmer's wife baked sweet cakes for us with white flour. When August's birthday suddenly came round she let him bind up the snout of a sucking-pig, so that it could not cry out, and stick it with a knife.

K

We roasted it during the night. She even made a crisp paste crust to go round it, as she had learned to do in the town where she had been a cook before the war. We had eaten it all up by the morning. Mienchen turned sick, but August, sitting in front of the smoking platter with his shirt-sleeves rolled up, crammed slice after slice into his mouth. The farmer's wife was holding him by the shoulder, whispering eagerly in his ear, " Go on, go on." She was wearing the fine dress my mother had given her, and her heavy hair was piled round her firm head in honey-coloured rolls. She sat solidly on her chair with her arm round August as he ate. She licked her lips every now and then. With her strong hands she poured out wine for August till the glass brimmed over. Mienchen was groaning out in the yard. She was being sick over the midden.

" How old are you to-day ? "

" Sixteen," said August, smacking his lips.

The farmer's wife lifted her glass and said : " Here's your health ! "

I went out into the yard. Mienchen was rinsing out her mouth at the pump.

" Oh, my dear, I'm feeling so ill." I steadied her and helped her to her room, which was just under the roof. I set her down on her bed, but when I turned to go she began to cry, and tumbled sideways. " Take my things off, sweetheart, I'm not able."— " But, Mienchen ! " I said, shocked, " I mustn't do that."—" Oh," she smiled wearily, " nobody will see. My mother and August want to be left alone together. Just take my things off. . . ."—" Mienchen ! " I cried indignantly, " what a thing to say about your mother." In reality I was afraid to take her clothes off. But she did not reply ; she had fallen asleep.

Gently I began to pull off her shoes. I thought, she can't stay in bed with them on, she'll make it all dirty. Then I drew off her rough black woollen stockings, and saw her brown legs. Their lines were beautiful, and still very young. Then I hesitated a long time before timidly slipping off her simple little skirt, and slowly drawing her blue smock from her body ; and there she lay in a thin chemise, breathing peacefully, with a plait of hair over her bosom. I trembled. But as I settled her comfortably I felt the warmth of her body. And again that novel feeling ran through me which I had felt when I gave her the second kiss. I did not dare to touch her. But drowsy with sleep she stretched out her hand towards a linen nightgown and murmured : " Pull off my chemise. . . ." I drew the chemise over her breast, pulled it gently up and uncovered her. She lay there naked on the bed and slept. I shrank from her naked body. There was a gust of wind outside ; the candle blew out.

" How lovely she is," I said to myself, looking at her brown body in the dusk.

The room was swept by a gust of wind, and the girl's bosom was a soft and gracious curve in the moonlight.

Then I realised that the Kalmuck had lied to me. The mystery was different, it could not be what the Kalmuck showed me behind the hedge. " It was the money—the money was to blame. Because I had stolen it, everything was horrible. . . ."

" Mienchen," I cried, stumbling to the bed, " Mienchen, dear Mienchen. . . ."

I wanted to kiss her, for her own sake and not for the sake of bacon, but she half sat up and whispered sleepily, " Oh, my dear, put on my nightgown." I took it and slipped it over her shoulders. "Mienchen," I whispered, and kissed her ear, but she rolled on her other side and breathed deeply and regularly.

The wind fell. The moon sank behind the byre. It grew quite dark. I sneaked out of the room on tiptoe. When I came downstairs the kitchen was empty. A tiny light was flickering under an image of the Madonna near the stove.

I went quietly into our room. August was not there. I undressed in the dark, and lay down naked on my bed. In the trees and hedges birds were twittering in their sleep.

Was it for hours I lay like that? Or was it only for a few minutes? I could see Mienchen's body— it was so lovely and harmonious, I believed that to put a hand on it would destroy its harmony. I thought certainly nobody had ever seen it before, else how could it be so lovely? And surely the mystery was only horrible when one was prying upon it?

But suddenly, when the strident church clock struck the hour, and called up the image of the church tower from which the bells had been removed a few days before to be melted down for cannon, I remembered the war.

At that moment the door moved gently, and August came in. He was carrying his jacket and his braces were trailing almost to the floor.

"August?" I said.

"Yes," he answered, "go to sleep."

He threw his jacket over the chair, then he began to undress. He smelt queer. A strange smell, but not a bad one.

"August," I said, "I've been waiting for you."

"I was in the byre." Then after a pause, "The cattle were restless."

I lay there naked. August took off his trousers very carefully.

"But there was no light in the byre."

"I hadn't a light there."

He stood naked before the bed, and said imploringly :

"Do make room for me." I shifted over.

August climbed carefully into bed. Then as he was lying beside me, after a few vain attempts to fall asleep he said in the darkness, which was very dense : "It's a lie I told you."

"Yes," said I, stretching my left leg for coolness out from the blanket. "I knew it was."

August turned round violently. He tried to catch my hand, but could not find it because I had it under my head.

"I wasn't in the byre at all. . . . And the cows weren't making a noise either. . . ."

I lifted my leg into the current of air which was coming in through the window.

"I've been with the farmer's wife—till now. . . ." My foot dropped. The air was chill. The dawn was coming.

We lay for a long time in silence.

Outside the glassy stillness of the sunrise lay over the fields.

I got up quietly and shut the window, for I was shivering.

Then, as if he felt himself safer with the window closed, August began slowly to talk.

"At first I was afraid of her, because she always stroked my hair and pressed her legs to mine when I sat beside her. But when I got my mother's letter and knew about Erni's rash I thought, oh well, what does it matter if she only gives me eggs? And she has given me a lot, more than you imagine. That was all right, so long as she left it at stroking my hair, and you were with us. But when the corn was sheaved and you and Mienchen went down to the village she set herself beside me behind a sheaf and grabbed my head and gave me a kiss. I never had a kiss like it, I can't tell you exactly what it was like, but I felt that I would either have to laugh and cry at once or fly into the air. At the same time she ran her hands in a queer way over me, and said if I sat quiet she would give me a ham too when I went away. So I sat quiet, but you and Mienchen came back sooner than she had expected, and she let me go.

"After that she made me always sit in the garden with her in the evenings and drink a lot of currant wine. She was very tender to me, but not a bit as if she were my mother. I kept thinking about the ham, and did whatever she told me."

August looked pale as he lay on his pillow. The first swallows wheeled outside the window. I crouched beside him and felt afraid.

"But then," went on August, "I suddenly began to like what she was doing. I felt myself grow so strong whenever I kissed her. She always used to lean back a little on the seat, and I had to bend over her and hold her tight. She shut her eyes and laughed in a queer way, pressing herself close to me. I liked that and I even forgot about the ham. . . .

"But once when it was nearly dark she whispered in my ear that I must come to her for a whole night sometime. Then she clasped me tight and didn't let me go for a long time. And when we went in I had to put my arm round her and give her another kiss on the stairs. That was the day before yesterday.

" So to-day she kept me with her. And when you and Mienchen went upstairs she stood up suddenly and turned the light out, and took me in the dark to her room and took off her clothes. I didn't know what I was supposed to do, but suddenly I stopped thinking and ran to her bed and kissed her. She pulled me closer and closer, and then we both began to take off my clothes quickly and I fell over her. . . .

" Then she bit me in the ear, and that made me terribly excited, and I had to seize hold of her, and I felt as if I were flying and could lift the hugest stones, I was so strong, and her skin smelt so good. It was wonderful, she moaned while we did it, but it sounded really as if she were singing to herself."

Both his hands were under his head, his mouth half open and his eyes shut as he lay there on the bed. I asked him, shaking, " Is the mystery beautiful ? "—" Yes," he answered, " it is beautiful—it makes one so strong."

The cocks began to crow outside. The first smoke eddied over the roofs. I sat beside August looking at him. His skin gleamed in the morning light.

When he opened his eyes and looked at me he began to cry. Bright and noiseless the tears welled out and ran down over his face on to his chest.

" August," I cried, " what's the matter ? "

But he said nothing, and his face quivered. Soon his whole body was quivering, and the tears rained down.

" August ! " I cried, and in great anxiety lay close to him, trying to comfort him in my arms. Then he flung his arm round me too, and when I whispered, " Why are you crying, if it was so beautiful ? " he

clutched me closer and stammered, " When I did it
the second time she cried out more and more wildly
and suddenly she shrieked a name, ' Schorsch !
Schorsch ! ' and clung to me. . . ."

" Schorsch ? " I asked, in a low voice.

" Yes," said August, suddenly ceasing to cry,
" that's her husband's name. . . . He hasn't had any
leave for over a year."

Silently we clung to each other. We held on tight,
for we were afraid we might fall into nothingness.

Then August freed himself and sat on the edge of
the bed. He had stopped crying. And as the
morning brightened and the cows in the byre grew
restless he said aloud as if for everybody to hear,
" She didn't mean me at all. They don't mean us
when they kiss us. We are only makeshifts. . . ."

" Makeshifts," he repeated, putting his arm round
my shoulders.

We sat like that until Mienchen called us.

That morning we stacked straw. The farmer's
wife never uttered a word. She only nodded when
August said with averted face : " We must go
away this afternoon. The school begins again
to-morrow."

When we were packing our bundles after dinner
there was a great ham laid beside August's clean
clothes.

" You take it," said he.

I would have taken it gladly, but I did not dare.

So August carried it down to the woman's bedroom and laid it on her bed.

The house was empty. The farmer's wife had
gone to the Mayor to apply for two Russian prisoners,
and had taken Mienchen with her. We went off to
the station.

When in a few hours' time the pale silhouette of our town appeared August said : " If they ask us why we haven't brought anything back, let's tell them the prices were too high, and we hadn't any money. . . ."

.   .   .   .   .   .

A month later Frau Kremmelbein and her children left our town, to go to Bavaria where her parents were. There was more to eat there. August became a labourer on a farm.

K *

CHAPTER XV

HOMER AND ANNA

ABOUT that time my father sent a letter from Kovno, the wording of which I remember exactly because it concerned me so closely. " I want my son to be taken from the modern school and sent to the classical school in D. There he will come into touch with the classical spirit, and learn to model himself on it. For in these difficult days I want him first of all to be a man of character ; English and the higher mathematics can always be learned later on. . . ."

I rebelled against this command. Although the war had taken the last of my friends from me I did not want to leave the town I knew, for I had not the courage to enter into new relationships with new people.

" Your son refuses to become a man of character," wrote my mother in reply to my father, for she was on my side. But his answer was pathetic. We could not stand out against its heroic sentimentality.

" If our young people do not realise that we are only trying to do our best for them, if they are scornful of our care and want to go their own ways, they do not deserve to have their fathers daily risking their lives out here for their future."

That scared us. That was the voice of the Front. That was the feeling of those men who used to be our fathers, but now after years of absence were like strangers to us, huge, terrifying and despotic figures with heavy shadows, oppressive as monuments. What did they know of us? They knew where we lived, but what we thought or looked like they knew no longer.

But they were better than we, they were risking their lives. We bowed before this fact, and I travelled daily with the early train to the classical academy of D. in order to become a man of character.

.   .   .   .   .   .

The academy was a red-brick building faced with grey sandstone. There were a few stunted lime trees lined up like soldiers in its grounds, and the whole was enclosed by a high iron railing, the bars of which resembled medieval lances, painted black and cemented into basalt sockets. Their stabbing points looked menacing in the hard, frosty winter air. They made every one who passed put on a grave and formal face. On the gable of the building " Knowledge is Power " was carved in huge marble letters.

The corridors inside were dark and echoing. Any light which was permitted to enter had a grey look. Even the light in the courtyards seemed to be dulled. Grey, too, were the walls and the windows, grey the tables, the jackets in which our books were bound, the faces of the pupils, the teachers' expressions, and the Headmaster's faded beard. It was forbidden

1. To run in the corridors.

2. To take more than one step of the staircase at a time.

3. To laugh during a lesson.

4. To open the windows without permission.

Hardly any of the teachers were less than fifty, and these all had some disease or other which made them even surlier than the old ones. All the sound teachers were at the front ; the pupils referred to them as the " good 'uns."

I was set back a class and had besides to take private coaching in Greek. The Professor who coached me suffered from gout. He was very proud of doing his " duty " in spite of that. His duty consisted in tormenting me and my schoolfellows every day with particles and irregular verbs.

The war did not affect the school at all. It was regarded as a chapter of history not yet finished, and therefore not suitable for the curriculum. Although it was a frequent occurrence for one of the boys' fathers to be killed, and an increasing number of the boys sat there with bands of crape round their arms, no reference was ever made to that by the teachers. They loomed over us like the towers of an officially regulated ideal of culture and allotted us marks in Greek and Latin while we were starving of hunger and stealing each other's bread between classes. And while outside in the square fronting the academy a convalescent company of soldiers from a Landsturm battalion were going through their field-drill, and the sharp commands of the officers came cutting through the air and the windows trembled at the insolent volleys of blank cartridge, we sat in the close atmosphere of the class-rooms discussing the weapons of Trojan heroes or of Cæsar's cavalry.

There were teachers who knew less than nothing about Verdun and its victims, but who were acquainted down to the last detail with the equipment of Achilles' myrmidons. If they were ever compelled to mention the war they made it sound like a translation from Homer. Only heroes came within their purview, all the rest were " foot-soldiers " whose

duty it was " to dye the fallow fields with blood."
If they had to celebrate a victory, they spoke only
of the generals whose names were given in the day's
bulletin. They distinguished them by Homeric epi-
thets : " the swift-footed " were those who were continuously advancing in Russia, without achieving
any of the war's ends, while those who kept at bay
the attacks in France were " the strong of hand."

So for the scholars the war was invariably falsified
into an allegory, whenever it was mentioned at all.

But by the time I arrived there even the scholars,
whose fathers were almost exclusively officers or
Government officials supporting the war, had grown
troubled and doubtful. They were beginning slowly
to rebel against the attitude of their teachers, who
would not suffer any allusion to the necessities of the
time.

This first became evident in the Homer lesson.
On one of the grey winter days of December 1917
—perhaps the hungriest month in the war—we were
reading the " Banquet of the Suitors " from the Odyssey.
Young Mahr, a shy boy, was up at the teacher's
desk translating fairly awkwardly the Homeric bill
of fare for this banquet. It was cold, and there was
very little fire ; we had our overcoats on. The
Professor stood rigidly at his desk and corrected
Mahr if he went wrong. We had our cribs under
our desks and were following the bill of fare with
trembling eagerness. And suddenly it began. First
a boy behind me started saying " A-ah ! " in a low
voice, then on my right I saw another secretly
smacking his lips, and others were running their
fingers eagerly along the savoury lines ; I myself
felt my mouth watering. Mahr stood in front translating.

Before our eyes danced a vision of roast chickens, oxen on the spit, Cyprus wine, butter sweet as a nut, and chines of boar-flesh whose fat spurted up hissing in rosy bubbles when one cut it ; we could taste the pungent impertinence of freshly cooked mutton, the dry flakiness of boiled fish, the savoury tenderness of the lambs of Ithaca, the exciting taste of the yolks of eggs robbed from nests in the cliff—we could hear the red wine pouring from the goatskin bottles, the lowing of the beeves, the frightened screams of the cocks, the dull stamping of the oxen that were slaughtered in the courtyard by sturdy half-naked menials, and rising above it the flute-playing of the scared musicians and the brave rioting of the suitors ; we wallowed in these lines, and rolled the luscious metaphors on our tongues, and though our limbs were puny, our blood thin, and our bones soft, we lived Homer through for the first time with all our bodily senses, as one should experience every great work of art, instead of taking it as a disagreeable task. Our mouths were watering, and in our starved imaginations we suddenly became those suitors dicing for a Scythian slave-girl with rich meat gravy trickling down our chins. . . . And like a stab the thin cold voice of the Professor roused us. " Mahr ! " he cried, " Mahr, ὅτι means ' that ' here and not ' because ' ! "

But Mahr said not a word. He had lowered the book, and when the Professor yelled at him to go on he muttered : " I can't go on."

This made the Professor get down from his desk and laugh maliciously. " Aha, you've come unprepared again ! Very well, sit down ! " and pushing back his glasses he marked a five in his note-book with great care and equally great satisfaction, so it seemed to me. But Mahr dared to answer back for the first time in his life. " I have prepared it, but I can't go on translating it ; I'm too hungry. . . ."

" Hungry ? " The Professor turned round as if this was the first time he had ever heard the word.

" Hungry—what has that got to do with the lesson ? "

Then he gave Mahr a push, saying, " Sit down," went back to his desk and began to announce in his piping voice : " We shall now go on to the next lay. It deals with the Death of the Suitors. You must pay especial attention to the divergences of the Ionic dialect from the Attic."

Mahr reeled back to his seat. The Professor began to beat out with his pointed finger the metre of the new hexameters he was reading. And the first revolt broke out. It began in the back benches. Booing. It continued and grew in volume. Some began to scrape too, and when the Professor shouted " Silence " he was met with an outburst of booing and scraping. We all kept our heads bent as if we were ashamed of ourselves, to avoid suspicion, but there was not one among us who did not boo.

With a celerity I should never have expected from him the Professor sprang up. We went on booing. He caught me at it, pulled me from my seat and boxed both my ears. But the booing went on. Some boys were already flinging ink-balls at him ; his collar was smirched, his spectacles awry. When he let me go I flung my indiarubber in his face, and his spectacles broke. The Professor ran out of the room and we yelled after him.

We had won. We had risen in rebellion. And when the Professor came back ten minutes later with the Head and we got two hours' detention after a long, abusive lecture, with two hours' extra detention for me, we took it cheerfully, for we had made our stand. But from that moment I was done for. I scored nothing but fives, and was soon the worst pupil in the class. I could learn well enough when I wanted to. But I soon desisted even from that futile activity, for a few weeks after this incident I had got to know Anna.

.   .   .   .   .   .

Anna was a guard. None of your Homeric guards, but a real one of to-day, a guard on the railway.

The recent combing-out had greatly diminished the supply of men, and employers tried taking on women to make good the deficiency. Anna was one of these experiments. She was in charge of Passenger Train A 7708, the train on which I travelled to D. every morning. I got to know her because of her voice.

The Christmas of 1917 was over, and even in our town it had been a hopeful one because of the Russian Revolution. There was still great hunger, but feeling was more cheerful; everybody thought the Russians had sprung a revolution simply to let Germany win after all. In the papers I read the proclamations of the Soviet, and they were very like the letter August's father had written about the war as a capitalistic swindle. I could not understand why our people were so delighted with these pro- clamations, for I had heard exactly the same senti- ments from the munition workers who travelled with me to D. every morning. Even the men on leave, who came home less and less frequently, said : " We really ought to do the same as the Russians. Then the swindle would be over." But they only grumbled; they did nothing.

It was on one of those cold grey mornings while I

was sitting among the tired munition workers that the name of a station was suddenly called out in such a clear ringing tone that we all looked up, although it was a station we knew well enough, some ordinary, stupid name or other ; but it sounded so new, it was trilled and carolled with such joyous glee in the bleak air of that hungry January morning that we all raised our heads and smiled with a kind of embarrassment. I let down the window and saw Anna standing on the platform in a brown jacket and tightly fitting breeches, with her cap tilted to one side and a lock of gleaming black hair on her forehead, a neat and assured figure. With her breath steaming in a soft vapour out into the frosty air she puffed her cheeks importantly, blew her whistle, threw a kiss to the surly stationmaster and jumped into the moving train with a joyous halloo.

I saw her every day after that. When the train came in I always waited in the middle of the platform in front of an oil-shed where her carriage usually stopped. It made me happy to see her ; I used to gloat over the prospect of seeing her all the way to the station. I always chose the compartment next to hers, even if I had to stand. I could hear her voice through the cracked sliding doors ; she often sang between the stations. Her favourite song was :

> "Why should I keep a lovely garden
> If others come in and pluck the flowers ? "

and also :

> " Here at the Front on cold hard stone
> I stretch my legs so weary. . . ."

She used to sing the last verse of that one over and over again with especial melancholy.

" And if a bullet shoots me dead
And I don't come home to mother,
Don't bother your pretty little head,
But go and find another.
Take a new lover, frank and free,
Anne Marie. . . .
But if you can help it, gal o' mine,
Don't let it be a pal o' mine,
A pal o' mine."

Outside the last clouds of night went racing over the
frosty fields, and inside on the benches of the compartment the workmen lay about sleeping. Their
clothes stank of oil and sweat. They often coughed
in their sleep, and their faces were as grey as the
morning and the saliva trickling from their mouths.
I peeped through the cracks in the door. Near me
under the pale gas-jet sat Anna singing.

Soon her voice would surprise me in my comfort-
less school hours, and her face would suddenly appear
on the blackboard where the Professor was setting
out the root forms of the irregular verbs. I got many
a black mark for inattention. In the afternoon when
school was over I ran straight to the station and
stood before the door of the fourth class waiting-
room watching Anna, who always sat there with
a few old guards supping her soup from a little can.
It made me very happy to see her. But I was
plunged into gloom if ever she exchanged a jest with
one of the passing soldiers.

My days took on a new perspective ; the few
hours during which I could see Anna were all that
mattered, the rest of the day I only filled in waiting
for her. Under pretext of doing my home work I
used to lock myself in my room, lie down on the
bed and dream of her. I could lie there for hours

thinking only of Anna. Time is boundless when one is in love.

I never expected to have the chance of speaking to her, but it was a great joy merely to see her every day. When I was lying on the bed calling up the image of her face I used often to experience that slight giddiness August spoke of—a desire to laugh and cry together, or to fly—and then shutting my eyes, hearing her voice and seeing her mouth I used to offer up to her image the usual secret sacrifice of boys, at once pleasurable and melancholy. I did not think of it as a sin, I thought nothing at all about it, I only saw Anna much more clearly during these whirling moments than at any other time, and that was what I wanted.

Weary and happy I would fall asleep, and my mother soon noticed these frequent dozes of mine and was very worried. She thought hunger was the reason.

But one bright morning—it was in March, when the last offensive in France was beginning—on one of these expectant mornings Anna waved to me as I stood looking at her beside the oil-shed and invited me into the guard's van. The train was overcrowded. I climbed in with my heart beating painfully, and waited until Anna had got the train off. When she sprang in, banging the door violently behind her, she clapped me on the shoulder and said : " Well, we know each other, don't we ? " I moved away in embarrassment and stammered, blushing up to the eyes, " Yes, I've seen you often. . . ." Anna laughed and sat down beside me. I looked secretly at her shapely legs, which even the puttees could not disguise, and at her face, in which the dark eyes moved constantly to and fro, while the mouth seemed to be waiting in quiet strength for something. She wore a large watch-chain on her breast, and the plaited cord of her whistle, with which she played.

There was an old guard also in the van, but he was gouty and slept mostly between the stations.

Suddenly Anna took off her cap and began to rearrange the heavy knot of her hair. I had to hold her combs and hair-pins. I sat there trembling beside her, but yet found the strength to secrete one of her hair-pins in my pocket. Anna did not see this, for we were just coming into a station, and she pulled the door open quickly, crying as she sprang from the step : " Only a minute—I'll be back in no time. . . ."

Stealthily I took the hair-pin out of my pocket and sniffed at it.

When she came back I felt much more courageous, and told her incidents from the school, the nicknames of our teachers, and such like, inventing pranks and giving free rein to my imagination—all because I could not bear to sit beside her without talking.

I tried to make her laugh, which was not difficult, for Anna liked a laugh.

When we reached D. she said to me : " Come in beside me every day if you like, for you're a nice boy. Just get in ; the old buffer there is much too boring for me. He hardly does anything but sleep. . . ."

That morning I got an hour's detention in the Greek class for persistent inattention.

.   .   .   .   .   .

So every morning I got into the van beside Anna. The old guard was won over by a packet of tobacco, and just went on sleeping. Even when he was awake he never said a word. If he was asked why, he screwed up his face, snapped his fingers contemptuously, and said : " There's no point in anything." The two sons he had were both killed.

Anna and I did not bother ourselves about the war. True, I soon discovered that she had a fiancé who was on the *Kemmel*, but she said she had quite forgotten what he looked like ; it was such a long time since she had seen him. Her work, which had set her free from the sordid overcrowding of a proletarian home, was like play to her. She smiled whenever she could, and when a soldiers' train passed used to wave her handkerchief. But the soldiers hardly acknowledged it. I was happy while I was beside her, and in between I thought of her.

I told her everything. Soon she knew all the Homeric heroes. Ajax appealed to her most—she liked his madness. She thought Achilles spoilt and conceited, but she appreciated Odysseus. " He was a sly old bird," she used to say about him. " Only I don't see how they could keep up the excitement about a woman for ten years—but maybe they hadn't anything else to be excited about. . . . Penelope was a goose," she decided, " she was only faithful because she had lots of suitors—but if she'd had only one. . . ." She looked at me with half-closed eyes and laughed.

I took her hand gently. She did not pull it away.

That was the day I played truant from school for the first time. Anna was off duty until twelve o'clock, and I went with her into the canteen. She ordered a glass of beer and five cigarettes from the buffet, and when the man put them before her she pointed to me and said : " Another one for my friend." I was very proud.

In the afternoon I wrote out in my room my first

forged note of excuse. After an hour's practice I could imitate my mother's signature with convincing accuracy, and I made ready some more notes for all emergencies and handed one in at school next morning. So every week when Anna was off duty I suffered alternately from sore throats, diarrhoea or fever, and spent the time in the canteen or walking in the woods with Anna.

She loved anemones, which were just in bloom at that time, and I picked them and laid thick bunches of them in her arms. We had no eyes for anything but the young green, and we often took hands and raced down a slope. The war ceased to be of any interest to me at all.

I was in love with Anna, and she liked me.

She often gave me cigarettes.

The Greek Professor prophesied that I would certainly not get my remove in the autumn. At Easter as a favour they had advanced me provisionally.

I was living in a different world with Anna— what did I care for the war and the irregular verbs ?

My mother was delighted to see me so merry when I came home after these walks in the woods. She saw that I was broadening out and becoming less nervous, and when my voice broke she was very proud and wrote to tell my father. In the town, where people were faint with hunger and feverish with waiting for the result of the offensive on which they had pinned their hopes of peace, I used to go whistling the songs I often sang with Anna. I liked best of all the one a man on leave had lately sung to her in the canteen.

> " In Hamburg I've been often seen
> In silks and satins like a queen."

The tune reminded me of Anna's hair.

It was the first time I had ever felt assured in my
life. Since knowing Anna I realised that the Kalmuck had lied to me. For I told myself that Anna's
mystery must be as lovely as she was. I wanted to
share it, because I loved her.

.   .   .   .   .   .

All the same, when I tried to pull her close to me
one morning in the van she gave me a push that
sent me flying, and said : " That's the kind of thing
anybody can try on."—" Anna ! " I cried imploringly. She embraced me then almost maternally and
said : " You mustn't be like that," looking at me as
if she wanted to save me from something. When I
managed in spite of her to touch her lips, she shut
her eyes a moment and yielded, then she jumped up
and stamped her foot, crying : " Stop it ! " The
old guard waked up with a start and said : " Are
we there ? "—" Very nearly," said Anna, sitting
down again and staring over my head. That morning we went into the wood. I sat down beside her
as she lay in the grass. She had only an hour off,
she had to be back on her shift at twelve. Suddenly
she took my hand and said once more : " You
mustn't be like that. . . ." Then she told me what
a difficult time she had, especially with the older
men, who pursued her everywhere, thinking that any
woman was theirs for the asking because many whose
husbands were at the front had surrendered themselves. But that was what she wouldn't do, not if
she were to burst. " And you see," she added,
" that's why I like you so much, because that's not
what you're after, because you're so different from
my fiancé when he came on leave a year ago ; all
he wanted me for was to go to bed with, and in the

daytime he never bothered about me at all, but just lay around in the public-houses."

When she stopped I saw that she was crying. She kept hold of my hand and stroked it.

" Anna ! " I cried, " Anna, I love you, and I'll love you for ever. I never knew what love was like until I met you. I always thought it was something beastly, but you, you're so lovely ! . . ." and while she put her arm round me in amazement at my earnestness I told her about the incident with the Kalmuck. Then she pressed me close, caressing my cheeks, my hair and my hands, and saying, " My poor boy, my poor fine young gentleman. . . ."

And I, enraptured by her quiet tenderness, laid my arm round her neck and whispered : " I love you, I do love you really." But when I tried to kiss her she fended me off and said : " If you really love me, you must prove it."

I jumped up crying, " And if I prove it will you love me absolutely ? "

She nodded, standing up to beat the grass from her puttees.

I picked her countless anemones.

.   .   .   .   .   .

A week later Anna's fiancé was killed. She was silent for many hours. When I tried to comfort her she said : " Leave me alone, you don't need to bother." She had his photograph enlarged and framed, and hung it in her parents' best room. Then she was just the same as ever again, even gayer. I kept cudgelling my brains to think how I could prove my love for her.

By the end of May the supplies of grain from the last harvest were rapidly running short. My mother

said : " If they only win the war soon now. . . ."
In school the classes took it in turn to go into the
woods and tear down the foliage from the trees,
which was used as cattle-fodder. The turnips were
all needed for the people.

On the advice of experts we went into the fields
and gathered nettles, which were cooked as vege-
tables. They tasted abominably, but the experts
averred that these weeds contained far more calories
and vitamins than more palatable plants. They
demostrated that by statistics, and since we were
Germans we believed the statistics.

If a horse stumbled in the street and hurt itself
mortally, crowds of women and children gathered
round it immediately and followed behind the cart
that took it into the yard of the Town Hall where it
was cut up and distributed.

Every morning when I climbed into the guard's
van Anna told me how hungry her little brothers
and sisters were. She said nothing about her own
hunger, although I could see that she was slowly
getting thinner and thinner. I forced her to share
my bread with me ; sometimes, thanks to Kathinka's
adventurous journeys into Franconia, there was
butter on it. But only on one side. Anna refused
it at first, but soon she yielded to my importunity.
" Do you really love me so much ? " she asked, and
bit eagerly into the bread.

Never in my life since then have I broken bread
with such joy and devotion. That was when she
gave me her first kiss.

Anna's high spirits began to flag, and she often fell
asleep unexpectedly. I used to sit wideawake and
grieving beside her, counting the breaths she drew.
I had to rouse her whenever we approached a

station, and she would call out its name, white-faced
and reeling with sleep. Her voice had lost much of
its richness.

It was only later that I discovered that she was
giving up the half of her rations to the younger
children, because they often cried when they were
hungry.

The weaker she became the stronger grew my
love for her. It was not only her beauty that bound
me to her, for that suffered too. It was Anna I loved.
But how could I prove it to her?

．　　．　　．　　．　　．

It was the end of July, and the offensive had come
to a deadlock. " Oh God," said my mother, " still
another winter ! " In our town the church bells
were taken away. Even the parson shed tears. The
Kalmuck had to join up ; he had hidden himself in
the ice-house when they came for him. Dysentery
was rampant in D. The first air raids were made,
and we had to go into the cellar whenever the alarm
was sounded in the school. That made the teachers
furious, for it meant interrupting the class-lessons.
August wrote home to me that his father, who had
got leave at last, had refused to go back to the front;
" yesterday they arrested him, thank God for that,"
wrote August. That was the time when my father
sent us a goose from Russia.

My mother had gone off to the neighbouring big
town where the man on furlough was staying who
had brought the goose with him. She left a note
for me telling me that she was coming by the last
train, and that I was to wait for her in M. Just
before entering the station she would fling the parcel
down the embankment, and I was to be there to
catch it. She would get out at M. and wait for me

at the station exit, and then we would smuggle the goose home together through the woods.

These measures were necessary, for there were double patrols of gendarmes standing in the station of our town.

In the evening I got ready and took the train to M., a little village of working-men which lay in voluntary darkness because in the last air raid a bomb had fallen on its outskirts and killed three children at play.

I crawled up to the embankment and hid myself in an empty potato-pit in a neighbouring field, which was warm enough because there was straw in it. There I lay for an hour.

When I saw the dimmed headlights of the train I threw myself flat against the embankment. It had a burnt smell ; the grass was singed.

I felt the ground grow uneasy, tremble, rock and thunder beneath me, and suddenly a jet of steam was let off over my head. It blinded my eyes and muffled my ears—and just at that moment, about two yards on my left, a parcel swished through the air and fell whack on the ground. I lay close to the earth listening keenly, but there was nobody near. Slowly the last red lights of the train vanished into the station.

I jumped up, grabbed the parcel in the dark and ran on tiptoe in a detour through the field towards the end of the village. There I hid behind a small bridge and waited for my mother.

When she came up we neither of us spoke a word. We avoided the main road and took a little path through the woods. The pine needles deadened our steps. Once my mother bent to me and whispered : " It weighs twelve pounds."

We quickened our pace.

We could hear the hooting of the owls, the cooing of the wild pigeons, the working of the sap in the trees, and the crackling of the brushwood which snapped under our shoes. We held our breath.

Just before the town I made another detour so as to slip in unnoticed by a side street on the north side. My mother took the direct way ; she wanted meanwhile to light a fire in the house, for we had decided to roast the goose that very night.

When I got into the kitchen my mother embraced me. Then she stuffed up the windows with tow to keep the neighbours from smelling anything. I went into the garden and cut some heads of lettuce. My mother stood before the stove, where a great hissing and sputtering was going on ; the air of the little kitchen was soon rich with the smell of melting fat.

When my mother began to cut up the goose I uncorked our last bottle of wine with a joyous pop. We had really been keeping it for my father's triumphant return home. It still had some genuine tinfoil on it.

Then we ate.

An hour later my mother groaned : " I can't do any more. . . ." Then she turned sick. I took her upstairs to her room ; we were so full that we forgot to wish each other good night.

When I got into bed, my head heavy with the fat savour of the unaccustomed food, I could not help thinking suddenly of Anna. I had a vision of her sitting asleep in the train, leaning her pale face against the wall and scarcely breathing.

Soon I was out of bed and sneaking down to the kitchen with wonderful sureness. I found the goose in the darkness, and ripped the last meat from its bones. I even found a drumstick left. I tore out some of the bones from which I could not prise the flesh.

My fingers were bleeding as I packed it all in a paper bag and sneaked back to my room.

" Anna," I thought, " Anna. . . ." Then I stuck the package into my school-bag between Homer and my grammar, making them both greasy.

Then I fell asleep. It was already light. Anna kissed me in my dreams.

Next morning I raced to the station, and got there a quarter of an hour too soon. When the train ran in I waved to Anna. I climbed in, and when we were at last under way I opened my bag and showed her the package. Tenderly I unfolded the paper bag and drew her attention to the fragrant meat. " Where did you get that ? " Her voice was very excited.

" Take it, do," I cajoled her, " it's for you ! "

" Where did you get it ? " cried Anna, seizing me by the shoulders.

" What does that matter ? " I stuttered, " it doesn't matter at all."

" No ! " she shouted, so that even the sleeping guard was disturbed, " no, I must know." With that she held my face firmly with her two hands and looked into it.

" Oh, Anna," said I, weakening under the power of her gaze, " oh, Anna—I stole it from my mother."

Then she gave a shrill cry and threw her arms round me and kissed me passionately and tenderly on the lips. " You do love me, you do love me," she cried, " oh, you do care for me. . . ."

. . . . . .

We kissed each other all the way to D. When we

got in Anna said she had an hour off until the next
shift. Then she climbed with supple ease on to the
last carriage and unhooked the tail signal.

I waited for her in front of the station.

She came out very quickly.

" My friend ! " she said, taking my arm.

Over the grey bridge where dirty steam was welling
up from the arches we went off into the wood.

We said nothing.

The wood began quite near the station. Its clear-
ings were crossed by viaducts. The tracks of the
goods station spoilt its privacy. It was not a proper
wood, it was a plantation of trees round the railway
depôt.

But we contented ourselves with that wood, for
we did not want to lose any time.

We hunted for a seat, and found one opposite a
signal-box.

Not far from us a Zeppelin hangar lay like the
cocoon of a butterfly. Trees and roads were painted
all over its body, leading into the sky. Anna laughed
and said it looked like a garden in fairyland.

We sat down.

There was nobody near us.

Carefully I produced the package from my bag
and laid it in Anna's lap. She did not touch it.

" What ? " I asked, " don't you want to eat
it ? "

She shook her head.

I moved close to her, opened the paper, and fished
out the drumstick. I twirled it round in the air.
Although the sky was dead white and still the fat
on the drumstick glistened.

" Anna," I coaxed, " isn't it a lovely bit I've
picked for you ? "

She smiled and took it from my hand. Then she patted me.

" It's not the food I'm so pleased about—that won't fill me up for more than one day. . . . But that you stole it,—that's the thing ; that you *stole* it. . . . "

She embraced me with a tenderness new in my experience of her, and laying her lips to my ear with marvellous gentleness she whispered : " Now I am yours completely—yours until death."

I did not dare to kiss her, for her voice sounded so solemn and her eyes were saint-like in their gentleness.

" We shall love each other," I said, in a firm voice. A thin echo answered us from a near-by viaduct.

Anna caught me to her passionately, as if to hide herself in me. She let me unfasten the collar of her uniform and kiss her on the breast above the plaited cord of her whistle. I could hear her heart beating.

She caressed me.

" On Sunday," I heard her say, " on Sunday I'm off duty. Then we can go on bicycles to a lovelier wood than this, where there are little meadows hidden away, and lots of bushes. Do you think your mother would let you go ? "

" Of course ! " I cried enthusiastically. " I'll tell her we have a school excursion."

Anna leaned back radiant.

" We'll love each other," she whispered.

I pressed close to her, and listened to her every movement.

Suddenly she began to cry. With trembling fingers she fastened her collar and sat up. Her face was quivering.

She stood up, looked at her watch and wanted to go.

I held her back. She resisted me.

I pulled her back on the seat.

I imprisoned her in my arms.

" Anna ? "

She bowed her head and wept.

I let her go, and sat beside her without stirring.

After a minute or two she seized my hand.

Without looking at me she said, " Don't laugh at me because I'm crying. It suddenly came over me when I thought of Sunday."

She laid her head on my shoulder and drew broad furrows in the sandy ground with the tip of her shoe.

" Now that I know you love me, I'm so troubled to think what happened with my fiancé. He did it with me the first time he came home on leave. But I couldn't help it, for that was the time when nobody could refuse the soldiers anything. Besides, he didn't stop to ask me long about it, he simply laid me on the sofa when my parents had gone to bed, and then he took what he wanted."

I did not understand her.

" What did he take from you on the sofa ? "

" My virginity."

Her face was white and fixed, but she had stopped crying.

I got up. I walked up and down, putting on a grave face. I even clasped my hands behind my back. For Anna had pronounced the word with such solemn earnestness that it was unquestionably something of great importance. ·

" I knew it," said Anna, rising wearily. " Now you don't love me any longer."

I stood still in alarm. I seized her hand, and while I blushed for shame at my ignorance I stam-

mered with averted face, " I don't know what that
is—the virginity your fiancé took from you. . . ."

Anna pulled me down on the seat, and grasped
my shoulders.

" Don't you really know ? "

" No," I replied, " how should I know ? Nobody
has ever mentioned virginity to me since the war
began."

That made Anna. laugh. She slapped her legs
with her left hand while she put her right arm round
my neck and drew my head down on her breast.

" And I thought you would despise me for not
being what girls should be in your circles before they
are loved. I was even afraid you would run away
from me next Sunday because I'm not a virgin any
longer. . . ."

Anna laughed, a laugh in which the last of her
tears were mingled.

" I love you," I cried, " what do I care about
your fiancé. . . ."

Then Anna embraced me, and while she kissed
me so passionately that my lips were bruised, she
sobbed in wild but glad emotion : " I'll make you
happy, my friend. . . ."

" And I you," I returned.

We held each other close.

A few minutes later I let her go, pushed her back
on the seat, and brought the drumstick once more
out of the paper which was lying on the grass.

" Here," I said, " you must eat this now ! "

" Yes," said Anna, " I'll eat it now."

She took the drumstick. Before sampling it she
held it up again to look at it, and sniffed at it.

I lay back expansively to watch her eat it in peace
and comfort.

L

I felt very grand.

.   .   .   .   .   .

Anna had just torn off with great skill a firm chunk from the pale bone when the harsh hooting of sirens came piercing through the air in a wild clamour from the town. We jumped to our feet. The sirens shrieked louder. All the factories were shrieking, as if great cats were springing over the roofs with their tails cut off.

" Is it twelve already ? " cried Anna, fishing her thick nickel watch excitedly out of her breast pocket.

It was five minutes to eleven.

Just then the first maroons exploded in the town, and hung in the air like clouds of pollen.

" Air raid ! " shrieked Anna, dropping the drumstick.

For one second we stood there as if petrified. Then Anna threw up her arms and cried : " Run ! "

I ran after her.

From the defence post by the Zeppelin hangar they were firing off the first shots. Shrapnel. In a few seconds it was hailing down through the trees under which we were running.

" Take cover ! " I cried, flinging myself down.

Over my head I could hear the mosquito-like hum of the enemy planes.

Anna ran on.

" Lie down ! " I yelled, " lie down ! "

But she did not hear me. She was running towards the nearest viaduct.

" That's madness ! " I roared, " that's sheer madness ! "

And I jumped up and stumbled over some roots as I tore after her to catch her and make her lie down.

I knew we were in a dangerous region. Not far from the station was an ammunition depôt. Besides that, two strategic railway lines crossed each other here.

I raced on.

" Lie down ! " I yelled, making a trumpet of my hands. " Lie down ! "

But Anna did not hear me.

To left and right of the path little puffs of dust sprang high. Shrapnel falling in the sandy ground.

The signalmen were rushing over the sleepers and clambering up the embankment like monkeys, making for the wood.

In front of the station a train-load of children on holiday stopped dead, and the children swarmed out of the doors and over the lines like confetti out of a burst bag.

I was caught in their rush. They were crowding towards the wood. I beat them with my fists to get through them, but they thrust me back by force of numbers.

" Anna," I shouted, " Anna ! "

I saw her running under a viaduct.

Then I collapsed.

The throng of children trampled over me. Some of them screamed when they saw me, for they thought I was dead already.

The aeroplanes sounded more and more distinctly. The metallic beat of their engines ate into the sky. From the Zeppelin hangar there was wild but aimless firing.

Then the first bomb fell. Near the signal-box. The rails were torn up. There was a hole in the embankment ; then it fell in like a rotten tooth. I bit the earth ; my nails broke in the grass ; my mouth was filled with sand. Before my eyes, which were wide open with fear, I could see two ants playing on the great beam of a pine needle, quiet and remote from humanity.

Near me whimpered the children from the excursion train. " A-ow my Gawd ! " they howled, " A-ow my Gawd ! " They were from Berlin.

The second bomb. In the middle of the wood. The iron splinters swept through the pine trunks. The children screamed.

" Dear Herr Jesus," prayed a sister of the Red Cross.

I got to my feet. I knew that for us in that part the danger was over. For flying machines cannot drop a bomb twice running on the same spot, owing to their speed and their radius of distribution.

The guns went on thundering from the Zeppelin hangar. The defending aeroplane squadron was circling over the town ; none of them got very high and two were shot down by the enemy. They came reeling over the wood like wingless gnats.

I stood still.

" Anna ! " I shouted into the iron-swept air.

" Anna ! "

But there was no answer.

One of the Red Cross sisters even screamed at me : " Get down again ! You'll attract the enemy's attention to us ! "

I ran on. Out of the wood. Towards the viaduct under which Anna had disappeared.

The aeroplanes were rioting over the town. The path in our bit of ground lay open.

I followed it, crying : " Anna ! Anna ! "

Nobody answered. There were men lying behind

the trees, workmen from the railway engineering shops. " Lie down ! " they yelled at me. " Take cover, man ! "

I ran on.

I was loking for Anna.

Suddenly I noticed that a wild barrage had begun in the middle of the town ; there was a glittering wall of smoke-puffs from exploding shells.

The enemy were approaching the Grand Duke's castle.

Soon they wheeled round and passed over the outer suburbs in a deadly knot.

I ducked. I could see them making for the station again.

The singing hum of their engines grew louder and louder.

" They're going away," yelled someone behind me, but I could see them already almost vertically over-head.

The Zeppelin hangar began to fire again.

I threw myself flat.

" Look out ! " shouted a man.

A hollow whistling sound came screwing through the air.

I pressed myself flat on the ground, as if nailed to it.

With a bright red flash a bridge went flying into the air.

The splinters went singing over my head, and struck into the trees, bringing out the resin.

The hum of the departing squadron grew fainter. In a few minutes the first sirens began to hoot at short intervals to show that the danger was over.

I rose up. The whole wood got to its feet.

It was thronged as if it were Sunday.

The Red Cross sisters whistled up their children, and formed them in line and numbered them off.

" One — Two — Three — Four — Five — Six — Seven — Eight — Nine — Ten — Eleven ——" came rattling through the wood much like shrapnel.

I moved off, crying : " Anna ! Anna ! " I shouted. I took to my heels. I ran down a tunnel.

It was red.

Then a small paved causeway.

It was torn up.

And strewn with concrete blown to dust.

The viaduct was barricaded off. Two Landsturm men were on guard.

" Anna ! " I screamed. " Anna ! "

But they said I was to turn back.

They seized me by the arm.

" It's forbidden ! " they said, " absolutely forbidden ! "

A motor-car drove up. From behind the frosted glass panes of its coachwork sprang two men with glazed caps.

They were carrying a stretcher.

" Is she dead ? " I asked quietly, standing on tiptoe.

" Yes," said one of the Landsturm men, " she's lying over there. . . ."

I followed with my eye his pointing gun. Between two shattered blocks of concrete I saw a heap of clothes. A brown ground-sheet was thrown over it. A few yards away Anna's service cap, undamaged, was lying in the blackened grass.

" Is that Anna ? " I asked in a hushed voice, shaking my head.

" Direct hit," answered the Landsturm man. " We've covered up all that's left of her. . . ."

THE END